Advance Praise for *Corn Poll*

"*Corn Poll* is a hoot and a holler for political reform. In the satirical tradition of Joe Klein's *Primary Colors* and Jane Smiley's *Moo*, this book will make you laugh and then think. In fact, what Zachary Michael Jack has to say might just make a difference in next year's Iowa caucuses…and wouldn't that be a good thing!"
—**Dr. Timothy Walch**, Director Emeritus, Herbert Hoover Presidential Library

"Zachary Michael Jack has given us a great book—one that somehow changes the perspective of the reader when looking at real-life politics. It keeps us guessing, thinking, and laughing."
—**Dr. Jeff Taylor**, Professor of Political Science, Dordt College (IA), author, *Politics on a Human Scale* and *Where Did the Party Go: William Jennings Bryan, Hubert Humphrey, and the Jeffersonian Legacy*

"A nice break from the grind of campaign news…. Beyond the spoofing of characters you'll recognize, there's a warm hope for something better in our political system."
—**David Yepsen**, Director, Paul Simon Public Policy Institute, Southern Illinois University

"A roll   rt
and ic   th
the hc   rn
popul

B   y
R

"Som   le
inside   x
chara   d
will fi   th
of Jac

N
F

"Love or hate the Iowa caucuses, Zachary Michael Jack's entertaining novel, *Corn Poll* turns them on their 'ear.' With one more of his many literary gifts to Iowa, Zachary Michael Jack continues to prove he is one of the finest writers the Midwest has to offer."

> —**Dr. Robert Leonard**, author, *Yellow Cab*, and KNIA/KRLS radio news editor

"The best political writing is as much about people, places and principles as it is about process and philosophy. Professor Jack deftly weaves together all of these elements in a thoughtful, provocative, but always entertaining story set in America's heartland…. The perceptive reader will see political commentary worth considering in this compelling work of fiction—a perfect combination: a beach book with big ideas."

> —**Dr. Thomas D. Cavenagh**, Schneller Sisters Professor of Leadership, Ethics, and Values, Professor of Law and Conflict Resolution, North Central College, coauthor, with Lucille M. Ponte of *Cyberjustice*

"Covering the Iowa Caucuses for nearly forty years has taught me the greatest untold story in the Caucuses is the story of the people who cover them, real people with real thoughts and emotions. This book captures that image and brings new life to a political event that has become a tradition in the nation's political life."

> —**Mike Glover**, former Associated Press Statehouse and Political Reporter, Managing Editor, the *Iowa Daily Democrat*

"*Corn Poll* is an engaging story…. It's an insightful, behind-the-scenes peek at Presidential candidates and the media personalities covering the campaign drama."

> —**Dean Borg**, host of *Iowa Press* on PBS, Iowa Public Radio correspondent, winner of the Jack Shelley Award for lifetime achievement from the Iowa Broadcast News Association

Corn Poll

A Novel of the Iowa Caucuses

Zachary Michael Jack

Tall Corn Books
North Liberty, Iowa

Corn Poll: A Novel of the Iowa Caucuses

Copyright © 2015 Zachary Michael Jack

Isbn 9781888160895

Library of Congress Control Number: 2015905202

Tall Corn Books, imprint of
Ice Cube Press, LLC (Est. 1993)
205 N. Front Street
North Liberty, Iowa 52317
319-594-6022
www.icecubepress.com
steve@icecubepress.com
twitter: @icecubepress

The paper used in this publication meets the minimum requirements of the American National Standard for Information Sciences—Permanence of Paper for Printed Library Materials, ANSI Z39.48-1992.

Manufactured in the United States of America.

This is a work of fiction. Names, characters, businesses, organizations, places, events, and incidents either are the product of the author's imagination or are used fictitiously. Any resemblance to actual persons, living or dead, events, or locales is entirely coincidental.

Photo appearing on the author biography page: "Calvin Coolidge on the Farm," Library of Congress, American Memory Collection

To the small-town family newspaper,
long may you run.
&
to the long-suffering American electorate,
may you forever vote your conscience.

One

Jacob Preston cruised into Iowa in a high-mileage Honda Accord wondering what on earth he would do with himself for the forty-some days until the election. Like the opening scene in some Middle Western, it was dusk, and Jake had been in the saddle since Denver, ten hours straight, minus a few coffee and pee breaks.

He had forgotten how pretty the Corn Belt could be on a balmy day in early October, the high hills of beige corn stubble quilted with the bright green pastures and waterways, the red-tailed hawks riding the thermals, eyeing a fresh meal in the newly harvested cornfields. The burbs booming back in Denver—Wheat Ridge, Cherry Hills, Greenwood—had pretty much been named after the thing they'd destroyed in the name of progress. Meanwhile, things here looked much the same as when he'd visited his grandparents as a kid.

It had been less than six weeks ago that he'd made the admittedly kneejerk decision to enter the contest to cover Iowa's first-in-the-nation presidential primary. At 1:00 AM and nearing the bottom of his third consecutive bowl of ice cream, he'd surfed to his favorite journalism job board—the one he'd visited countless times since taking his first, entry-level copyeditor's gig in Denver—and there it'd been, a banner ad taken out by the Iowa Republican Party and the bigger fish at the Republican National

Committee in Washington. *Unparalleled access to the candidates,* the contest advert had promised. *Help take your publication's political coverage to the next level.* Jake had chuckled at the wishful hyperbole, scooped up the dregs of his mint chocolate chip from the bottom of the bowl, and commenced to filling out the fields in the online entry:

Name—Jacob Truman Preston
Position—Political Correspondent
Publication—*Rocky Mountain Partisan*
Circulation—65,000

Everything but his name and the name of the rag he wrote for had been a white lie. Truth be told, he'd rarely left his suburban copyeditor's desk to cover "politics," which in Denver consisted of mind-numbing FYI briefings at the governor's office and press conferences hastily called by this or that aggrieved interest group. A decade and a half after graduating at the top of his class, he'd counted himself lucky to be plying his trade at a cluttered desk at a struggling publication in a strip mall in Golden, Colorado, attempting to pass off rewarmed, barely rewritten releases as insider news for diehard politicos.

Ironically, a few weeks after filling out the online contest entry, he'd received the clean-out-your-desk notice straight from Corporate. He'd been vaguely expecting the downsizing, but when the shoe dropped it'd left unexpectedly deep tread marks—the kind that had made him want to say *to hell with it* and drink the last of the good beers in the fridge before they up and flew the coop, too.

Twenty-four hours after receiving his pink slip, he'd received a second unexpected communiqué, this one a text from his now ex-editor at the *Partisan* that read: "Meet me down at the office in an hour. Press, I've got news for you."

The text was vintage Geoff Hickenlooper—stoical and close to the vest. Jake was "Press"—short for Preston—and Hickenlooper was simply "Hick." In the dog-eat-dog world of journalism, a first name was best regarded as a privilege.

"Ever been to Iowa?" the editor had asked when Jake had arrived shortly after 9 PM to find the office door unlocked.

"My grandparents had a farm there before they moved to Phoenix. Why?"

"Because you, my friend, are the lucky winner of the Politics Up Close contest," he'd said, sliding the notification across the conference table, his tone the usual mixture of fatigue laced with more compassion than was good for the head honcho of a newsroom.

"Hick, you're not allowed to let me work here anymore, remember? The Big Boss gave me the axe."

"And you still don't work here…at least not on paper. I'm asking you to go as a favor to me, Press, and to yourself."

"To Iowa?"

Hick nodded. "You applied to the contest before your termination, so you're grandfathered in as I see it. All reimbursements for meals, mileage, and lodging go through me and only me. So, no, you won't officially be on the payroll, but I can keep your gas tank and your stomach full for a while…at least until Corporate hits us with the next round of budget cuts."

"And you'd do this for me because…?"

"Because you deserve better than a pink slip, Jacob. Because when I was about your age I had the privilege of covering the Iowa Caucuses, and I've never forgotten it. I'm too old to go myself, too tied down here in Denver with the kids, but you, Press, you're ripe for a life restart. You've got nothing to lose."

"So says you and Janis Joplin…. Is this a pep talk, boss, because if it is, I didn't know you had it in you."

Hick had offered Jake his hand then, solemnizing their deal with the faint uptick of the lower lip that passed in the newsroom for a smile.

It was good to get out of Golden, Jake reminded himself now, as he piloted his Accord downhill past a few dozen hand-lettered signs bearing upbeat messages like "Welcome Candidates!" and "Choose Hereford!" into the one-horse town that had become the nation's unlikely political ground zero. Exactly 1923 flags, one for each of the denizens of the little town that could, decorated his and every other journalist's entry into the Twilight Zone.

On First Street the Stars and Bars gave way to old-fashioned red, white, and blue festoons, and a huge "Welcome to Hereford…Where the Cows Come Home" vinyl sign hung from a guy-wire supporting the town's only stoplight. The burg looked pretty much like all the farm towns he recalled from his childhood visits—three blocks of turn-of-the-century, red-brick storefronts badly in need of tuckpointing, and above the plate-glass shop windows, walk-up apartments with oversized air conditioners tipped precariously toward the sidewalk below.

All the outposts of civilization appeared to be locked up tight at 7:31 PM on a Sunday night save for the town's only bar, the aptly named Wagon Wheel, and a greasy spoon called the Cal Coolidge Café, where the word OPEN flickered in neon, promising high-carb manna in a political promised land. A hardware store, a bakery, an antique shop or two, several churches, offices for the town's only insurance agent, lawyer, and CPA, and a newspaper, the *Hereford Gate*, completed the downtown set. Of the dozen or so unoccupied storefronts, at least half, it seemed to Jake, had been commandeered by campaign staffs, repurposed as headquarters, and plastered over with signs and slogans in favor of their respective presidential candidates.

Jake hadn't eaten anything, he realized, since devouring an undersized bag of Sun Chips somewhere north of North Platte. His intention had been to book into a nice Midwestern hotel on the highway—some low-ceilinged, Ma-and-Pa affair redolent of sweetly smelling bar soap and replete with Western-themed rooms, plaid sheets, and cable television. But the three prospects he'd tried en route had been solidly booked, and so he'd found himself, instead, drifting inexorably toward downtown Hereford: *Cowtown*, his friends in Denver had jokingly called it when he'd informed them of his destination.

He parked the car, swung the Cal Coolidge Café's plate-glass door open to the jingling of bells, and sat down heavily in a booth facing the gloaming on First Street. The full menu— breakfast all day, potatoes anyway you liked them, picnic-style sides—caused him to smile. Back in Colorado, his now ex-co-workers at the *Partisan* had needled him endlessly for his love of "breakfast food." And it was true—he could eat egg sandwiches, pancakes, and bacon all day every day and exist in something akin to culinary bliss.

"You're here for our election, I take it?" remarked the strawberry blonde waitress who intercepted him just inside the door and ushered him into a booth along the far wall.

"Just what you need, right? Another no-account journalist hogging the best booth."

She smiled enigmatically as she scribbled down his order: a fried-egg sandwich and tall stack of pancakes. "I don't so much mind the hogging of booths. I'm just not much of a fan of political pork," she said, then walked away.

In her wake Jake pulled out the informational packet that had been sent him by the chair of the state Republican party, Matt Pitchford, a youngish, vaguely Nordic-looking blonde with a prematurely receding hairline and a smug grin who claimed to be a farmer's son but who looked to Jake more like a horse's ass.

> Dear Jacob Preston:
> Over 500,000 registered Iowa Republicans congratulate you on winning our party's inaugural Politics Up Close contest. We are pleased to grant you full access to the many events of the iconic Caucuses, America's First-in-the-Nation vote. As chairman I am delighted to play a central role in furthering our party's goal of increasing national access to our one-of-a-kind political process.

The cover letter was followed by a short-but-sweet missive from the national RNC chair, Prince Reebus, the precocious head honcho from Minnesota. Jake had long wondered what the party elites had seen in Reebus beyond the obvious fact that he'd hailed from a swing state—perhaps that he was young and vaguely ethnic-looking, and therefore appealing to a party eager to drop a damningly homogeneous image. Or maybe he was tapped because he was plainly at ease in front of the mic and quick with squeaky-clean jibes and one-liners aimed at the Democrats.

At the bottom of the manila mailer Jake uncovered the usual welcome wagon paraphernalia—vitals about Hereford—population 1,923, 95.3 percent white. Half of Herefordians, he learned, claimed to attend a house of worship at least once per month. Other need-to-know info included the name of the local high school mascot—The Fightin' Plowmen—and the town motto, "Acres and acres of promise." At the bottom of the prize package waited a lanyard bearing his full legal name and the name of his publication, the *Rocky Mountain Partisan*.

The Cal Coolidge Café was clean as button—not quaint or cozy exactly, but surprisingly modern. Above each booth hung signed photos of what Jake assumed to be highlights of the local scenery—covered bridges, dewy brown-eyed Susans, sky-blue chicory volunteering in yellow-green ditches. Above the table immediately behind him hung a Norman Rockwellian shot taken directly down a flag-draped First Street on what had presumably been Hereford's Fourth of July celebration. The photo above his own booth showed a fine morning mist rising above a silvery river. Its caption, "Morning on the Skunk," left Jake scratching his head.

"Don't know whether to laugh or cry, do you?"

Jake whirled around to see a youngish woman tucked in a booth along the wall opposite his, a French fry poised at the edge of her lips. He swung his arm over the back of the booth to get a better look, as much as his car-weary lower lumbar would allow, anyway. "FYI," she added, "the Skunk is a river that runs about an hour from here, not far from Long Dick Creek."

"You're joking."

"Wish I were," she said. "Look it up in your Iowa gazetteer, mouseketeer." She paused to nibble on a fry. "Well, you are the lucky sweepstakes winner, aren't you? Doesn't your golden ticket mean you get to join our plucky little club covering the corn poll otherwise known as the Iowa Caucuses?" She whipped the straw out of her glass of Coke, waving it back and forth as if she were conducting an invisible brass band:

"Hey there, hi there, ho there, you're as welcome as can be. M-I-C-K-E-Y … M-O-U-S-E!"

She drew out the last "e" like the last kid left singing at a birthday party. "Shall I continue with the jazz hands?"

Jake waved the white napkin of surrender. "I suppose that little marching song means you're somehow part of the reporters' club, too?"

"Yeah, and I didn't even have to send in ten proofs of purchase."

She was in her thirties, he guessed, a butterflies-inducing, button-down kind of beauty that made him immediately self-conscious. She said, "Why don't you bring your Happy Meal over here, and let's you and me talk shop," and motioned him over with the hand that wasn't busy with her Freedom Fries.

When he arrived tableside she gave him a firm handshake and a recitation of her vitals. "Amethyst Gilchrest. Eyes: Green; Height: 5'9"; Size: 2; Graduate: Vassar College; Employment: 7 years at the *Times*. First Iowa Caucus…last time I eat cold French fries. You?"

Jake regarded her with a mixture of apprehension and fascination. "Ditto," he said.

"Fancy that. Two of a kind in a little ol' Hereford." She sized him up with eyes twice as alive as any he'd seen back in the Denver burbs. "You ready for tomorrow?"

"What's tomorrow?"

"The same as yesterday, and the day before," she said pointing the tines of her fork absentmindedly toward the ceiling—"and the day before that…. You know, shameless pandering, awkward stump speeches, bad catering, and tragically weak coffee."

"How long have you been in town?"

Her eyes drifted toward the ceiling. "How long have I been doing hard time? Let me see here…. I arrived in Des Moines in early August in time to eat fried butter on a stick and witness Milt Cloward actually break a sweat atop the soapbox at the State Fair."

"That must have been a sight."

"T'was. That was back when the frontrunners were all happily headquartered in Des Moines."

The freckled waitress—nametag Katherine—returned with Jake's tall stack of hotcakes and sandwich in time to shoot him a disapproving look for his unilateral decision to switch tables.

"Remind me again how they all ended up in Hereford." Jake poured the syrup slowly, savoring the high-fructose corn syrup IV he'd be hooked up to for the next forty days. "Pretty much unheard of, isn't it?"

"Literally," his dinnermate said. She caught the eye of the waitress, raised her glass to signal a refill, and leaned in conspiratorially close. "This campaign is so far off the rails there's no telling what could happen next. I've never seen anything like it and neither have any of the other newsies, not even McGreedy."

"Mort McGreedy is here... in Hereford?"

"All 300 newly-divorced pounds of him. He's taken to calling his reporterly exile in Iowa his Alimony Tour.... So back to my little back-story. McGreedy and I and the rest of the reporters are packed into a town-hall meeting hoping against hope that Milt Cloward will prove he's actually not a robot, and up stands this gray-haired geezer in glasses who asks, 'Why Des Moines?' Milt, unfailingly polite, replies, 'Why Des Moines what, sir?' So the guy, who by now has sat his ass back down to listen to Cloward's answer, stands back up again and says, 'You know there's more to Iowa than our cities.' At which Cloward asks the gray-hair what town he's from, and the gray-hair replies, 'Hereford, and we'd be pleased if you'd come visit us.' So the next day the party's media relations guru...this guy named Chuck Sousage..."

"Sausage?"

"Rhymes with *corsage*. It's French, or so he claims. Anyway, the next day Chuckles clambers up to the podium at campaign headquarters to report that Milt Cloward is delighted to accept the invitation to visit Hereford. Turns out the grumpy old guy who'd posed the question is the editor of this one-horse town's newspaper, the aptly named *Hereford Gate*."

"And…?" Jake prompted, soaking up the last of the syrup with his flapjack.

"And Milt goes gaga over the place. Says it's the kind of burg where the last true Americans reside…says it made him feel like he was a boy again back in Michigan. Right there in the press conference he blows a big ol' bubble from some vintage brand of chewing gum he claims to have acquired at the little corner drugstore in town, and that smells of clove and licorice and a dash of seraphim from the glory days when even our junk food was purer. Then he grins this big, goofy grin, and announces, campaign advisors be damned, that he's moving all his in-state operations to the town named after the world's most popular breed of cattle—Hereford—where, badly punneth he, *the bull must stop*."

Jake rolled his eyes. "Yeah, we ran that quote in the *Partisan*. Pretty priceless stuff."

"Crazy is more like it." Amethyst took off her glasses and held them up toward the light, revealing a pair of too-mischievous green eyes. "There are no coincidences in politics, young grasshopper. As it turns out, the state party chair, this jackass named Matt Pitchford, grew up right here in Hereford County as close as the next own over, Goodacre. Put those two apparent coinkydinks together, and two weeks later the venerable *Register* has Cloward ten points up in the polls. A week later it's like an airfare price-war with all the other yahoos in the field practically tripping over themselves to match him. Mike Santoro sets up shop in Goodacre, Brad Charger says he's "temporarily relocating" from Hollywood to Sweet Loam, and Renard Kane and the wife no one has ever really seen buy the old church in Hereford and turn it into his Iowa headquarters. That, in a nutshell, kernel, and ear, is the twisted tale of how we find ourselves here, *Jacob Preston*," she concluded, reading the nametag from his welcome kit.

Jake caught his hands playing nervously with the sugar packets on the table, and forced them back into his lap. "My friends call me Press," he said.

"So, Press, what kind of per diem does that rag you write for—the *Rocky Mountain High*—offer youngish bucks like you anyway?"

"*Rocky Mountain Partisan*," he corrected her. "And it's $20 a day for meals; $200 a week lodging."

She whistled. "You'd live like a king in Mexico City, but here in the land of ethanol and Big Ag that won't get you a hotel room anywhere within sixty miles of Hereford, not with the media hordes waiting to get into our little walled city." She paused dramatically. "Unless of course…"

"Unless of course what?"

"Unless you pay your per diem to me and shack up at my luxurious penthouse apartment above the Sweetheart Bakery across the street."

Jake cocked an eyebrow.

"Listen, I'm dying for intelligent conversation, and I could use the extra cash to wire the place for Wi-Fi. The cell phone signal out here in tall-corn country sucks donkeys. Anyhow, no pressure, but I do have an extra room to let, two of them in fact. I'm paying a fifth of what I paid for a studio back in New York, and I've got ten times the room. Now that's living in the real economy."

Over Amethyst's shoulder Jake watched the obviously eavesdropping waitress attack his original table with a wet rag. Unfortunately, he'd left behind a conspicuous water ring and no apology.

"And you'd trust me to bunk with you because…?"

She looked at him like he must be the village idiot. "Your name has been plastered on every Republican party press release since last Friday; I don't think you're going to steal my press credentials and rob me of my virginity, at least not in that order. Besides, both have already been stolen at least once anyway." She winked. "Do we have a deal?"

"Deal," he said, shaking her hand for the second time in their brief, impromptu meal.

"What say we go back to my place then?" she said, making her eyebrows dance above her glasses. "Oh, and one more thing. In return for our little bargain, you agree, henceforth, to pick up any and all tabs at the artery-hardening Cal Coolidge Café."

$17.13 for a dinner for two—Jake dug deep into the back pocket of his Levis and laid down an Andrew Jackson on the table. Then, thinking better of it, he doubled the tip, leaving another few bucks at his original table. He considered once more the "Morning Over the Skunk" photo, noting that the photographer's signature beneath it read, in an artfully flowing script, *Katherine Genevieve Clarke*.

He glanced one more time at the waitress, as she, frowning, commenced cleaning up the mess they'd left behind. He hadn't exactly gotten off to a good start with the natives.

Jake woke the next morning to the sound of one-hundred-year-old radiators pinging and the smell of high-octane coffee being burned in the kitchen. He heard the bedroom door swing open on its rusty hinges before Amethyst Gilchrest's voice reached him with a question: "Hey, do you have any boxers I could borrow? My panties aren't dry yet."

He heard footfalls approach where he lay, sprawled out on the air mattress, and opened his eyes to a pair of pink stockinged feet directly in front of his nose. Remembering where he was, and with whom, he hastily pulled the blankets overtop of him.

"Self-conscious, are we?" She bent down for a closer examination. "Blue eyes and dark brown hair fringed with what just might be a few flecks of gray…. Tell me, did a Siberian Husky sneak into your mother's bed or are you, in fact, the child of the milkman? And speaking of Siberia, Jacob Preston, riddle me this: what's the difference between Siberia and Iowa?"

Jake groaned and put his palms over his eyes.

"I give up…what?"

"Iowa doesn't have vodka bars…otherwise I submit to you that they are one and the same place." She winked. "All and all you're not too bad a guy who eats fried-egg sandwiches at 8:00 PM on a Sunday night and washes them down with a tall stack of flapjacks. Nope, I'd say you're about the finest guy in town, which, trust me, isn't saying much."

Jake raised himself half up in the guest bed, running his finger through a prodigious bed-head. "Finer than Mort McGreedy?"

"As a body, totally; as a writer, not even close. Anyway, Sleepyhead, check out today's headline in the *Times*." She handed him her iPad, and he dutifully scrolled to the big, bold type: "Preston Presses Political Luck in Hereford."

"When did you have time to write this?"

"After you hit the hay last night," she said, snatching her tablet back. "What's a red-blooded American girl supposed to do when her new roomie retires to his own bed at 10:00 PM… Cross-stitch?"

Jake snatched the tablet back and read the article aloud, his voice sounding hollow in the high-ceilinged apartment:

> Jake Preston ate his favorite meal in Hereford Sunday night long after the candidates and the candidates' men had gone back to their Cowtown compounds. The total? A whopping $17.13. Not bad for a downpayment on forty days of the most topsy-turvy season of retail politics God-fearing Americans may ever see again.
>
> "I never expected to be where I am right now," Preston said, playing the part of the humble Everyman. "But I'm looking forward to the unparalleled access offered by Politics Up Close."

Jake put down the machine, miffed. "I didn't say that."

"You did," countered Amethyst, "in so many words. Besides, you should be thanking me for giving a shout-out to your sponsors. If you had any sense, you would have shined Matt Pitchford's and Prince Reebus's shoes twice already this morning."

Jake read the remainder of the article with an admixture of agitation and bemusement. Thankfully, it was pretty much harmless back-page stuff.

"I know what you're thinking, sport," interrupted Amethyst, "but let me remind you that is the *Times* you're holding in your ungrateful hands, the world's only go-to newspaper. And the foxy chick that spent those lines of copy on your sappy, Cinderella story happens to be a pretty big deal in certain journalistic circles. So, are you going to get up and drink some joe, or just sit in your boxers contemplating your expanding waistline?"

"You've rendered me speechless," he said, and it was true.

She tossed his phone to a cushioned landing beside him on the air mattress. "I had to check my email on it…hope you don't mind. Your data signal is *way* stronger than mine. Oh, and you got a message from Matt Pitchford. He's called a lunchtime press conference for you, which means you've got exactly two and a half hours to figure out what you want to tell the world about the undeserved privilege of covering the nation's first presidential scrimmage." With a wink Amethyst Gilchrest closed the heavy door behind her, adding through its solid oak, "Hotcakes are on the table, courtesy of this hottie with an assist from Mother Bisquick."

As soon as the door clicked shut Jake pulled on some sweats and read through the email from Pitchford—blah blah blah… *press conference, Hereford High School auditorium…all of the candidates' campaign managers will be there…here's a draft of a short statement I'll read congratulating you and the* Rocky Mountain Partisan *on your contest win.*

He'd forgotten to bring shampoo, Jake realized a few minutes later, climbing into the apartment's coral pink tiled shower whose last update, he could tell, had been in the Eisenhower administration. By necessity he would be showing up to give his first-ever press conference smelling like either Amethyst Gilchrest's Mango Madness or her Passion Fruit Decadence.

"Passion Fruit…definitely," she said, poking her head into the steamy bathroom. "And don't you dare close this door again, you fruit. There's just the right amount of humidity in here to steam the wrinkles out of my poly blends."

Jake's hand hovered momentarily over the Passion Fruit before opting for the Mango Madness. It was going to be a season of difficult choices, he figured. Might as well embrace the Madness from the beginning.

"How you feeling, champ?"

Amethyst had agreed to "speed walk" him to the high school gymnasium. His new roommate, he was beginning to realize, did everything at warp speed.

"Consider yourself lucky," she prattled on. "I spent my first six years of political writing in Gotham trying to get the movers and shakers to remember my name. People are going to know who you are from Day One."

She pointed down the street to where the Depression-era, red-brick high school towered above a spacious lawn, looking more like an old-fashioned insane asylum than a temple of learning. "Good ol' Hereford High, home of the Fightin' Plow-men, a mandatory Pledge of Allegiance, and no doubt plenty of heavy petting," said Amethyst, breaking the spell. "That's Matt Pitchford pressing flesh out front, the little blonde brown-noser. I don't want to blow your rep on your first day at school, so I'll leave you here and see you afterward. Break a leg, Press, and hey, don't color too much outside the lines, okay?"

He watched as she power-walked toward what he gathered was the press entrance. Press entrances were always backstage, backdoor affairs…cigarette butts and cracks-in-the-asphalt kinds of places you wouldn't hang around after dark unless your job depended on it.

Almost overnight Jake Preston had become a Front-Door Guy.

Pitchford met him with a firm handshake and an over-produced, overeager smile. "Welcome to the Hawkeye State…. Matt Pitchford, chair of the state Republican party."

"I know," Jake said. "I recognize your picture from the welcome packet."

Pitchford's eyebrows knit together in momentary puzzlement. "Oh, that…. Just a little primer on our state and some ground rules for your stay in Hereford."

"Ground rules?"

The party chair waved off the question like so many barnyard flies. "The contest wouldn't be legit unless it came with a whole hell of a lot of fine print. How was your ride in from Colorado?"

"Smooth sailing," Jake replied. "East of Denver it's flat as a dish pan."

"Glad to hear it," Pitchford said, clearly distracted by the steady stream of VIPs flowing into the gymnasium. Jake watched as the party chair's eyes, accustomed to picking out important people from the crowd, roved for potential flesh-pressings. "In a minute I'll walk you inside and get this clambake started. I'm going to say a few words about the Politics Up Close contest, then I'll introduce you. You go by Jake or Jacob?"

"Jake to my friends."

"Let's stick with Jacob," Pitchford suggested, trespassing well into Jake's personal space. "Makes you sound more pro-fessional." The party boss stepped back to survey him. "Don't have too many gray hairs on your head yet, do you? Well, that'll change come the second week in November."

"So," he continued, "after the intros, we'll open it up to a few softball questions. Half of the media are already in Sioux City for tomorrow night's big debate." He paused, reading the question forming on Jake's lips. "Don't worry. Your Politics Up Close pass will get you into that debate and pretty much any other media event over the next forty days—unless you want to see Milt Cloward on the shitter, that is."

"Wouldn't dream of it," Jake said.

The party chair dialed up an obligatory grin. "If you have any trouble over the next few weeks, you call me, you hear?" He pushed a business card brusquely into Jake's hand. "I'm all about leveling the playing field between the big fish in the media and the marginal players like yourself. Now let's go in and get you mic'd up."

Jake followed Pitchford through the door, down a long hallway of polished linoleum, passing what seemed far too many lockers for a school the size of Hereford High. "After you," said his host once they'd reached the door marked "Theater." Jake went first into a darkened backstage cluttered with the kind of dusty props that suggested the Fightin' Plowmen theater department had performed *The Music Man* and *A Midsummer Night's Dream* a few too many times in the past forty years. "Graduated from a school about this size myself…over in Goodacre." Pitchford's too-loud voice seemed incongruous in the semi-darkness. "Our basketball court wasn't even regulation. If you wanted to try an NBA three-pointer, you had to let fly from the bleachers."

Together they climbed a short flight of stairs to the stage, where an earnest-looking intern waited. "In about five we'll open the curtain and introduce you to the world," Pitchford said, watching as the intern pulled Jake's unruly bangs this way and that until she had no choice but to surrender. "I'll say a few words, then it'll be showtime. Are we good?" He reached out to give Jake a go-get-'em punch on the shoulder.

A few minutes later the intern who'd given him the once-over tugged on an old rope and the curtain creaked open to reveal a crowd of perhaps thirty reporterly types—80% of them guys who looked like they could use a little more Pilates in their life. As promised, Pitchford warmed them up with a slightly paraphrased version of the pep talk he'd given Jake a few minutes earlier concerning the importance of the press to participatory democracy, about the party's abiding belief in the little guy working at the little newspaper in an era of media consolidation, about how this first-in-the-nation vote gave everyone—farmer, mechanic, schoolteacher—a chance to size-up the candidates in person and test the firmness of their handshake, if not their ham hocks.

It wasn't Winston Churchill, but in Hereford it would pass as oratory.

En route to the podium Jake raised his hand to acknowledge the onlookers seated in the kind of Cold War-era folding chairs frugal school districts like this one had insisted on deploying well into the new millennium. At the podium he turned to survey the huge vinyl sign hung behind him that read "Politics Up Close" printed alongside the state Republican party seal.

From the wings Pitchford gave Jake an overzealous thumbs-up before disappearing into the backstage darkness. It was showtime.

"Thanks…thanks again for having me," Jake sputtered, the microphone emitting ear-splitting feedback. "To be honest, I'm more accustomed to reporting the news than making it." He paused, waiting in vain for at least a sympathetic nod. "Look, I know you all have important deadlines, so I'll keep this brief. I'd just like to say thank you to the party for giving a correspondent at a weekly a chance to hobnob with the Mort McGreedys of the world—the razor-sharp political journalists I grew up reading and dreamed of one day becoming."

Someone in the front row nudged the sleepy behemoth seated next to him—Mort McGreedy in the flesh, Jake realized, with a flush of excitement. "I'm honored to be in your midst, and pleased to be in Iowa, where my grandparents once owned a farm. Iowa's a long way from Bradenton, Florida, where I grew up, but I feel strangely at home here, and I'm looking forward to the next forty days. I'm sure we'd all agree that anything can happen from here on out, and probably anything will." Jake caught Pitchford's eye, and the party chair gave him another thumbs-up and a hurry-up sign in such close proximity it looked to Jake as if he was being signaled to steal third base. "So, in closing, thank you all for coming. Can I…can I answer any questions?"

Mort McGreedy didn't wait to be called on. "Who do you like in the race?" he asked.

"I wouldn't be much of a political reporter if I let that cat out of the bag this early, would I?" The crowd laughed, more at Jake's good-natured sparring with McGreedy, he imagined, than at his wit behind the mic.

"If you were much of a reporter, you wouldn't need to win a sweepstakes to be here," McGreedy fired back, and the crowd of newsies laughed again, this time with relish.

"What question do you intend to pose in tomorrow night's debate?" a disheveled scribbler in the second row asked.

"I didn't realize I would be granted a question," Jake confessed, his eyes searching the auditorium for Pitchford. "I need to think on it some more, I guess," he conceded, covering his ass. The reporter who had posed the question sat down, clearly disappointed with the non-answer, while out of the corner of his eye Jake saw a familiar face in the back row rising to throw what he hoped would be the softball he had been waiting for.

"So where will you be staying?" asked Amethyst Gilchrest, sitting down with her notepad immediately after she'd floated the question.

Jake paused, temporarily flummoxed. What was he supposed to say, that he was sleeping on the floor of the apartment of the very journalist who'd just called the question. "I…I haven't found a permanent place yet, but I'm hoping to find a room here in Hereford." He paused. "Anyone have any leads?" he asked, forcing an awkward laugh.

Amethyst stood again. "Follow-up, if I might…. Is there a woman in your life?"

The crowd of jaded, guy-journalists groaned. Some half-swiveled in their seats to shoot their young female colleague a disapproving look. Still, when they turned around to look at Jake again, their eyes told him they expected an answer.

Jake bit his lip. "Not yet. Maybe I ought to put that in the classified, too."

Pitchford hustled back onto the stage, apparently to put Jake out of his misery. "Thank you, Jacob," he said, resting his arm on his shoulder and grinning amiably. "Maybe if you play your cards right you'll end up finding a Midwest girl somewhere on the campaign trail." Pitchford checked his watch and faced the crowd. "Folks, we've got time for just a couple more questions. Yes, Mrs. Meyers."

A plump, matronly woman with eyes that reminded Jake of his grandmother's stood to be recognized. "Marianne Meyers, occasional columnist for the *Hereford Gate* and local grade school teacher…. Let me be the first local to welcome you to our town, Mr. Preston."

Jake nodded his thanks, as Marianne Meyers tapped a pen against her pursed lips, apparently deep in thought. "I've been hoping to ask you, Mr. Preston, do you know how our caucuses work?"

Jake glanced nervously at Pitchford who hastened back in front of the microphone again. These were supposed to have been routine infield flies.

"Mrs. Meyers asks an excellent question," Pitchford said, brushing his blonde bangs back from a forehead already glistening with sweat. "But we respectfully ask that you confine your questions to the Up Close Politics contest and to tomorrow night's debate."

Below where they stood on the stage, a rail-thin man, gray-haired and bespectacled, stood to introduce himself. "Herb Clarke, executive publisher of the *Hereford Gate* and Mrs. Meyers's grateful editor." The elderly newsman paused, looking down at the polished gymnasium floor as he gathered his thoughts. "I've been chagrined to discover that the majority of the national media who descend on our town don't know our primary system from a hole in the ground…. That's a little troubling for an old fossil like me. I guess I don't give two shakes for what Mr. Pitchford considers out-of-bounds or off-base, so I'm going to put Mrs. Meyers's fine and fair question to the sweeptsakes winner once again…just what do you know about our first-in-the-nation caucuses."

"I know a little bit about them," Jake offered hesitantly.

"I'm not getting any younger, young man. Tell us what you know."

"Well, I know you've got to show up at your polling place if you want your vote to count. You can't go absentee."

"But do you know, son, what actually happens on caucus night?" Jake glanced at the ancient clock behind the bleachers, wishing the bell would ring and save him from the hotseat. "Do you know, Mr. Preston, how the delegates to our state convention are chosen? Do you know the demographics of our caucus-goers?"

Mort McGreedy and his buddies turned to get a good look at the local sharpshooter. Once they had, they snorted derisively before wheeling around to stare daggers at Jake again. Meanwhile, Pitchford was doing his best to whisper something Jake couldn't quite make out.

"I'm not going to lie to you, Mr. Clarke..."

"Would that the candidates follow your example."

"I don't know everything about how your caucuses work, but that's what I'm here to learn, right?"

Clarke frowned. "It's an honest answer, Mr. Preston, but honesty doesn't make up for ignorance. If you were a rookie sportscaster covering the World Series, it would be fair to assume you would know a balk when you saw one, am I right?"

Jake stood stock-still at the front of the room, wondering what he'd done to deserve this kind of public flogging. Meanwhile, the editor reared back to throw him some more high heat. "And wouldn't it be more than a bit presumptuous if you hoped your viewers would pardon your ignorance by allowing you to learn about baseball on the job, at their expense?"

"I suppose it would."

"Well then, being a contest-winner entails more than just showing up at the stadium to collect your laurels and wave at your fans, now doesn't it?" Satisfied, Clarke took his seat and jotted down a few crisp notes before putting his arms politely in his lap like a regular good Samaritan.

The sound of feet shuffling and metal chairs scuffing the polished gymnasium floor all but drowned out Pitchford at the podium, as he struggled to salvage what not so many moments ago had been a positively golden PR moment for his party.

"Should you decide to upload a story on this afternoon's press conference to your respective publications, remember that we at the state Republican party would appreciate your sending us a copy for our files. Have a great day on the campaign trail and see you all in Sioux City for the tomorrow night's debate. Remember, drive safe, watch out for bucks, and don't take any bull."

It was Pitchford's signature closing, but it was, to extend Herb Clarke's trenchant baseball analogy, a swing and a miss.

"How bad was it?"

As promised, Amethyst met Jake on the corner of School Street and Washington for the post-mortem.

"I'm not going to lie," she replied. "It was pretty awful."

"Like how awful?"

"Like being on the wrong end of a no-hitter awful."

"That's what I thought," Jake confessed. "What's with that guy anyway?"

"Herb Clarke? Oh, he's just an incorrigible grump. The candidates go out of their way to steer clear of him. Mostly because they know he'll ask them tough questions."

"What's his angle?"

"Don't think he has one. Basically, I think he's had this town to himself a little too long. And he's pissed that he has to share it."

"He seems sort of mean."

"*Mean* as in unable or unwilling to bullshit like the rest of us," remarked Amethyst. "So he's unwilling to shine sunshine up your ass, or take it easy on you because you're Charlie Bucket holding the Golden Ticket. So sue him."

"And what about Marianne Meyers?"

Amethyst answered without missing a beat. "Local schoolteacher who dabbles in writing a weekly column for Clarke called 'The People's Corner.' Mostly it's inspirational bit and bobs from a woman-about-town…feel-good, civic do-gooding stuff, you might say, mixed with a bit of sunshine and the old-time Socials column that died a quiet death in any self-respecting newspaper long before we were born. You know, 'So and so visited so and so at the Women's Auxiliary League, and gee ain't that swell.'"

"And yet that sweet, smiley grandmother was the first to fire a shot across my bow."

"Gotta hand it to her," Amethyst admitted, "school marm's got spunk. I've made reading her fluffy columns a guilty pleasure the past six weeks, God help me, but they've definitely gotten edgier since Cloward headquartered his campaign here after Labor Day." Amethyst whirled around in the street to face her newfound sidekick. "But forget Marianne Meyers. What I want to know is why you didn't tell Mort McGreedy and everyone else in that gymnasium that you were bedding down in the *casita* of the cutest, sweetest reporter this side of Goodacre."

She batted her eyelashes as mock-sweetly as if she'd just agreed to wear Jake's letter jacket to the Hereford High homecoming. "Anyway, I know you well enough to know you won't answer me, you prude, and I'm hungry enough to eat a horse, as they say in these parts, so what say you 'n' me saddle up, partner, and ride on in to lift us some greasy spoons at the Cal Coolidge Café?"

"Not until you tell me what your headline from today's disaster-of-a-press conference will be."

"*Press Grills Press?* Nah, probably too punny, too *Kramer vs. Kramer.* Let me see here…how about *Sweepstakes Winner Loses Tough Opener With Press.*"

"Too wordy," Jake interjected.

"*Bachelor Winner Seeks Lesson in How Politics Work….* No, still too long? How about your basic wordplay, something like *Journalist Stupefied by Politics Up Close.*"

"You're too kind."

"It's not my job to be kind," she reminded him. "Still, maybe we do need a headline to humanize you, help readers understand you're just a small-town reporter in way over your head. *Up Close Winner Admits Lots to Learn on Campaign Trail.* Is that vanilla enough for you?"

"I can live with that."

"You'll have to," Amethyst said, breaking into a run. "C'mon slowpoke. I want to get there before they take down the lunch specials. Last one there is a deviled egg."

"Or a bum steer," Jake said, jogging after her. It was the first time he could remember running after anything other than one of the windblown credit card receipts that roiled out of his car.

He had to admit…he sort of liked the chase.

Two

"Who do you think will bite it in the debate tonight?"

Beside him in the passenger seat of Jake's rusted-out Accord, Amethyst Gilchrest filed her nails as nonchalantly as if she'd just committed political murder.

"C'mon, Am, it's not a heavyweight bout."

"There's where you're wrong, mister. Remember you're the latecomer to this political Rumble in the Jungle…or should I say this Tussle in the Tall Corn. I was ringside at the first two title fights. And there's already been two knock-outs."

"More like an Agatha Christie murder mystery than a fight, isn't it?" Jake offered. "What's the name of the one where, one after another, the suspects get axed?"

"*And Then There Were None.* Trust me, it's *way* more gloves-off than that. A better analogy would be Ultimate Fighter."

"You didn't really think Tom Polenta had a chance, did you?"

Amethyst ceased her nail-filing to scowl at him. "He was a former governor of Minnesota. I would have at least expected him to be competitive in a neighboring state."

"You think the voters punished him for going after Rochelle Boxman in the first debate?"

"Probably. Every politician knows there's hell to pay if you go after a woman. But if you're a woman you're allowed to perform like a little pit bull. Boxman goes after Polenta, and she's tough, not bitchy. Polenta goes after Boxman, and he's an incorrigible prick. Classic double standard."

In the rear-view Jake caught himself smirking. "I assumed a feminist would see it the other way around."

"Are you kidding? I could find a gendered double standard in an electrical bill. A minor in Women's Studies has got to be good for something."

"So who do you think will crash and burn tonight?"

"The smart money says Brad Charger," Amethyst declared, assuming a new direction in her quest to outflank her stubborn hangnail. "I mean what chance does a gay Republican have in an evangelical state?"

"Remember, though, this was one of the first states to legalize gay marriage."

"Yeah, and they promptly recalled the poor Supreme Court justices who voted for it. I mean, good for Charger for running on principle, but how long can his funding hold out? He's barely polling two percent. The only reason he got into tonight's debate is because Pitchford thought it would make his not-so-compassionate conservatives look tolerant."

"Do you think Renard Kane can stay in the race?"

"It's another Big Ask, if you ask me," Amethyst said. "An African American Republican on a presidential ticket is as rare as hen's teeth, and probably about as electable as hen's teeth, too…whatever the hell they are." She paused to look out the window. "No, for me tonight's big unknown is what Mr. Politics Up Close is going to ask for his token question."

"Been thinking about it all day." Outside Jake's window a seemingly endless number of farmsteads drifted by. "I want it to be something original, but not totally out of leftfield either, you know?"

"I'm pickin' up what you're puttin' down," his seatmate replied, putting her feet up on the dashboard. "I'd be having the same dilemma if I were in your totally unhip shoes."

"No you wouldn't. You'd ask them if they had a girlfriend."

"Yeah, and probably half of them do…that is, in addition to their wife."

"I'd like to ask them something about the place they're campaigning rather than the generic stuff Donna Sawyers and George Agropolis are going to ask them."

"Ask them about farm policy then."

"Can't," Jake said. "Don't know enough about it"

Amethyst frowned. "I thought your grandparents farmed."

"They did…. And I was usually only there long enough to eat the sweetcorn."

Amethyst dug deep in her purse, coming up with paydirt. "I'll read you some blurbs from today's *Register*, okay, and you tell me if any of these butters your bread. Here's headline numero uno: 'Hawkeyes questionable at running back versus Clones.' You could always pitch them a football question, you manly man."

"'Fraid They wouldn't be dumb enough to fumble a football question. If they don't know their pigskin by now, they're pretty much toast with Middle American male voters."

"Fair point," Amethyst conceded. She twirled her bangs around her index finger while she scanned the newsprint for another prospect. "Here's one. Seems all the football fans are pooh-poohing the new Interstate Pigskin Trophy sponsored by the Ag Bureau. Says here they're miffed that the trophy design doesn't have anything to do with football. It's cast in the shape of a silver steer."

"Is it wearing a helmet?"

"Very funny."

"Keep looking."

"Here's one…the League of Cities says small-town graft is at an all-time high. Goodbye, Norman Rockwell and Apple Pie, hello stolen laptops."

"Maybe I'm better off just cooking something up on the spot."

"Right, because that worked so well for you at the press conference yesterday."

"I survived it, didn't I?"

"Just by the skin of your Hawkeye."

"Quiet you, or I'll force you to listen to Rush Limbaugh." Jake punched "scan" on the AM dial and, lo and behold, five of the first seven stations featured El Rushbo.

"Don't tell me you actually listen to that cigar-smoking chauvinist pig."

"Someone out here in farm country sure does," Jake pointed out. "It's all Rush, all the time."

"Does it have to be Rush during our drive-time, though?" his seatmate whined, reaching for the dial.

"Hey, it's research," Jake replied, playfully swatting her hand away. "Whatever happened to when in Rome, do as the Romans do?"

Amethyst frowned. "The same thing that happened to Rome. FYI, you insist on listening to his bullpucky, and I'll make good on my threat to power nap."

"Oh no, not that," Jake teased, as on the radio Rush jumped on some poor welfare mom's case.

"Do me a favor then, will you, Mr. Dittohead? Wake me up when we're in Sioux City, okay?" Am mumbled before clamping her eyelids shut.

"*Wake Me Up When We're in Sioux City.* Isn't there some croony old jazz standard by that title?"

"If there is I pray to God I never hear it."

After five minutes of Limbaugh lullabies Amethyst Gilchrest had made good on her campaign promise to saw some serious logs. When her first bead of drool began its inevitable decline in the polls, Jake switched the radio off and basked in what he'd been driving at all along: silence.

Amethyst shivered, pulling a shawl over her shoulders. They had rolled into town early, it was cold, and she was fit to be tied.

"Let's go over to the hotel and get us a hot toddy," she coaxed, tugging Jake by the sleeve of his sport coat. "All the political scribblers will be bellied up to the bar until right before the curtain goes up on the debutante ball."

Inside the Hotel Sioux City, Jake discovered she was right. All the reporters were there, including Mort McGreedy, who was holding court as the usual retinue of remoras circled the biggest fish in the press pool.

McGreedy waved them over when he spotted them. He was sweating profusely, Jake noticed, his glasses either smudged-over or fogged-up, it was hard to tell. Overall, he looked as if he'd been on a pretty newsworthy three-day bender.

"Pull up a chair," he growled, brushing back the ring of admirers with a bear paw while fixing Jake in his walleyed gaze. "Jake Preston," he said, raising his glass, "welcome to the big-time."

"Welcome to the big-time!" one of the acolytes parroted, and it was down the hatch all around the table. McGreedy clapped Jake on the back with enough force to knock the whiskey right out of him. "So what chestnuts do you two fresh-faced newsies have for us grizzled veterans?" McGreedy looked around the table at the scrum of gray-haired, bespectacled men that qualified as his groupies.

"Cut the old-man shtick, will you, McGreedy," Amethyst said, returning serve. "I'm just as jaded as you and your Middle-Aged Men's Club about this dog-and-pony-show. Jake here might just be gullible enough to be sucked in by it though," she added, taking an impish pull on her Tom Collins through a red plastic straw.

Jake hesitated. "I don't know quite what to think yet."

McGreedy smiled ruefully. "Now that's profound. With gems like that you'll go far in this business."

"What I mean," Jake continued, "is that for me it's innocent until proven guilty. So, they're all thespians…so what? We fault candidates for being bland if they aren't Mr. Charismatic. And if they're dramatic we fault them for not being more sober."

"He's right," Amethyst agreed. "And speaking of the so-not-sober, remember covering your first presidential debate, McGreedy? What was it again…Lincoln versus Douglas?"

"Very funny, Gilchrest."

"Just saying…you were jazzed, right? You believed anyone had the chance to win. You believed with your whole, not-yet-hardened heart that the candidates were seeing the questions for the first time, that they all liked or at least respected one another, and that they hadn't rehearsed every quip and barbed rebuttal in advance."

Across the table McGreedy nodded.

"And good for you," Amethyst continued, "because you believed in the system. Look, the process is pretty much the same now as it was when you first crawled out from under your rock, McGreedy, give or take. It's we around this table who've changed."

McGreedy leaned back in his chair stool until it appeared to Jake as if the whole thing would give way under the weight. "Wish I could agree with you, however, I was never under any illusions about 'the process.' Remember, I broke into this business just after Watergate. And as bad as Nixon and the White House Plumbers were, it's been pretty much downhill ever since."

"You really think so?"

"I *know* so. Super PACS, bought judges, less campaigning and more fundraising, half of the amount of time spent on the ground in states like Iowa…and now comes the latest and greatest form of grassroots manipulation: social media. I'd have retired from this charade months ago, were it not for the alimony and a kid to put through college." McGreedy swirled his whiskey. "On the positive side these clowns give a political writer the best material he could ever want, and then some. I owe my living to their perennial buffoonery." The journalistic giant swiveled dramatically in his chair until he was facing Jake. "Tonight Preston here gets his first real taste of the once-every-four-years cloak-and-dagger. Let's see if he leaves feeling better about the state of participatory democracy or if he's ready to commit Hari Kari in the spinroom afterward."

The larger-than-life reporter slammed his tumbler down to the table with a sharp thwack, cracking the night's first sick smile. "Anyway, this debate will have to wait until after the debate. It's almost 7:30. Journalists, to your battle stations."

By the time they made it to the pressroom in the Hotel Sioux City, the folding tables had already filled with newsies and the cheesy potato hot dish catered in from the local grocery store had mostly been devoured. At each media station a small table tent listed the name of the reporter's publication, and Jake was weirdly startled to see his own rag, the *Rocky Mountain Partisan*, spelled out for him in all-caps. In the few days since he'd left Denver he'd forgotten he had a pseudo-employer at all.

Meanwhile, three seats down from him, Amethyst Gilchrest gnawed on sunflower seeds like a manager of a particularly pathetic baseball team, spitting out the hulls into a homemade spittoon she'd fashioned from some repurposed hotel glassware.

"No, I haven't forgotten you, Press," she said in answer to Jake's unspoken question. She pinched a seed between her freshly lip-balmed lips. "Is someone feeling a little bit needy?"

"No," Jake countered automatically, though in truth he was alarmed by Am's ability to read his mind.

"As soon as you're done soothing your damaged masculine ego, feast your eyes on the boob tube over there. Donna Sawyers and George Agropolis are coming out now to shake hands. George is kinda cute, in that small, hairy, Greek bobblehead sort of way, don't you think?"

"Wouldn't know," Jake replied, salving what remained of his male ego. He located the nearest big-screen and settled in for what he expected would be a two-hour-long marathon. Luckily, tonight's caterer had been smart enough to provide kettle corn. It was hell on the keyboards, but good for the soul.

"Welcome, all, to the third in our series of Republican presidential debates," Donna Sawyers, the former beauty queen turned broadcast journalist, began, smiling beatifically into the camera. "And welcome to Iowa, where Caucus voters will be going to the polls a little over a month from now. The economy and foreign policy will be our focus tonight, as voters in this state and around the nation hope to learn more about this fascinating cadre of candidates…. George, if you're ready…"

"Ready as ever, Donna."

"I pass the baton to you for the night's first question."

Agropolis grinned with the smart-as-a-whip smugness he had become famous for—a smile that made you think he had all the answers stowed away in that oversized cranium of his.

"Good evening to each of you, candidates. As Donna alluded to, many voters report feeling as if they don't know you yet. So let's go down the line, and have each of you re-introduce yourself, telling us why you're running for your party's nomination. Share with us something that makes you stand out from the crowded field. Let's begin with the only woman on our stage tonight, Congresswoman Rochelle Boxman. Congresswoman Boxman, thirty seconds."

"Oh my God," Amethyst said, momentarily choking on her sunflower seeds, "the munchkin brought her own little box to stand on. Can you see it?" The newsroom erupted in a series of guffaws and catcalls so derisive it sounded like the Houses of Parliament. "I know she's vertically challenged, but…her own personal riser? Please!"

"Thank you, George, and thanks to the people of the Heartland and to the network for hosting this important debate. I'm honored to be here, and honored to be standing up for true conservative values. I'm a farmer's daughter from just across the river in South Dakota, so I know a load of bull when I see it. Voters in the Midwest and throughout the country can count on me to sniff out 'stuff' of the kind emanating from this White House."

"Thank you, Congresswoman," said Agropolis. "Next up is Rich Priestly, former governor of the great state of Oklahoma. "Governor Priestly, take it away."

Priestly smiled big, opening his broad arms as if to wrap the entire convention center in a humongous man-hug. "I'm askin' the good people of this state for their vote because, well, I'm just a simple country boy from Salt Lick, who somehow growed up, married his high school sweetheart, and made good. I'm pretty much exactly like the rest of y'all in the audience tonight."

"Ain't that the truth," Amethyst muttered darkly.

Agropolis jotted down a note. "Next up is businessman, preacher, and radio personality Renard Kane. Mr. Kane?"

"Thank ya, George, thank ya, Donna, and thanks to all the good folk who've joined our campaign. Listen, I'm a businessman, and businesspeople know all about making a judgment call 'bout whether or not whatever's gonna fly. That's what I'm prepared to do in the Oval Office—make the is-it-gonna-fly decisions. That's what the hardworking folks in this auditorium are gonna do on caucus night when they make the call in their livin' rooms, and firehouses, and school gymnasiums about who they want as their nominee for president. I'm hopin' they're gonna put me in the game, and if they do, I promise I'll catch the last-minute Hail-Mary pass they're gonna throw me and run it in for a score. I'll sink that three-pointer at the buzzer and point right back at 'em in gratitude for the assist, givin' credit where credit is due."

"Thank you, Mr. Kane, for that athletic answer. And now it's your turn, Congressman Paul Paule."

"Thank you, George. My name is Paul Paule, and I'm the only strict Constitutionalist on this stage. Voters are tired of the government playing king and usurping their God-given rights. They know that I've been in Congress for more than three decades consistently calling Big Government on its abuses, and they know I don't plan to stop anytime soon."

"Thank you, Mr. Paule," Agropolis said, while on stage Paule cracked a wizened if not slightly unsettling grin. "Next we have Dolph Heinrich."

"Let me just echo what's been said earlier, about the importance of this election. As a former history professor, college president, and congressman, I understand all too well the magnitude of the historical moment. I submit to you that just as Lincoln debated Douglas, the country would be well served should I have the privilege of being the nominee to debate the current occupant of the White House. I'd be happy to inform him that his economic policies have been disastrous…the worst, in fact, since the Great Depression. It takes some historical perspective to realize just what a God-awful mess our current Commander-in-Chief has put us in."

"A sobering perspective, to be sure," Agropolis replied, ad-libbing. "Let me turn the reigns back over to Donna now to take us through the rest of the candidate introductions. Donna?"

"Thank you, George. Mr. Charger, your turn. What do American voters need to know about you, perhaps the most unknown of the candidates onstage tonight."

"Donna, I may not be well-known by American voters, but American television viewers may remember me from the work I did on *Starsky and Hutch* and *Welcome Back, Kotter*, in the 1970s. They'll want to know that I come from a long tradition of conservative Hollywood actors in the mold of Ronald Reagan, Clint Eastwood, and Arnold Schwarzenegger. And I'm proud to say I'm the only candidate standing on the stage tonight who embraces same-sex unions as the first-ever openly gay candidate for President of these United States."

"Gay? No way!" Wisecracked Amethyst, pointing to the lavender Oxford beneath Charger's navy blue sport coat.

Onstage the unflappable Donna Sawyers moved on. "Next up is the senator from Ohio, Mike Santoro. Senator?"

"Thanks for this opportunity, Donna, to speak directly to the American people, and to remind them that a vote for Santoro is like getting your antifreeze and your diapers and your potato chips all in one. I'm your one-stop-shopping Republican... strong on defense, strong on family values, strong on the rights of the unborn, and strong in defense of the sanctity of marriage. The people out there in this great hall tonight and at home in front of their televisions eating the last of the old maids from the bottom of the popcorn bowl should know that with me what you see is what you get—a working-class son of Italian immigrants who pulled themselves up the right way...the American way...by the bootstraps, only expecting from the government what they absolutely could not provide for themselves."

"Last but not least, we come to the man most polls show as the frontrunner, former governor of Connecticut, Milt Cloward. Governor Cloward, the mic is all yours."

On screen Cloward's pearly whites gleamed and his black hair glistened.

"Donna, I can't remember the last time I got called last in roll call. That doesn't happen very often when you're a guy whose last name begins with a 'C.'" Cloward chuckled amiably. "Let me just say how pleased I am to meet the voters of Sioux City tonight, this historic cattle town on the banks of the mighty Missouri River. On a night like this I'm reminded of the greatness of our rivers, and of our people, and of all the good and wholesome products We the People have brought to market over the centuries since we settled this once-wild frontier. And that's really what I'm all about…markets…free-markets…and making sure we're trading our goods with partners who don't manipulate their currency or slap unfair tariffs on our imports. When America competes on a level playing field, there's no other country on the face of God's green earth that can top us. That's why I'm here tonight, Donna, to remind us that folks in places like this settled harsh and unforgiving lands in order to bring the best products of the land to customers willing to purchase the fruits of their labor. That's a good and worthy thing to stand for. And I intend to stand for it. Thank you."

"Pretty presidential," Jake heard himself muttering, while catching an eye-roll from Amethyst.

"Reminds me of Thomas Dewey," said a gruff voice that Jake recognized immediately as belonging to Herb Clarke, the editor of the *Hereford Gate* who had uncharitably grilled him the day before about the ins and outs of the caucus system. "But I don't suppose you remember Dewey, do you, Mr. Preston? Probably weren't even born when he died."

Jake wasn't sure whether he should be offended at the dig the old man had dealt him or whether he should apologize for not noticing the crusty curmudgeon in the first place. So he simply said, "Didn't see you there, Mr. Clarke."

"That's what makes me dangerous, Mr. Preston. Unlike Mr. McGreedy over there, I don't call attention to myself." The inscrutable editor nodded toward the big-screen, a cue that the coverage was about to recommence.

Donna Sawyers turned serious as the camera zoomed in. "As we gather here tonight in this beautiful convention hall, in this bountiful Midwestern state, storm clouds gather in the Middle East. Just yesterday the U.N. atomic watchdog group warned that Iran was once again flaunting IEAA inspections by moving forward aggressively with a nuclear weapons program. Paul Paule, what would you say to a resurgent Iran?"

Paul Paule looked to Jake like he'd just swallowed a handful of spiders. "What would I do? Why, I'd talk to those poor people who have been suffering under the rule of a repressive regime since Americans were wearing bell bottoms. Of course their regime isn't much more repressive than our own. Those people over there deserve to be talked to, and what do we do? Like a big bully baby we refuse to talk to 'em…. Let 'em have their bomb. They're not a threat to our national security. How would we treat a country that tried to tell us what weapons we could and could not have in our arsenal? It's the Golden Rule."

"What in the hell is a big bully baby?" Amethyst asked, scratching her head, while out in the convention center Donna Sawyers continued with the cattle call.

"Mr. Charger," she said, unexpectedly turning to the darkhorse candidate, "what would you do about the worsening situation in Iran?"

"As a Reagan Republican I believe in a strong defense," Charger said soberly. "But as a gay man I believe the best defense is a good offense. I understand better than most what it's like to live in an atmosphere of fear and distrust, and that's why we can't tolerate loose nukes in Iran. Because the same mullahs who would shut down the newspapers and the cybercafés, would also squelch individual liberties and the right to express and live out one's sexual destiny."

"Tell me he didn't just go there," Amethyst said, bringing the legs of her chair crashing back down to the floor of the pressroom. "That's one for the annals, or should I say anals, of presidential history. Oh, baby, this is gettin' good."

"A penetrating comment, Mr. Charger. Now to Senator Santoro…. What would you do about the rise of Iranian power in a volatile region?"

"I'd snuff it out like Smokey snuffs out wildfires. Ladies and gentlemen, what we have in the Middle East is a smoldering conflagration, and, if Iran succeeds in getting nukes, we could all wake-up one morning to find ourselves burned like so many scorched s'mores. Look, Paul Paule means well, but his views on Iran are simply dangerous. If he were President he'd be over in Tehran playing checkers with the Iranian president and swapping stories about how God-awful America is. Paul, you and I come from different generations, and in the generation I come from, checkers is a game for losers and nerds. Let me be clear, nothing—and I do mean nothing—will be as painful as the hurt I, as President, would put on Iran."

"Milt Cloward, as the leader in the polls, I'd like to give you the last word on this important issue," Sawyers intoned.

Cloward swallowed hard and stared into the camera. "America has the strongest military the world has ever known. As President, rest assured, I would have no problem pulling the trigger whenever, and wherever, terror threatens our way of life, at home or abroad. I'll fight fire with fire and that…"

"Are you saying you would give the go-ahead to the Joint Chiefs to launch a preemptive strike on Tehran?" Agropolis interjected.

"George, you've been in this business long enough to know that a President never says never."

"But does he ever say ever?"

"Every so often," Cloward said, grinning at their thrust and parry. "But then again, forever may never come."

"Isn't that a James Bond movie?" Amethyst quipped, pacing the room while simultaneously forking catered cubes of cantaloupe into her mouth with a toothpick.

"Yeah," McGreedy deadpanned, "It's the one after *Trigger Finger*, starring Mike Santoro, *Dr. No*, starring Paul Paule, and *Casino Imbecile*, starring Rich Priestly."

"Nope, it was the totally forgettable sequel to *Idiots Are Forever*," Amethyst said, wadding up a campaign press release and shooting it into the trashcan for a definite score. "What about you, Press, what's your personal James Bond movie going to be called…*Muckraker?*"

"*Live and Let Cry*," McGreedy piped up, piling on.

"*From Iowa With Love*," Herb Clarke pitched in from out of nowhere, "that will be the name of Mr. Preston's Bond film, don't you think?"

"Coming up after the commercial break we'll have a special question from Politics Up Close winner Jacob Preston. You won't want to miss it."

"Oh my God," Amethyst exclaimed, "it's time for your question, you big bully baby! Have you decided?"

Jake shook his head, and the whole press corps rained down abuses on him. They worked too hard, tirelessly following the candidates cross the country to get in so much as a question, to see this interloper, this ingrate, fritter away such journalistic manna.

Amethyst massaged his shoulders like a corner man in a heavyweight bout where her man was losing badly. "They're coming back from commercial break in a sec, Press. For once in your slothful life, think fast."

"We're back," George Agropolis said after what seemed to Jake the shortest commercial break in history. "And now, let's go to the pressroom, where the winner of the Politics Up Close contest, Jacob Preston, is standing by with our next question. Are you there?"

Jake watched on screen as, out in the convention hall, Agropolis looked anxiously at his monitor. "Jake, are you with us?"

"I'm with you," he managed.

"Great. Go ahead with your question."

Frantically, Jake racked his brain, and the only thing he could think of was the headline Am had read him en route to Sioux City—the story about the derelict football trophy. What was it called again?

"Jake?"

"Yes, George…. Uh, I read in the newspaper today that the trophy for the Interstate Football Series…the Silver Steer… has come under fire. So my question is…if there was a trophy for winning the first-in-the-nation vote, what do you think it should be?"

Jake watched on the big-screen as his unorthodox—okay, pathetic—question registered with Agropolis and Sawyers.

"There you have it, candidates," Agropolis said after a long and difficult pause. "The sweepstakes winner wants to know what trophy you would suggest for this presidential contest. Mr. Charger, why don't we start with you?"

Brad Charger adjusted his frameless glasses. "A rainbow," he said.

"A rainbow because…" Agropolis followed up, "…because it's a sign of tolerance?"

"Well, yes, there is that. And rainbows are hopeful."

"How would you cast one in silver?" Agropolis persisted, nonplussed.

"I'm afraid I have to call time on what would no doubt have been a fascinating answer," Sawyers chimed in. "Mr. Heinrich," she said, turning to the one-time history professor turned candidate, "what would your trophy look like?"

"The bust of Lincoln," Heinrich intoned. "And I would consult it before each and every decision I took in the interest of the American public."

"Okay," Sawyers said, raising a professionally dubious eyebrow, "back to you, George."

"Paul Paule, what would be a fitting prize in your mind for this presidential race?"

Paul Paule blinked twice. "I wouldn't have a prize," he said flatly. "Trophies cost money. What good is some cheap plastic bauble when we'd have to borrow money to pay for something they probably made in Red China in the first place."

Sawyers shook her head. "Now that's thrifty. No money in the federal coffers for so much as a trophy. Mr. Paule, you certainly are a true fiscal conservative. Congresswoman Boxman, what say you to this most intriguing question?"

Rochelle Boxman batted her eyelashes, wide-eyed at the possibilities. "That's a tough one, Donna. I'd say just having the privilege to represent people like these hardworking Iowans would be reward enough for this South Dakota farmer's daughter."

"Isn't that just precious," Amethyst said, disgusted. "I suppose she wants world peace, too."

"Are you kidding," McGreedy piped up. "She's a hawk. She'd rather have a hot little war on her hands."

"George, back to you to pose the question of the hour to our early frontrunners."

"Renard Kane," Agropolis said, picking up the hot potato while it was still warm. "We're all dying to know…what would your trophy be?"

"A six pack of Coke and a dinner at McDonalds with my wife, Candy," Kane said, cracking a slightly sideways grin.

Agropolis looked down at his notes. "Mr. Santoro, how about you?"

Santoro cocked his head quizzically, as if he were Joe the Plumber contemplating an abstract expressionist painting. "As the only real deficit hawk on this stage besides Paul Paule, I'd say let's put that existing trophy to good use, especially if the football teams don't want to put it into the game. Let's turn to the old-fashioned American work ethic that once made us famous around the world and repurpose that sucker. It's either that or the Silver Steer goes back to the foundry, right, and ends up as somebody's tooth filling. What's wrong with a statue of a proud head of cattle made at a factory right here in the Heartland from American materials? There's something so right in the symbolism of the mighty steer—proud, free, and totally ticked off."

"If it was offered as a campaign prize for the victor, you would accept the Silver Steer then?" prompted Agropolis.

Santoro nodded. "With pride, George."

Sawyers leaned in again. "Governor Cloward, what would you think of that idea?"

Milt Cloward looked like he was suffering a particularly noxious round of indigestion. "Donna, am I not going to get the same chance my fellow candidates received to answer on my own terms?"

"See there," Paul Paule barked from across the stage. "Everything has got to be on the Governor's terms."

"Mr. Paule," Agropolis interrupted, tut-tutting. "Your time is up. Let's let the Governor speak for himself."

"George…Donna, will you permit me the chance to answer the question according to my dictates?"

"Go ahead," Agropolis said, unblinking.

Cloward gazed in earnest over the audience. "My own choice for a trophy would be a one-on-one communion with my God, the heavenly father. My religion teaches us that it's wicked to worship false idols."

"With all due respect, no one's talking about false idols, Governor," Sawyers said, gently but firmly. "Now if we might return for a moment to Senator Santoro's premise…. Would there be a place for the Silver Steer in a Cloward administration?"

"Donna, as you know, it's not my policy to answer hypotheticals. But, sure, if Mr. Santoro wants to compete for the likeness of an infertile bull cast in silver, he's entitled. It's a free country."

Beside Cloward, Santoro agitated. "Are you saying, Milt, that you're too good to compete for a football trophy?"

"Not at all, Mike," Cloward shot back. "But I would be remiss not to point out that even the football teams don't want to play for it."

Santoro checked his notes. "So you're saying we should just put the Silver Steer out to pasture just like you did with all those businesses you downsized and off-shored?"

Cloward swung around to face his opponent, who had just landed the night's first blow. "Senator, that's ridiculous. This isn't about American manufacturing. It's about an imitation bovine…"

"…That just happens to have been fabricated and cast right here in America by American workers and given out as a prize for excellence in a truly American sport."

"I'm simply saying that I don't believe in false idols."

"And that, ladies and gentlemen, is where we're going to have to leave it. Candidates, thanks once again from George and me for participating in this high-spirited debate wherein our candidates truly locked horns. Thanks to the people of Sioux City for your immaculate hosting. Thanks to the state Republican party for sponsoring tonight's debate, and a shout-out to Jacob Preston, winner of the Politics Up Close Contest, for that most provocative question. I have to admit, George, when I first heard it I thought it might be a bum steer."

"Me, too, Donna. I found myself wondering where was the substance…where was the beef?"

"Well, it just goes to show not to judge a heifer by its hide. Goodnight, all, from here in Sioux City."

In the pressroom Jake breathed a sigh of relief as a few of his fellow reporters clapped him on the back. The storm had passed, the first major obstacle had been overcome, and now only a two-hour drive stood between him and the ultimate bed of hay…the blissful, American-made air mattress awaiting him above the Sweetheart Bakery.

Hereford was black as a political consultant's soul as the Accord nosed its way down First Street in the wee hours of the morning. Beside Jake, Amethyst Gilchrest stirred in her sleep.

"Are we there yet?"

"Not quite," Jake answered, looking over at her for what seemed like the hundredth time tonight. It was unbelievable to him how much it felt like they were already a couple, though he had only known her for a couple of days. He could almost hear his friends' reactions back home. *You met her when? You're staying where?* There was something about Amethyst Gilchrest that made everything seem not just possible but inevitable, like it couldn't possibly happen any other way.

Jake eased the Honda down the alley behind Am's apartment, hoping to avoid waking any of the other apartment-dwellers who inhabited the second stories above Hereford's few dozen storefronts. The town appeared palpably different by night. Removed of the light hustle and bustle of daytime, it seemed mysterious, if not a bit melancholic, to him.

"Home again, home again," he said softly, putting the car in park once he felt the tires softly kiss the curb. Amethyst stirred, making groaning noises like a girl who didn't want to go to school.

"Carry me," she mumbled.

"Carry you?"

"Carry me," she said sleepily.

"I can't carry you," Jake said.

"Pleeeease."

"No can do, Princess," he said, smiling in the dark at the odd request. "Now, c'mon, let's get you up to bed."

"Not going," Amethyst said stubbornly.

A particularly brazen raccoon rifled through the neighbor's trash as Jake contemplated what should be his next move.

"Amethyst," he said, gently shaking her awake, "you know you can't stay out here all night, right?"

"Can, too," she mumbled. She turned over in her seat like an obstinate child.

If he tried to sleep in the car beside her, Jake knew, neither of them would get so much as a wink. Between the Colorado plates on his car, and the nosey neighbors, they were sure to be woken up at dawn by Officer Friendly if not the early shift at the Sweetheart Bakery. He could go inside, but he probably wouldn't be able to sleep worrying about Amethyst in the car. Who did she think she was anyway, and why did she insist on tormenting him?

After his first attempt to recline in the driver's seat had failed, Jake leaned over and whispered, "Amethyst, I'm going inside. Will you come in with me?" Shaking his head at her stubborn silence, Jake closed the car door gently, locked it for safety, cracked a window to let the fresh, night air in, and climbed the stairs up to the apartment.

A few minutes later, teeth brushed and fully into his skivvies, his conscience got the better of him. He pulled on his sweats, slipped on his flip-flops and clambered carefully down the impossibly dark flight of stairs to the parking lot where he found her exactly as he'd left her, drooling onto the upholstery, her face lit beautifully by the moonlight.

He opened the passenger door, unbuckled her seatbelt, and scooped her up, groaning as her arms reached instinctively up and around his neck. The polyester weave of her blouse scratched his cheek as he staggered toward the door.

A few backbreaking minutes later he nudged the door to the apartment open with his foot, and stumbled across the threshold into Am's room, where he half dropped her, half threw her on the bed, his arms quivering with the effort.

"Kiss me," she said, sounding like a sleepy girl again.

Jake bent down and gave her a peck on the cheek. Amethyst smacked her lips a couple of times, rolled over, and buried her head in the down comforter.

He watched her for a moment from the threshold, smiling in spite of himself, before cutting the light and closing the door.

There would be no shortage of headlines in the morning.

Three

Thx for the lift last nite. Out shaking corn for a lead and weeding out the corn bores. (Get it?) See ya when the cows come home.—Am

Jake dropped the note back on the kitchen table and shook his head at the memory of the previous night—lifting a fully-grown woman up a Victorian walk-up after the most stress-inducing night of his quasi-professional life. Not surprisingly, he had slept hard. When he'd powered up his phone it had been nearly 10 AM and the whole place smelled of sweet rolls from the bakery below.

Waiting for him had been a text message from Matt Pitchford bearing a time stamp of 7:50 AM. Whatever it was, it must have been important. There were few professional courtesies extended journalists anymore, but calling before 8:00 AM somehow endured as a serious social faux pas.

The text read: *meeting tween u and Sousage at café. 10:00 AM B there.*

Jake snorted. Sure, the guy was the chair of a state Republican party, but a state most people got confused with Idaho, or Ohio…a state that seemed to lose a seat in Congress with every Census because so many of its young people moved away. He could either blow off the meeting completely or he could make a half-assed attempt to pull a comb through his hair, throw on an Oxford, and make a bee-line for the Cal Coolidge Café. Had there been some decent breakfast food around Am's apartment, he might just have played hooky and maybe tried to peck out a doomed story for his saintly ex-editor back in Golden—Hick, the man who would be picking up the tab for his $1.99 short stack. But there was nothing much in the cabinets besides some ancient rotini, and little in the fridge beyond some barely used condiments, so he put on his shoes and left.

A healthy dose of foot traffic awaited Jake on First Street, as he stepped out the door headed in the direction of the Cal Coolidge. The best dressed among the passersby, Jake suspected, were campaign staffers and rent-a-wonks, though they never identified themselves as such, only summoned their best lukewarm smile in passing before briskly going on about their business.

As he opened the door to the café Jake wondered whether he would be able to pick Chuck Sousage out of a crowd, but there was little doubt when he saw a middle-aged man sporting a healthy head of hair and a freshly pressed suit jacket hung on the hook beside the booth.

"Chuck?" Jake approached the table hesitantly as if this was more of an awkward blind date than a political tete a tete.

The man stood up to offer him a meaty hand. "Welcome to Hereford. Have a seat, Chief."

Jake groaned as he lowered himself into the booth.

"Jesus, Jacob," Chuck Sousage commented. "You look like a pack of hungry lionesses worked you over last night. What gives?"

"Bad back," Jake replied, reaching around to massage his lower lumbar.

"You slip a disc scooping all that horseshit from the debate last night?"

Jake chuckled ruefully. "That and lifting a particularly heavy load to a second-story apartment."

"Man, you've got to take care of yourself. You're a celebrity now." Sousage pushed several front pages across the table at him. "Do you want to read about yourself in the *Times*, the *Tribune*, or the *Journal*. You're the belle of the ball, kid."

Jake glanced down at the headlines, his eyes landing on the phrase "most revealing question of the night" and "especially memorable debate," while Sousage motored on. "Of course tomorrow the same hacks who today are blowing sunshine up your ass will crucify you. Enjoy the fame while it lasts, that's my advice. Because, Jake…it won't last."

"Don't expect it to," he replied, putting down the news rags in favor of a menu.

"Sousage," Chuck said when the freckled, strawberry blonde waitress—Katherine again—stood before them with her short-order pad at the ready.

"Eggs with your patties?" she asked.

Jake's breakfast partner smiled ruefully. "No, I mean my name is Sousage. And this is Jacob Preston."

Katherine blushed—beautifully, Jake noticed. "Pleased to meet you," she said. "Sorry for the mix-up on the name."

"Don't think a thing about it, darlin'" Sousage dripped, pushing the charm button again. "Happens all the time, believe me…. Anyhow, just a coffee and an English muffin for me," he said, patting his belly. "Trying to get back to my fightin' weight."

"Fried-egg sandwich, hotcakes, and home fries," Jake said, stacking up the menus neatly before passing them off to the waitress.

"I think you may want to keep this." She returned to him a rumpled broadsheet that had accidentally found its way between the menus. "Your grandkids may want to tease you about it some day."

"Got to have kids first," Jake said, smiling as brightly as he could.

"She's a looker," Chuck commented when Katherine left for the short-order window. "You married, Jake?"

"That's a negative."

Chuck raised his eyebrows provocatively. "So you ready to talk about the sport that's second only to sex?"

Jake looked on silently as Sousage steamrolled ahead.

"I mean politics, man…. Suffice it to say, last night was the bomb. I've been trying to generate that kind of PR for the party for years, and you do it all in a single night with one dumb-ass question." Sousage paused, gauging Jake's reaction. "Every sorry rag from the *Dill Weed Daily* to the *Podunk Pilot* to the *Shit-can Sentinel* has mentioned the Iowa Republican Party and the Politics Up Close contest by name this morning. I'm telling you it's a brander's dream, my friend! And last night's ratings were… well, let's just say they were as good as any primetime football game this season. So all and all we're riding pretty goddamn high on the hog."

"Wish I could say the same thing for myself," Jake said, reaching around in another failed attempt at self-massage.

Sousage stuck a fleshy pair of elbows on the table. "We feel fortunate to have you on our side, Jake, and blessed, believe me, that you won our little contest. Hell, it could have been Bubba T. Flubba from Dayton, Ohio, but, no, we were lucky enough to get a youngish, not unattractive, pretty much perfectly unobtrusive writer who's stumbled into the political promised land." Jake looked down at the table, nervously hydroplaning his cup of water in wayward circles while he listened to Sousage monologue. "What I'm driving at here, is that we feel like our mutually beneficial relationship has pretty much peaked. You've been good for us. We've been good for you."

"Chuck, I've only been on the ground in Iowa a few days."

The ad-man chuckled. "Don't worry, partner, we're not gonna cut you loose, at least not yet. We just want you to dial back the political rhetoric, keep a lower profile from here to the finish line." He spread his napkin across his lap, patting it down twice for good measure. "Three days, one press conference, a question on national television, and now your name splashed across Page One. You gotta admit, that's some heady stuff. A lot of small-market scribblers would just ride off into the sunset."

Beneath the table Jake's stomach rumbled.

Sousage eyed him critically. "Look, it might not be a bad idea to just sort of blend into the press pool for a while, take some road trips around the state… treat this electoral stint like a little vacay." He took a pull from his coffee and let it burn its way down his throat. "We just don't want any bells and whistles—no extra publicity or anything going forward. Capiche?"

"I'm not looking for political stardom," Jake said, as he watched Sousage chomp greedily on the English muffin Katherine had delivered to him. "I'm here to do my job, see a little bit of the country…"

Sousage dabbed roughly at the corners of his mouth with a napkin. The English muffin was history. "Then we understand one another." He tossed a twenty down on the table and stood to go. "Hate to do this to you, Jacob, but I really gotta run," he said, extending his hand again. "Breakfast is on me. Be sure to give that sweet-ass waitress a healthy tip for me." Sousage smiled, winked, and walked past him out the door, leaving Jake with a half-finished breakfast and an unspent Andrew Jackson.

"What was his hurry?" Katherine said, swooping in to pick up the crumb-strewn plate the overscheduled Sousage had left in his wake.

"Busy man, I guess," Jake said. "He's the media relations guy for the state Republican Party. Tough racket these days to sell an election hosted by white, conservative, evangelicals as representative of an entire nation."

"Ouch," the waitress said, stacking the plates expertly in the crook of her arm. "I'll try not to take that personally."

"That came off sounding like an ugly out-of-stater, didn't it?"

"It did," she replied, "and my friends call me Kate…or Katie.

"Katie as in photographer of 'Summer Patriots on Main,' 'Morning on the Skunk,' and 'Chicory in Bloom,'" Jake asked, pointing to the photos on the wall that had caught his eye on his first visit to the Cal Coolidge Café.

"One and the same," the waitress said. "Though I wouldn't call myself a photographer."

"You should," he said. "They're good…. I mean, they're not the Rocky Mountains, but they're pretty…for Iowa."

"You mean like a girl is pretty…without quite being beautiful."

"Yes," he said, automatically wishing he could have the words back.

"I hear that a lot," she said. "I've had tourists come through here tell me I could be charging hundreds for my prints at the galleries in the cities where they come from. Here, I can only get about as much for them as a steak dinner for two."

"So why don't you send some with them then?"

"Because," she said, half-turning to indicate the interior of the café lit up with late-morning light, "this is my gallery… always has been, always will be." She looked down at the stack of newspapers Sousage had left in his wake. "Half of those are about you, is that right?"

"Apparently," Jake said. "Only they're more about last night's fireworks at the debate. Did you watch it?"

"Wouldn't miss it…. My dad and I are the world's biggest political junkies."

"Big political family?"

"I guess you could say, that," Katie said. "I suppose I probably should have kept up the family tradition and gone into journalism, but, much to my father's dismay, I minored in journalism and majored in political science. I actually got to serve as a research assistant at Central Iowa University for one of the most famous political historians in the country, Anne Templeton."

"And now you're waitressing…." Jake checked himself as a hint of a frown flashed across Katie's pretty face. "I didn't mean that to sound condescending."

"Actually, I'm a café *manager* who just happens to double as a waitress who is unfortunately at the beck and call of ignorant, fly-by-night journalists like you, so…strike two." For a second Jake feared his server might just hurl the remnants of Sousage's breakfast platter right back at him. Instead she held the plates in one hand while flipping through the rejected newspapers with the other.

"This one is definitely a keeper."

"Which one is it?" He leaned over in his booth to get a better look. "The *Times*?"

"Nope."

"The *Journal*?"

"*The Hereford Gate.*"

"I get it," Jake said, "the hometown favorite."

"No," Kate said, "the best articles…and the best writers."

"Like who?"

"Like my father, Herb Clarke."

Jake stared after her as she spun on her heels and walked to the kitchen, realizing not only that he had made an ass out of himself for the third time in their three-minute-long conversation, but that by some accident of fate the bright, strawberry blonde waitress was the daughter of the impossibly crotchety old newspaperman.

Feeling penitent, Jake picked the *Hereford Gate* from the top of the stack and dutifully read the article in full.

The Silver Steer...And Why Not?"
By Marianne Meyers with Herb Clarke

Last night Iowa and America watched as a coven of practiced politicians offered more pabulum to a cynical electorate that, more than ever, deserves to hear the truth. That is, until a neophyte journalist named Jacob Preston—the winner of the equally fraudulent Politics Up Close contest, blundered into the first real question of the campaign.

Why real? Because it was local, not high falutin'. Because the candidates couldn't possibly have scripted their answers in advance. Because it had absolutely nothing to do with the "hot-button issues" speechwriters and strategists drill their men on before each and every campaign stop. Real because an unassuming little query caused them to take off the masks that had frozen into grins as alarming as the Joker's.

Make no mistake, Jacob Preston is no Batman or Boy Wonder but only the most recent in a long line of fools who've been made to feel, for publicity's sake, that they're making a real difference on the political landscape. Still, from fools sometimes comes gold.

Now, thanks to this accidental political tourist from the Rocky Mountain State, we have campaign gold, or rather silver, in the form of a piece of hardware rejected by our bloated state universities, which, like the candidates themselves, are now mostly bought by out-of-state dollars. It seems Iowa football fans don't cotton much to steers anymore, even though it was corn, beans, cows, and sows that made their uncommon commonwealth what it is, and what promises to keep it going long into the future. Sources leaked to the press just yesterday informed us that the perennially unsexy Ag Bureau had been dropped as the trophy's underwriter, while Principled Insurance had been brought in as a more demographically-relevant title sponsor. After all, precious few of us farm anymore, but plenty of us are in the business of, as they say, "protecting our assets." The trophy, too, is reportedly in line for a makeover, and will allegedly feature a young boy tossing a football in the air, as if playing catch with himself.

So much for our agricultural heritage. So much for the parents and grandparents and siblings we used to toss the pigskin around with. They're all passé, apparently. The future belongs to actuaries, life expectancies, not-so-recoverable losses, unceremoniously denied claims, and the lesser art of playing with ourselves.

At the risk of seeming impertinent, why not the Silver Steer? As we Iowans know better than most, the political process is a farce, a circus sold to the highest bidder while being pitched to the public as a timeless exercise in participatory democracy. Competing for an actual prize—a trophy akin to those you and I once sought in our bowling leagues and softball tournaments—might actually help put the whole hyped-up and garish affair in the proper light, reminding us to be credulous when fools and knaves attempt to buy our vote with baubles and trinkets and blow-dried, one-hundred-dollar haircuts.

This idea of Preston's may yet have legs. Mike Santoro is for it. The orphaned steer trophy, currently out to pasture and awaiting a new owner, is surely out standing in the field for it.

Outstanding in the field...now there's something we could use more of from our purportedly distinguished cadre of candidates.

The question is, are you for it?

What a poison pen this grade school teacher and her small-town editor wielded in their spare time. If there was an article from his time in Iowa that he would one day be sharing with his hypothetical grandkids, Jake felt sure it would be this one—the one that had succeeded in basically burning him and the other pretenders to the crown at the stake...or the steak.

"Just so you know," Katie Clarke said, poking her head through the short-order window as Jake sat staring at the unsolicited commentary, "Daddy claims to think the Silver Steer is a bunch of bunk, a 'political charade.' She paused to push a few wayward strands of auburn hair from her eyes. "Or was it 'political chimera'.... I don't remember which. Anyway, he doesn't much like it."

Jake let the newspaper fall back down to the table. "Then why did he lend his name to the article?"

"Because Mrs. Meyers has been writing a column for him for almost 15 years, and never...not once...asked anything of him…not even payment. And because Mrs. Meyers, in her other calling as our third-grade teacher, has taught nearly all of his nieces and nephews how to write about the world and how to do their times tables. And because unlike me and unlike Daddy, Marianne Meyers still has a big enough heart to believe that an out-of-state, accidental journalist like yourself might actually know his head from a hole in the ground."

That evening Amethyst came home full of news, saying nothing about the events of the night prior. She had been pounding the pavement, she said, in search of every Tom, Dick, and Harry's reaction to the debate. Most agreed it was a total zero except for the trophy question. Absolutely nobody, Amethyst relayed with a laugh as she poured herself a glass of red wine and handed one to Jake, liked Brad Charger's idea of a rainbow.

"He's toast," Amethyst concluded. "I don't care how much he has in that Hollywood nest egg of his, or how much money he's getting from the gay lobby out in Cali. There's no way that guy can last."

"That's what they said about Jimmy Carter," Jake pointed out.

Am brought her glass back down to the table. "So how in the hell was your day, Press?"

"First time you've ever asked me that," Jake said, brightening as Amethyst rolled her eyes at what she had already repeatedly dismissed as her roommate's *overly sensitive behavior*. "Well, the day started with Matt Pitchford setting up a meeting for me on two hour's notice with Chuck Sousage."

"He didn't," Am said, taking off her scarf and draping it over the back of the chair as she listened.

"Oh yes, he did."

"Damage control, I suppose."

"Actually he thanked me for generating all the free publicity for the party."

"As he should."

"But he made it clear that I should dial it back."

"Of course he did. You're getting to be too big an item to fit into the box they made for you. You've gone from being a marginal utility player to a big-time slugger, and all because of the question I gifted you with in the car."

"I should thank you for that."

"That," she said, "remains to be seen. In any case, it's gotten you more PR than I've achieved in seven years of shaking trees in New York City."

"If you'd like me to credit you for the idea, I'd be happy to…"

"That ship has already sailed," his roommate replied. "Or should I say that steer has already left the barn? A simple thanks would suffice."

"You know I never wanted this, right?"

"That's what you say. But I haven't exactly seen you out renouncing the infamous question."

"What's the point?" Jake countered. "It's the question that's getting the attention, not me. I'm just a sidelight."

"A sidelight who's getting the lion's share of the limelight," Am pointed out. "Anyhow, my point is this: if you're really not digging the attention, what's stopping you from riding back into the sunset to good ol' Golden, Colorado? Rescind your acceptance of the Up Close contest. Point your Accord back toward Denver and carry on with your mediocre, Middle American life."

Jake swallowed hard. She had a point.

"You see," Am continued, "you're not-so-secretly enjoying your fifteen minutes of fame, and, hey, I don't blame you. Ride the wave, Press, but don't go around being all aw-shucks about it. Cut the bullshit, if you'll pardon the pun."

"If I'm so famous," Jake responded, "how come my phone isn't ringing off the hook? How come the producers from *Late Night* and the *Tonight Show* aren't tripping over themselves to book me? The only contact with the wider world I've had today was the text from Pitchford and a ten-minute-long power breakfast with a guy whose last name is synonymous with a breakfast meat."

"Good one." Amethyst pointed her wineglass at Jake in acknowledgment of the jibe. "Know what?"

"What?"

"I sooo don't want to stay in tonight."

"Me neither," he confessed.

"Where do you want to go then, Press?"

"Someplace quiet."

"Are you kidding? That's exactly what I don't want." Am tapped her index finger against her nose, thinking. "How about we go down to the Wagon Wheel. There's sure to be some scribblers there after a night like we all had last night. They'll all be requiring some serious beer therapy."

"I'm almost afraid to ask, but what, pray tell, is the Wagon Wheel?"

Am widened her eyes. "Gee, Press, it's only the bestest, most coolest watering hole in three counties, and the most groovy, too…. Seriously, you've got to get a load of the new owner… this guy called Mad. He's one of, like, two 'young entrepreneurs' I've met since I've been here that's supposed to ride in on his silver steed and raise small-town American backwaters like this one up from the economic swamp. Trouble is, Mad is pretty much only interested in three things so far as a I can tell."

"And what would those be?"

"Brewing beer, sticking it to the Man, and all things Wisconsin, though not necessarily in that order."

"Wisconsin?"

"That's where he claims to be from, though I've got my money on either Nazareth or Galilee. You've got to see this dude, Press…. Black beard down to here," she said, pointing to the bottom of her pretty plunging neckline, "and a complexion just a shade darker than bright white office paper."

"I don't know if I'm up for that degree of excitement tonight."

"Suit yourself," she said, draping her scarf around her neck again. "I for one could use a little Karaoke cure, and I'm not too proud to admit it."

"Alright," Jake conceded, "hold your horses. I'm coming with."

When they arrived at the Wheel, as Am called it for short, the owner of the town's only Karaoke machine, a mustachioed middle-aged man named Artie Shaw, was busy setting up shop on what passed for a stage. From the looks of the empty pitchers at the journalists' table, the scribblers had been self-medicating for a good long while.

"Prepare yourself for a serious snarkfest, Press," Amethyst instructed as she called over to the table. "Can you fit us in, McGreedy?"

"That's what she said," McGreedy deadpanned. "Yeah, 'I'll fit you in,' as you so indelicately put it, if you'd be so kind as to buy me another Jameson's."

"Such a gentlemen," Am muttered, giving the seriously over-sized reporter a hefty pat on the back. "Hey, Jake…there's a little tradition among us political reporters…guy who gets to ask the question on national television has to buy the next pitcher," she said, pushing him in the direction of the bar. "And if he fails to deliver said beer, we eat him like the cannibals we truly are."

"Of the two options I'll take the beer run," Jake replied, drifting toward a bar fronted by patched vinyl-and-chrome stools that had no doubt been there since the Bay of Pigs, along with a few of the crusty patrons presently occupying them.

"Welcome to the Wheel, friend," the bartender called out, he of the much ballyhooed, quasi-Biblical beard. "I'm Mad…. I mean my name is Mad, though I'm pretty pissed off, too," he added as an afterthought, "strictly politically, I mean."

"Jake Preston." He reached out to take the hand Mad had extended him.

"Saw you on TV last night, dude. Beers on the house for keeping those Ken Dolls and Barbies on their toes. So what can

I wet your whistle with?" Mad set aside a dull pencil and what looked to be a half-finished word puzzle, clapping his hands together in anticipation. Jake squinted into the half-light in an attempt to make out the labels as the barman read him the list. "I got the Fightin' Bob La Follette Populist Pale Ale, the Joseph McCarthy Blacklist Lager, the Russ Feingold Prefers Blondes Honey Blonde Ale, the Paul Ryan Deficit Hawk Amber Bock, and then the two most recent additions to our Cheesehead politician line-up, the Scott Walker Union Bustin' Bad-Ass I.P.A. and the Scott Walker Half-Ass Harley Hawg Honey Weiss.... Can't decide which of the last two suits the Governor better."

"What do you recommend?"

"The Fightin' Bob Pale Ale, but that's just me. Of the four, he's the only Cheesehead politician to really fight the good fight, you know. Feingold looked promising, before he started throwing away wives like expired cheeses."

"I'll take a pitcher of Fightin' Bob," Jake said, looking around at the Green Bay Packers and Wisconsin Badgers memorabilia hanging on the walls alongside image after image of Fightin' Bob himself striking various and sundry poses of hellfire and indignation.

"If you're thinking I've got a bit of a man-crush on La Follete," Mad said, drawing forth a pitcher full of frothy brew, "you'd be right. Last true Republican who actually gave a rip, or lived up to the billing of compassionate conservatism. Also, the last presidential candidate from 'Sconsin who stood a snowball's chance of getting elected Prez. Even a lot of the homefolks don't know he racked up almost 20% of the vote against Coolidge in 1924. Beat Coolidge's ass bad in Wisconsin, actually."

"They don't make 'em like that anymore, do they?"

"Sure as hell don't. Most of your pale ales are watered down for the foodies and beer snobs."

Jake smiled. "No, I meant they don't make politicians like La Follete."

"Or beers either," Mad said, sitting back down to work on whatever word puzzle he had been working on when Jake had bellied up to the bar.

"What's that?" Jake asked. He pointed the overflowing pitcher in the direction of the tavern-keepers' stationary-sized sheet.

"This little number is the weekly 'Mad's Libs' I write to keep my more politically cynical patrons amused…. Here, have a look," he said, pushing the half-completed sheet across the beer-slick countertop.

Mad's Libs

On Sunday Senator _Shitweasel_ **(noun)** announced he was going to run for President on the _Bullshit_ **(noun)** Ticket, even though his detractors nearly _shat_ **(verb)** at the news. Despite some of the Senator's own colleagues denouncing him as a _shit-eating_ **(adjective)** _shitshow_ **(noun)**, Senator _Shitweasal_ **(proper noun)** refused to give a _shit_ **(noun)** about their condemnation, declaring that his "Walk Softly and Carry a _Big Shit_" **(adjective)** grassroots campaign would continue despite the opposition….

"I could probably use a little more variety in my responses," Mad conceded, flashing the briefest of grins as he stroked a beard that would put Grizzly Adams to shame, "but why change horses midstream, you know?"

"It's a good all-purpose word," Jake acknowledged, trying hard to think of something positive to say to cheer up the brooding barman. "Anyway, thanks for the generous pour," he said, excusing himself for Mort McGreedy's table as Artie Shaw's Karaoke warmed up in the background.

"Alright, everybody," the deejay enthused, getting too close to the mic. "In honor of the distinguished candidates who've descended on our humble little town, tonight's sing-along theme is…politics!" The crew of rowdies at McGreedy's table roared with approval. "Now I know this isn't much of a political crowd," Artie continued, administering the needle.

Hisses from the scribblers' table.

"And I know most of you could give a rip about who's up or who's down in the polls."

Boos this time—a lusty roomful of them.

Artie of Artie's Karaoke smiled so big the sheer force of the grin lifted his handlebar mustache up to within a few whiskers of his nose. "We'll start with a lightnin' round of Presidential Anthems. If you can name it, you can sure as heck get your sweet little patootie up here and sing it."

"This should be good," Amethyst said, noisily sucking the head from her first glass of Fightin' Bob. "Now that's a beer that won't take it laying down," she enthused, appreciatively puckering. "Anyway, where are my manners…. Let me introduce you to tonight's honored guest and my new roommate. Everyone, this is Jake."

"Hi, Jake," said everyone. Jake gave his best nondescript wave.

"Jake, that's Dan over there from the *Monitor*, Mort McGreedy you already know. Next to The Inglorious Morton is my friend Loretta Draper from some 'Sconsin left-wing news rag with an unfortunate moniker no one's ever even heard of, *The Weekly Badger*…. I call her the Sexy Badger. And last but not least that foxy, wonky geek down at the end of the table is Alex from the *News*. Mort, why don't you introduce your old-fogey posse."

McGreedy stared into his Scotch. "That's Jim. That's Bob. And that grizzled veteran over there is Kevin. Their wives haven't slept with them in six months."

"Great stuff last night, Jake," Kevin said.

"He doesn't really mean it," McGreedy grumbled.

"Actually I don't," Kev admitted. "Really, I thought the debate was a joke and your question sucked ass."

"Thanks," Jake said, raising his glass. "At least you're honest." He was already wishing he'd stayed home to watch PBS and sort through his unopened bank statements. Mercifully, though, Artie of Artie's Karaoke was ready with Round One of Presidential Anthems.

"Okay, let's get started with something easy, wonks and wonkettes. What was Barack Obama's campaign theme song in 2008?

"'Sign, Sealed, Delivered, I'm Yours,'" screamed Loretta Draper.

"Yes indeedy. C'mon up here, young lady, and favor us with a soulful rendition of that classic Soul."

Loretta had some decent pipes and a few Motown moves Jake found mildly endearing. She was drunk as a skunk, clearly, but having a good time letting off a little campaign steam, and who could blame her.

"Okay, let's up the difficulty level, Smarty Pants. How about 'No, I Won't Back Down'?"

"Al Gore," Alex said smugly.

"Close," replied the emcee.

"It's Bush," Amethyst whispered too loudly into Jake's ear.

"What's that, young lady?"

"Nothing," Amethyst said, turning red.

"She said 'Bush,'" Loretta piped up. "I heard her."

"Bush is right! Will the mystery lady in the scarf please come up here and regale us with her rendition?"

"No the mystery lady will not," Am said, turning a shade more crimson.

"Does the mystery lady wanna be banned from the Wheel for the rest of the campaign drinking season and bad-mouthed all around town by the ex-mayor of this here cowtown," Artie drawled.

Amethyst sighed, letting her head loll side to side. "Fine, but I won't do it unless Loretta, the little tattle-tale weasel, or badger, or whatever the hell varmint she is, comes up to sing a duet with me."

"Serves 'er right for snitching!" Artie declared. "Alrighty then, folks, here are Loretta not-to-be-confused-with-Lynn and the Mystery Girl singing Tom Petty's 'No, I Won't Back Down.'"

"Petty had the good sense to sue Bush for using it, too," McGreedy mumbled darkly into his drink. "Neil Young threatened to do the same when Donald Trump co-opted 'Rockin' in the Free World' for his campaign launch."

Ordinarily Jake counted himself a huge Tom Petty fan, but he couldn't help but cringe at the Amethyst-Loretta butchering of one of his favorite tunes. Mercifully, the girls had begun laughing too hard to make it much past the first chorus.

"Here's a tough one for you whippersnappers in the press corps whose earliest memory of William Jefferson Clinton is asking your parents what the word *fellatio* meant. Can any of you babes out there in Politicsland tell ol' Artie the name of Fat Howard Taft's theme song?"

Pin drop. Then a gruff voice floated their direction from a distant booth.

"'Get on a Raft with Taft.'"

"Well, well," Artie said, swinging around to see who had answered the stumper. "Will the Jurassic specimen who correctly answered the question now please walk forward on his hind legs?"

Jake watched as Herb Clarke stepped out of the back booth to stride briskly to the stage. "Well, if it isn't our illustrious editor of the *Hereford Gate*," Artie gee-whizzed. "Herbie and me go way back to the days when I was mayor of this one-horse town, before I grew out my 'stache and came to my senses. Dropped glad-handing politics in favor of banjo-pickin' and record-spin-nin', didn't I, Herbie? Well, if I'd 'ave known you were in the house, Mr. Clarke, I would have brought the Genius Edition. Now, for Final Jeopardy, can you recite me a verse—any verse—from that long ago classic, 'Get on a Raft with Taft?'"

"Go on, Herbie," Artie coaxed, "recite a few bars for these ingrateful political whippersnappers."

> Get on a raft with Taft, boys
> Get on the winning boat
> The man worthwhile with the friendly smile
> Will get the honest vote
> He'll save the country sure, boys
> From Bryan, Hearst, and graft
> So all join in, we're sure to win
> Get on a raft with Taft!

"The irony is you would have never wanted to get on a raft with Taft.... He weighed 354 pounds on inauguration day," Clarke said matter-of-factly before taking a slight bow and walking stiffly back to the booth where his one and only daughter patted him on the back.

"Well-done, you old geezer, you," Artie enthused. "Now for our next round of Presidential musicology, I'm goin' to give you the name of a recent president, and you, the peanut gallery, shout out what cha think *shoulda* been their unofficial theme song. If the record fits, I'll spin it.... Let's start with William Jefferson Clinton."

"'I've Got Friends in Low Places' by Garth Brooks," McGreedy's buddy Jim called out.

"Yeah, friends with benefits," quipped Loretta Draper.

"'Your Cheatin' Heart' as sung by Ray Charles," Amethyst hollered, riding a post-Karaoke adrenaline high and the liberating effects of her second Fightin' Bob.

"Now there's a winner!" Hereford's ex-mayor-turned-deejay enthused. "Let me spin it for ya, sister."

Ray Charles possessed jou jou sufficient to cripple even the most stalwart heart with regret, Jake wholly and sincerely believed. Tonight that theory held true, as the right reverend's mournful stirrings put the whole bar in a temporary melancholy until Artie's circus-barker act brought them back from the depths. "Next up on our list of Commanders-in-Chief is JFK."

"JFK, blown away, what else do I have to say," Dan piped up, adding smartly, Billy Joel's 'We Didn't Start the Fire.'"

"A capital choice," Artie said, "but since you two troubadours have already sung the choicest lines, we'll need us a runner-up."

"'Happy Birthday, Mr. President' by Marilyn Monroe," McGreedy growled, knocking the ball out of the park, per usual.

"Say no more, preacher McGreedy, say no more," Artie said, and the Wheel filled up with the sultry purr of the blonde bombshell and presidential-undoer herself.

On stage Artie mouthed the words, miming the smoothing down of a ruffled skirt caught in a flirtatious updraft. "Okay, everyone, last call before we end the thematic portion of tonight's show. Do any of you hopeless political junkies have a song you'd like to nominate as the campaign theme for the next sucker gullible enough to occupy the People's House? Anyone? No? How about a song then, any song, ripe for the political season?"

"I've got one," McGreedy piped up.

"Okay then, Big Fella, just lemme know what you need for accompaniment…"

Groaning with effort, McGreedy raised himself up from the table and dragged his carcass over to the stage, where he whispered something into Artie's ear.

"I've only got a few verses jotted down," Mort said, producing a tattered napkin covered in writing from the pocket of his jeans. "Here it is, though, sung to the tune of 'Desperado' by the Eagles. Artie, go ahead and hit it."

Morton McGreedy let rip a surprisingly soulful baritone:

> Jacob Preston, why don't you come to your senses?
> You been out askin' questions for too long now
> Oh, you're a cool one
> For any political season
> Those campaign promises that are teasin' you
> Are gonna hurt you somehow.
>
> Don't you believe the bullshitters in this world
> They'll dupe you if they're able.
> You know the Silver Steer is the better cow to
>   catch.
>
> Now it seems to me some very fine hotcakes.
> Have been flipped upon your table,
> But you only want the ones that you can't catch.

Jacob Preston, oh, you ain't gettin' no younger.
Your pain and your hunger have carried you far
    from Denver
And freedom, oh freedom, well that's just some
    voter's problem
Your prison is waking up in Cowtown all alone.

Desperate Preston, why don't you come to your
    senses?
Take down your fences, open the *Hereford Gate*
It may be rainin', but there's a Hawkeye here that
    loves you
Don't you let some politician fool you, or it'll
    soon be too late.

And with that Mort McGreedy, baritone, swashbuckler,
political cynic, drunken wreck, brought the house down.

Four

"Someone tell me this isn't really happening," Amethyst Gilchrest opined at Jake's side.

In front of them Mike Santoro had arrived at the podium. Santoro's team had sent out notice of the press conference just a few hours earlier. Apparently, a couple other dozen reporters, including Dan, Loretta, Alex, Kevin and, of course Mort McGreedy, had likewise received summons and scrapped what plans they may have had in order to attend. Santoro's people were fond of calling eleventh-hour pressers, but they seldom called them on this short of notice.

The wind whipped Santoro's tie as he stood beside a makeshift podium hastily erected in front of the county courthouse in Goodacre. "Check…check" some staffer kept saying into the microphone, while the north wind played havoc with Santoro's moment, not to mention his carefully coiffed hair.

At 2:30 PM—a full half-hour after the scheduled start-time— Santoro took to the mic wearing a Cheshire grin.

"Well," the candidate began, mock-shivering, "they don't make October quite so cold in Ohio, where Howard Taft and I come from, as they do here in the Hawkeye State. I gotta say, though, ol' Howie's extra layers of blubber were a way better insulator than my awesomely large wardrobe of Bill Cosby sweaters."

The handful of reporters and Goodacre residents in attendance winced, whether at the sudden gust of north wind that blew, unimpeded, across the courthouse lawn, or at the pitch-deaf reference to Cosby, it was hard to be certain.

On stage Santoro wore the grin of a man who had just gone one-up in a rubber match. "I called you here today to relay a news flash crucial to this campaign." Santoro looked side to side dramatically before reaching deep into the recesses of his lectern. "I have it," he shouted above the wind, holding something large and metallic aloft. "The Silver Steer!"

"Now I know what you all must be thinking…. 'How in the heck did Santoro get his Ohio Buckeye on the most talked-about trophy in the Hawkeye State? Well, my wife Christine and I have made a number of friends in high places during my six months of living on the ground amongst the Iowawegians, and one of them just happens to be the higher-up at the Ag Bureau who commissioned this little castrated, cast-off beauty." Santoro held the prize aloft, stroking it with his gloved hands in a fashion reminiscent of O.J. Simpson. "In the debate the other night my opponent, Milt Cloward, suggested that a trophy like this one would somehow diminish the presidential race and the men and woman in it. I couldn't disagree more. Does the Lombardi Trophy detract from the sanctity of the Super Bowl… heck no! Does an Oscar belittle the film industry? No, friends, an Oscar *epitomizes* the film industry."

"My opponent suggested playing for a trophy like this one might be beneath him. Well, the critics and pundits who've weighed in these last few days are right to say such comments reveal a candidate increasingly out of touch with the American middle class. I say they don't just make him *look* out of touch...I say he *is* out of touch. In fact, I'm willing to bet you Milt Cloward has never competed for, much less won, so much as a bowling trophy. I'm willing to bet he thinks football is an inferior religion...fit only for obese, TV-obsessed fans drinking the Champagne of Beers on a Sunday afternoon when they ought to be at their local temple. Well, Governor Cloward, while I may not be as well-born as you, I'm proud to say I've bowled league and detasseled corn. I'm proud to say I enjoy a good game of smash-mouth football as much as any other Joe, and I don't mind tipping back the Champagne of Beers before, during, and after kickoff. Where I come from we'd drink our brewskis right out of the Silver Steer if it could hold liquor."

Santoro perched his political prize on the edge of the podium, looking pointedly into the bank of cameras. "I've come here today to say three things to America, to Iowa, and to my opponents.

"First, we are not above competition. As Republicans all of us claim we are in favor of a competitive marketplace. Here's our chance to walk our political talk."

"Second, Jake Preston asked a brave question the other night, brave mostly because it was simple. So I say to Jake Preston, thank you, buddy, because without even knowing it, you stood up for Lanny the League Bowler and Betty the Blue-Ribbon Pie-maker at the State Fair, who proudly say to people like Milt Cloward, 'Earning a trophy for my troubles makes the competition—the race—all the sweeter.'"

"Third, to my opponents I say remember Akron and Dayton and Cleveland and all the other working-class places where folks wake up every day in factory towns and steel-mill burgs to put on twice-worn, once-washed uniforms and pack their lunch to save their hard-earned cash. These folks compete day in and day out against the likes of Japan, Germany, South Korea, and China in a contest of very real consequences. And they glory in it. They proudly say, 'We make the kind of product here that's gonna bring home the bacon.' They say what I'm saying now, and what they say on the playgrounds of Columbus and Cincinnati, Akron and Dayton and Cleveland. They say, 'Bring it, Dawg. Game on!'"

"So today I say to my opponents, 'Bring it! I've got the Silver Steer, and if you want it, you'll have to come take it!'"

Santoro pointed straight at the cameras, unblinking, looking for a moment like a younger, raven-haired, hatless version of Uncle Sam himself, before breaking pose to answer the assembled reporters' questions.

The man of the hour scanned the nearly hypothermic press corps. "How you guys and gals doing out there…cold enough for you? Folks, the only reason I can stay warm up here is that I've got enough belly fat to keep me fed until Groundhog Day. That and all the political hot air. But in all seriousness, fire away with your questions!" Santoro rested his palm atop the steer's quicksilver head, directly between the horns. The statue itself, Jake realized, seeing it for the first time now on the hoof, and in the flesh, was twice as large as he had imagined. Its head was the size of a grapefruit and its horns were easily the length of a Number 2 pencil. No doubt they were just as sharp.

"Do you anticipate the Silver Steer becoming a significant part of your campaign?" Jake asked.

The candidate paused to admire his prize. "You heard what I said, Jake. I'm making the Silver Steer here the symbol of my candidacy from now until election night or until the cows come home, whichever comes first. I relate deeply to the steer's fighting spirit, its pride…"

"…its impotence," Amethyst mumbled under her breath, while raising her hand to ask Santoro a follow-up.

"Do you feel it's risky to be out in front of the public on this? They haven't exactly been clamoring for the candidates to compete for a trophy, at least not yet."

Santoro wagged a finger at her. "I predict they will once they realize all that's at stake…no pun intended…. Seriously, it's a politician's job to lead, and the steer represents a major issue I have with the hypocrisy of campaigning, where a lot of guys… and gals for that matter…act like they want to win, but not enough to roll up their sleeves and really fight for it. Hey, it's a loose ball out there, folks, and I'm willing to get down on the floor and scrap for it. So, no, I know where you're going with the question, but I don't mind being out in front. I relish it, actually."

Santoro re-scanned the crowd of frozen faces. "Any other questions from my media friends…. The steer here grows restless."

"What if Milt Cloward takes you up on your offer?" McGreedy asked. He was wearing what looked to be an enormous parka—like something Jake had seen the Broncos fans in Denver wearing in the middle of a January playoff game. "Are you prepared for where this could lead?"

"Mort," Santoro said, pointing at himself and looking more than a bit aggrieved. "As long as you've been following politics, and covering my career, you should know the answer to that question. Sure, I've discussed the steer briefly with my inner circle, but I'm a passionate, off-the-cuff guy who calls them like he sees 'em even when he's on the horns of a dilemma. So no, I haven't beaten this dead horse over and over with my strategy team. What you're seeing up here is the unadorned, unaffected…"

"…unhinged," Amethyst whispered under her breath.

"…uncensored me. As to the second part of your question, do I know where the steer might take me, or any of us? Absolutely not, and therein lies the beauty. As I've said all along a campaign is a journey with an uncertain destination. The trick is to enjoy yourself along the way."

"Where will you be keeping the steer?"

"Suffice it to say I'm keeping this big guy close to the vest until the final votes are tallied on caucus night. As I said, if any of my competitors want to come get it, they're going to have to storm Castle Santoro and take it by force."

"Where have you been, stranger?" Kate Clarke asked when Jake stopped off for some mid-afternoon pancake therapy at the Cal

Coolidge Café on his way back from Santoro's impromptu news conference in Goodacre. Amethyst had a lead on a story over in Ames, the closest university town, and this meant Jake was free to do as he pleased without the endless barrage of acidic commentary he had come to expect from his new roommate. He found he couldn't stand it when Amethyst was around and missed her when she was gone. The whole friendship thing they had going struck him as perilously close to a relationship.

"Doing my best to live up to Chuck Sousage's charge," Jake replied. "Sort of a difficult thing he asked me to do. I don't know too many reporters under directives not to ask questions."

"So did you ask any?" Kate asked, not looking up from what appeared to be the paper-cutting task she had set herself at the table next to his.

"Just one, and that was mainly to keep myself from getting rusty." Jake took a sip of coffee and let it warm him. "What're you up to?"

"Cutting the clippings of Mrs. Meyers's and Daddy's Silver Steer article. It got picked up by the *Register*, the *Star*, and the *Trib*. This is pretty much Daddy's dream come true." She pointed the scissors at him. "And it wouldn't have been possible without your question."

"How's the old man taking his newspaper's newfound fame?"

"We'll see," she said, sliding the newsprint behind a poster frame. "He agreed to help Mrs. Meyers write a sequel."

On the flat-screen in the corner of the café, the one positioned directly above the salad bar, Jake saw the image of a wind-whipped Santoro on CSPAN. "This must be the tape-delayed broadcast of Santoro's presser. Turn it up."

Kate pointed the remote at the screen, and Santoro's exuberant voice filled the all-but-deserted restaurant.

"He looked like some high-schooler gloating over winning first prize at a debate tournament," Kate remarked once the speech had concluded.

"So do you think the idea has legs?"

"I think it has hooves," she deadpanned.

"Didn't Santoro do exactly what Mrs. Meyers called for in her article?"

"I think Mr. Santoro may have missed the irony," commented Katie. "Marianne was saying that since the whole primary system has become such a farce, and since the fields are made up of such uninteresting and irrelevant candidates, why not add the Silver Steer to the three-ring circus. At least it's tangible rather than abstract. It's something more than just another empty promise in a lackluster campaign season."

"Spoken like a true poly sci major," Jake said. "So maybe Mrs. Meyers and your pop meant more of what they said than you might think."

"Maybe," Kate admitted. "Daddy can be pretty inscrutable, I'll admit. I've never completely been able to pin him down politically. On the one hand, as a newspaper editor he should be a raging liberal, right? On the other hand, as a farm owner in a totally Red county like this one you'd expect him to be a tried and true conservative. I've been trying to figure him out since high school, and I still don't have an answer."

"Which caucus does he attend," Jake asked.

"Depends on the election. Mostly Republican, but then again I remember him and mom voting in plenty of Democratic caucuses when I was a girl."

"Do you know what you are?" Jake asked.

Kate paused, considering. "I guess I'm more like him than I like to think, because I don't identify with either party, at least not exclusively. I identify with people, and places, and principles. You?"

"I lean Democratic," Jake said. "But I'm open. The more I hear a candidate speak…any candidate, the more convinced I am by them."

Kate smiled. "That's because they're professional convincers."

"Like newspapermen?" Jake asked.

"Like newspapermen," Kate echoed, adding, "only with fewer scruples…. So yes, I could see how Santoro might milk a week or two out of the Silver Steer. I could even see how he could use it to help paint his rivals as out-of-touch. But if this news event is anything like those that follow, the Silver Steer will be on life support in a few days and hung out to dry in the slaughterhouse by this time next week…. Then again, I've been wrong before."

"You don't strike me as someone who's wrong much," Jake said, hoping he didn't sound too flirty. Actually, he felt sort of flirty when he didn't allow himself to think about the pseudo girlfriend-colleague-platonic roommate who'd be waiting to abuse him when he got back to their shared apartment above the Sweetheart Bakery. Already, Amethyst Gilchrest had complicated his life more than he cared to admit.

"I'm as wrong as anybody else," Katie said. "Probably wronger. Anyway, as you so undiplomatically put it the other night, if I've got such a great political mind, why am I not working as a paid campaign consultant instead of a waitress managing her dad's restaurant."

"Herb Clarke owns this place?"

"Who else but a seventy-something-year-old newspaperman would name a café The Cal Coolidge?"

"Fair point," Jake conceded.

"Anyway, no rest for the wicked. I've got to get going if I'm going to make it back here before the dinner rush."

"Where are you going?"

"A little forward in your line of questioning, aren't you?" Katie commented. "I don't ask you where you're going everytime you leave, do I?"

"No, but then again you already know I'm not going anywhere."

"If you must know, I'm headed out to the cemetery to visit my mom."

"Can I come with?" Jake asked, struck by his own rare moment of courage. "I haven't had a chance to put Hereford in perspective yet."

"The cemetery would be a good place for that," Kate admitted, grabbing her jacket from a hook by the front door. "You can see for miles and miles."

"Let's go then," Jake offered, donning the oversized Fightin'
Plowmen sweater and matching stocking cap that had been his
first non-food purchase in town. "Can I leave my recorder and
notebook here?"

"Daddy always says a good reporter takes his notebook with
him everywhere he goes," she said. "What if you get a hot lead?"

"From cold corpses? I think I'll take my chances."

The aptly named Cemetery Road meandered its way up the
town's only real hill, past the Hereford water tower, before it
turned to gravel. Already, the maples that clung to the road as
it climbed had begun to yellow. In the rural Midwest fall was a
different sort of phenomenon; it failed to produce the kind of
striking autumnal colors found in New England photo shoots.
Instead, autumn in farm country featured a sort of gradual
draining of chlorophyll from the land that had once been satu-
rated in it, followed by a less-than-spectacular yellowing. These
weren't the trees of the suburbs, pre-selected for their pleasing
palette of spring and fall color and transplanted along wide bou-
levards with an eye toward aesthetics, but what farmers called
"volunteers,"—trees that had sprung up beside their parents in
the ditch and along the fencerows and had done their best to
hold on ever since.

When they pulled into the graveyard's macadam parking
lot the trees had thinned to a handful of ramrod-straight hard-
woods scattered on the hillside. Below them the view of the
town looked almost storybook. From here, the strict geometry
on which the town had been founded was clear. The streets

named after presidents, trees, and states in the Union ran at right angles to the numbered routes running on a north-south axis. The water tower, by far the tallest structure on the landscape, reared up in the foreground on a lesser hill between the cemetery and town. Farther south, thousands upon thousands of freshly harvested, golden acres lay all the way to the highway.

Kate had brought a pair of mums with her, one bright yellow, one bright orange, and a small spade to set them in the ground with. The summer had been unusually dry, she had told Jake on their way, and harvest time even more so. On windier days since he'd come to town Jake had been surprised to see dust devils whipping up and the occasional tumbleweed blowing through the street, as if the little burg he'd chosen to hang his hat in was closer to Dodge City, Kansas, than Des Moines, Iowa. The community needed some relief, but the broken-record dry weather showed little promise of relenting.

The newspaper editor's daughter led him wordlessly down avenues of newer gravestones until she stopped, knelt down, and began troweling out the previous set of mums the drought had caused to wither. Jake watched as her strong, slender hands pulled the mums from the pot, stripped the excess dirt, and placed them in the ground with a firm, practiced push, tucking the soil around the roots to keep them warm. "There," she said when she was through, "that should spruce things up for the next few weeks anyway." The name on the tombstone before them read *Genevieve Grace Clarke*, and Jake noted she had passed away decades ago, in the fall.

"How old were you when you lost her?" he asked after a moment of silence had passed between them.

"About eight," she explained. "Old enough to have clear memories."

"What was she like?"

"Tall, beautiful, theatrical, warm. The stage where you gave your first press conference…at the high school…that was her home away from home. She was the theater director at Hereford High for almost a decade. She was unfazed, basically, by anything and everything, until the cancer came along. Isn't that always the way?" she said, turning to Jake as her eyes began to well up. "It's always the people who are the most capable who are struck down. It's like someone, somewhere, decides that the strongest should get the strongest tests. Mom didn't make it, but it wasn't for lack of trying." She wiped a tear from her cheek. "I'm sorry to get emotional in front of you. That's why I always come here by myself or with Daddy."

"It's fine," Jake said, casting his eyes downward. "I understand."

"Do you?" Kate said. "Have you lost a parent?"

"No," Jake admitted, "only figuratively, I guess. I'm an only child, and my folks, well, they've mostly been about themselves. I don't know whether it's because they both grew up on farms that they wanted to live it up a little, or whether it was the Sixties that did it to them. But they couldn't wait to leave Iowa. They meant each other in college in California, moved to Chicago shortly after having me, then moved us to Bradenton in Florida in time for me to enter first grade. When I left home at 18 to go to college in Boulder, I felt pretty much alone. I knew I was starting over, and that I could never live the way they had— gate-guarded communities, tennis clubs, the *New Yorker* and the *Wall Street Journal* delivered to the door. Don't get me wrong, they're good people—smart, caring, involved—but sometimes I feel like there must have been a mix-up at the maternity ward. Know what I mean?"

"No," Kate replied flatly.

Jake looked out across the countryside, searching for the right words. "You can love something, but feel distant from it at the same time, right?"

"I don't think so," Kate said quietly. "I don't think you can feel removed from the places and the people you love."

"Naturally, you would think that," Jake pointed out. "Growing up here, amid all these Clarkes"—he motioned down the long row of family tombstones dating back to the Civil War—"love would be closeness, just like for me love might mean distance. Remember, Colorado is the closest thing to home I've ever really known, and I've only been there, off and on, for fifteen years. Your people have been here for more than 150 years."

"They *fought* to be here," Kate said firmly, her eyes not moving from his. "They *chose* to be here. My dad always says that people boil down to stayers and goers, and that you can understand most of what you need to know about someone by the choice they make."

"Does that mean that people like me are somehow a lesser breed because we didn't have what you had…a pedigree, a family plot in a pioneer cemetery, a stake in the town newspaper, a family name that people recognize and respect at a glance? Did your dad ever figure out what good the rest of us are?"

"The rest of you," Kate said, a steeliness entering her voice Jake had not heard before, "will go where you're most needed and happily hang your shingle. You'll find work where there is work, and find love where you can get it. That's what he says."

"And what do you say?"

"I say he's right," she said, walking away.

Jake felt a swell of something perilously close to anger. "So the rest of us are just careerists…professional whores?"

"You said it, not me," Kate said, quickening her pace. The sun had begun to set and what had been a golden afternoon had turned a marbled gray. "I wish…I wish you hadn't come along," she said over her shoulder. "I wanted to focus on Mom while I was here, not have a debate with you or anyone else."

They rode the rest of the way back to town in silence, Kate gripping the wheel with both hands, occasionally dabbing at her nose with a Kleenex.

They entered the café through the back door, the one that opened up on the alley, and Jake watched as Kate hung her jacket up on the hook in the break-room without inviting him to do the same. She sat down at the office computer, her back turned to him. "Better get your things from the booth," she advised, motioning toward the seating area out front. "The booths will be filling up for dinner soon."

"Katie, I'm sorry if offended you," he said.

"I'm sorry for taking you," she replied. "It…it just wasn't a good decision."

"See you tomorrow then?"

"Maybe."

"Have a good shift tonight, okay," he said, stopping on his way to the front door to pick up the things he'd left in the booth.

When he opened the plate-glass door a rush of suddenly cool air blew down First Street, unimpeded. A cold front had passed through, and he could feel winter in it—snowpack and ice storms and brutal, unrelenting winds—and that thought made him want to hurry back to Amethyst's brightly lit apartment, where CNN would be on, and where there would always be good-natured banter, plenty of beer and chatter, and a room he felt he could almost call his own.

"So how was your day at school?" Amethyst Gilchrest had slipped into what she called her "cozy clothes"—form-fitting yoga pants and an equally form-fitting long-sleeved made of some space-agey stretch material. In their first few days together in the apartment, it had been hard for Jake not to be distracted by her get-up. For every other woman he had ever known, comfy clothes meant baggy sweats, but these....these comfy clothes accentuated her curves rather than disguised them.

"Okay, I guess," Jake answered, not much appreciating the implication of her question—that he had been screwing around like some kid while she had been out being an adult. "Stopped at the Cal Coolidge for lunch after the press conference, and ended up getting in a fight with the waitress."

"The strawberry blonde?"

"Yep."

"She's a tough customer, that one."

"I don't get it, Am. I don't understand while the locals don't give us more of a chance. Christ, can I help it if I'm not from here?"

"Thank God you're *not* from here. Every day you wake up you should remind yourself how lucky you are that you didn't grow up in a backwater town like this. Where would you be if you had? You'd be getting minimum wage setting type for Herb Clarke at the *Hereford Gate*, who's had a bug up his ass for the last fifty years without ever bothering to tell anyone why."

"I think he's probably a good guy at heart," Jake offered.

"Yeah, if you like intractable, inscrutable, inexplicable old-guy bitterness," Am fired back. "Actually, allow me to correct myself—he's grumpy for a very good reason. He's pissed off because he's spent the last five decades of his professional life wasting his considerable talent writing copy in Cowtown about the woman who won the blue ribbon at the county fair and why the local businesses are up in arms about watering the geranium planters on First Street. Meanwhile, his long-suffering wife is condemned to work for him at the newspaper, if she's allowed to work at all, and has to get her kicks reading *US Magazine* at the check-out line of their wretched little grocery store."

"I don't think he has a wife…at least not any longer."

"She probably wised up, divorced him, and left for the city."

"She passed away. From cancer, I think. She was the high school theater director."

"Anyway, you get my point. Herb Clarke is pissed off because he's watched the guys he went to school with, who no doubt had half as much raw writing ability as he had, pull in six figures in places like Chicago and Minneapolis and Kansas City while sending their kids off to the Ivy League. Meanwhile, he can barely pay for the ink at the paper, his wife is dead, and his daughter is bussing tables. I'd be pissed, too."

"I don't think that's entirely fair," Jake ventured. "I'm sure the Clarkes have their reasons. I mean, you don't just up and leave a place your family has lived in for one hundred and fifty years."

"Sure you do," Am countered. "Do you think Herb Clarke's kin sprang from the good Iowa soil in 1859 by some act of immaculate conception? I can almost guarantee you their family did what every other frontier family did back then—left New York or Ohio or Pennsylvania after they burned out the soil and wore out their welcome, moved west until they found people who basically looked and acted the same way they did, begged, borrowed, bought, or stole some decent land, then set about putting corn in the ground and inseminating cattle. We're all from somewhere else, Press. Anyway, what gives with all the Clarke talk? That waitress…what's her name again…really got under your skin, didn't she?"

"It's Katherine…but she goes by Kate or Katie."

"Does she now?" Amethyst said, arching an eyebrow. Jake looked down at the table while Am reloaded. "Lucky for you, I've arranged somewhere else for us to be tonight other than between these increasingly claustrophobic walls."

"Where?"

"I scored us tickets to the high school homecoming game… Hereford's version of Friday Night Lights."

"You have to buy tickets to go to a high school football game?"

"Duh, where have you been for like the last ten years? Tickets are what pay for the fancy uniforms and the practice facilities. Besides, a little birdie told me Milt Cloward and his lovely wife Blanche are supposed to put in a surprise appearance."

"A little birdie who weighs over 300 pounds and answers to the name McGreedy?"

"Precisely."

"Mort likes you, doesn't he?"

"What's not to like?" Am replied, flashing her best killer smile. "Granted, my ass is starting to sag a bit"—she reached around to give one cheek a diagnostic lift—"but otherwise I'd say I'm a damn fine catch. Have you seen the women around here, Press? Compared to them I'm in the 99.99 percentile. I gotta say, it's starting to go to my head."

"It's not a contest, Am."

"Really? Silly me, I thought that was the whole point of love and politics. May the best man, or woman, win. Anyway, throw on some pantaloons, roommate of mine, we're steppin' out on the town. And while you wait for me to get all bundled up in my too-cute-to-resist papoose coat, get a load of this… Marianne Meyers's latest 'People's Corner' column fresh from the otherwise stale pages of the *Hereford Gate* and cornier than ever, if that's even possible."

Jake glanced down at the newsprint Am had flung in his lap. "But this is a poem…"

"Very good," Amethyst called from the bathroom, "and in Hereford poems count as serious political commentary apparently." Bundled in her North Face coat, Amethyst leaned over the back of the couch, hovering so close Jake could feel her hot breath on the back of his neck. "Will you read it aloud, Press? I haven't had my recommended daily allowance of small-town schmaltz yet."

AN ODE TO THE SILVER STEER

By Brandon Frazier
Mrs. Meyers's Third Grade Class
Hereford Elementary

Whoever stares into your blazing eyes
Looks to see the truth
You help us see through politicians' lies
You offer us every possible proof.

Good guys and bad guys you help us sort out
You give us something for which to cheer
Silver Steer, we have nothing to worry about
For from you we have nothing to fear

Unless it is ourselves we need fear
reflected in your silvery mirror.

Amethyst let her scarf dangle playfully between Jake and the political verse. "Do you see what you've done to our poor Mrs. Meyers? Before you rolled into town in your Honda Accord, she could be counted on to produce my weekly dose of small-town gossip and civic do-gooder fluff. No, she's running the unedited, socially conscious poems of her class of little political activists. If it weren't disgusting, it might almost be inspiring. Bottom line, Press…you've invaded these poor children's psyches, not to mention their sweet, caring, doting teacher's. You've succeeded in creating a modern Midwestern legend, damn you."

"You mean like Paul Bunyan."

"More like his Big Blue Ox," she said, making two makeshift horns with her gloved fingers, and herding him out the door.

The high winds of the daytime had settled by the time Jake and Amethyst emerged from the apartment above the Sweetheart Bakery, so they opted to walk the ten minutes to the stadium, whose ambient light they could see glowing from the apartment like a beacon. The marching band was already tuning up, and as they drew nearer to the packed stands, Jake could just make out the chorus of the homespun fight song:

> Hail, Hail, Hereford High
> Fightin' Plowmen do abide
> Through wind, water, and darkness too
> Fightin' Plowmen see it through.

They found McGreedy slumped in the corner near the top of the stands, wearing the overstuffed parka that made him look like Admiral Perry at the North Pole, while drinking—decaf coffee he claimed, though his breath said otherwise—heartily from an oversized thermos. "Pull up a chair," he joked when finally they had climbed the bleachers to his windswept over-look.

"You couldn't get much farther from the action," Jake observed, looking down at the boys of Hereford High as they completed their pre-game warm-ups.

"The wind isn't quite so bad in this corner, under the press box," McGreedy explained.

"Any word about the possibility of a Milt Cloward flash mob?" Amethyst asked, plunking down beside the journalistic giant in the stands.

McGreedy shook his head. "Trust me on this one, Gilchrest. It comes from a source close to the campaign, as they say."

Amethyst spread her scarf out beneath her to take the sting out of the cold metal bleachers. "I don't see how you know these things," she marveled. "Is there some special Mort McGreedy hotline—you know, something like the Batphone—that lights up anytime something politically gigantic is about to happen?"

McGreedy smirked. "I won that battle by attrition. You stick around in a profession long enough and the people who spent twenty years successfully avoiding you can't anymore. The new ones are so intimidated by your gray hairs and alleged gravitas, they spill the beans before you even think to ask them."

Am scooted in close to the oversized reporter, either using him as a windbreak or stealing some of his body heat, it was hard for Jake to be certain. "Anyhow, here we go. Looks like good ol' Hereford High has won the coin toss," she said.

The first half of the game seemed to take forever, what with its endless run-it-up-the-gut plays broken only by the occasional short slant or screen pass. All of Hereford High's gains were modest—four yards here, six yards there—but they marched down the field twice to score two touchdowns compared to arch rival Goodacre's pair of field goals.

Just before halftime Jake noticed a flurry of activity on the Hereford sidelines and the full head of blow-dried salt-and-pepper hair that could only belong to Milt Cloward. Cloward sported a brown leather jacket, its collar stylishly upturned while his best gal and trophy wife, Blanche, followed behind in a creamy fleece coat with fur hood. Both wore blue jeans. Making their way up the home team's sidelines, they stopped and shook hands with the various cheerleaders, coaches, and Fightin' Plowmen who stood between them and the appointed rendezvous at the fifty-yard line.

"Make a pretty convincing First Couple, don't they?" McGreedy commented.

"I'm going down to get a closer look," Jake said, but the truth was he had spied a local in the stands with whom he desperately wanted an audience.

Herb Clarke sat alone near the bottom of the bleachers, a blanket spread across his lap. Jake excused his way through the crowd until finally he had scooted his way so close that the editor had little choice but to acknowledge him.

"Mr. Clarke," he ventured, in what came out sounding more like a question than a proper greeting. He felt now as he remembered feeling when he addressed his date's father on prom night back when he was scarcely older than the boys on the field.

"Oh, it's you," Clarke replied, only half-turning to look at him.

Oh, it's you. There were many greetings Jake had prepared himself for en route to an audience with the prickly editor. *So you're the jerk who made my daughter cry this afternoon.... Well if it isn't the dunderhead who introduced the asinine notion of the Silver Steer at the last debate. How fares the lucky winner of that fraudulent sweepstakes?*

What he hadn't counted on was *Oh, it's you.*

"Can I sit?" Jake asked.

"Suit yourself."

"I wanted to get a good view of the halftime festivities."

"You mean the crowning of our homecoming king and queen, I take it," remarked the editor.

For a second Jake thought the old newspaperman was yanking his chain.

"Yeah," Jake remarked, playing along, "how about those candidates?"

He followed Clarke's lead and stood when the boys from Hereford High sprinted off the field at the half, clinging to a seven-point lead. After the last straggling Plowman had entered the tunnel, a voice boomed over the P.A. system.

"The students of Hereford High invite you to join them as they elect their king and queen from their homecoming court. Candidates, please make your way now to the fifty-yard line."

The crowd cheered as, two by two, arm in arm, the candidates walked proudly to the oversized image of the Fightin' Plowmen mascot painted at midfield—a wild-eyed, grizzly old farmer wielding a wicked-looking plowshare. The dude looked a lot like Artie Shaw, Jake thought—the graying handlebar mustache and Martin Van Buren-styled mutton chops—and a moment later the announcer confirmed Jake's suspicions. Karaoke nights, trivia at the Wheel, a dab of homespun political consulting on the side—was there anything Hereford's ex-mayor-turned-banjo-picker didn't have his hands in, covertly, overtly, or otherwise?

The announcer read down the list of names of the finalists—good, solid, northern European names—Peterson, Vanderburg, Smith, Jensen, Langen, O'Connor, De Vries and, of course, Clarke. Cynda Clarke.

"Any relation?" Jake asked.

"Katie's second cousin."

"Looks like a bright girl."

"She didn't have much of a choice," Clarke replied flatly.

Didn't have much of a choice? For the life of him, Jake couldn't read Herbert Jefferson Clarke. *Didn't have much of a choice* because her overdemanding parents wouldn't tolerate less than perfection…in other words, a negative connotation? Or *didn't have much of a choice* because the family was so thoroughly steeped in Plowmen pride Cynda Clarke wouldn't have accepted anything less than homecoming court? Jake suspected the latter. After seven generations of kicking ass and taking names in Hereford County, why would this Clarke, of all Clarkes, be any different?

In the end, though, Cynda finished runner up to the lovely Samantha De Vries, the captain of the cheerleading squad, who had had to leave her post on the sidelines to don her tiara.

Cynda, however, beamed just as broadly as if she had won first prize when the runner-up sash was lifted over her shoulders.

"Hard to believe she's only a junior " Jake said to his still-silent seatmate.

"Nothing but a popularity contest," Clarke muttered, while in the background the P.A. announcer revved up the already keyed-up crowd. "Please direct your attention now to the south end zone for a special homecoming treat. Ladies and gentlemen, Governor Milt Cloward and his lovely wife Blanche!"

Jake followed the fingertips of the excited parents in front of him, as they pointed toward a pioneer wagon drawn by two beautiful horses. Riding atop stood the other couple of the hour, this one seeming an older, more moneyed version of the younger, Jake thought, as he watched the cart driven slowly up and down the sideline by some old geezer—a local character no doubt—dressed to play the part of the Fightin' Plowman himself. After the schooner had made its way in front of the home-team bleachers, it hung a hard right and headed out to midfield, under the brightest arc of stadium lights, and the drum major from the pep band hustled up with some mobile steps to help the First Couple safely down to the turf.

Homecoming king Robert Buchanan, holding his scepter in one hand and a microphone in the other, was first to speak. He thanked his coaches and teachers and classmates for their support, adding how totally cool it was to be sharing the field with one of his idols, Milt Cloward. Samantha De Vries was then given her moment, which she used to thank God for giving her this opportunity, her parents for their sacrifice, and her teachers and coaches for making her what she was today. It was cliché but still moving stuff, Jake thought, impressed in spite of himself by the sincerity of the young people's words and by their poise. At their age he was sure he would have been a stuttering, shaking, incomprehensible wreck, even if a presidential candidate had not been there to witness his insecurities played out in public.

Once the King and Queen of Hereford High had spoken their separate peace, they stepped aside to let the Clowards, Milt and Blanche, wave to their fans on both sides of the stadium, including to the visitors from Goodacre occupying the East side of the field. The band director produced a microphone, and Milt Cloward cleared his throat to speak.

"Thank you…thank you so much…for this incredibly warm reception. Blanche and I are thrilled, just thrilled, to be here with you tonight. You know it wasn't so long ago that I was Robert Buchanan." The crowd laughed, not entirely sure if the usually stoical Cloward was being serious or jokey. "Folks, that's the God's honest truth. Unlike Robert here, however, I wasn't popular enough to make homecoming court, though I'm proud to report that my date tonight, the lovely Blanche Cloward, was. And though she danced that night with the homecoming king rather than with me, I ended up winning the big game in the end…the contest for the heart of Blanche Davison." From the stands came a collective sigh. They loved this aw-shuck's Milt, not the one who had off-shored and downsized folks like them by the tens of thousands in his days as a corporate robber baron. "So while I may not be homecoming king material, the woman beside me will always be my queen."

As if on cue, the Hereford High cheerleaders broke into a spirited cheer:

The Fightin' Plowmen of Hereford High

Love Milt. Milt, Milt, Milt Cloward

Who's the apple of Hereford's eye?

Love Milt. Milt, Milt, Milt Cloward

Who's the hero of Hereford High?

It's Milt. Milt, Milt, Milt Cloward

Who's gonna win your vote on caucus night?

It's Milt, Milt, Milt, Milt Cloward

Back on the turf Milt held up his hand, all bashful prince. "Thank you. That was great. Maybe I can get my people to chant that each morning at our staff meetings. What do you think?"

The crowd cheered again, this time more boisterously than before.

"You know," the candidate opined, "there's been a lot of talk lately about the Silver Steer…"

Some nutcase in the stands shouted, "Yeah, Steer!"

"Yes, thanks for your enthusiasm, sir. But what I wanted to say is how much a night like tonight reminds me of the importance of tradition in communities like yours, places where milk is still delivered to the door, and boys still steal kisses from girls in the backseat…"

"And we all still drive Model T's," groused Herb Clarke, as, out on the field, Cloward continued to wax nostalgic.

"…and where candidates for President are still elected by pencil and paper, not held hostage to some rejected piece of hardware made for a football game."

"You're just chicken, Cloward!" someone yelled from the opposing sidelines. Jake could just barely make out the figure of a man standing in his jeans and Carhart jacket to give the candidate an earful.

Milt Cloward smiled ruefully. "Well, I see Senator Santoro is in the stands tonight. Folks, do you know who Mr. Santoro is, or shall I introduce him?"

The stands erupted in a round of raucous laughter mixed with good-natured booing.

"Milt, you're a poser and you know it," Santoro called out while someone on the Goodacre side of the field fetched the senator a microphone. "Why don't you tell these good people what a quarterback draw is, or a fade route, if you know so much about the pigskin."

The crowd howled now as Cloward looked down at the green grass as if the answer to Santoro's unexpected throw-down might be printed there.

"The Senator from Ohio doesn't seem to understand that politics isn't blood sport. It's not fisticuffs at the bar. It's civil people talking about pressing issues, not catcalling from the sidelines."

"You talk a good game, Miltie, but you wouldn't recognize a Statue of Liberty play if it up and bit you in the "—Santoro paused to smile sheepishly—"in the *grass*. Now why don't you answer these folks since you've interrupted the most important game of the season to convince them that you're all Ma 'n' Apple pie."

Beside her husband, Blanche Cloward had, true to her namesake, blanched. This was clearly not what she had been led to expect, and the few cameramen who, like McGreedy, had been tipped off to tonight's surprise appearance zoomed in tight on the former homecoming queen. Cloward was just about to open his mouth when the Fightin' Plowmen began to sprint back onto the field after halftime, only to have their coach shout "Whoa, boys!" and hold them up in the end zone when he spied Cloward on the fifty-yard line vamping. It looked for a moment like a very real stampede might be in the offing.

"You know, it doesn't always have to be about you, Senator. Why don't you save the low blows for tomorrow night's debate and sit on your hands so your friends from Goodacre can see the game they, unlike you, paid to attend."

Santoro waved dismissively at his rival, as if he was contesting a joke call made by some wayward referee, and sat back down in the stands to high fives from the Goodacre faithful who had rallied behind him.

"I must say, this is getting rather interesting, isn't it, Jacob?" Herb Clarke remarked. The editor's normally implacable face had broken into a grin. "The men are finally coming out from behind the machine."

As Milt and Blanche rode off the field in their chariot to a surfeit of waving, clapping, and no small amount of booing, Jake ventured the question that had been on his mind at least as much as the night's guest appearance. "Where's your daughter tonight?"

"She didn't feel like coming out," Clarke said flatly.

"Is she not feeling well?" Jake asked, opting to press the issue. "I'm sure she wouldn't want to miss her second cousin winning runner-up homecoming queen."

The older man turned to look Jake in the eye for the first time all evening. "Actually, Mr. Preston, she's recovering from a rather unfortunate run-in with a member of the press today. Perhaps you know him…out-of-state reporter from Colorado. Pretty much representative of his species."

"I'm sorry about that," Jake managed. "Sometimes I forget that I'm still a visitor here."

"You would be wise to remember that when you tread where you're not wanted," Clarke said. "Excuse me, Mr. Preston, while I go fetch some hot cocoa. Unlike you, I am here for the long haul."

It was painfully clear that Herb Clarke would not be rejoining him anytime soon, if he could help it, and for a moment Jake sat there, cursing his luck and licking his wounds, before recalling that he had promised McGreedy and Amethyst that he would only be gone a few minutes.

When he rejoined them a moment later, he could tell from their rosy cheeks and the empty thermos at McGreedy's side that Amethyst and McGreedy had gotten closer in the time he'd been away. In fact, they were sharing a blanket.

"Tuck in here, Press," Am offered, "there's plenty of room for a third."

"Nah," Jake replied, "I think I've had enough pigskin weather for one night. I'm gonna call it a night."

"Of course you are," she replied. "You always do. See you at the debate in Des Moines on Saturday night then?"

For some reason that he couldn't quite fathom, Amethyst Gilchrest was pretending as if Jake wasn't living with her. It was

Friday not Saturday, of course, and he would be seeing her in an hour tops…as soon as the game was over.

Whatever, he told himself climbing back down the bleachers, through the turnstiles, past a couple of teenagers nuzzling one another in the parking lot, and into the dark streets of Hereford, where he recalled that he had asked Amethyst to bring her set of keys to the game so he wouldn't have to carry his in his pocket.

He walked slowly back to the apartment, listening to the distant sounds of the game—delayed by the halftime debacle— behind him. Everything in the town was shut up except the Git-It-Kwik convenience store, and he didn't feel like loitering in front of the energy drinks for an hour while he waited for Am to return with her key.

Instead, he walked back to where his car was parked on the street a few storefronts down from the Sweetheart Bakery, figuring he would go for a long drive with the heat on full blast until his roomie returned from the game. It was a good plan, until he remembered for the second time that evening that he had forgotten his key ring and, with it, the ignition key to the Accord.

So he reached in his back pocket for his stocking cap, zipped up his windbreaker as high and tight as he could manage, and reclined in the driver's seat, figuring he'd catch a few Zs until Am and the cows came home. What else could he do?

Sometime later he awoke to someone—Am?—tapping at the driver's side window. He glanced at his watch—he had been asleep for a little over a half hour. Whoever she was, she was wrapped up so tightly in her scarf it looked more like a burka.

He rolled down the fogged-up window, blinking into the bright streetlights overhead.

"Do all political journalists sleep in their cars?" Katie Clarke asked, her voice a mixture of good humor laced with genuine concern. "You're going to freeze out here."

Jake's mind shifted into high gear. How was he going to explain this? He hadn't told Kate he was staying at Am's place—only that he was staying with a fellow reporter until he could find more permanent digs.

"Uh, I…" Jake stuttered, stalling for a plausible explanation, "I was at the football game with a few friends, decided to come home early, and realized I'd forgotten my keys. I'm just waiting here until…until my buddies get back."

"The game won't be over for another hour yet," she said, checking her watch. "Daddy is there, and I just got a phone update from him."

Jake tried his best to sound casual. "I don't mind waiting here. It's sort of nice, actually, in a brisk sort of way."

"I could unlock the café for you…"

"I couldn't ask you to do that."

"You just did," she said. "C'mon we'll be able to see the scoreboard from the roof. When Daddy called he said the game was headed into overtime."

The Cal Coolidge Café was ghostly—all the half-lit, hulking appliances and Coca-Cola signs glowing for no one to see. Katie switched on the light in the kitchen, leaving the rest of the eatery in darkness. She had learned from experience, she told him, not to turn on the lights in the seating area after-hours. The first and only time she had made that mistake a hungry local from across the street had come over asking if he was too late to get dinner.

Kate grabbed the radio and a flashlight, and together they ascended the two flights of stairs to a walk-out roof bathed in chilly moonshine. In front of them, casting shadows, sat two well-used lawn chairs.

"Expecting company?" Jake asked, pointing to the two seats arranged side by side.

"Daddy and I sometimes come up here to solve the world's problems. We were here last night, in fact."

"What problem were you solving?"

"None of your business," she said, and in the dark Jake realized he found the daughter's tone as inscrutable as the father's. She pointed at the halo of lights off to the southwest, handing Jake a pair of binoculars. "It's almost as good a play by play. You can see the scoreboard, time left, down, yards to go. Where do we stand?"

"Still knotted in a tie. Good Guys 21, Bad Guys 21."

She shook her head woefully. "The Fightin' Plowmen will break your heart every time, just like the Hawkeyes and the Cubs. They're a lose-from-ahead team."

"FYI, your second cousin Cynda won runner-up homecoming queen tonight."

"She lost to Samantha De Vries, right?"

"How'd you know?"

"There are certain universal laws. One, blondes always win, and, two, politicians always lie."

"What's the third?"

"Journalists always lose."

He mulled it over. "Seems like a pretty sound philosophy to me."

"It's not a philosophy," Kate corrected him. "It's a truism."

"How do you know?" Jake asked, figuring he was treading on thin ice again with the small-town saint who had just rescued him, freezing, from his car. But here in the dark, looking at the glow of the distant stadium lights, he felt emboldened, ebullient to be alive and talking rather than cold and shivering.

"My dad has a saying," Kate told him, "'Often wrong but never in doubt.' I subscribe to that notion, too."

"What I mean is, how did you arrive at such cosmic certainties while the rest of us are still trying to figure everything out?"

"I'm an old soul in a younger woman's body," she replied. "I've always known my own mind."

"And apparently other people's." Even in the gloaming, Jake swore he could see her eyes flashing.

"You've got a funny way of talking to someone who just rescued you," she said.

In the distance they heard an enormous roar. "That's got to be a touchdown for Hereford!" she exclaimed.

Jake looked through the field glasses and relayed the score 24-21, in favor of the Fightin' Plowmen. The time remaining read four goose eggs. "That's all she wrote," he said. "Your alma mater wins."

"Daddy will be pleased," she said, more to herself than to him. "He loves it when they clean Goodacre's clock."

"What does he have against the good people of Goodacre? They can't be all bad if Santoro set up his campaign office there."

"In his opinion they've sold out—they've got a Walmart, a Sonic, an Applebee's, and a branch office of the big hospital based in Des Moines."

"Right, those hospitals are public enemy number one," Jake teased.

"Actually, there's plenty wrong with hospitals, and if you want to know why Daddy feels the way he does about them, why don't you ask him yourself." Kate folded up the blanket she'd put in her lap and stood to go. "You might find yourself enlightened."

"I apologize," Jake said. "Don't go. We haven't even savored the home-team victory yet."

"And we won't…not tonight. Daddy will be home before too long, and I don't want him to wonder where I am…. Look," she added, "I don't know what your living situation is, and I'm too polite to ask, but you are welcome to sleep on the couch in the break-room tonight, as long as you're gone by 5:00 AM when Beverly comes in to bake the pies. Just leave the key in the letterbox beside the door, and I'll get it tomorrow morning when I come in for my shift."

"Thanks," Jake said. "I'm grateful for it."

"I like to think you would do the same for me," she replied. "Just promise me you won't be sitting in my booth, unshowered, at 6:00 AM tomorrow morning when I walk through the front door."

"I might be unshowered," Jake said, smiling in spite of himself. "But I promise I won't be comatose in your booth."

"Here," she added, throwing him the blanket, "you might want this. As soon as they power down the stadium lights, the stars up here are incredible, but that's also when you really start to feel the cold."

"Is this what those British air raid officers felt like in World War II," Jake wondered aloud, "just sitting up on the roofs with a light and a blanket waiting for the German Air Force to drop another night's worth of bombs."

"Could be," she said. "What are you waiting for?"

"A compassionate conservative," Jake quipped, "or a shooting star."

"Or a silver steer," Kate fired back, and when Jake turned to compliment her on the comeback, she was gone.

Below him on First Street he heard Katie's beater pickup truck drive away, leaving him in momentary silence until the cars streamed out of Fighting Plowmen Stadium and spilled into the streets with horns blaring and hip-hop busting out of the kinds of subwoofers he wouldn't have imagined small-town kids like these to have.

Beneath Katie's blanket he shivered, listening to the dulcet voice of the Fightin' Plowmen's radio play-by-play guy reviewing the game's highlights, including both a blow-by-blow of the homecoming vote and the Milt Cloward, Mike Santoro throwdown. For most of the fans in the stadium two of the most powerful men in America were minor sidenotes, second or third in order of importance where the night's events were concerned.

And maybe that's the way it should be. Maybe all the political junkies listening 24-7 to Fox News, and CNN, and MSNBC listened because they needed a team to root for. Maybe the farther apart people drifted from their homes and their families, the harder they pulled for, and the closer they watched the spectator sport of politics, where folks like Milt Cloward and Mike Santoro made passable substitutes for both the long-gone boys-next-door and the real American heroes in every community who once spent their days doing good deeds. Rightly or wrongly, politics in the TV era had become about faces—whose you liked, whose you didn't, whose reminded you of a face you once knew, and trusted.

Lost in his own thoughts, Jake walked to the edge of the roof of the Cal Coolidge, making sure to stay far enough back that he would not be mistaken for a kamikaze journalist attempting to end it all at the end of this, his first week on the ground in Iowa. From here he could see a light on in the apartment across the street, a light that could only mean one thing—Am was home.

He turned to leave, but a voice inside him he didn't quite understand caused him to re-train the binoculars on the apartment's signature bay window. This time the field glasses revealed to him the figure of Mort McGreedy raising a toast—whiskey no doubt—and Amethyst beside him, laughing lustily.

For a moment he couldn't turn away, so completely unexpected and yet weirdly predictable was the spectacle that, like a train wreck, it kept him transfixed. Didn't Amethyst realize he couldn't possibly be in his room? Wouldn't she have checked? And if she hadn't, wouldn't she at least have resolved to keep quiet, maybe given McGreedy a rain check out of sympathy for her new roomie? And, why, of all people to invite back to your place, did she invite McGreedy?

Whatever else McGreedy's visit might mean, practically, it meant that Jake would not be returning to his room anytime soon, at least not until he was sure of not running into either McGreedy or Amethyst. He would wait for the lights to go off, check that McGreedy's car was no longer parked out front of the Sweetheart Bakery, then walk over to see if Am had left the door unlocked for him.

He turned the radio back up, listening to the headline news for the first time since his arrival. Things had moved so quickly that aside from the copies of the *Times* Amethyst brought home each night, and whatever breakfast-stained broadsheets he could find at the café, Jake found himself in a bigger news black-out here than he had ever been in before, at exactly the time he was more plugged-in to the political process than ever. It wasn't easy getting the *Wall Street Journal* or the *New York Times* in Hereford, and he was strangely glad for it.

"Our top story tonight is an apparent shouting match between challenger Mike Santoro and frontrunner Milt Cloward during halftime of a homecoming game in Hereford, Iowa. The conflict apparently stemmed from a disagreement over an orphaned football trophy known as the Silver Steer. Santoro and others have claimed that the cast sterling trophy should become the de facto prize for the first-in-the-nation primaries scheduled this year for their earliest date ever—the second Tuesday in November."

Jake chuckled. He had forgotten just how far the media version of events diverged from reality. It had not been a "shouting match," though it was, so far as he knew, unprecedented. He turned the radio down, remembering to look up at the stars Kate had begged him consider.

What would his friends back in Denver say if they could see him now, struggling to pick out Orion for the first time since grade school, sitting alone with a radio on the roof of a café named for a forgotten president best remembered for relishing his afternoon naps, after a day of twice alienating the most intriguing woman he'd ever met who just happened to be the daughter of the town's biggest grump.

And yet somehow, for all the strangeness of his new life, he had never been happier. Not even the image of the oversized Mort McGreedy yucking it up in his living room could spoil the goodness of the moment, as he pulled the blanket tightly around him and drifted off to sleep.

Five

"Preston, Sousage here."

Every time he heard Chuck's voice, Jake pictured a life-sized breakfast patty holding a cell phone.

"What's up?"

"You're back in the game, friend," the PR guru enthused on the other end.

"What game?"

"The only game in town, man. Tonight's debate in Des Moines."

"I thought you wanted me to keep a low profile."

"I did, and Pitchford did, but the party boss in DC, Prince Reebus saw it differently."

It was Saturday morning, the day of the big debate, and Jake Preston hadn't been home in twenty-four hours.

"What's going on with you, kid? You sound like hell."

"Didn't get much sleep last night," Jake admitted, letting the convenience-store coffee from the Git-It-Kwik lift the fog away.

"Those Hereford gals must be wearing you out. Get a nap, Casanova. We need you sharp tonight. Can you handle it?"

"Guess I'll have to."

"That's the spirit," Sousage said sarcastically. "My God, you're a regular Gipper." He paused. "Your job is to do your best to look hip and to rep the youthful side of the Republican party."

"Wait a sec," Jake cautioned, throwing up the red flag. "Remember, I'm a journalist not a member of the party faithful."

"Right, and I'm the Pope. Listen, you won a contest sponsored by the state Republican party. So far as we're concerned you're our man, and we're your party, at least for the next... uh, let me see now, the next twenty-one days of our arranged marriage. We're not asking you to change your stripes, just to fulfill your end of the contract, wherein you agreed, in writing, to appear at any event of our choosing. So we're choosing. You also agreed not to do anything that might, in some tangible way, affect the outcome of the race. I reviewed the fine print of our little agreement last night over a rot-gut bottle of Scotch, and it seems your question about the Silver Steer already has you treading on some thin legal ice."

"Explain to me how mentioning the Silver Steer has materially impacted the race."

"Where do you want me to begin? In the last seven days Cloward is down five points among likely voters and Santoro is up eight. We'll have some more detailed polling and focus group data after tonight's battle royale, but it's hard to chalk up that kind of momentum shift to mere coincidence, don't you think?"

On the other end of the line Mr. Breakfast Patty paused to clear a phlegmatic throat. "So tonight you're going to retract your question, admit that you intended it as a jest, and say that you are as surprised as anyone that the voters of Iowa have taken it so seriously. You're going to suggest that the Silver Steer is, at base, a very un-American notion. And then you're going to ask a serious, issues-oriented question of the kind that would make George Agropolis green with envy. Do I make myself clear?"

Jake considered the quid pro quo. "I'm not making any promises."

"You've already made your promises, son, and I have the signatures to prove it. Show up at the debate hall an hour early. Sawyer and Agropolis are hosting, and thanks to a call from Reebus, you're an eleventh-hour addition to a small roundtable of editors from the state newspaper association. The focus is on regional issues impacting farm communities and small towns. Better use the next few hours to bone up so you don't make us all look stupid."

When Jake asked *Are you still there, Chuck?* and his question met with radio silence, he realized he'd been abruptly hung up on by the man whose last named rhymed with *Corsage*. Jake shoved the phone back in his pocket and rolled out of the gas station parking lot headed toward home. He wanted to see what the party girl had to say for herself, but mostly he wanted a good warm shower and a long, slow toothbrush.

He found the door to Am's apartment locked. On the third knock, the door opened just wide enough for his roommate's head to poke out. She was still in her negligee.

"Jesus, Press. You just about scared the Milt Cloward out of me. Well, are you going to get in here or are you going to stand there like a Jehovah's Witness?"

She opened the door wide, disappeared into the bathroom momentarily, and returned wearing a robe and some fuzzy slippers twice the size of her feet. Jake sat down on the couch and waited for the shoe to fall. "Where were you last night?" she asked once she had settled in. "I was worried sick!"

"But not so worried as to postpone a slumber party with Mort McGreedy?"

Am folded her arms defiantly. "It's bad enough that you go to bed at 10:00 PM, but now you're controlling whom I can have over and whom I can't. Hereford's turned somebody into a little control freak."

"So you somehow thought I was peacefully snoozing away in my room while you were out here in the living room laughing your head off?"

"I figured you were sound asleep. You'd left the ballgame an hour and half before we did, your car was parked just down the street, and the lights in mi casa were already off. And if perchance you weren't already in dreamland, I hoped you'd have the decency to come out and join us for a nightcap."

"At midnight? After I'd supposedly been asleep for two hours?"

"I can't help it that you're a Debbie Downer. Anyway, why are we arguing about this? It's clear, isn't it, that you were not in your room, which raises the question, where in the hell were you?"

Jake was just tired enough, and sufficiently pissed, to give some flak back to Amethyst Gilchrest. "And I suppose because you 'rent' a room to me, you control where I go and when I come back?" He watched with satisfaction as Am frowned at the taste of her own medicine. "Actually, if you must know, a good Samaritan saw me sleeping in my car, and offered me a place to crash, which is more than I can say for you. By the way, how was McGreedy?"

"Ouch," Amethyst said, tightening the sash around her robe. "Actually, Mr. Preston, I don't care for your insinuation. I did not sleep with Mort McGreedy, if that's what you're implying. Because a girl invites a colleague over to her home for drinks does not mean she lets him in her pants, or is that too difficult for you to comprehend?"

Jake was too weary to play the name-calling game. "What's your angle, Am? What do you want with McGreedy?"

"Two for two on presumptuous questions, Mr. Preston.... Suppose I want from McGreedy what any ambitious young professional in her field would want from a veteran—advice, strategy, wisdom."

"And an inside tip or two, right?" Jake added. "That's pretty self-serving, even for you."

Am put her slippered feet up on the coffee table, looking at them instead of her roommate. "So what do you say we agree to chalk up the events of last night to a mutual misunderstanding, and go on being friends?"

"The trouble is, I don't believe a goddamn word you just said, Amethyst. I believe you were pissed at me for leaving the game early, that you remembered full well that I left my keys behind, and that you figured I was out there somewhere, roaming the streets of Hereford, and would surely arrive to find the house lit up and you and McGreedy having a gay old time. That would have been exactly your way of exacting revenge."

"Is that what you think of me, Jacob, that I'm so obsessed with you that I spend my nights weaving sinister webs, contemplating how I can make your life miserable until you inevitably become infatuated with me? It may come as a blow to your male ego, but your approval, or disapproval, does not motivate my actions…not last night, not ever."

They sat in an uncomfortable silence. Finally, Amethyst stuck out her hand. "So, can I offer you a laurel leaf? Can't we just agree to disagree?"

Jake took a long second before he answered. "No," he said finally.

"What do you mean, 'No.'"

"I mean no I'm not okay with what you did last night, so why don't you go ahead and plan on driving yourself to the debate tonight."

"I would," Amethyst said, "but I don't have a car."

"You have a car," Jake said firmly. "I've ridden in it."

"I *had* a car," she corrected him. "And I returned it to the rental car agency yesterday for a partial refund. There was no use both of us having cars."

"So you returned the rental that the *Times* paid for so you could bum mileage depreciation off me, while you pocketed the expense account money that should, by rights, go for your transportation? Do I have your Ponzi scheme about right?"

"Fine," Am said, commencing a serious pout. "I'll hitch a ride with McGreedy. And when he's not regaling me with stories about traveling with the President, and making me laugh so hard

I'm wetting my pants, I'll consider whether I want to extend the generous offer of renting my extra bedroom to you. Fair?"

"Totally," Jake said.

"Good," Am said. "Then we're clear. So why don't you leave me alone now so I can get on with my day. Some of us occasionally have some reporting to do." She walked halfway to the kitchen before turning around. "I'll only be here for another twenty minutes, and then you can have this place to yourself for endless moping and self-pitying. Oh, and the heartless bitch you live with made coffee cake as a special treat this morning, and she saved you some in the fridge. Bon appétit."

"And another thing," Am added from the hallway. "The only candidate gayer than you are, Brad Charger, dropped out of the race this morning."

"Welcome back to the latest in our exclusive series of candidate debates," Donna Sawyers enthused from what would have once been the orchestra pit in the old auditorium. "Tonight's debate is brought to you by our fabulous network, right George…"

"Right, Donna."

"And by the Iowa Newspaper Association. Hello, Des Moines!" the former beauty queen bubbled, turning around in her seat to give the packed house a wave. "We're delighted to be here on this historic campus, in this grand old auditorium. George, this hall is simply stunning. I could live in here."

"And you just might if this race gets any closer. Polls out today show the race tightening, with a virtual dead heat between Milt Cloward and Mike Santoro, with Renard Kane, Rochelle

Boxman and Paul Paule not far behind. And that brings me to who's not on the stage tonight, most notably Brad Charger, who suspended his campaign earlier today. According to the rule established and agreed to in advance, only candidates polling at 5% or better in official polls have been invited to the table tonight. So we'll be welcoming Milt Cloward, Mike Santoro, Rochelle Boxman, Paul Paule, Renard Kane, and Rich Priestly."

"Another programming note before our eager candidates take the stage," Sawyers added. "George and I will pose the questions in the opening two segments, with the third and final portion belonging exclusively to four journalists who will focus their questions on economy and governance in the region's many small towns and rural places."

"Ah, the small-town newspaper editor," Agropolis waxed, "that relic of an earlier age when the press held politicians in check, and served as a necessary counterweight to overzealous government."

"Just like you read about in your civics textbooks," Sawyers chimed in. "But before we zoom in on a region in crisis, we need to take a commercial break. When we come back we'll begin with the big picture, hearing from the candidates on issues ranging from domestic security to economic policy and immigration."

Backstage Jake listened as the candidates, fresh from commercial break, delivered their usual carefully rehearsed talking points. He had been following the race now for almost nine months, eight and a half of them from Denver. After about the third week, the candidates had ceased to surprise him. He knew exactly how they were going to answer, and he knew that each of them, and their campaign staffs, lived in fear of political suicide, the left-handed comment made at some Podunk stop somewhere that, if taken the wrong way, could effectively end their campaigns and leave their donors running for the door. To prevent just that inglorious end, campaign advisors and coaches drilled them for hours on talking points, each carefully and liberally sprinkled with words that focus groups had demonstrated would yield positive results, pinging just the right part of the voter brain—*entitlements, second amendment, entrepreneur, small business, American exceptionalism, secure our borders, defer to the generals, class warfare, unconstitutional mandate, war on terror*— he knew the list of buzzwords almost as well as the candidates themselves. When one of the candidates opened their mouth, what Jake heard boiled down to catchphrases pinging his hippocampus like some strange political drug. *Blah Blah Blah Blah Blah ENTITLEMENTS. Blah Blah Blah IMMIGRATION REFORM and LIMITED GOVERNMENT.*

What he longed for were the unscripted moments, and these, he knew, were many times more likely to occur in the pressure cooker of the big debates than anywhere else. And judging from the handful of protesters on the other side of the police barricades as he walked in, he knew he wasn't the only one disappointed with the woefully predictable, some would say inexorable, process by which the candidate with the most money and the biggest private donors and political action committees would take a comfortable lead in the primaries sometime around September. Voters who never much liked the frontrunner would then grow tired of being told about the "presumptive nominee," and they would buck, looking desperately up and down the field for an underdog they could temporarily elevate to make the presumptive nominee work to earn their votes. They would find someone, Jake knew, they always did, and that person's stock would rise as rapidly as some hot dot.com suddenly proffered for public offering. That individual would then shoot up in the polls like a meteor before closer scrutiny and tougher lines of questioning revealed them to be the second-rate, second-tier candidate everyone had always known them to be.

And yet somehow through all that seeming unpredictability, the candidates never put themselves in a vulnerable place, never had to really work for it in anything more informal than an Oxford rolled at the sleeves or a hardhat obligingly donned for a brief factory visit. The only time voters came close to seeing them in head-to-head competition came at the debates, where the nature of the questions was almost always known in advance, and where the candidates predictably clashed in ways they had clashed a thousand times before.

"Lost in thought, I see." Herb Clarke strolled into the Green Room and stood before Jake, interrupting his feedback loop. "Too much thinking is bound to get you in trouble."

For a second the cat had Jake's tongue. "I…I didn't know you were on the panel, Mr. Clarke."

The editor laughed. "I was, then I wasn't. I was until a couple of days ago when suddenly the Republican party decided they needed to create a last-minute spot for the Politics Up Close sweepstakes winner—some greenhorn reporter from Denver.

Then I wasn't. Then I threatened to file a formal protest with both the party and the network, and suddenly I was again. Chuck Sousage called me personally to say, 'Hey, no hard feelings. The more the merrier, right?' So now I'll be sitting next to the young guy, who, if the party had had their way, would have taken the old guy's place. It's an interesting parable for an old man like me to consider." The editor sat down heavily in the chair next to his own.

Jake wasn't sure whether he ought to be flat-out insulted, mildly pissed off, or completely apologetic. He opted for the latter.

"I had nothing to do with it, I swear. I just found out myself this morning that I would be on the panel."

"No hard feelings, Mr. Preston. I gathered that you were nothing more than a puppet content to have your strings pulled. The important thing is that we both have the opportunity we have been waiting for to ask the candidates our all-too carefully vetted questions." Herb Clarke looked up at the giant television screen as, out in the auditorium, Rochelle Boxman talked tough on tax reform.

Clarke cleared his throat before he continued. "So, as the Bard once said, we're about to have our fifteen minutes of fame. My suggestion, young man, is that you make the most of it." And with that he rose from his chair, speared a couple of pieces of pineapple from the complimentary fruit plate, and walked briskly out of the room just as one of the network producers poked his head through the open door.

"On in two!" the guy called in, disappearing as quickly as he had come. His visage was followed shortly by the round, preternaturally tan face of Chuck Sousage, who likewise opened the door just enough so that Jake could see only the top half of him…the top half of the Sousage, as it were.

"You set with your question, bub?"

"It's not really a question, is it?" Jake said flatly. "It's more like a statement."

"So we're good then?"

"Yes," Jake replied, annoyed that Pitchford had sent his minion to make sure he was still all in.

"Better get your game on. Your colleagues are already lining up out here like pigs in a chute." Sousage winked conspiratorially before he too was gone.

Jake gathered up the few note cards he had brought with, fumbled for his pen, and hustled into the darkened line of editors. He found himself experiencing flashbacks to high school basketball, where he and the other four members of the starting five would agitate in the tunnel, shaking their legs out and talking smack, before coach would give them the signal and they would sprint out onto the floor for warm-ups before, inevitably, losing by 20. Tonight, the three editors in front of him weren't Division One prospects, but graying oldsters who'd spent their lives setting type, weeding out semi-colons, and attending city council meetings where leaf-burning amendments qualified as landmark legislation.

Tonight, however, thanks to some big bucks put forward by their professional organization, these sharpshooters were suddenly buzzer-beaters at the NBA finals. The make-up intern came by, giving each of the gray-hairs one last dusting of cover-up before addressing any and all potential wardrobe malfunctions. The job of introing the editors fell to Sawyers and, as always, she dispatched her duties with the social graces of a former debutante who had spent her professional life sweet-talking the camera.

"We're back now with the final portion of tonight's debate, a roundtable Q and A with the traditional opinion-makers in the Heartland's many small towns and rural places. That's right, it's the editors of your local small-town newspapers holding the candidates' collective feet to the flame this evening. We are pleased to have with us tonight Sue Donald from the *Register*, Herb Clarke from the *Hereford Gate*, Buzz Brooks from *The Conservative*, and, of course, representing the *Rocky Mountain Partisan,* the winner of the Politics Up Close competition, Jacob Preston."

Jake felt the sweat building on his forehead.

"Donna and I plan to yield the floor in this segment," clarified Agropolis, "so as to let these professionals do what they do best…ask the tough questions concerning the communities where they hang their hats…. Sue Donald, first question goes to you."

Donald nodded, squaring up the corners of the sheaf of papers laying before her on the table. "I'd like to start with you, Congresswoman Boxman. You've made a point of championing your small-town roots in this campaign…"

"…yes, I have Sue," Boxman said, interrupting, per usual.

"And yet two years ago you and your husband sold your home outside Sioux Falls and moved your permanent residence to Washington D.C. Are there any ways in which your move has compromised your ability to advocate for your primarily rural district?"

Boxman looked like she wanted to tear Sue Donald's liberal arm off, salt and butter it, and eat it for dinner. "Absolutely not, Sue. In fact, my move to Washington has allowed me to better represent the farmers, ranchers, manufacturers, and small business people of my home district. Think of it this way. If the boy's club in Washington is gathering to make closed-door deals, wouldn't you want to be there to stick your hand in the door and say, 'Wait a minute, fellas, what's going on back here that you don't want the little lady to see?' If I were back home in Sioux Falls, shady deals like these would have gone down while I was stuck changing planes in Chicago. Now I'm just a few blocks away from Congress, and if something dirty is about to hit the floor, or the fan, they can count on Rochelle Boxman being there to raise a stink about it."

"At the same time, Congresswoman, and with all due respect, your children are not attending a small Midwestern school as you and your husband once did, the kind you credit in your memoir for having shaped you into the strong and principled leader you are today. Instead, they are enrolled in a private academy in one of the largest metropolitan areas in the United States. Does that trouble your conscience?"

"My kids are learning what it's like to have a mom who's willing to go wherever it takes to represent her convictions, and they're receiving a first-class education with students from all over the world. What conscientious mom would be the least bit troubled by that?"

"Thank you, Congresswoman Boxman. Next question goes to you, Mr. Brookings."

"Mr. Kane," Buzz Brookings drawled, "my readership is made up primarily of farmers and cattlemen who appreciate plain-spokeness. There are many aspects of your economic plan that appeal to my constituency, but they're worried that it's too big a change to the current tax structure and to existing revenue projections, and as successful business people themselves they don't want to be left footing the bill for urban America, as they did during the mortgage crisis. What could you say to ease the fears of cautious, risk-adverse readers like mine regarding your economic plan?"

Renard Kane nodded, meeting the question head on, as was his habit. "As a no-nonsense businessman, I share your readers' appreciation for straight-shootin'. It's like the words of the old spiritual tell us, 'Tis a gift to be simple, Tis a gift to be free.' I called my economic plan the Common Sense plan, in part to pay tribute to that great American patriot Thomas Paine, who wrote the original *Common Sense*, and in part because my program for economic recovery just makes good sense. I could have called it the No Brainer Plan. Basically, Buzz, it's this: Implement a national sales tax, institute a flat tax, decrease the corporate tax to under 10 percent and, last but not least, rewrite the Tax Code using the government standard for Plain English that Bill Clinton called for. In a Renard Kane administration folks who are perfectly capable of reading and understanding their local newspaper could file their own taxes. Let's start honoring the intelligence of our voters by giving them a fair, unbiased tax system they don't need an accountant or an attorney to understand."

"A follow up on that, if I could, Mr. Kane. Out on the campaign trail you've sometimes called your program for tax simplification the 'Duh Plan.' Do you think in some ways that kind of language might be viewed as an insult to the intelligence of the very voters you're trying to appeal to?"

"I do not believe it is insulting," Kane answered flatly. "In the African American community, we believe in tellin' it like it is."

"And why exactly is the term 'Duh' fitting as a moniker for your common-sense plan?"

"All's I've got to say to that is, 'Duh, Buzz.'"

Mercifully Agropolis intervened. "A tough line of questioning from Buzz Brooks and an equally firm response from Mr. Kane. Looks like we're off to an engaging start, Donna."

"Yes indeed, George. Now we come to the third member of our distinguished panel tonight, Herb Clarke of the Little Paper That Could, the *Hereford Gate*. Now many of you watching this debate across the country tonight have never heard—or should I say *herd*—of Hereford, Iowa. But this small town out on the edge of the prairie has become the unlikely national headquarters for the Milt Cloward campaign and, up until recently, the nerve center for Brad Charger's recently suspended run for office. Mr. Clarke has recently found his newspaper's fiery columns reprinted across the region as he writes from the sleepy farm town turned political ground zero where his family has hung their hats for a century and a half. Herb, why don't you begin by telling America a little bit about your hometown."

"I appreciate the opportunity to do so," Clarke said. Jake wondered whether he had been prepped in advance for this moment. Either way, Herb Clarke would be ready. "We're a town of just under two thousand hearty souls located about ninety minutes equidistant from two cities your viewers may have heard of: Des Moines and Sioux City. In a rapidly urbanizing state and region, we remain a farm community tied to our agricultural heritage. We're a proud, self-reliant people, the kind of folks many of your viewers probably think exist only in history books and stories about prairie schooners and grasshopper plagues. We're not yokels, hicks, rednecks, isolationists, provincials, or any of the other unfair stereotypes we're saddled with. We boast a small municipal airport, run our harvesters by GPS, and make do with the health care available to us at our twenty-five-bed critical-access hospital. You can order a vegetarian burger and a spinach salad at our local café, and our town library contains over twenty thousand volumes. But for all that, our population peaked in the 1960s, and we currently have about five hundred fewer people living within our city limits than when Cal Coolidge took office. Many of the people watching tonight would be surprised to learn the poverty level in my proud little town equals or exceeds the rate in some of the country's most hard-pressed inner cities."

Donna Sawyers raised an eyebrow. "Thank you, Mr. Clarke, for that impassioned and educational introduction." Jake could almost hear the television sets across the nation clicking off at Clarke's overtruthful intro. "Go ahead when you're ready with your question," Sawyers instructed.

"Mr. Santoro and Mr. Priestly, I'd like to hear from each of you regarding what you would do to help curtail the so-called Brain Drain devastating small towns across Middle America as we gather here tonight," Clarke said. "As both of you are well aware, the most dramatic symptom of this plague is the alarming rate at which our youngest, best educated citizens move away to the region's cities as soon as they have their college degree in hand."

"Let me start by thanking Mr. Clarke for his convictions," Santoro said, leaping in first. "Suffice it to say, I'd plug the drain. I'd do it by rebuilding an America whose small towns and villages not so long ago made many things. You know, I come from a Midwestern state, Ohio, where not long ago we had a balanced agricultural and industrial base. Tragically, the trade policies favored by presidents of both parties in the last two decades have meant that many of our once thriving towns are now mightily struggling. I understand that, I've lived that, and I'm committed to changing that. That's why I moved my family and my campaign headquarters to a town just down the road from Hereford, a little village called Goodacre, Iowa, six months ago. That's why I attended the Hereford High homecoming game last night and had the time of my life. A Santoro administration would see to it that communities like those I cheered for last night have a fair and equitable chance to thrive."

"Mr. Priestly?"

"Look, you're talkin' to an Okie. We Sooners understand workin' the land and its resources better than anybody. Here's the thing…Brain Drain is caused by lack of economic opportunity. Plain 'n' simple. Give young people a chance at findin' a good job close to home and most of 'em will gladly put down roots. That's why Oklahoma, with one of the fastest rates of economic growth in the nation and some of the lowest taxes, is a state young people are finally comin' to—some to work in oil and gas, some in farmin' and ranchin', some just to appreciate all the culture available to 'em in Tulsa or Oklahoma City. Our goal with our various college scholarship programs has been to keep our best talent in-state for their higher education, then work hard to make sure there's a job waiting for 'em when they graduate."

"Thank you, candidates, for your thoughtful answers. Now, for this segment's final question, we come to a new face on the political landscape, one many of you saw for the first time, as George and I did, at last weekend's debate on the other side of the state. Jacob Preston, welcome to this fascinating, topsy-turvy exercise we call American electoral politics."

"Thanks, Donna. Glad to be here," Jake said. Underneath the table he attempted to wring the sweat from his hands.

"Why don't you tell the folks at home who missed last week's debate about the Politics Up Close contest—the competition that you won in order to join us here on stage tonight. Tell them how you came to sit with us in this front-row seat."

"I applied online," Jake said.

Sawyers smiled broadly. "Hear that, folks? It's just like your parents taught you...you can't win if you don't play. So you submitted an application, then what?"

"My editor at the *Rocky Mountain Partisan* called me to tell me he had some news for me."

"Boy did he ever, right?"

"I loaded up my Honda Accord and set off for the Hawkeye State."

"And how many miles does that Honda have on it, Jacob."

"210,000."

"Wow. Now that's an economical ride. Maybe the candidates on the stage tonight could learn a thing or two from your frugality."

"Maybe," Jake said, doing his best to smile.

"Now, I understand you'd like to talk more about the Silver Steer, this orphaned football trophy you suggested might be used as a kind of prize for the winner of the first-in-the-nation vote. Do I have that right?"

"Sort of," Jake began. "Actually, when I asked what the candidates would choose as a trophy, Mr. Santoro was the one to suggest he would choose the Silver Steer."

On stage, Santoro nodded energetically, all too willing to accept credit.

"And it seems that idea has achieved some real traction among voters this past week, powering Mr. Santoro's rise in the polls. So what would you like to add to the debate tonight?" Jake wondered whether Pitchford or maybe Prince Reebus had given Sawyers a heads-up about the retraction they had scripted for him, so she could have her segue ready.

"Over the past several days I've begun to reconsider my question from last week," Jake began, doing his best to follow the notes Sousage had handed him. He looked out in the audience and caught the eye of Katie Clarke sitting in the second row, and for a moment he lost his resolve. "I guess, what I mean to say is, the idea of these respected men and women competing for a prize has inserted a lot of volatility into the race."

"So much so that I understand there was a shouting match last night between two of the candidates at a homecoming football game. Is that right?"

"I wouldn't call it a shouting match," Jake explained, only to find himself interrupted by Herb Clarke.

"Donna, I was at the homecoming game last night...my daughter's second cousin was on the court, actually."

"Congratulations," Sawyers bubbled. "You must be one proud family member."

"I am indeed," the editor avowed. "What I saw last night wasn't a shouting match at all but a good-spirited debate of the kind that we used to have all the time in this country. We only commenced calling such public discourse 'shouting matches' when the powers-that-be started picking our frontrunners for us in advance."

"Mr. Preston," Agropolis said, turning his bobblehead back to Jake. "I understand you were at the game last night as well. Do you agree with Mr. Clarke that last night's exchange at the ballgame piqued your interest?"

"Definitely," Jake said.

"Why don't we open the discussion up to the two men embroiled in this...in this whatever it is," Agropolis suggested, swiveling his chair back toward the stage to point his pen at

Milt Cloward, who seemed mildly confused at the direction the conversation appeared to be taking. "Mr. Cloward, voters are giving the Silver Steer idea a real endorsement. In the last week they've logged in and called up to report, by a 2 to 1 margin, that they would tune in more closely to the race if the Silver Steer were up for grabs. Given those kinds of majorities, have you at all reconsidered the lukewarm sentiments you expressed in last week's debate?"

On stage Milt Cloward stood ramrod straight, wearing a smile suspended somewhere between mild disapproval and barely concealed disdain. "As a matter of fact I have, George. You see, in thinking back to my school days playing sports…"

"And which sports were those, for the record?" Agropolis asked as Cloward frowned, visibly bothered by the interruption.

"I played a little polo and some handball, as I recall, and I rowed on our crew team. To be truthful, I wasn't much good at any of them, but, let me tell you, I loved to compete for that prize, whatever it was! And you know, last night's victory by the Fightin' Plowmen of Hereford High had me thinking about how satisfying it is to hold a trophy over your head as a symbol of good things hard won. So, yes, I'd be pleased to compete with Senator Santoro and others for the Silver Steer, though I don't know that I'd recognize this trophy everyone is talking about even if I saw it."

"No problem, Milt," Santoro piped up. "I've got it right here." The former senator reached underneath his podium and, with both hands, raised the Silver Steer to oohs and ahhs from the crowd. Under the auditorium spotlights, the statue seemed even more talismanic than it had when Jake had first seen it in the flesh, and on the hoof, a few days before in Goodacre. "Worth fighting for, isn't it?"

"Certainly," Cloward said, stepping back from the podium for a better view. "It's a symbol of some things America once stood for and can stand for again if Milt Cloward is President."

"Just to make sure everyone at home gathered around their TV sets is clear on this," Donna Sawyers jumped in, sensing her moment. "From this point forward you officially agree to compete with Mr. Santoro and the other candidates on stage tonight for the prize of the Silver Steer?"

Cloward blinked. "Now of course we must do so within the existing electoral framework. That said, surely there is room in the primary process for some additional good-natured competition."

"What do you say, folks," prompted Sawyers, turning to the audience seated behind her. "Would you be interested in seeing the candidates on stage compete for this magnificent trophy?"

Applause. Whistles. And somewhere in the auditorium, a rogue cow bell. "I think, gentlemen and lady, you have yourself a competition," Sawyers enthused.

Jake breathed an audible sigh of relief into the microphone.

"Mr. Preston, this news seems to come as some relief to you."

"It does, Donna. It's just that…well, I worried somehow that I had misspoken at the last debate. And that the Silver Steer might detract from the process."

"Ladies and gentlemen," Agropolis interrupted, "I think we have another election-year first here…a self-conscious journalist. Jake are you sure you're a hardboiled presidential journalist in real life?"

"Maybe I just play one on TV," Jake said, and the crowd broke into laughter.

"And so the upstart journalist gets tonight's last word," Donna Sawyers declared. "Thanks once again from George and me to all these deserving candidates, to the newspapermen and woman on tonight's panel, and to the Silver Steer here for making this yet another fascinating and high-spirited evening."

"Well, you survived, young man," Herb Clarke said as soon as the producers signaled they were off-air.

Jake dabbed at the sweat beads forming on his forehead. "Barely," he said. "I'm afraid Sousage won't be very happy with me. I didn't get out exactly what he needed me to say."

Clarke raised an inquisitive eyebrow. "Is that so?"

"I think the state Republican party would like to put the Silver Steer out to pasture, and me along with it," Jake said.

"I can imagine they might," the editor replied. It was the first trace of compassion Jake had heard in Clarke's voice. "We've made some progress tonight, son, and don't let anyone tell you otherwise."

Backstage in the Green Room Chuck Sousage was livid. "You screwed the pooch, son!" he shouted, running his hands through his movie-star head of hair over and over again.

"I tried to get it out," Jake defended himself. "I got interrupted, first by Herb Clarke, then by Agropolis."

"So what...so I'm supposed to feel sorry for you? Christ, Preston, you're a professional journalist. It's like you're some goddamned freshman quarterback telling his coach that he would have passed the ball, only he got tackled first. Throw the goddamned ball before you get tackled!"

"Maybe you're right."

"Of course I'm right! In my line of work, you either shit or get off the pot. This doesn't bode well for you, Mr. Sweepstakes Winner; it doesn't bode well at all. Instead of putting this Silver Steer thing to bed, you've fed and watered the goddamn thing and given it new life."

Sousage continued to fume. "Preebus and Pitchford are gonna chew my ass on our conference call tomorrow. I'll be surprised if heads don't roll over this. It might be mine. It might be yours. Or it might be both of ours. And if it is, I'm holding you personally responsible. I've got a daughter in college, Preston. This isn't some game to me...it's a livelihood. You come between a man and his livelihood, watch out!" Sousage shouted, shoving a meaty finger in Jake's face.

Six

It took just two work days for the Silver Steer to hit the fan.

On Monday Jake received written notice, full of legalese, informing him that he had violated the terms of the Politics Up Close contest and, pursuant to that violation, all privileges associated with the contest would be revoked, effective immediately. Less than forty-eight hours after his face had been broadcast to sixty million primetime viewers, his career, such as it was, lay in ruins. And since the only thing that had kept him in touch with the *Rocky Mountain Partisan* had been his status as the contest winner, he had lost his last legit press affiliation in the process.

The whole thing had gone down while Amethyst was away covering an immigration raid in Sioux Falls, and it came as something of a surprise to Jake that he missed her, and missed her badly. In her absence the apartment seemed lifeless, the town drab and boring, as if the color itself had leaked out, leaving the whole thing in monochrome again. A girl like Amethyst, Jake realized, as he held down the bar by himself at the Wagon Wheel on Monday night, was all too easily underappreciated. Sure she was obnoxious, opinionated, self-obsessed, and occasionally disingenuous, but she had joie de vivre. Amethyst was a force, plain and simple—a verb rather than a noun. She would be a silver-haired diva at 85 and live to be 100. Her funeral would be packed to overflowing with hundreds of people who both loved and hated her, but who were bound to her nonetheless. By contrast, his own funeral would be attended by whom...his parents, one or two ex girlfriends maybe, a few close friends, and, he noted with an inward grin, good old Geoff Hickenlooper, his unfailingly loyal, now ex-editor at the *Partisan*—the man who had been quietly and covertly footing the bill for Jake's low-budget dip into the shallow end of Middle American politics.

He thought about texting Am, something subtle and appropriately morose like, "put out to pasture" or punny, as in "on the Sousage cutting room floor." Taking a deep pull on his Joe McCarthy Blacklist Lager, Jake chuckled darkly at this new digital medium for neediness. He had left his fair share of overlong, self-pitying, woe-is-me voicemail messages over the years, but here, here was a new method that had the power to keep anyone and everyone feeling sorry for you no matter how far away they were.

"Life on the campaign trail got you down?" Mad said, reaching out with a rag to wipe up the foamy head that had overtopped Jake's frosty mug and pooled on the counter, unbeknownst to him.

"You could say that," Jake said, grateful for the interruption. "I've just been stripped of my caucus credentials."

"Big hairy deal," Mad said. "Look at me. The only credential I got is brewmaster, and I'm totally making a difference."

"Uh-huh," Jake mumbled into his beer, "how's that?"

The barman tossed the towel over his broad shoulder. "Take your average Herefordian..."

"I'd rather not," Jake replied glumly.

"Guarantee you they spend ten times as many hours at the Wagon Wheel having their breakfast coffee klatch, eating their burger and fries and slaw here at lunch, or drinking their beer in the booth after supper than they do in the City Council chambers. If you give people a place to talk to one another, and compare notes…you know, like the British pub or the old New England Tavern…that's a recipe for revolution. If people stay home with their eyes glued to their screens they never know what their neighbor is thinking, or feeling, or whether the government they elected is working as shittily for their neighbor as it is for them."

"Hate to break it to you," Jake said, "but most people don't come to the bar to brush up on their civics. They come to play video poker, fling darts, flirt with someone else's spouse, shoot some stick, and leave stone cold drunk."

"Maybe," Mad said, stroking his beard, "if that's all the credit you give 'em. But if you ask 'em to use their brains or their hearts at the tavern, they're just as happy, if not happier, doing that than playin' poker and pukin' in the stalls. Example…last night I had a political group in here watching the debate in the back…sort of an after-hours thing, ya know. Guarantee you just about every other bar had the football game on, but we had you on the big-screen last night, Jake, and when you and Herb and Agropolis started holding the candidates' feet to the flame on the Silver Steer deal, this place went ape-shit…in a good way."

"Really?"

"Dude, people are so sick and tired of these Eddie Haskell types with the trophy wives and their perfect hair promising them things they know will never come to pass. You don't need a credential to throw a wrench in that fakery, man. You just need to bring people together and remind them what they're missing."

The bartender held up his index finger. "Another in case point…this fallen down old bar, right? So three months ago I'm up in 'Sconsin kinda at loose ends, and I read in *Ad Busters* that Milt Cloward is planning to move his campaign headquarters to some dot on the map called Hereford, Iowa. I Google the place and the eleventh or twelfth hit on the list is some old rambling tavern for sale for, like, twenty-five grand. I mean, the roof is leaking like a sieve, the cooler is busted, the felt on the pool table is in shreds. So I empty out my savings, buy the dump, and I'm thinking what in the hell have I done…I'm not an M.B.A. or a C.P.A…I'm just a certified idiot. Three months later, I've fixed every freakin' electrical short and water leak in this place by bartering with my customers. The thing is, I discovered the regulars wanted a nicer place to spend their time in just as badly as I wanted that for 'em, and they'd only been waiting for an invitation to roll up their sleeves and get to it…. They'd had the skills all along."

"Now look at this place," the burly brewer continued, gesturing toward the Wagon Wheel in all its Middle American grandeur. "Dude, this shit *is* the grassroots—way more than the council chambers, I'm tellin' you. These four walls belong to everyone who had a hand in makin' the rusty old Wheel roll again…not just the few dozen old ladies who read cat mysteries and check out cake pans from the library or the guy who visits the council chambers every week 'cause he wants to understand why he can't build an eight-foot fence so he never has to lay eyes on his neighbors. You don't have to drink to feel at home in the Wheel…you just have to think and commune. Once we grew that kind of spirit in here, the hard-core drunks moved on without anyone ever having to say boo."

Jake moved his brew in small concentric circles atop his beer mat. "You're a brewmaster…I'm a journalist, least I'm supposed to be. A journalist doesn't have any power to influence the process positively unless he has a mouthpiece, and an audience, any more than a bar does without a keg to tap. Basically, minus the press pass, I'm a barman without any beer to sling."

"'Cept you're forgetting the big picture, dude. And I'm not just sayin' this cause I'm from 'Sconsin, but it's all about the cheese, man…where it's at and how people get it. People don't read the newspaper because you wrote the article, or Amethyst Gilchrest or Herb Clarke or Loretta freakin' Draper. They read 'cause they want to feel a certain way—smarter, more involved, more civically engaged, you know, or whatever. Same with what I do. Every kid who's ever taken a sip of his dad's beer knows it tastes like warmed-over horse piss. Folks don't drink it for the taste, they drink it for the way it makes them feel…chatty, clever, carefree, what have you…it's whatever it is they'd be if they didn't feel so fenced in all the time, so stuck in their rut."

Mad paused to look intently at his down-in-the-mouth customer before he continued. "Number one rule of tendin' bar…. Everybody carries a secret around with 'em they're just about dyin' to tell. Could be a hidden talent, or dream they don't dare tell the missuses, or some career aspiration, or some deep dark confession. Long and short of it…people are usually much more, not less, than whatcha think."

"So what's your secret?" Jake asked.

Mad grinned "Don't have enough beer in me to spill it. Besides, I'm on duty. Bottom line, Jake my man, is who gives a rat's ass if you have a credential. You find out what people need, and want, and are inclined to appreciate, and you make *that thing* happen for 'em…then you're gold, man. You've gone and built yourself an audience that doesn't depend on the The Man or his media."

Jake grinned wryly, dropped a healthy tip on the counter, and stood to leave. "I've got a feeling I'm not going to get you to come over to my side on this one, Mad," Jake said, turning toward the door.

"Hey man, before you turn tail and slink outa here like a raccoon in the night, you should try my latest promotion… eight different autumnal brews, one named for each of the Republican candidates, including that quitter Brad Charger. Whenever a customer orders and empties a pint of one of these babies, his cup counts as one vote. By election night, if we even make it that far, the stacks of empties should call the winner way before Donna Sawyers and George Agropolis do."

"What do you mean 'if we even make it that far'? You expecting the Four Horsemen to swoop down riding fire-breathing steers?"

"Just sayin'," the barman added, "I got a feeling anything could happen in the last twenty days of this race…*anything*."

He winked. "So you gonna cast your vote in my little beer poll or not?"

Jake chuckled darkly. "You already have my vote in your hand. That's one for the road…and one for Mr. Blacklist himself, Joseph McCarthy."

The following morning, despite the unsolicited pep talk from Mad, Jake did not go to the Cal Coolidge for breakfast as he had the Tuesday before. What would he have to offer Kate Clarke? He could talk some smack, pretend as if he still had an insider's track. To fake it would be relatively easy. He was still on the e-mail list for all the campaign announcements and press releases. Still, it wouldn't feel right. There were some people you couldn't feel good bullshitting in life, and Katie Clarke was one of those.

Instead he sat on the floor of his room, Indian style, weighing his options. He could return to the Denver burbs, re-post his resumé online, and hold out for a nibble or a bona fide bite. He could go back home to Bradenton, camp out with his parents, and hope for something to fall in his lap in the Tampa area. Or he could pack it all up, apply for unemployment, and travel around the country until he had his head screwed on straight again. Things always seemed to make more sense when he had the pavement underneath his wheels and drive-by vistas to contemplate. Or he could continue to live with Amethyst and attempt to free-lance from Hereford. But who would hire him? Maybe some Internet outfit that would pay him a dime a word. Enough to buy some mac and cheese at the local Save-U-Mart, if he really hustled, but not enough to pay the rent. And that was the other thing…the miniscule per diem from Geoff Hickenlooper at the *Partisan*, and from which he had been paying Am for the dubious privilege of apartment-sharing with her, had been nixed as soon as the national Republican party had stripped him of his access.

At noon he took a walk down First Street, hoping some social contact, or at least the sight of other people leading normal lives, would do him some good. His habitual route took him past the offices of the *Hereford Gate*, and for a while he considered detouring, but the balm of routine had kept him from the abyss before, and hopefully it would save him again.

He lingered for a moment in front of the plate-glass façade of the *Hereford Gate*, admiring the latest of the school-spirit window paintings that had become a weekly fixture there. "Go, Fight, Win, Fightin' Plowmen!" the latest caption cheered, followed by a perfectly gratuitous number of exclamation marks. Beneath the big bubbly letters of the school cheer, some teenage Van Gogh in the Pep Club had brushed in the likeness of the Fightin' Plowman himself, a wild-eyed, grizzly old farmer wielding a wicked-looking plowshare. The dude in the cartoon looked a little like Herb Clarke, Jake thought, what with the same unruly mane of silver hair, aquiline nose, and hawk-like tufts of eyebrows above a coolly discerning pair of blue eyes. A sharp rap from the other side of the window startled Jake from his musings, and when he pressed his nose to the glass for a better view, he saw the newspaper editor inside, motioning him in.

The editor greeted him from behind a pile of spiral bound recipe books at the front desk, where the Hereford Ladies Club was selling their annual *Hungry Plowman* cookbook for $9.95. "Out for a noontime constitutional, are we?"

"Yeah," Jake replied, trying not to belie how desperate he felt. "Thought some fresh air would help the former celebrity clear his head."

"Slow news day?"

"You could say that," Jake said before the guilt overtook him and he decided to come straight out with. "Actually, it's a no-news day. Just got relieved of my badge. Looks like the first-in-the-nation vote will have to go on without me."

Across the counter Clarke waved Jake's news away. "Already knew," he said, "it's all over the news."

"What is?"

"I take it you haven't been anywhere near a newspaper or a computer this morning?"

Jake shook his head. "The wound is still too fresh."

The editor pushed several front pages across the desk at him. "Apparently the mics picked up the little conversation you and I had after the debate ended Saturday night." Jake frantically searched his memory banks. What exactly had he said?

"Remember you told me that the state Republican party had asked you to distance yourself from the Silver Steer? How you were worried that Sousage would retire you and the Steer. Well, the audio clip leaked, and the party has released a statement confirming that you have indeed been stripped of any and all privileges associated with the prize. They're citing a violation of the agreement you signed. But that editor of yours back home in Denver must really like you, because he stuck his neck out and dug up the original signed contest documents, and it's pretty clear to anyone and everyone who's read it that the Grand Old Party did a hatchet job on you." Clarke paused to catch his breath. "I suppose you haven't had your phone on this morning either?" Jake shook his head, still trying to comprehend what the crusty old newsman was trying to convey to him. "I would imagine your voicemail is completely full by now with national reporters seeking comment."

Jake stared at Clarke, unsure what to do next. "Go ahead," the editor directed, "switch that contraption of yours on…. I'll wait." Clarke watched intently as Jake powered up the smartphone. "How many messages, Jacob?"

"Twenty."

"Would you entertain a little advice form an old man?" Jake lowered his head in assent. "Take this seriously, Mr. Preston. Yes, you've lost your job, but for a shrewd man there's tremendous opportunity in a clean slate. If I were you I'd listen to every message, decide which half of the calls are most worth responding to, and reply to them quickly before the moment passes. The statement released by the Republican party announced that Sousage has submitted his resignation, which means he was fired. So you can bet that son of a gun is going to be out spinning his side of the story, if not spinning yours for you, too. You need to tell your side yourself, son, and you need to take advantage of every reasonable opportunity to tell it. Do you understand me?"

Jake said he did.

"Hop to it then. As Silent Cal Coolidge once said, 'Do the day's work. If it be to protect the rights of the weak, whoever objects, do it…. Don't hesitate to be… revolutionary.' Now, I don't want to see you moping by my office window anytime during the next twelve hours unless you're working the phones!" Clarke made a motion like he was shooing Jake out the front door. "And Mr. Preston," he said when Jake had reached the threshold, "after you've done all that, feel free to drop by and tell me the latest. I don't get out much, you know."

"Will do," Jake said, leaving the offices of the *Hereford Gate* in something of an electoral dither.

The old newspaperman had been right. Sousage was quoted in the afternoon papers as saying he was considering legal action against the party and would not comment further until he had decided on the appropriate course of action. His silence would buy Jake a little time and, following Clarke's advice, he resolved to take full advantage.

In less than six hours he had booked four solid interviews—one with the *Times*, one with the *Register*, one with the *Post*, and a TV appearance on a popular morning show called *The Scoop*. He was amazed at how quickly people had gotten back to him.

Just after dinner a text message lit up his phone while he was reading the day's papers and doing his best to chew on some undercooked pasta. It was Amethyst:

Times sending me home to interview u! WTF??!!

He smiled at the vintage Gilchrest text. As plugged in as Am was she would surely have the scoop by now. He had not talked to her at the debate after she had hitched a ride home with McGreedy. When Jake had gotten back late from the Chuck Sousage lambasting and rest of the post-debate fall-out, she had already been sound asleep. The next morning he had woken up late to a note on the kitchen table informing him that she'd been sent out to report on an immigration sting at a meat-packing plant across the Missouri River and would let him know when she would be returning

By now, the third week in October, darkness fell by seven o'clock, and after nearly a half dozen hours spent working the phones, Jake decided to reward himself with some pancakes. He could get a short stack at the Cal Coolidge for $1.99—less than he could buy a frozen meal for at the grocery store in town, the Save-U-Mart, or the Save-Yr-Appetite as Jake had begun to call it. Now, too, he had something other than woe and misery to report to Katie Clarke, when, inevitably, she asked him how his day covering the campaign trail had gone. Doubtless, she had already heard about the post-debate fracas, and this, too, would save him the awkward explanations that had caused him to stay away from the café the last couple of days.

A minute later he walked into the Cal Coolidge feeling a bit less like a mole and more like a man. "Look who's here," Kate said, walking toward him as the bells strapped to the door jingled festively, "America's favorite sacked journalist." The gray-haired man with his back to the door turned, and Jake saw that it was Herb Clarke, wearing a cloth napkin like a bib. "You make those calls?" he asked, gravy stuck comically to the corner of his mouth.

"Sure did, boss," Jake said, sitting down across from him. "Followed your advice exactly."

The editor hovered his knife and fork above his steak plate, looking up at Jake over the rims of his glasses. "I meant to tell you not to take any money for your appearances, at least not initially. The party will claim that you're using this whole controversy to build a golden parachute for yourself, and, if you've taken compensation for your interviews, people will start to believe them."

"'Fraid I couldn't even if I wanted to, Herb," Jake said, bemused by the fact that he'd inadvertently called the old curmudgeon by his first name. "When I signed the contest agreement I pledged I wouldn't use my Up Close access for financial gain."

"So you're still among the righteously poor," Clarke translated, flashing a hint of a grin Jake's direction.

"Still poor," Jake conceded, "but not poor enough to swear off the pancakes, at least not yet."

"Well, if this isn't a sight I thought I'd never see," Kate said when she came around to take Jake's order. "The town's too most infuriating journalists sitting down at the same table together." She smiled, tossing a wet rag over her shoulder. "I kind of like it."

"Me, I'd like some pancakes," Jake said, adding, "as fluffy as you can make 'em."

"Plate of fluff coming right up," she called out, heading back toward the kitchen.

"So how'd it go this afternoon?" Clarke asked through a mouthful of Grade A Iowa beef. "How many interviews did you agree to do?"

"Four," Jake said, "beginning tomorrow."

"And what are you going to say?"

"What do you suggest?"

Herb Clarke swallowed a particularly knotty chunk of sirloin. "Keep it positive. They might try to bait you into the equivalent of a he-said, she-said…don't do it. You don't have anything in writing from Sousage or Pitchford or Preebus, do you, in which they ask you to cease and desist?" Jake shook his head. "I didn't think so. They're all too cunning to put anything in print. At this point it's your word against theirs. Clearly the public will be inclined to believe you, as they should. You would have had nothing to gain by telling a fib to me when you clearly thought the microphones had been turned off. Still, you can't go impugning the party, and you shouldn't. They would tear you limb from limb."

"So keep it real, eh?"

Clarke looked puzzled. "If by that you mean be honest and be yourself, yes. I'd expect nothing less."

Jake looked closely at his dinnermate. "Why are you helping me with this?"

"I'm taking pity on you," Clarke said, chewing with the vigor of a man eating his last meal, "and don't mistake it for anything else. That and I know how the political machine works. In a state like this they're not malicious, at least not openly. You're not likely to find yourself at the bottom of a lake with concrete strapped to your shoes like you might in Chicago. But the bigwigs will set your career back a decade if you rile them up enough, and without remorse. Over the years they've tried to retire me plenty of times."

Jake raised an eyebrow at the editor's hinted-at war stories. "Yes sir, they have, but that's all water under the bridge by now, and you, Mr. Preston, are very much of the now. Suffice it to say, I have some experience in these matters, and if you can benefit from my experience, I'm happy to share it. Consider it my own unique form of hospitality to an out-of-town guest. Since I didn't put a fruit basket at your door when you moved to town, at least I can lay some advice at your feet."

"I appreciate it," Jake said.

"It's nothing really," the editor said sawing at his steak. "Nothing you wouldn't do for me, Katie, or anyone else, I'm sure, if the situation were reversed. Speaking of, here comes my number-one daughter with what looks to be a rather prodigious plate of pancakes."

Katie swatted her father playfully on the head. "You mean your only daughter."

"A mere technicality," the old man said, cracking a playful grin.

"Check this out," Katie said, handing Jake her phone, "there's already a Facebook fan page in your honor called '*Free Press*.' I take it 'Press' is your nickname?" She cleared her throat and began to read. "'Formed to call for the reinstatement and recre-dentialing of slandered small-market journalist Jacob 'Press' Preston, our goal is to raise public awareness of this politically motivated assassination attempt on one journalist's right to free speech. What can you do to *Free Press*? Call up his employer, the *Rocky Mountain Partisan*, and let them know you want him back on the job. Phone, e-mail, or tweet Iowa Republican party chair Matt Pitchford to make your feelings known about their breach of contract. But whatever you do, don't swallow your tongue. Speaking out, and speaking up, is the best way to *FREE PRESS*.'"

Kate looked at him curiously. "You've gone viral."

"Not the first time I've been compared to a highly infectious disease," Jake quipped.

"I could make a joke on that," Herb Clarke interjected. "But fatherly decency prevents me."

"Any interviews you're especially looking forward to?" Katie asked him.

"Bambi Bloomberg and Venus Jones on *The Scoop*."

"You mean you're going to sit down on the couch with those two gossips?" Herb Clarke asked disapprovingly.

"They're doing a special election broadcast from Des Moines this week, so I could hardly refuse."

"Any newspapers?"

"A few," Jake told the editor. "The *Times* is doing an piece. You two know Amethyst Gilchrest, right?"

"Tough as nails," Clarke said almost admiringly, "and a damn fine writer."

"And then there's one or two others. By the time I get to those, I imagine the TV folks will have done what TV folks always do…moved on to chase the next White Whale…and I'll be allowed to return to my life of not-so-genteel poverty."

"How long will your expense money hold out?"

"The expense money is no more, I'm afraid. But I have a few hundred dollars left in savings. Once that's used up, I'll have to find some other unsuspecting Midwestern town to terrorize."

Herb Clarke threw his napkin down on the table, his plate cleaned completely. "Take it one day at a time. Things may look very different by Friday."

"We can always feed you scraps from the kitchen," Katie joked. "Daddy and I used to take them home to our boar on the farm, didn't we Daddy? Now the bore is coming to us."

"Hey now," Jake said. "My self-esteem is fragile these days."

"Seriously, if the fussy owner of the café here will permit me," Katie said resting her hand gently atop her father's perpetually disheveled head of hair, "I think we can at least keep you in pancakes."

Jake looked forward to Amethyst's return with anticipation coupled with a quiet kind of dread.

When she opened the door to the apartment and found him standing in the kitchen she marched directly toward him, pushed him in the chest like a schoolyard bully, and shouted, "Press, you're in at least one newspaper in every grocery store from here to Sioux Falls, South Dakota!" She paused to gather herself. "I've got a handle on the basics of the story, but, quick, sit right down and tell me the juicy stuff."

"Off the record?"

"Sure, yeah, whatever…off the record. Now sock it to me, Sister."

Jake sat down at the couch with Amethyst eagerly on his heels, ever the newshound. "So Sousage told me after the cat…er…

the Silver Steer…got out of the bag in the first debate, to lay low, you know. Then Mr. Breakfast Patty calls me up the morning of the debate and tells me a spot has opened up for me on the Iowa Newspaper Association panel portion of the debate…"

"So now you have a spot on the big show…"

"Actually, I think Sousage basically created me a spot."

"Duh, do you think so?"

"And he wants me to put the Silver Steer to a quiet death."

"Euthanize the poor, dumb beast when it's barely begun to breathe life."

"Pretty much"

"And let me guess, you said, 'Sure, no problem, Chuckles.'"

"I didn't promise anything. Breakfast Patty pretty much talked right through me."

"I think I've got it from here," Am said. "I was, after all, at the debate. So Sousage probably tore you a new one afterwards, and word came down from on high…probably from Prince Reebus himself, that Mr. Politics Up Close was about to become Mr. Politics Out in the Cold…. What I haven't figured out yet is exactly how the story leaked."

"Someone must have turned in the audio clip to the network. I know it didn't make it into the regular broadcast, because I recorded the debate and watched it myself at three times," Jake confessed.

Am kicked off her flats and draped herself across the couch like a rag doll. "So are you going to give your one-and-only-roomie an exclusive?"

Jake shook his head. "No can do. I've got a TV show tomorrow, and I've already agreed to an interview with the *Register*. You can have me, you'll just have to share me," he replied, grinning.

"How about we do the interview right now. I promised my editor I'd have something to him by tomorrow's deadline." She held up her Diana Ross stop hand to quiet Jake's attempted protest. "I haven't gotten where I am now by being as chickenshit as you are, Jacob Preston. I promised the man a story; I give the man a story. Now come on. I helped you out when you rolled into town without a place to hang your hat."

"I didn't ask you for help."

"You did if extreme piteousness counts as asking. And it does in this girl's book."

"I'm exhausted, Am. It's been a long, long day."

"Yeah, you had it real rough, didn't you? You got to stay in the apartment all day being a celebrity for making a dumb-ass, bonehead media neophyte move, and I'm eating McDonald's out of a bag on my way to interview a roomful of Hispanic illegals who've been working for slave wages in a slaughterhouse for five years and are now on the brink of getting deported."

"Are you more sorry for them, or for you?"

Amethyst stared daggers at him. "I'm sorry for both of us, if you must know. So I certainly don't care to hear you bitch and moan."

"Alright," Jake said, withering under her onslaught, per usual. "I'll try the interview, but no promises."

"Oh, goodie," Amethyst exclaimed with mock-schoolgirl joy. "Let me get my notebook so I can record all of your fascinating thoughts, you media mogul, you." She pulled her little composition book out of her back pocket, as if she'd been expecting to score the interview all along. "Okay, let's start with the basics, shall we, hmmm? Favorite food?"

"Pancakes."

"See there, you're doing just fine, Press. Hold still and this won't hurt a bit."

"Name of prom date?"

"Seriously?

"Serious."

"Mandy Jorgensen?"

"Kiss or no kiss?"

"Peck on the check."

"Okay, so I'm writing, 'no sex on prom night.'"

"Favorite Presidents?"

"Harry Truman and Abraham Lincoln."

"Interesting," Am mused. "A Democrat and a Republican. Why those two?"

"Because they were both failures before they weren't failures."

"Ahh, I see," she said doing her best imitation of a German shrink but sounding more like Dr. Ruth. "A martyr complex mixed with an acute fear of failure."

"That's me."

"Okay, next question: party affiliation?

"Independent."

"C'mon, you cop-out," she said, tossing her notebook down on the couch. "Who got your vote in the Obama versus Romney grudge match?"

"Romney."

"And who did you vote for in Obama v. McCain."

"Obama."

Am threw up her hands. "Okay, so maybe you really are a mixed-up Independent." She paused to make a note. "Now that we've got the get-to-know-you formalities out of the way, tell me what you thought when Chuck Sousage, a.k.a. Mr. Breakfast Patty, told you to ceremonially slay the Silver Steer."

Jake opened his mouth to launch into the story, but as he did he felt the last ounce of energy leak out of him. "Amethyst," he said wearily. "I just can't do this. It's late, and I've got to leave at 6:00 AM tomorrow morning to go do *The Scoop* down in Des Moines, and I really, sincerely, don't want Tired Me saying a whole bunch of things he's bound to regret. Can you understand that?"

"No," she said flatly.

"I'm not saying I won't do the interview with you. It just feels weird right now. Like getting interviewed by one of your friends."

"So it's okay to sleep on the floor of my extra bedroom and drink beer with my friends, but when it's time to actually be a friend, you're on your way to doing an interview with *The Scoop*. Jake, if I don't get this story turned in tomorrow, I'm going to have some serious egg on my face back in Gotham."

"Just like if I didn't drive you to the debate the other night you wouldn't be able to file your story? That turned out not to be true. Or just like if I didn't go to the homecoming game with you, you'd have no one to sit with? I just can't do it, Am, not yet.

If you need to hate me for a couple days go ahead. Right now I need some serious shut-eye."

"I want my rent," Am said firmly.

"But it's not even the end of the month."

"We never agreed to waiting until the end of the month. C'mon, I want it. At this point you're a risk to run, and I'd be out 300 bucks if you up and leave like a raccoon in the night."

"You seriously think I'd stiff you for 300 bucks?"

"You don't have a job, do you, or any source of income?"

"Am," Jake replied, looking her directly in the eye. "I'd give up eating before I'd not make good on the rent, you know that."

"I'd like my rent, please," she said, holding out her hand.

"For real?"

"For real."

"Okay," Jake said finally, "let me walk down to the ATM and withdraw your ransom."

"If you're expecting me to say, 'Oh no, Jacob, I trust you. Don't go out of your way,' I'm not going to."

"I'm not expecting anything," he said, throwing on his coat. "Except a warm bed to sleep in. And even that hasn't always been made available to me, has it?"

He slammed the door behind him, feeling instantly better when the cold air hit his lungs. The apartment had seemed to shrink in the last few days, as if there weren't enough oxygen in it for both him and Amethyst.

On his way to the cash machine he replayed what had just happened, and each time he did it grew more and more ridiculous. What a willful person Amethyst Gilchrest was! Sure, he probably could have given her ten or fifteen more minutes of an interview, but she had bullied him into it in the first place.

As he walked down First Street he noticed a light on in the offices of the *Hereford Gate*. Was Katie in late, doing the books? Or was it Darlene, the receptionist upfront? But what would she be doing there at this late an hour? Jake crossed the street and tried the door, only to find it open.

"Hello?" he called out, poking his head in. "Anybody here?"

A familiar voice called back, "Nobody here but us chickens."

"Oh, it's you, Herb," Jake said, relieved, as the editor met him at the door. "Saw the light on and wondered if maybe the White House plumbers were rifling through your filing cabinets."

"That's a very neighborly gesture," Clarke said, clapping him on the back. "We may turn you into a honorary Herefordian yet." The editor paused to polish his glasses. "Out on another constitutional I see."

"This one's a bit more involuntary," Jake confessed.

"Fame will cause a man take a lot of walks…and so will failure. Lincoln was a walker, you know."

"But did he ever have to walk six blocks to the ATM at midnight to withdraw his rent money?… So what's with burning all this midnight oil, Mr. Editor?"

"Just got an email blast from the Santoro camp. They're calling another press conference for tomorrow. It's urgent, apparently."

"You know what it's about?"

"If I did, would I be here now? Still, I'd be willing to bet the farm it has something to do with the Silver Steer."

"Our next guest on *The Scoop* is an overnight political sensation. Well, not an overnight sensation exactly, more like a seven-day sensation?" quipped the show's hostess, Bambi Bloomberg, as Jake Preston looked on. "Do you like politics, Venus?" Bambi asked her co-host.

"About as much as I like gettin' poked by my gynecologist," Venus Jones replied to a roar of incredulous laughter from the studio audience. "Is that seven-day sensation anything like the seven-year itch?"

"Could be," replied Bambi. "Anyway, you saw him in the presidential debate a few nights ago, but what you may not know is that due to a microphone malfunction, Jake Preston is now in the middle of a political controversy so hot it has the presidential primary season and the G.O.P. bigwigs fully bothered."

"Jake this whole thing started when you won the Politics Up Close contest, as I'm sure many of our viewers know if they haven't been living in a nuclear fall-out shelter the past few weeks. It heated up when in an earlier debate you asked if the candidates might consider competing not just for votes, but for a trophy. And it got downright hot, as in a hot potato, a few nights ago when a mic overheard you saying that you were asked to take the fall by the state Republican party chair for the runaway popularity of your idea. Do I have the scoop straight?"

"Just about," Jake allowed, nervously crossing and uncrossing his legs.

"Why don't you tell our viewers why they shouldn't assume you're not just another crazy white dude sellin' some kind of self-promotional snake oil," Venus chimed in, irreverent as ever. "Why should they go for this Silver Steer thing?"

Jake felt the studio lights bearing down on him. "I'm not saying they should or they shouldn't. I mean, it's up to each of them to decide for themselves."

"Well, ain't that big of him," Venus said, widening her eyes and letting them rove her audience. "Ya'll hear that? White boy's not gonna tell you what *you* need to do with your votes."

Jake smiled weakly and tried again. "What I mean to say is, I was never advocating the Silver Steer…"

"Now hold on, boyfriend," Venus said. "Rewind your bad self and start at the beginning. What is the Silver Steer?"

"The Silver Steer is…well, it's a silver steer."

"Some crazy-ass statute, right?"

Jake nodded. "It was originally designed to be a trophy for the Interstate Rivalry football series between Iowa and Iowa State."

"Lemme hear you Hawkeyes in the room make some noise," Venus said cupping her hand to her ear. "Now how 'bout you Iowa State Cyclones raise some roof?"

Jake did his best to press on through the raucousness. "Anyway, it's about so big," he said, talking with his hands.

"Here we go," Bambi chimed in. "Our producers have just posted an image of it."

"That's it," Jake confirmed. "That's the Silver Steer."

"Is that what all the fuss is about," Venus said, putting her talk-to-the-hand hand up. "Shoot, I wouldn't play pinochle for that."

Another image flashed up on the screen—the image of an Academy Award. "Would you play for an Oscar, Venus?" Bambi asked her co-host.

"Damn straight. I'd do anything for that little naked man." She raised her eyebrows. "And I do mean anything,"

"That's sort of the idea," Jake said. "A lot of the trophies athletes and entertainers compete for must have seemed pretty silly at one time or another." He paused, searching for an example. "I mean, look at the Green Jacket that golfers compete for at the Masters."

"There you go gettin' all white man on us again," Venus said. "But I'm pickin' up what you're puttin' down."

"The whole idea probably wouldn't have gone anywhere if the candidates had just answered my question honestly in the first place," Jake pointed out. "But if you roll the clip, you'll see that half of the candidates ducked the question. They wouldn't or couldn't say what they would play for."

"And yet they are soooo competitive," Bambi interjected. "I know, I've covered Bill Clinton."

"Uhhh-huh," said Venus, shaking a her naughty finger at her co-host, "and I bet he covered you, too, eh Bambi?"

"My confusion was similar to Bambi's," Jake went on. "Until I realized that most of these folks are so focused on their presidential ambitions…. It's like the rest of us—the voters—become this weird kind of abstraction for them, you know? So they spend their life preparing to compete for the prize of the nation's highest office, but they couldn't imagine competing for a trophy. The whole thing sort of highlighted for me a hypocrisy."

"That's a pretty big word to throw around," Bambi said, turning serious.

"I know," Jake admitted. "Still, I think it's accurate. So that's sort of how the Silver Steer idea got started. Mike Santoro was for it from the beginning, and I have a feeling the whole thing would have been a dead issue had Milt Cloward, Renard Kane, Rochelle Boxman, Paul Paule, Rich Priestly, and the rest of them just answered the question straight-up."

Jake let his eyes wander out into the studio audience as he continued. "So the whole idea has taken on a life of its own. People seem to really embrace the idea of the folks who want the job of President not being above some good-natured competition for a real, tangible prize, just like folks do all the time at everything from bowling leagues to pie-eating contests."

"And this story really caught fire when the mic picked up comments you made to small-town newspaper editor Herb Clarke about being compelled by the state party to retract the whole idea and rescind your question. Can we roll that clip?"

For the first time since Saturday's debate Jake heard the replay of his supposedly off-mic conversation with Herb Clarke: *I think the state Republican party would like to put the Silver Steer out to pasture, and me along with it.*

"Jake, the next time you get unintentionally recorded, can you speak a little more clearly," Bambi kidded.

"Damn straight," Venus said. "It sounded like you had that mic shoved down your pants.'"

"What exactly did you mean that the Republican party would like to 'put you out to pasture?' Have there been threats made against you?"

"Of a sort," Jake replied cautiously.

"Can you tell us exactly what methods were used to hush you up?"

"I'd rather not point fingers," Jake said. "I'll let the party's actions speak for themselves. Clearly, if they revoked my press credentials and scrapped the contest, they felt threatened by the idea of the Silver Steer. I'd just like to keep things positive and celebrate the fact that people have gotten behind an idea that will make the race a lot more engaging, more exciting, and in a weird way, more humane."

"And what will become of you?"

"One thing I want your viewers to know is that the agreement I signed when I won the Politics Up Close contest stipulated that I could not in any way benefit financially from my status as a contest-winner, and I intend to honor that. So one thing I won't be doing is offering any candidate endorsements or doing commercials or anything of the sort."

"So you gonna lay around in your boxers dreaming of Milt Cloward," Venus needled.

"Maybe," Jake said, breaking into a grin for the first time in the interview he had laid awake the night before both anticipating and dreading. "Mostly, I want to follow the Silver Steer through to the end. Who knows where it's going to lead, but I think it has a lot of life in it."

"And as we come up on commercial break, is there anything else you'd like our loyal fans to know as the first-in-the-nation vote approaches?"

Jake felt the camera zoom in tight. "Just that there's a lot of room for our political process to be opened up, so that everyone—not just the political junkies and the wonks—find it compelling. There's more room for all of us—politicians, journalists, editors, constituents, volunteers—to express our true selves and not just follow the party line because things have always been a certain way and show no signs of changing. If we'll let it be, the Silver Steer can be a vehicle for our collective political desires for reform…how we'd prefer things. It can literally be whatever we the people want it to be. It's our prize…we determine what the candidates must do to earn it and our respect. That used to be the democratic ideal. Now politicians don't necessarily earn it as much as we hand it to them by default, because, hey, we had to vote for someone, right?"

"Uh-huh, pick your poison," Venus said, nodding sagely.

"Well," Bambi said, turning back to the camera, "there's some philosophical fodder for us. When we come back, we'll hear more from Jake Preston, and we'll spend some time with a surprise guest. So stick around."

"Are we off-mic now?" Jake playfully asked his hostesses.

"Yeah," replied Venus. "We're cool."

"Who's the special guest?"

"Wouldn't you like to know," Venus said. Her eyebrows danced.

"Alright," Jake conceded, "I'll roll with it."

"Okay, we're back in 10!" one of the show's crewmembers shouted from the other side of the set. "And 5, 4, 3,2,1."

"Welcome back to *The Scoop* everyone. Now before the commercial break we promised Jake Preston, upstart journalist, that we'd have a special guest for him. He tried to worm their identity out of us during break, but Venus and I don't give it away that easily, do we Venus?"

"We don't give it away unless they're payin', Bambi, and payin' good. You know what I'm sayin'?"

"So here we go. Special Guest, come on out and join us."

Jake watched with morbid interest as out of the wings strode Rochelle Boxman, wearing some stylishly chunky heels, a stars and bars knee-length skirt, and a navy blue blazer. The pint-sized dynamo reached up to give Bambi and Venus a warm hug and gave Jake a firm handshake before they all settled back into the soft seats.

"Whoooeee," Venus said, looking at Boxman. "Girlfriend, you just keeping gettin' prettier every time I see you. What are you, like 36 or something?"

"I'm 55, Venus," Boxman said, blinking into the studio lights.

"That's just sick," Venus said. "Before I put my make-up on, I look like I'm 97."

"The two of you know one another, right?" Bambi said, looking back and forth between her two guests awkwardly sharing the couch.

"Yes," Boxman weighed in, "we sure do, though I have to admit, not so long ago, I didn't know who Jake was. But now I feel like he's as familiar as an old friend. I really appreciate Mr. Preston for shaking up this race and giving an anti-establishment candidate like me a fighting chance."

"So you're down with the whole Silver Steer thing?" asked Venus.

"Absolutely," Boxman enthused. "I'm looking forward very much to competing for that handsome beefcake."

"You mean Jake or the steer," Venus quipped.

"They're both handsome, aren't they?" Boxman replied, appearing to blush. "But what I meant is that lovely piece of sirloin up on your screen."

"So what would you like the Silver Steer, and by extension the voters, to know about you? Look into the camera there, and tell us what would you tell the steer if you were sitting down to a steak dinner with him."

"I'd say, 'Mr. Steer, you and I share a common spirit. We're both proud, dignified, timeless beings who understand that reputation and history matter. We share a farm background, me a girl from a farm outside of Sioux Falls, South Dakota, you likewise born and reared in a barnyard. You and I know firsthand the nobility that exists in rural life, and we appreciate the salt of the earth people who run those farms in places like Minnesota, South Dakota, Nebraska, Kansas, and Iowa. As a young girl who learned to chore on her parents' farm, I took care of you and your brothers and sisters and you in turn took care of me and my family. That's what you and I understand that the Washington DC types will never understand. Their relationships are built on distrust, whereas on the farm where you and I first came to mutual respect, our knowledge of one another is built on reciprocal understanding, care, and concern, even when we had to load you up and take you to the slaughterhouse." Boxman turned back to her host, looking pleased with herself. "That's what I'd say to him, Bambi."

"How do you know it's a he, girl?" asked Venus.

"Because a steer is a bull who's been castrated," Boxman explained matter-of-factly, "so he's gotta be a guy...just a guy who's missing some of his...equipment."

Venus Jones looked surprised. "Daaaamn, girl, that's some kind of bummer for all them lady cows."

"Maybe so, Venus," said Boxman, "but, speaking from experience, it makes them a whole lot easier to handle."

"You talkin' men or castrated bulls?" quipped Venus, turning back to Jake. "I guess they're one and the same thing, am I right, Bambi?"

"And did I hear, Jacob, that you actually live in a town named after a breed of cattle?" Bambi asked.

"Hereford, Iowa. Yes, mam, guilty as charged."

"Who-wheee," Venus exclaimed again. "What is it with you Middle American white folk with your cowtown names and your castrated animals?"

"Well, Venus," Bambi said, taking the reigns again, "that's about all the time we have for today's *Scoop*. Special thanks to Jake Preston for coming to tell us more about the Silver Steer controversy. As always, props to Congresswoman Boxman for coming to the studio to share her thoughts on this perplexing race. We'll see you tomorrow, when we'll talk about what's hot, and what's not, in boots for the coming winter, and we'll check back on developments in the campaign. Until then, may all your bulls be easy to lead."

"And easy to ride," Venus added.

"Great show!" Boxman enthused, reaching over to shake Bambi's and Venus's hands once the producers had given the off-air signal. "I'm just about your biggest fan."

"Mike Santoro's on-air from his campaign headquarters in five," one of the production assistants shouted at Bambi. "We'll be going there live."

"Do you know what Santoro's press conference is about?" Bambi asked her guests.

"Not exactly," Jake conceded. "Though I can guess it has to do with the Silver Steer."

Boxman shook her head. "My people haven't had any contact with the Santoro campaign today."

"If you two could stand by while we switch over to the news-feed, that would be great," Bambi said. "I can use you as my expert panel." She stopped to point at several screens in front of them, all showing what looked to be a hayrack decorated with bales of hay, from which Santoro was beginning his press conference:

> Thank you. Thank you for that kind applause. I've called you all here today to report that the Silver Steer, which was last in my possession, has disappeared.

My campaign wishes to make it clear that we did not voluntary yield the steer nor consent to its removal, and are treating this as an act of theft. The steer vanished shortly after the last debate and we concluded it would be more prudent to wait a few days to see if the culprit came forward or if any of our leads proved credible. We are asking any and all concerned citizens with information about the Silver Steer to call our campaign offices or visit our campaign website. All serious tips will either be referred to law enforcement officials, or, where appropriate, followed up on by my campaign staff.

I know you're all wondering what effect, if any, this will have on the race. I have the same question. Days ago we convinced Milt Cloward to bring his campaign back down to earth and compete fair and square. Then, just as our prize bull won the battle for hearts and minds, it disappears and along with it a major focal point for the developing campaign.

Friends, I've never much believed in conspiracy theories. I believe Elvis is dead. I believe Neil Armstrong landed on the moon and that Neil Harvey Oswald was acting pretty much alone. But the timing of the Silver Steer's disappearance strikes even me as political cloak and dagger, and maybe even skullduggery. I leave it for you at home and you in media to guess whodunit. As for me, I have a couple of frontrunners among my suspects.

Let me close by saying this matter should be treated seriously, as seriously as any threatened disruption of the vote. And please, if you have any information regarding the whereabouts of the Silver Steer, do not hesitate to come forward and claim your reward. Thank you, and may God bless.

On screen Santoro shook hands with a sea of advisors and well-wishers queuing on either side of him, waved one last time to the crowd, and flashed a wan smile before clambering down from the hay bales and into a waiting SUV.

"Alright, Bambi," the producer butted in, "let's get some reactions from your guests in…five, four, three, two, one and go."

"You've just seen an extraordinary live press conference from the Santoro camp, and I'm so grateful that candidate Rochelle Boxman and journalist Jake Preston have agreed to stick around to help us digest this puzzling new development."

Boxman looked wide-eyed into the camera. "I think it's just awful. And the timing couldn't be worse, given the consensus we reached on the Silver Steer, or appeared to reach, at our last debate. Personally, I can't imagine who would do such a thing. I mean, on the one hand, we haven't known the Silver Steer very long, but it sort of feels like a celebrity kidnapping."

"What about you, Jake? This is sort of…well, it's sort of your baby."

Jake paused, searching for words to describe what he was feeling. "I'm a little bit shocked to tell you the truth. But then again I'm not surprised either."

Bambi's eyebrows knit together, signaling her intrigue. "What do you mean?"

"I mean, suddenly this…this trophy has gone from being a reject to becoming very, very valuable as a status symbol. At the debate Ms. Boxman and the other candidates basically agreed to compete for it. At that point it should probably have been in the possession of a third party rather than being carted around by Senator Santoro to be trotted out at each and every campaign fundraiser. Don't get me wrong, I think with every hand that rubs it, it gets luckier…more meaningful…"

"Like a djinni," Bambi chimed in.

"…so that by now it sort of belongs to all of us, which also means it sort of doesn't belong to any of us."

"Will the apparent theft change your campaign strategy going forward, Ms. Boxman?"

"Not at all, Bambi. We're still going to be driving that Boxman Express bus around the state, shaking hands, sharing coffees, eating donuts, and attending town hall meetings to witness for a better Midwest and a stronger America."

"Well there you have it," Bambi summarized. "Two takes on perhaps the oddest event yet in this already unorthodox campaign season. Stay with us here on *The Scoop* as we bring you ongoing coverage of 'The Stolen Steer.' Rochelle Boxman, Jake Preston, best of luck to both of you on the campaign trail."

Bambi Bloomberg smiled one last time for the camera, holding her pose perfectly until she received the signal they had gone to commercial. "Great stuff," she enthused, reaching out to shake their hands. "We couldn't have ordered up that Santoro drama if we'd tried…. The folks who say live television is dead haven't met the Silver Steer apparently."

From the wings Boxman's campaign manager walked briskly onto the set to offer his congratulations and to save his candidate from the overzealous interns attempting to liberate her from her wireless microphone. "Dick Folsome," he said, reaching out to pump Jake's hand. "You two looked great together up there." Folsome stopped, wheeling around to look at the various screens scattered around the studio. "That's a whole hell of a lot of eyeballs." He looked back down at Jake, still sitting in the overstuffed couch that had made *The Scoop* a household name. "Son, looks like you got some followers of your own down there." Folsome walked toward the bank of windows facing Grande Avenue below, and motioned Jake to follow. "Kind of a ragtag bunch, though."

Ringing the studio entrance below were a dozen folks who looked like they hadn't showered in a week. One, a big man wearing a Richard Nixon mask, held up a sign that read "*Free Press.*"

"Gotta admit, I don't get that one," Folsome mused, scratching his head.

"'Press' is short for Preston. It's my nickname," Jake explained.

"I see," the campaign manager said slowly. "And what exactly do they want to free you from, if ya don't mind my askin'?"

Jake looked at the amateurish illustration scrawled above the sign's angry red lettering. It showed a man crudely drawn to look like Jake, with a gag over his mouth.

"From the gag rule I'm under, apparently. You know they've rescinded the Politics Up Close contest, right, and along with it my campaign access?"

"Heard something about that," Folsome drawled, looking down at the crowd through the soundproof, double-paned glass. "Now that one I get." Smiling, he pointed in the direction of another bedraggled protester holding aloft a picture of an oversized bovine beneath which was scrawled: "RNC, *Steering Us in the Wrong Direction.*"

Folsome chuckled. "Welcome to the circus, son," he said, leaving Jake at the window to ponder who these people were, and why they had wasted some perfectly good poster board and Sharpies on him.

"Go down there and meet your public," Folsome called over his shoulder. "I keep tellin' Rochelle when she's feelin' low…. You get the people on your side and, man alive, anything is possible."

Jake nodded, thanked Bambi and Boxman one last time for being good sports, grabbed the only jacket he'd brought with him from Denver, and headed for the lobby, where a couple of burly guys—studio security, he gathered—stood waiting for him.

"Ms. Bloomberg asked us to escort you to your car," explained the shorter of the two men. Jake peered through the glass doors at the small crowd looking eagerly inside, apparently awaiting his exit. Under ordinary circumstances he would have fought the rock-star treatment tooth and nail, but today he could stand to be delivered safely and without incident to his trusty Accord. "Alright," he said to the rent-a-cops, "let's go."

The minute he saw Jake, the man who appeared to be the ringleader of the group—the tall guy wearing the Tricky Dick get-up—began chanting, "*Free Press, Free Press, Free Press*" as the guards shuffled Jake along. Two television cameras appeared on either side of him, the faceless men behind them hurling questions rapid-fire. *Are you surprised by the public show of support? What's your reaction to the news of the Silver Steer's disappearance?*

When Jake looked up he realized the tidal force of the crowd was pushing him inexorably in the direction of the ringleader. A minute later he was practically face to face with the masked man, who abruptly reached for him. And in the chaos Jake felt his clenched hand gently but firmly opened and a slip of paper tucked inside. He looked up again, wondering what gives, but the dude dressed as Nixon only took up the cheer again. *Free Press. Free Press. Free Press.*

Mercifully, the demonstrators did not pursue him into the parking lot, where, moments later, the security guys delivered him, with apologies for the chaos. "That's as packed as I've ever seen the plaza," the taller of the two said, glancing anxiously over his shoulder before turning back to Jake sitting safely behind the wheel of the Honda. "Anyways, safe travels and…hey, by the way, we're totally behind you on the Silver Steer."

"Thanks," Jake said. He saluted the boys in blue, turned the key in the ignition and breathed a sigh of relief as his experienced car sputtered to life.

Hereford at high noon reminded Jake of the old Westerns he had seen on television as a kid—townsfolk hurrying along on errands as if moved by some unspoken urgency, business-owners and bankers stepping outside their front doors for a breath of fresh air, blinking into the sun, and a few civic types—always women, it seemed—talking openly on the sidewalk in front of the concrete flower boxes full of impatiens that had thus far been dealt only the most glancing of blows from Jack Frost.

Today the Wild West vibe was heightened, as Jake rolled into town carrying what felt like a burning secret. Did any of the folks out buying milk and eggs and fertilizer and cigarettes realize that in less than twenty days they would be electing the man or woman likely to be the next leader of the free world? Could any of them possibly comprehend just how many schemes and strategies were being hatched by overpaid politicos and underpaid journalists in between the walls of the rambling downtown buildings that temporarily housed what the media called "the political class."

If anyone understood what was happening to their town, it was Kate and Herb Clarke, Jake concluded, easing his Accord into the open parking spot directly in front of the Cal Coolidge Café. Nibbling on the cheese plate that had been put out for his and Boxman's interview on *The Scoop* had only heightened his breakfast food craving.

"Imagine the new star of daytime television eating at our little restaurant," Kate teased as she watched him sit down heavily in the booth.

Jake smiled. This kind of abuse was exactly what he'd come for.

"So how'd I do on a scale of 1 to 10?"

"About a 6," Kate said, tapping the tip of her nose thoughtfully with her ink pen. "Maybe a 6.5"

Jake shook his head. "Why is everything is a 6 with you Midwesterners?"

"Because we're afraid of facing the mediocrity of a 5, and wary of the optimism of a 7…. Isn't it the same everywhere?"

"Thank goodness no," Jake said, grinning as he looked up from his menu. "So I maybe managed a 6.5, huh?"

"Maybe," she said.

"What did you think of Boxman?"

"A definite 7. With the whole Santoro thing playing out while she was sitting in one of those comfy chairs looking radiant, she came off as being above the fray."

"You think she has a chance?"

"*Anyone* has a chance," Kate said, pausing to consider. "Though you may be a bit of long-shot, especially after this." She snapped open a copy of the *Times* and spread it out on the table in front of him. "I draw your attention to the article, "Journalism's Boy-next-door…Almost."

Jake swallowed hard when he saw the byline, Amethyst Gilchrest. *She didn't,* Jake thought.

But she had.

> Journalism's Boy-next-door … Almost
> by Amethyst Gilchrest
>
> Jake Preston managed to make it to his high school prom in Bradenton, Florida, with Mandy Jorgensen, but he didn't kiss her.
>
> This fact may go further than any focus group or opinion poll in helping America understand what's going down in this wild and wooly caucus season in the Hawkeye State, where a silver statue of a cow has become the latest campaign hot button, and its poster

child, a previously unknown political journalist, has emerged as a real political player.

Meeting Jake Preston, as I did recently, one can't help but think of a Gen X version of the Jimmy Stewart character in *Mr. Smith Goes to Washington*. In his first-ever press conference in the unlikely farm town, Hereford, Iowa, that has become the region's new political ground zero, Preston, or "Press," as he's called, admitted to reporters that he didn't quite understand himself how these confounded caucuses worked. One day later, tasked by party officials with posing a substantive question to the contenders for the nation's highest office in their Sioux City debate, Preston looked flummoxed, before finally grasping at the straw of what was then a minor news item, a rejected football trophy nicknamed the Silver Steer. Somehow, some way, Preston emerged smelling like roses.

Maybe folks here identify with Jake Preston because he seems blinkered by the process itself, a victim of larger political forces he can't quite understand. Or maybe it's because we all secretly fantasize about being lifted from our unbearably mundane existences by some cosmic act of fate, and thrust into the prominence we secretly thought we deserved all along. It's powerful stuff, and dangerous.

As Jake Preston's accidental fame tour comes to a television set near you this week, you'll learn all sorts of endearing things about this peculiarly American character—how he can't quite decide between Truman and Lincoln as his most admired president, how his favorite food is an extra-tall order of flapjacks, how he hasn't yet found the woman of his dreams, and why he thinks the Silver Steer should matter to us all.

He's entitled to his fifteen minutes of course, and as political Pollyannas go, he's harmless enough. But should you decide to get on the *Free Press* Express, consider how often ignorance comes cloaked as innocence. Not so long ago veteran political reporters who paid their dues, played by the rules, and earned their promotions were understood as the gold standard. They could be counted on to get the complete story and to understand its complexities. The simple fact that they understood the blood sport they'd agreed to report didn't compromise them; it ennobled them.

As anyone who's fallen in love with a pipedream can attest, willful innocence is a dangerous thing, and heartbreak is its only likely outcome. Politics is now gladiatorial, and just as the Soviets once demonstrated to the world that the nail that sticks up must be hammered down, Midwesterners know that the inexperienced cowhand is certain to get himself trampled. And when, not if, he bites the dust, sentimentalists and cynics are more likely than ever to denounce the carnage they've witnessed as simple meanness, and to turn away, in many cases permanently, from the process.

Me, I'm sticking with the more experienced cowboys this campaign season, the ones who've long roped the steers, and rustled them through the gates. The ones who not only managed to take Mandy Jorgensen to the prom, but also, as they say out here on the range, danced with the one that brung them.

"She's an amazing writer," Kate offered, filling the silence as she waited pensively for Jake's reaction.

"I suppose so," Jake conceded, "if you like poison pens."

Katie sat down in the booth opposite him. "How do you feel?"

"Tired. Exposed…. And more than a little pissed off."

"The article may backfire on her. It comes off as a bit vindictive." Kate paused. "What did you do to that poor girl anyway?"

"Nothing," Jake replied wearily. "At least nothing that I know of."

"You didn't hide her favorite pair of Australian leather boots?"

"No,"

"Flatten her tires?"

"She doesn't have any wheels."

"Kick her dog?"

"It's currently kenneled in New York."

"Challenge her politics?"

"She's too jaded to have any."

"So what gives?"

"I'll let you know when I find out," Jake said, desperate to talk about anything other than Amethyst. "So what's new in town?"

"Well, we're low on Worchester sauce, Thousand Island, and Iceberg lettuce."

"Now there's a headline. What else?"

"My old political history professor at Central e-mailed me. Naturally, I was her favorite student." Katie smiled playfully. "We've traded a few emails every year since I graduated. This year she's extra enthused, now that our little Hereford has become the political capital of the prairie. Oh, and she asked if I knew Jake Preston."

"What'd you tell her?"

"I told her you get your campaign fuel at this very café…. She wants to meet you."

"Why?"

"Because you're becoming a celebrity, and because her expertise is in electoral history. This year she's seeing something play out she's never seen before… the kind of thing that'll make even an old scholar feel her oats, she claims…. And now there's the big mystery of the little steer gone missing to contend with."

Jake dug eagerly into the stack of hotcakes that Bev, house cook, kitchen mistress, and resident pie-baker, had brought over to him. "What do you make of The Case of the Purloined Steer?"

"I know one thing…Daddy will be overjoyed. He always says the best stories are the kind you couldn't make up in a million years, even if you tried."

"Like a mediocre small-market reporter no one had ever heard of a week ago spilling his guts before a national TV audience."

"On Bambi Bloomberg's couch, no less," Katie added, completing the thought.

Jake swabbed up the last of the maple syrup with what remained of his flapjacks. "Guess this cowboy better steel himself to go off and get trampled then," he said, cracking a rueful grin.

"What do you mean?"

"I mean," Jake said, grabbing up the *Times* and his windbreaker in one big scoop. "I'm about to go looking for the Black

Hat of this cowtown, Amethyst Gilchrest. But before I do, I should get your opinion on this little piece of evidence."

He fished around in his pocket for tip-money, retrieving a sweaty dollar bill and the crushed slip of white paper he had read, and re-read, dozens of times on the long drive back from Des Moines. "Some guy gave this to me…one of my supporters, I guess…"

"One of your supporters?"

"There were like a dozen of them, outside the TV studio, when I walked to my car."

Katie nodded toward the crumpled mess in Jake's hand. "Well go on, tell me what it says!"

He passed the crumpled note to Kate and listened as she read it back to him:

We know where the beef is. Meet us at the meatlocker
in Holstein at 10 PM sharp —WOPP

"Jake, Holstein is only forty-five minutes from here. And these people…this 'WOPP'…this organization…this whatever-it-is, know where the Silver Steer is!"

"Pardon me for asking the obvious, but what, pray tell, is a WOPP?"

"No clue," Katie confessed. She stared out the plate-glass window onto First Street. "I mean, technically a wop is an ethnic slur for Italians."

"And I'm guessing rural Iowa isn't known for its high concentration of Italian immigrants."

"You'd have to drive sixty miles from here to order a calzone." She put a freckled hand on her hip, deep in thought.

"This almost reads like a ransom note. I hate to say it, Press, but you should probably go to Holstein, at least if you want to call yourself a reporter. But you shouldn't go by yourself."

"Who am I supposed to take? You read the note. If what they want is to give me a scoop…. I can't exactly take Mort McGreedy."

"No, but you could take me," Kate Clarke said, throwing a wet rag over her shoulder rakishly.

"I don't know, Katie. This thing"—Jake waved the offending paper between them—"smacks of a hoax. I may not have been as long in the saddle as McGreedy, but every journalist is taught to check his facts before he gets himself, or anyone else, in over their heads. Sure, 'WOPP' might tip me off as to the where-abouts of the Steer, but they might also give me a fat lip and a one-way ticket back to Denver…in a body bag." Jake paused to consider. "Can I sleep on it?"

"You mean sleeping on it like how you've slept on my break-room couch and on the roof of my café?"

"Exactly," Jake grinned, taking her rag and cleaning the table himself. "You should count yourself lucky that I haven't slept on a bed of your best iceberg lettuce."

When Jake walked through the door of the apartment Amethyst Gilchrest didn't even bother looking up.

He walked up to the kitchen table and laid the rumpled *Times* broadsheet down in front of her. "Do you always write your articles before the subject consents to a full interview."

"Not usually," she admitted, continuing to read her news-paper in what struck Jake as a gesture of feigned indifference.

"But then again most of my sources aren't intransigent, sancti-monious pricks who begin an interview then whine about being too much of a wuss to finish it."

"Ouch," Jake said, sitting down beside her. "Did I deserve that?"

"Yes, you did," Amethyst retorted, really looking at him for the first time since he'd walked in. "When you actually learn something about journalism you'll learn that you either make reporters your friend, or you make them your enemy. Contrary to what you've been led to believe, you're not above the rules of your profession."

"Then I'd rather be your friend," he said. "The trouble is, I don't have any other friendships where it's the norm to trash one's pals in the pages of the nation's top newspaper."

"Then maybe you don't have very interesting friends."

"Look, Am, I know I haven't done anything to deserve all this…" he looked around the room as if the word for which he was searching was a housefly buzzing somewhere just beyond his reach, "…this attention. But I never really asked for it either."

"Which does not absolve you from having to deal with it."

"Let me also point out that I have no home, no job, and no money. It's not as if I'm making out a like a bandit."

"What you have," she said, "is fame, or infamy, and in this messed-up country that's worth more than all of the other things you mentioned combined." Amethyst's eyes flashed. "Let me ask *you* a question. Have you stopped to consider the irony that I've worked for almost eight years for the most respected newspaper in America, and no one really knows who I am. I can walk down the street to my local co-op in New York City in my yoga pants to buy some arugula without the slightest worry that anyone will recognize me. Then there's you. You sit on a couch with two women 'journalists' whose names sound more like porn stars than reporters…"

"Bambi and Venus?"

"Exactly. And all of a sudden your face is piped into the living rooms of sixty million viewers. Meanwhile, you're living in my apartment, eating my food, and using my minty fresh toothpaste. You've made it plenty easy to hate you."

Jake winced at the word *hate*, a word his mother had taught him never to use unless he meant it irrevocably. "You really mean that?"

"Yes," Am said flatly, returning to her newspaper.

Jake pushed away from the table. "I can't stay here then."

"Looks like it," Am said, unmoved.

"When do you want me out by?"

"You see!" she said, throwing down the paper. "That's why I hate you. I write an article that pretty much guts you like a carp. Then I tell you I hate you, and you stand up, sigh, and ask me when I want you to leave. Can't you handle even that decision without my input?"

"And by the way," she added, her anger rising to a boil, "a letter came for you today. Since when is it okay for a jobless squatter who's behind on his rent to have his mail sent to a place where he's not even on the lease. You know, you've got a lot of gall, Jake Preston." She threw the letter at him. "It's probably from one of your stupid admirers!"

Jake retreated to his room, holding the letter in hand, and sat down heavily on the air mattress that had been his home for over two weeks. He opened the letter to find a typewritten note:

We found the beef. Come and find us. We're on your
side, Press. —WOPP

That settled it; he was going. Jake threw the note into his duffel bag. He had de-camped this way more than a few times since graduating college—always in haste, usually after some dust-up he'd felt powerless to stop—a psycho landlord, a girlfriend who had decided to move on, a once-promising job come to an untimely end. He had the fifteen-minute pack down to a science.

Amethyst was still sitting at the kitchen table when he emerged, exactly fifteen minutes later, decidedly packed. "I'll be back in a couple of days to get the rest of my things," he said. "I'm sorry…I don't have anywhere else to put them."

"Where are you going?" she asked, unmoved as always.

"Out of town…on a story. I figured we could use a break from one another."

"And what if I find a new roommate while you're gone?"

"Like McGreedy," Jake said, unable to resist the parting shot. "Just take my stuff over and give it to Bev at the café. She'll put it behind the counter or something."

"Who's Bev?" Am asked flatly.

"The cook."

"Making friends in high places, aren't we?"

"Apparently I have a gift for that," Jake said, shutting the door quietly but firmly behind him.

Seven

"I haven't been on a real adventure in years," Katie Clarke said, happily riding shotgun beside him.

"I would have thought your dad would have dragged you along on all sorts of stories."

She laughed. "They don't call it a *local newspaper* for nothing."

"Did you travel much during college?"

"Not much," she replied, staring out the window. "A lot of my girlfriends did, though. I guess I never much saw the point. And besides, Daddy gave every extra penny he had to help me pay for school. He would have helped me study abroad, I suppose, if I'd asked, but I couldn't bear asking, not after seeing how hard he worked for what we have."

"So where have you been?"

"Let's see," she said, counting off the locales on her fingers, "Minnesota, the Wisconsin Dells, Galena, the Black Hills in South Dakota once. That's it, really."

"That leaves a lot of world left to see."

She looked out the window at the endlessly rolling fields of harvested corn. "Daddy was stationed overseas during the war, so I grew up hearing his mantra that all of the most beautiful things in the world could just as easily be found within five miles of home. In a lot of ways, he's right."

Jake tapped his palm on the steering wheel. "Maybe," he said, "and then again maybe not. What about the pyramids, or the Haggia Sophia, or the Sydney Operahouse? You can't see those things in Hereford or Goodacre."

"I always did want to see the pyramids," she said softly.

"I couldn't help but notice all the back issues of *National Geographic* in the breakroom of the café. I think I used the 2012 editions as a pillow, actually."

She looked at him as if he had just discovered her most shameful secret. "I only read them on breaks. *National Geographic* is my *US Weekly* and *People* rolled into one."

"Why not escape in real-life then?"

"Because," she said, her voice taking on some of the fierceness Jake had come to expect from her old man. "That's what we're told we're supposed to want…. Jacob, I used to volunteer at the Hereford Library, and one of my jobs was to sort through all the old magazines the patrons dropped off for donations."

"That explains your hoarding."

She nodded. "Most reporters assume the average person in a place like Hereford is basically a rube. *Boobus Americanus* I think H. L. Mencken called us once. But you'd be shocked at how many of our farmers read *U.S News and World Report* and *Time*. You'd be surprised to learn how many of our schoolteachers and widowers read *Smithsonian*. Look up the literacy rates sometime, and you'll find places like Iowa and Wisconsin at the top of the list and New York and California buried somewhere in the middle."

She paused, catching her breath. "In most of the glossies I sorted through, the number one thing being sold was the idea that there was a better life awaiting you somewhere else. It wasn't just the stories—Best Places to Live in America…10 Places You Should See Before You Die…Secrets of the World's Healthiest Places. It was the ads, too, all the cruises, and tours, and travel agents, and time-shares, and eco-adventures. As soon as people in places like Hereford retire and finally have a little mad money to spend, what do they do? They book a flight to one of those seemingly exotic places to do one of the apparently exotic things the ad men have been pushing them to do all along. Daddy always said it was as predictable as our young people leaving after college."

"And so you take pictures of the local wonders around you… like the Raccoon River…as a form of protest, is that it?"

"Ah, the mighty Raccoon," she said, and when Jake looked over he was relieved to see Katie Clarke wearing a rare smile. "Isn't that life, Jacob, and light…seeing the beauty in the people and things around you…not wasting your days quietly wishing you were elsewhere. My photos are a way of reminding people, including me, of the romance right under their nose."

"Is that part of why you stayed so close to home for school?"

"That and it was way cheaper, and"—she paused—"after losing mom I always sort of feared I'd lose Daddy if I went far away."

Jake lifted his palm momentarily from the steering wheel to check his speed…sixty-four miles per hour. Not quite ten over the limit and the road ahead straight as a string. "I'm really sorry, by the way," he said, "about what happened in the cemetery. I should have recognized what that ritual meant to you."

"I miss her…I miss her terribly…. But I'm lucky to have Daddy and I'm lucky to have the café."

"It can be kind of limiting, though, right?"

"Yes," she conceded, "but then again I'm not in debt. How many people my age could say that?"

"Not many."

"I make my own hours and manage things as I see fit."

"That you do," Jake acknowledged, thinking of the tight ship the newspaper editor's daughter ran.

"And most of all, I have a group of people that depend on me…that would miss me terribly if I were gone. Do you know what that feels like, Jake?"

"Not really," he said, considering. "Would my readers miss me if I moved on? I got axed a month ago, and beyond Geoff Hickenlooper, my saintly editor back in Golden, I don't think there's much of a Bring Jake Back movement afoot."

"And yet you've been here all of what…three weeks? And just like that you have a Facebook group and a dozen people holding pickets signs to come to your defense. Have you thought about how something like that could be possible?"

"Barely had time to," Jake confessed, taking note of the road sign telling him they were now within five miles of Holstein. "You're right about one thing…it's different out here."

"It's different because you matter here…because people want to know who and what you are. And that desire to know what you're all about has nothing to do with winning the Politics Up

Close contest. Every four years thousands of reporters descend on us, and you'd be surprised how many of them don't want to leave once caucus night is over."

Jake wasn't buying it, at least not completely. "Maybe, but for all the people who want to stay and become a Hawkeye, I'll bet there are at least as many who can't wait to get the hell back to New York or San Francisco or Los Angeles, where they can drink their skinny lattes and take their Shih-tzu for a walk in the doggie park…people like Amethyst Gilchrest."

In the seat next to him Katie Clarke wrinkled her nose. "She doesn't like Hereford?"

"I don't think she necessarily likes it anywhere. I'm not sure she knows where she wants to be."

"And you do?" asked Kate, looking at him intently.

Jake chuckled. "Maybe I'm more like Amethyst than I care to admit."

"Maybe," Kate said quietly. "You've been staying with her, haven't you?"

Jake nodded his head in quiet assent, taking care to keep his eyes on the road. "What gave me away?"

"I overheard her inviting you to sleep in her extra room that first night in the café. That was a pretty strong indicator, don't you think? And I couldn't help but notice that you walk into the café every morning smelling like her shampoo."

"Ah yes, the Mango Madness…"

"And you're almost always wearing one of her hairs on your sweater when you come in. She does have beautiful hair."

"She's a beautiful girl."

"Yes, she is," Kate agreed. "There aren't many like her in Hereford."

"I don't think there would be room enough for them," Jake said, holding his breath as he veered left to pass an endlessly long grain truck on the rapidly darkening two-lane highway. "Amethyst pretty much takes up all the air in the room."

"Do you like living with her?"

"Better to ask *did* I like living with her. She kicked me out this morning."

"Why?"

"Now that I'm officially unemployed, I'm not a good investment. That, and I think she really needs her space."

"Does she even need your money?"

"I think I'm mostly mad money to her…some extra cash for Wi-Fi or maybe a new pair of Jimmy Choos…. She's on a per diem most reporters would die for."

"Maybe you're someone for her to talk to."

Jake signaled to make a right turn onto Highway 59. "Well, here we are. Another town named after a breed of cattle. There's the meatlocker up ahead and there, if I'm not mistaken, is our contact."

Jake pulled to the curb, locked the doors, and rolled the window down as a small, shadowy figure under the streetlights moved toward them.

"Jake Preston?" a woman's voice asked, and a hand came through the driver's side window for Jake to shake. "Ripon," she said. She peered curiously into the car at Jake's companion. "Who's your copilot?"

Katie leaned over into the driver's seat to get a better look at the young woman in the baggy hoodie. "I'm Kate…. Jake's partner in crime."

Ripon nodded silently. "Park your car around back of the locker, and I'll let you in."

"How about you tell us what this is all about before we step into a darkened warehouse with you," Jake insisted.

Ripon laughed. "We'll talk more inside, but, in a nutshell, we asked you here to talk about the Silver Steer."

"What about it?"

"We have it," she said, motioning for them to follow.

Their host opened the door to a concrete-floored locker lit entirely by fluorescent lights.

"Welcome to Little Wisconsin."

All around them were stacked cardboard boxes labeled with more kinds of beef jerky than Jake had ever known existed—Beef Pepper, Teriyaki, and something disturbingly called Whole Muscle. He wondered what other mystery meats might be lurking in the walk-in freezers lining the walls. Between the smell of blood and the sight of coffin-like wood crates piled here and there, it felt like they had entered a morgue.

"Let me take your coats," Ripon offered.

"I'll keep mine, thanks," Kate said, shivering.

Jake hunched his shoulders against the deep freeze. He felt like he was on the sidelines for a December game at Lambeau Field.

"It's everything but the oompah band," Ripon replied after a long silence, running her hand through the head of dishwater blonde hair that had emerg.. ! from beneath the hoodie. "Nothing says 'Sconsin like cured meats, warm beer, and cold concrete floors. Anyways, the other WOPPs have gone home for the night…too ass-cold in here to overnight in the locker."

"WOPPs?" Jake asked.

"It's an acronym… Wisconsinites Opposed to Partisan Politics."

"So you're some sort of out-of-state political organization?" Katie ventured, connecting the dots.

"We're more of a movement than an organization."

"How many of there are you?" Jake asked.

"Between our members back home and on the ground here, we're in the thousands, easy."

"Members back home?"

"Yeah, the WOPP natives—WOPP-NATS we call 'em— make up more than half of our numbers. They're the ones who support our cause financially but haven't been able to commit to joining our ground forces here in Iowa. They're the ones keeping us fed and with a roof over our heads."

"Your cause," Jake prompted, "is what exactly? I mean, besides opposing partisan politics and loitering in shady meatlockers."

"Our name is probably more vague than our mission," Ripon conceded. "Our most immediate objective is to alter the outcome of the first-in-the-nation vote. Basically we're here to throw our weight behind the candidate the media and the party bosses have dismissed as 'unelectable' or 'underresourced' or both."

Ripon motioned for them to take a seat on what appeared to be several gift boxes of meats that had been stacked together to form a crude couch. "But you can't vote," Kate pointed out, wrapping herself tighter in her scarf.

"That's news to us." Ripon grinned.

"You can't if you're from Wisconsin…. You're not residents here."

"There's where you're wrong. Most of us have been here at least sixty days, others nearly six months. The legal codes made our cross-border voting bloc almost too easy to bring to fruition. If you move to this state, even without a job, you can get a license after thirty days. Once you have license, it's child's play to register to vote. And that's in a regular election. The Caucuses are even easier. The election officials are so freakin' terrified of being charged with voter discrimination or intimidation, they don't even ask for a photo ID."

"What do you use as an address?"

"Oh, we've got addresses galore," she laughed, as if addresses were the easiest thing to come by in the world. "All the State requires is something official with your address on it…like a utility bill. Do you know how many out-of-state property owners there are in this state…a hell of a lot, I can tell you, because our head honcho asked me to look up the numbers. Just counting the Iowa land owned by our more liberal supporters in Milwaukee and Chicago we easily have a few thousand addresses where we can legitimately receive mail. Actually, we're a bit of a hot commodity among all our absentee owner friends. While they're busy making the big bucks in Madison and Milwaukee we're keeping an eye on their acreages, raking the leaves and cutting the grass, giving the place that 'lived in look,' and all while advancing the political causes they share but lack the time to enact. It's what the politicos call a 'win-win situation.'"

"Who organized this…this thing?" Jake asked, letting his eyes roam around the deserted warehouse.

"You mean The Big Cheese?" Ripon said, grinning. "If I spilled the beans on that it'd give you the impression that we have a leader. Up until now we've prided ourselves in being a mostly leaderless organization…though that could change soon." Ripon paused, eyeing them intently. "Listen, I'd love to show you both something before we go." She motioned them inside the cooler. "You first, Jacob."

"No thanks," he said, stepping back from the threshold. "I've watched too many Scooby Doo episodes to be the first to walk into an ice chest in a room full of meat cleavers. You first, Ripon."

"Dude, I'm such a big Scooby fan," she enthused, leading the way. "Just be sure to close the door behind you. The Cheesehead who owns this place is a real Scrooge where electrical bills are concerned."

She swung the door open wide to reveal the Silver Steer, looking as chaste and cold as an ice statue in Menomonee.

"WOPP nicked it," Kate muttered under her breath.

"Damn straight we did," Ripon admitted. "Santoro's so proud of the thing he's been carting it around to every town-hall meeting and meet-and-greet his ego could overschedule. You put a politician in a crowded room with a hundred hands to squeeze and suddenly nobody's watching the cash cow. One of our bolder members swiped it for us."

"And what's why I'm here, isn't it?" Jake said, thinking aloud. "I'm the one most closely identified with our Ice Cow here."

"Better not let him hear you say that," Ripon joked, admiring the statue. "Now what do you say we find somewhere a little warmer to carve up this Kielbasa?"

They followed Ripon's car down a series of winding gravel roads that ran north and east along a river too miniscule and muddy to merit any signage. Autumn leaves swirled in Jake's field of vision, crowding and crazing the scant illumination offered by his low-beams.

As they turned their eighth mile on the odometer, their host's beat-up pickup truck rolled to a stop in front of a large, four-square farmhouse with an enormous red dairy barn. When Jake and Kate opened the doors to the Accord, a chorus of barking dogs announced their arrival.

"Farm mutts mostly," Ripon explained sheepishly. "But they make for good watchdogs. C'mon in the barn and get yourselves warmed up."

She opened the door to a rush of warm air produced by two stoves whose chimneys ran up and out of the old hayloft. Several dozen mostly 20-somethings milled around the stoves in various states of amusement. Some read paperback books positioned atop quilts in their laps. A few others played a spirited game of ping-pong on a makeshift table made out of a couple of sawhorses and a sheet of plywood. A couple of young woman appeared to be busily knitting.

When Jake walked into the room everyone in the barn began to clap. He raised an embarrassed hand, his face reddening not just from the blast of oven-like air coming from the corn stove, but at the undeserved adulation itself. *Free Press,* a bearded, college-aged kid in a knit cap said, nodding at Jake as if to say *right on, man.*

Ripon picked up the thread. "About thirty of us bunk out here, a dozen or so bed down in the farmhouse, and another handful stay at the locker in town when the temperature allows. This particular cell…" She paused to slap herself on the forehead. "I'm supposed to quit calling them that… . The Big Cheese claims the word *cell* makes us sound more like an Al Qaeda group in Yemen than a group of progressive-minded Independents from the Frozen North. Holstein is one of a dozen statewide 'headquarters' for us, including one very close to you."

"Why Holstein?"

"Because we're from the Dairy State and Holsteins are the world's largest breed of dairy cattle. It's both an homage to our roots, and a statement about the breadth of what we believe our reach may be."

"And because it shares a name with a town in Wisconsin, right?" Kate ventured. "I had a college friend from Holstein, Wisconsin."

"New Holstein," Ripon corrected her. "But close enough. Anyway, if we stay out here in the Commons you're likely to get mobbed by WOPPs. Let's step into an office, shall we?"

Acknowledging a few good-natured exhortations of "give 'em hell, Rip" with a friendly wave, their host led them into a converted dairy stable. Sheathing had been screwed to the beams to make four walls, while a space heater kept the barnyard cubicle toasty. There, a familiar-looking young woman with short-cropped dark hair sat waiting for them under a bare bulb strung from the ceiling.

"Jake, Kate…meet Loretta Draper. She's one of our founding members."

Jake squinted into the bright light at the young woman who stood to greet them. "You were at the Wagon Wheel the other night. Amethyst's friend, right…the one who writes for the *Daily Beast*?"

"The *Weekly Badger*," Loretta corrected him, extending her hand in greeting. "And, yeah, who doesn't know Amethyst Gilchrest? Throw a gorgeous girl like that in the middle of a small town chock full of male reporters and men-farmers, and she tends to stand out. I like her…she's got guts, not to mention good taste in shoes. Who wouldn't have at least a little bit of a crush on her?"

Jake let the provocative question hang in the air, unanswered. "So what's a national political reporter doing in a barn in the middle of nowhere?"

"I could ask you the same thing."

"You could, but then again I'm not a national reporter, at least not technically." Jake replied, pausing to consider just exactly what he was, or had become, in the last few weeks. "I didn't even know the *Weekly Badger* existed."

"I've never heard of it either," Kate echoed. Behind her, raucous cheers arose from the threshing room floor…. probably a decisive point played in the passionate game of ping-pong in progress beyond the door.

Loretta's eyes flashed. "That's because *The Badger* is a chimera…. It doesn't really exist…. Well, more accurately, it exists on my laptop, on the Internet, and in my imagination. These days that trinity is good enough to make it real."

Her eyes stayed locked on Jake's. "I introduce myself as Loretta Draper from the *Weekly Badger*, a little newspaper in a town in northern Wisconsin you've never heard of…. And hocus-pocus, alacadabra, and shazam, that's what I am. Add in a set of business cards ordered online, and you're new identity is pretty much solidified. It won't get me into the national debates, mind you, or into the big-media-only press conferences, but everything else is mostly a confidence game."

"Amazing," Katie said quietly. "I wonder what Daddy would make of this brave new world of pseudo journalism."

"Oh, it's far from pseudo journalism," Draper replied defensively. "It's the real thing. I've been pissed off enough to write every day about this stolen presidential primary—the one that Milt Cloward is destined to win whether we like it or not. Even the homegrown evangelicals who used to control the caucus winners in this state on the Republican side of the ticket have lost their pull to the Super PACs and big-time donors on the Coasts."

Loretta Draper shifted her gaze from Jake to Kate as she continued. "A journalist is as a journalist does, right? If journalism is sitting on your butt parroting official press releases for fear of your media conglomerate bosses firing your ass, then you're right…I'm no journalist. If it's having your eyeballs bought by some soulless newspaper chain while your head and heart are someplace else, then I'm also not a journalist. But if a journalist writes her own conscience, and makes her own independent judgments after really listening to people without censoring them, I'd argue I'm more of a journalist than anybody covering this race."

"So why do you need me then?" Jake asked.

Ripon joined the conversation. "We need you in a thousand ways, actually. But most urgently we need you to announce to the rest of the world that WOPP's sleeper cells…" Ripon paused to check herself, "…I mean its *local chapters*…have woken up to become a serious electoral player. And what we intend to give you in return, Jake, is a shot at what may be the biggest scoop of this entire election season."

"And what about the Silver Steer?"

"Here's the deal," Ripon said, breaking it down for him. "After successfully breaking our story in a national newspaper, we allow you and you alone to return our little stolen trophy here to the cold fish at the Republican party."

"And what if they refuse to play?"

"They won't," she said flatly. "At this point the Steer is the only thing standing between them and a disappointingly low turn-out on election night, and the inevitable downgrading of the caucuses from first-in-the-nation to, like, fifth-in-the-nation. Besides, each of the candidates has pledged on national television that they'll compete for the trophy. If the beef's not there, it's another promise broken to the voters, who, believe me, are in no mood to be have the cheese moved on them again.

They've experienced enough bait and switch from politicians to last them a lifetime."

"What are you going to do when public opinion turns against you?" Katie asked. "A lot of our voters are going to be angry when they learn their election is being influenced by out-of-staters."

"And yet we *are* Iowans," Ripon countered, "at least as far as the state election commission is concerned. We're here, and we're not going anywhere until our voice is heard. No one bats an eyelash when anonymous, out-of-state, monied interests play kingmaker by snatching up all the ads and airtime, basically buying the election well before caucus night. Compared to those jerks, we WOPPers are saints; we're exercising a legitimate, Constitutionally-protected, on-the-ground influence. Everything we've done…everything we're doing…is completely legal…. That much we're confident of."

Ripon let a small silence sink in before she continued. "Jake, we don't want to give you a hard sell. WOPP thinks you're a breath of fresh air in this race…a kindred, soul, a brother in progressive Populism." She rose from the bale of hay she'd been sitting on. "Give our proposition some serious thought. We've got a few second-runners-up in the chute if you need or want to refuse….journalists with a large enough platform to let the rest of the country know about WOPP…. So no worries either way, okay."

"Like who?"

"Like Mort McGreedy," Loretta Draper volunteered, "and other, equally talented prospects."

"Look, it's getting late," Ripon said, shooting her colleague a look that said *I'll take it from here, sister.* "And I'm willing to bet you two have pretty much ODed on politics today. It's totally okay if you need to hit the road, but our foot soldiers would be stoked if you'd take few minutes to dig our new favorite pastime."

"What's that?" Jake asked.

"Cow-chip toss," Ripon enthused, heading back toward the threshing floor. "It's way cooler than bags, and Greener, too."

"Can I ask you a question before we fling the chips?" Kate asked. "When you introduced yourself to us you said your name was Ripon.... And your name," she said, turning to the tenacious one-woman show that was the *Weekly Badger*, "is Loretta... Loretta Draper. So am I crazy to think you're all named after a town in Wisconsin?"

Ripon grinned crazily. "Put Katie here in the Showcase Showdown. She cracked our little code."

"How do you know so much about 'Sconsin," Draper asked, her eyes belying her bemusement. "You an honorary member of the Cheesehead mafia or something?"

"Practically," Kate chuckled. "Remember, I got my B.A. at Central Iowa, where there are almost as many Minnesotans and Wisconsiners as Iowans. Add to that a major in political science with a concentration in political geography, and, yeah, I can tell you that Loretta and Draper are two sister cities heading east on Highway 70 near Bruce, and Tony, Ingram, Glen Flora, and Kennah."

"Sounds like the names of a fraternity-sorority mixer," Jake joked.

"I must say," Katie said, picking up a choice cow chip from the pile and hefting it for size, "I feel sorry for Kronenwetter and Fond du Lac.

Eight

"I need your help, McGreedy."

Jake Preston sat opposite the outsized legend in an especially dingy corner of the Wagon Wheel. It was a few minutes before midnight—late enough that the Cloward campaign staffers had already been in for their hard liquor and the thirty- and forty-something political correspondents had consumed their pitchers of cheep swill and staggered home to their apartments with an economical buzz.

On the way back from Holstein, Katie Clarke had made it known she was against Jake's going to McGreedy, and the unquestionable clout his national newspaper offered, with the WOPP scoop. "My dad will give you a byline, I'm sure of it," she'd said on the long drive back to Hereford.

But for all the attention Herb Clarke had stirred up, the newswires would be reluctant, Jake knew, to pick up an admittedly fanciful story from such a small fish.

He had, he'd figured, two possible lifelines: Amethyst Gilchrest or Mort McGreedy. It was like choosing between arsenic and strychnine.

He'd chosen strychnine. Hence the Jameson's he had just purchased for McGreedy. Hence the pitch he was about to make to the most celebrated, most loathed, political journalist of his generation.

"What could I possibly offer journalism's Wonder Boy?" McGreedy asked, tongue firmly in cheek.

"I'd like to let you in on what I guarantee is the biggest, strangest scoop of this, and maybe any other, primary season."

McGreedy's caterpillar eyebrows lifted. "Bigger than the Silver Steer?"

"Not bigger necessarily," Jake cautioned, "but stranger."

"And tell me again why you want to share this bit of newsworthy deliciousness with a rival scribbler?"

"I don't consider you a rival," Jake replied. It was true; he didn't put himself in McGreedy's company…not even close.

"Then what do you consider me?"

The word *mentor* jumped into Jake's tired mind, but he stopped short of saying it. Mort McGreedy was many things, but he was nobody's mentor. Nor was he anybody's fool.

"I consider you a professional," Jake said finally.

"A professional!" Mort McGreedy practically spit up his whiskey. "I don't know whether I should be honored or offended."

"You've got something very few of the rest of us have…a reputation."

McGreedy snorted. "There's no arguing that." He took a drink. "So this story is so big, so huge, that you need Mort McGreedy's name on it to make it legit. Is that it?" The big man leaned in. "Do tell…what is it?"

"Are you willing to cowrite the story with me…share the byline? I've made promises directly to the source that I intend to keep."

"Come on, Preston, I'm an old man and it's getting late. You either pitch fast or you hustle up to the bar and make Mad pour me another Jameson's to augment my patience."

"What if I told you there's something happening on the ground, here in Iowa, that has the potential to alter the outcome of the presidential race?"

"I'd be interested," McGreedy said, finishing off his first whiskey while motioning Mad behind the bar for another.

"And what if I told you there were clandestine organizations…movements actually."

"I'd be doubly interested…. Are we talking terrorists or anarchists or fellatists?"

"None of the above," Jake said. "Qualified voters."

McGreedy's eyebrows knit in confusion. "How could qualified voters throw an election when they're already in the polling data?"

"What if they weren't from the state in which they were voting? And what if no one knew they existed yet."

"Sleeper cells?"

"Exactly," Jake said.

"What are you two, cheap-ass Woodward and Bernsteins whispering about?" Mad interrupted, ferrying McGreedy's whiskey to the table along with a half-pint of something that looked like beer.

"More like Abbot and Costello," McGreedy deadpanned.

"A Jameson's for the legend and a complimentary sample of my Dolphus Heinrich Stout for the legend-in-the-making. Tell me what you think of my latest flavor, Press."

Jake held the beer up to the light and smiled. "How'd you squeeze ol' rotund Dolph in there?"

"A lot of elbow grease and a helluva lot of hops and WD-40," the barman fired back. "I figured a hefty politician carrying some serious academic clout needed a stout seasonal brew. What do you suppose Ol' Dolphus weighs…two and a quarter?"

"Hey now," McGreedy grumbled, patting his own sizable gut. "Watch the weight discrimination. Used to be men of size were considered men of stature. Ask Howard Taft."

"Bad analogy," Jake quipped. "You can't have your president stuck in the bathtub when the red phone is ringing. Look at Obama. You could fit two of him in the tub."

"Taft would have eaten him for breakfast," shot back McGreedy.

Mad grinned, enjoying the good-natured back and forth. "So what're you two muckrakers over here whispering about? It's okay…you can tell your barman or your priest anything."

"Jake here has a powerful secret," McGreedy said, impishly cocking an eyebrow, "that he regrets he cannot share with me until I make him a star."

"Good for Jake," Mad said, reaching over the table to pick up McGreedy's first empty. "A man's gotta keep something to himself in this world. Once the last little bit of mystery has leaked outa his life, he's pretty much done for. "

"I'm telling you this one is big," Jake avowed, knocking on wood—in this case, the bar's wood wainscoting—to avoid tempting fate. "Have I lost my mind, or did someone on the other side of that wall just knock back?"

"Must be the raccoons," joked the barman. "At least they've got the good sense to wear masks when they're on about their secrets."

McGreedy waved his big bear paw good-naturedly at the barman. "If I'm gonna get the skinny on the skinny reporter's skinny story, you're gonna have to make like a tree. Ol' McGreedy needs to see whether Preston's lead has any meat on its bones."

"So…" McGreedy continued once the tender was safely out of earshot, "where…and how many?"

"All over the state, a thousand….maybe more…easily enough to swing an election that usually comes down to a few percentage points."

"What do they call themselves?"

"WOPP," Jake told McGreedy, almost embarrassed to utter the word in public. "Wisconsinites Opposed to Partisan Politics. They're radical cheesehead Progressives and Independents."

McGreedy's open palm slapped the table. "You're shitting me."

"I promise you I'm not."

"And there are what… a thousand of them you say?"

"Maybe more."

"How in the hell did you, of all people, land the mother-of-all-scoops?"

"Apparently, they've adopted me as an emblem of their cause. They invited me to their headquarters."

McGreedy snorted derisively. "What cause? Abject stupidity?"

"More like audacity," Jake said firmly.

"That I'll grant you," McGreedy conceded. "So when can we go meet these nut jobs?"

"Been there done that. Just got back a couple of hours ago. I've got everything we need right here." Jake withdrew a manila folder from his lap and set it on the table. "Their mission statement, quotes, the whole works. The article will practically write itself."

McGreedy put his elbows on the table. "You 100% sure about this, Preston? Good…because Amethyst Gilchrest just walked in the door and she's headed our way. And I'm a way better liar when I'm compelled to fabricate a story to protect the almighty scoop."

"We were just revealing secrets," McGreedy continued, as Am walked up to their table. She was wearing an Iowa Hawkeye jersey, sweats, and thigh-high suede boots—a cross between her comfy clothes and her going-out-to-get-take-out wardrobe.

"Were you now? I've got to say you're the last two people I'd thought I'd find on a cozy little date at the Wheel tonight. Tell me, who asked whom out?"

"Preston here propositioned me." McGreedy cracked a wizened grin.

"Tell me, Jacob, when did this crush begin?"

"When I fell in love with his first column," Jake told her, deciding it was easier to play along.

"An intergenerational relationship between two total smart asses…well ain't that something," Amethyst said, stepping back from the table to take it all in.

"What're you doing here, Gilchrest?" McGreedy asked.

"Ever had their breaded cheeseballs? Let me tell you, sex is nothing by comparison."

"Not much I guy can say to that," McGreedy retorted.

"No there isn't.... Anyway, I should let you two divas back to your date while I satisfy my late-night munchies. Watch out, Jake," she said turning toward her former roommate, "he might take advantage of you."

And with that Amethyst Gilchrest turned on her heels, dragged her boots across the Wagon Wheel's brazenly red carpet, and, tucking her take-out order of deep-fried balls under her arm, let the door swing shut behind her without so much as a goodnight wave.

McGreedy watched her go. "Nice ass."

"More like a smart ass."

"You lived with her for, what, couple weeks, right? What's she like?"

"Am?"

"No, Tinkerbelle. Who else would I be talking about?"

"She's okay."

"Is she?" McGreedy pressed.

"I mean, she can be infuriating, but she's smart as a whip. And pretty much always on fire."

"Wear you out, huh?"

"Sometimes...okay, maybe most of the time."

McGreedy leaned in. "You sleep with her?"

Jake grimaced. "No."

"Missed opportunity, Bub."

"Did you?" Jake asked.

"That's a negative," McGreedy said, drawing circles on the table with the sweat from the bottom of his whiskey on the rocks. "But I did regale her into the wee hours with tales of horror and woe from the White House press corps."

"You mean that night after the homecoming game, right? I'd assumed..."

McGreedy shook his head. "I may be a professional, as you call it, but I'm not a cheater."

"But you divorced your wife last year…"

"More accurately, she divorced me. In any case, excellent background research," the oversized scribbler conceded, raising his glass to Jake in a mock-toast.

"So technically you're free to pursue Amethyst."

"Technically, yes I am, and—technically—so are you."

They stared at each other.

"Would you?" McGreedy repeated.

"I don't think so," Jake told him. "Though I have to admit there's something about her I find intoxicating and maddening all at once."

"Me too," agreed McGreedy. "Some people call it love."

"And some people call it torment."

"Don't be so hard on her," McGreedy advised, leaning back in the booth again. "A girl like Amethyst Gilchrest is a creature of ambition. She wanted to work at the *Times* since she was at Vassar, and she plotted a path to get what she wanted. I was exactly the same way at her age."

"Maybe I'm just not as much of a tactician as the two of you," Jake concluded, nursing his Dolphus Heinrich Presidential Stout.

"If that's so, how did you engineer our little meeting tonight," asked McGreedy. "Ambition is an easy target, Press, because the people who don't have it, or never had it, or have given up on ever having it, resent it when they find it in others. To hear most people tell it, you'd think their most ambitious friends are also their wickedest. But the same folks that live their life by some kind of messed-up Tao of Mediocrity make a point of tuning in the Barack Obamas, the Oprah Winfreys, and the Hillary Clintons of the world every single day—the most goddamned ambitious people you would ever want to meet. So yeah, Amethyst may be ambitious, but that doesn't make her wicked."

"I never said it did."

"No, but you implied it," countered McGreedy. "And speaking of ambition, what say we return to your hot little proposition." The big man toyed idly with the beer mat in front of him. "Listen, if this turns out to be a hoax, and I put my name to it, I'm as good as early retired." His face broke into a broad grin. "But hell, I'm probably a year away from retirement anyway…. Alright then, Press, let's you and me get down to business."

"Is it just me, or is there a very large, pancake-loving squirrel living on the second floor of this café?" Katie Clarke wondered aloud to Bev, her short-order cook. She sat down next to Jake in the booth, bright as the sunshine filtering in through the picture windows.

He shrugged. "I didn't finish my story until 2 AM Then I slipped into the new temporary digs you've lended me, quiet as a church mouse."

"Was it an 'I' or a 'We' that wrote that story?" Katie asked, sniffing the air. "Doth I detect on thee a note of whiskey?"

"Quite possibly. McGreedy and I finished the story about a minute before last call at the Wheel. Honest Abe's got nothing on us. We actually started drafting our magnum opus right there in the booth, on Mad's napkins."

"And McGreedy filed it?"

"He sure as heck better have. Recall that the only thing I could file a story in right now would be a trash can. I'm officially a horseless cowboy, which is another way of saying an unaffiliated journalist." He paused. "So what's this meeting with your dad all about?"

She shrugged. "He has it in his head that he wants to sit down with you one-on-one. And when Daddy gets an idea, he doesn't let it go."

"Bulldog Clarke" Jake said, mulling it over as a potential calling card.

"Speak of the devil," Katie said. She nodded in the direction of the door and quietly took her exit.

In her wake Herb Clarke scooted into the booth opposite Jake holding a still-steaming mug of dark coffee. "Mornin', Jacob," he said, tucking a napkin in his lap. "Katie tells me the two of you had quite an interesting evening last night in Holstein." He looked up from fixing his napkin in his lap. "Still, not even my own flesh-and-blood daughter would tell me why. So much for freedom of information." He smiled ruefully. "Naturally, I've come to pump you for information."

"I'm sworn to secrecy, Herb," Jake countered, making like he was zipping his lip.

"Sworn to secrecy my foot!" exclaimed the editor. "You've already told McGreedy."

"Had to." Jake took a conspiratorial pull from his coffee. "The big fella was my best ticket to get the thing in print."

"You know I would have run it, and gladly."

"And I appreciate that. But I think this one is beyond even us."

"Bigger than the *Hereford Gate*," Clarke replied, grinning. "Say it ain't so."

"It ain't so," Jake said, returning the grin. "So did you come here merely to heighten my already elevated sense of guilt?"

"As a matter of fact I did not…" the newspaperman mused, as if reminding himself of his original purpose. "I came here to make you an offer."

"Are you proposing?"

"In a manner of speaking, yes. Jacob, Katie tells me you've been sleeping upstairs in the café these past few days."

"Guilty as charged."

"I gather you lost your roommate."

"You could say that."

"And have you succeeded in obtaining permanent lodging elsewhere?"

"I figured I'd get to that as soon as my big story breaks."

"And squat in the storage rooms above my restaurant in the meantime? I won't have it, least of all for the insurance headache it's bound to cause me." Herb Clarke took off his glasses and rubbed at the pair of tired eyes underneath. "Why don't you come stay with Katie and me on the farm?"

"I couldn't," Jake said, suddenly and inexplicably terrified by the idea of sleeping under Herb Clarke's roof.

"We've plenty of room."

"What would I pay you with?"

"Your talents," he said.

"Don't have any."

"Come now, Mr. Preston. This is no time to be unduly modest. If you'll help me with some of the legwork at the newspaper from now until the election, we'll call it even. If no money changes hands, you can maintain your journalistic independence, and blow wherever the political winds take you. And Jacob, they will take you."

"What about Katie?"

Clarke smiled broadly. "She'll have two stubborn journalists to sit down to supper with."

Jake eyed the editor curiously. "I thought farmers never allowed strangers into their homes for fear of the lodger running off with the farmer's daughter."

"True enough. But I'm not exactly a farmer anymore, am I, unless you count raising some sweetcorn, puttering around in my tomato patch, and housing a dried-up old milk cow."

Jake mulled it over. "No other strings attached?"

"None whatsoever."

"Not even me spilling my secret before it hits the presses tomorrow."

"Not even that." Clarke reached amiably across the table. "Deal?"

"Deal," Jake echoed.

"Fine then, your chores begin tonight."

"Chores?"

Herb Clarke smiled. "You can't very well live on a farm without doing chores."

"Wait a minute," Jake said. "You just said…"

"…that I had a sizable tomato patch, yes indeedy," interrupted the editor. "Tonight we're picking the rest of the Green Zebras. Weatherman's calling for a heavy frost overnight, and I don't want to lose the crop I've been doting on this whole summer like a mother hen." The veteran newspaperman swallowed his last drop of coffee. "See you in the tomato patch, then."

As soon as the door swung shut behind Herb Clarke, his daughter returned to her roost on the side of the booth opposite Jake.

"So?"

"So I've been conscripted to help with the tomato harvest."

"Good for you. The only sure way to know whether Daddy likes you is if he puts you to work." She wiped at a spot on the table. "When do you start?"

"Tonight."

"Can you cook?" Katie asked.

"Yeah, I can actually."

"That makes one of us."

"And yet you work at a restaurant. Go figure."

"Frying foods and chopping salads is not cooking. Actually, Daddy's a fine cook in his own right. Did some cooking overseas in the Army, or so he claims."

"I'm not surprised," Jake said. "Whatever Herb Clarke sets his mind to, he seems to achieve. For God's sake, here we sit in a town of two thousand people that forty days ago no one had ever heard of, until that old man of yours gets up in a press briefing and chews Milt Cloward out for walling himself off from salt-of-the-earth people. Four weeks later Cloward is based here; Santoro is just down the road in Goodacre, and Rochelle Boxman is running around flaunting her credentials as a Midwest farmer's daughter."

"He's a pretty persuasive fellow," Kate Clarke allowed. "But then I imagine you can be, too."

"Let's hope so," Jake said. "I'm due to talk politics in Mrs. Meyers's third grade classroom in less than an hour."

How long had it been since he'd actually been in a room full of nine-year-olds, Jake wondered. Did they talk on cell phones? Did they know who the President was? Did they still believe in Santa Claus or was he just another cartoon character to them?

Marianne Meyers met him outside her classroom door with a warm handshake and a heartfelt so-nice-you-could-come-the-children-will-love-you before leading Jake inside the lion's den. "Children," she said, actually leading Jake by the wrist to a position squarely in front of the blackboard. This is Mr. Preston. He's a nationally famous political journalist."

"I saw him on *The Scoop*," one of the girls piped up. "He was pretty cool."

"If we're lucky, he still will be…cool, that is," Mrs. Meyers said, smiling the smile of all beatific third-grade teachers, even those who wrote whip-smart political commentary in their spare time. "Now I've asked you all to write down at least one question for Mr. Preston concerning either his life or his career. Who wants to go first? Yes, Cheyenne."

"Is Milt Cloward really the most boring person in the world?"

Of all the candidates Jake felt like he knew Milt Cloward the least. "He seems really calm to me," Jake said, measuring his words carefully. "Level-headed. I don't know…what do you think?"

"He's tall," Cheyenne observed, and Jake couldn't help but nod. A pretty fair first lesson in politics, if he did say so himself: tall equals noticeable equals electable.

"What's the coolest thing about your job?" a boy whose nametag read Chris asked. An awkward question, Jake thought, considering he didn't actually have a job. "Getting to ask tough questions of really important people," he said, strangely satisfied with his answer.

"Do you have a girlfriend?" A little blonde girl asked in the front row.

"Riley," Mrs. Meyers interjected. "Remember when we practiced the difference between appropriate and inappropriate questions?"

Jake waved it off. "It's okay," he said, looking down at Riley and seeing a youthful version of Amethyst Gilchrest. "I'm afraid not," he admitted, figuring honesty was the best policy.

"Do you want one?" the girl said, lisping through two missing front teeth.

"Some day," Jake said, letting it go at that.

"Who's the best athlete of all the candidates," asked a boy named Terrance.

"Probably Renard Kane. He played basketball when he was in high school. That's supposedly how he met his wife, Candy, who came one night to watch her older brother play against Mr. Kane's team."

"Sweet," Terrance said.

"I've got a question for our guest," Mrs. Meyers chimed in. "What does he think of the Silver Steer's sudden disappearance?"

The kids buzzed with excited approval. Their teacher had asked a keeper.

"It's a mystery," Jake said, looking all around the room. "The Silver Steer has become very valuable…and you know what often happens to valuables in mystery stories."

"They get swiped," interrupted Terrance.

"That's right. And to avoid just that, people hide their valuables away in lockboxes, or have them insured for thousands of dollars."

"Gazillions of dollars!" some kid shouted from the back of the room.

"We got too careless with the Silver Steer, and maybe now we'll be forced to pay the price," Jake added.

"Do you think we'll find it?" nametag Kari asked from the second row.

"I'm fairly certain we will, dear," Mrs. Meyers said knowingly. "Now don't you worry."

"We'd better," Kari replied. "Cuz, I'm really worried about him. I put him in my prayers every night."

"You do?" Jake asked

"Uh-huh."

"We shouldn't keep Mr. Preston from his work, children. But we'd like to ask him if he has time to hear the winning entry in our Silver Steer writing contest."

"Mr. Preston certainly does have time," Jake said, amused at the third-person reference.

"Wonderful," bubbled Mrs. Meyers, "the children and I have been talking all fall about the origins of our unique political system, and what we can do to make it better for everyone—a cause the Silver Steer would surely approve of. Emily, do you want to come up and read your first place entry, 'The Silver Star.'"

On cue an impossibly cute redhead minced her way to the front of the room, half turning toward Jake in preparation for her recitation. Once at the head of the class she cleared her throat, waited for the go-ahead nod from her smiling teacher, and began.

The Silver Star

One year there was a boy bull born in Hereford whose coat was so white and gray it looked like silver. "I'll call you Silver Star," its owner, said, putting Silver out to graze in his very best pasture.

Before long, people were driving from as far away as Goodacre and Sweet Loam just to see this magnificent creature. They parked up and down the farmer's gravel road until the farmer couldn't even squeeze his tractor between the parked cars to plow his fields anymore. "I'm going to have to get rid of you one of these days, old friend," the farmer told his prize cattle. "Or I won't be able to plant my corn."

One day a businessman from Connecticut pulled up in a fancy limousine whose license plates read "FutrePrz." This very wealthy man with the perfect head of hair offered the farmer millions of dollars for his Silver Star. The farmer thought about it long and hard and finally declared, "My neighbors would be mighty sad if I up and sold Silver here. He's the one thing that gives them the most pride. And besides, who would stop at their roadside stands and buy their honey, and their apples, and their sweetcorn if the Silver Star went with you to shine in Connecticut."

The farmer thought long and hard about the rich man's offer. "I'll tell you what I will do, though. I'll sell the Silver Star's likeness to you; that way I can keep 'im, and you can use 'im as a symbol on all the things your company makes that are of the highest quality, like my Silver Star here."

A few years later a reporter came to town whose name was Jacob Preston. One day he was out driving and saw the Silver Star for himself, and thought, wow, what a fabulous creature. Everyone should know the Silver Star is more than a picture on somebody's fancy car or someone else's fine salad dressing. So he stopped at the farmhouse and asked if he could share Silver's story with the world.

The farmer was glad to have Jacob spread the word about his amazing breed, so glad that when Jacob stopped back with another idea he was more than ready to listen. "I notice the contract you signed with the businessman gives you the right to take back the image of the Silver Star after four years have passed," Jake told the farmer. "Why don't we have a contest each and every four years right here in Iowa, where the very best people in each town, the ones who work super hard for their community, each win a trophy in the shape of Silver Star."

"I'll go you one better than that, Jacob," the farmer said. "We'll give a Silver Steer trophy to each and every one of those important people. Then we'll gather those good folks together and have everyone in all the towns across the land vote on who's done the very most to help their neighbors. Whoever wins will have the honor of keeping the real Silver Star in their pasture for a whole summer, so that all the citizens in their hometown can see them for themselves what pride looks like."

Many years passed, and the idea Jacob and the farmer came up with that day worked famously. Meanwhile, Silver Star grew older and wiser with each passing year. By the time Silver had celebrated his twenty-fifth birthday, people were coming to him directly for advice on all the tough problems their community couldn't solve by itself. Silver Star was pretty amazing as an advice-giver, too, though like all cows, he couldn't talk. But he could lo and moo and whatever he mooed appeared to work because everyone seemed to go home with the answers to their problems.

Some claimed Silver Star was a miracle breed of cattle that could speak in tongues. Others said he hypnotized people then slipped them the answers when they weren't paying attention. But Jacob and the farmer always said the people visiting the steer knew best all along, and that the real beauty of Silver Star was that it reflected back to the people the answers they already knew to be true in their hearts.

—THE END

"Isn't that just a wonderful political parable?" effused the always effusive Mrs. Meyers.

"It's nothing short of amazing," Jake told the girl. "Did you write that all yourself?"

"We wrote it together, didn't we, Emily?" Marianne Meyers volunteered before turning to Jake to whisper under her breath, "Forgive me. Where We the People are concerned, my passions sometimes run away with me, though I try to hold back when I'm with the children."

"No need to apologize," Jake replied. "I know exactly how you feel. And besides, since when did standing up for your rights become synonymous with biting your tongue?"

Mrs. Meyers smiled demurely, turning her attention back to her gifted pupil. "Emily might have inherited some of her talents," she explained to the class. "Her great uncle runs our very own *Hereford Gate* and owns a farm himself."

"Is that the old dude who wears glasses and walks down First Street like he's really, really ticked off about something?"

"Yes, Terrance. That's our Mr. Clarke. He's been our newspaper editor here for as long as anyone can remember, and when I write my newspaper columns, he's my boss."

"He's soooo old."

"We don't say *old*, Terrance," Mrs. Meyers corrected him. "We say *elderly* or *senior citizen*. It's true Mr. Clarke is a senior citizen, but he doesn't seem old to me. Does he to you, Mr. Preston?"

"Not in the least," Jake said. "In fact, he has more energy than I do."

"You see there, kids. Mr. Preston has shared with us another valuable lesson. You can't judge a book by its cover. For example, I may look like a sweet old third-grade teacher to you, but where citizens' rights are concerned, I'm not afraid of jumping up on a table like this," Mrs. Meyers said, clambering atop the nearest table, "and proclaiming to everyone in Hereford County that we won't take any more nonsense from these visiting politicians."

The children looked from their suddenly animated teacher back to Jake, who shrugged his shoulders and said, "Looks like your teacher isn't afraid to take the bull by the horns. You'd all better behave for her."

"Or else what?" Terrance asked.

"Or else the Silver Steer is gonna get you," Jake replied, pleased for once at his scare tactic.

When he arrived at the Clarke's Century Farm, Jake found the door unlocked and, after calling out a few times to no avail, let himself in through the front door, though the living room, back to the kitchen, and still he found no answer.

In sum the old house surprised him in its modesty…the oak floorboards had been worn to a cherry patina, the horsehair plaster in the walls and ceiling had cracked badly, and here and there the Clarkes had tacked up plastic sheeting over the old sash windows to keep out the chilly autumnal air. An old divan, a parlor piano, an ancient television, a badly outdated personal computer, stacks upon stacks of newspapers and magazines, and plenty of dusty black-and-white photos of the Clarke's unsmiling ancestors completed the décor.

Exiting through the back door Jake found the red-faced newspaperman up to his chest in the tomato patch, an overgrown jungle of low-hanging fruit already ripened on the vine.

"I'm afraid I've let my patch get ahead of me," the editor lamented. He made a painful attempt to straighten his back, and wiped a bead of sweat from his forehead with the back of a hand stained black from the good garden soil.

Jake paused at the edge of the garden. He had never seen tomatoes like these—row after row hung with plump green fruit the size of baseballs, vining this way and that. "Jesus, Herb," he exclaimed. "What are these…mutants?"

"They're my Green Zebras," he said, groaning at the hitch in his back. "Funny thing, I don't even like the taste of 'em all that well. They're the bees knees in a fresh salad, but they're hell to cook with unless you like a steady diet of gazpacho or green salsa for weeks on end."

"Then why on earth do you grow them?" Jake fetched the extra empty bucket and began picking, not quite sure what the perfect Zebra looked like, but duly resolved to fine one all the same.

"Because I can," Clarke said. "With all this land I don't know how I'd look myself in the mirror if I let it lay fallow. Do you know what I mean, Jacob?"

"Not really." Jake tossed a keeper in his bucket. "What do you do with all this fruit? There's way more than you and Katie could ever use."

"True, though I'll have you know I make a mean cold tomato soup and an even meaner Caprese salad. What we can't use at the restaurant we give to the local food bank, or sell at the farmer's market in town. We don't make a dime by the time it's all said and done, but it helps the community. Here, try one." The editor opened up a dirt-stained palm to reveal one of the zebra-striped aliens, and watched as Jake took a tentative bite.

"It's a tomato, alright," he said. "Never been a big fan."

Clarke chuckled. "I can see from your face that it's an acquired taste. You're accustomed to the big beefsteak tomatoes you pick up from the supermarkets back in Denver. These are grown from heirloom seeds I get from a little farm up in the northeastern corner of the state that's built themselves a world-class seed bank. This one here, for instance, was bred by a guy named Tom Wagner. It's only about thirty years old, which is young as seeds go. Over on the other side of the garden I've got some Eva's Purple Balls. They were brought over from Germany in the 1800s. A little further down the way I've got some Aunt Ruby's German Green."

"Sounds like they're all old-lady varietals."

Clarke stopped picking, turning a thoughtful eye toward his conscripted help. "You're right. While the men have been off doing so-called important things for the last one hundred and fifty years—by which I mean leveling forests, fighting wars, and poisoning the earth from which they nevertheless hoped to wrest a living, the women have been cultivating seeds for their children and grandchildren. And for the last thirty years anyway, they've been outvoting men, not to mention staffing the library boards and PTAs and doing most of the teaching and child-rearing and caring for their community. Do you know women have voted in greater numbers than men in every election since you were a little boy? So yes, we'll take your old-lady comment as a compliment."

"I thought the whole idea of farming was progress," Jake said, his curiosity piqued now as he fell into his own picking rhythm. "Why would anyone plant a one-hundred-and-fifty-year old seed?"

Clarke emitted the laugh Jake had come to recognize as a mixture of wry amusement laced with barely latent ferocity. "I fear I've misled you. My Eva's Purple Balls aren't actually as old as Abe Lincoln, but their seed stock is. They've survived, genetically unaltered, by the good graces of people who've planted them, harvested them, and saved their seeds every year since that unredeemable drunk from Illinois, Ulysses S. Grant, took office after the Civil War."

Sorting through the best of his Zebras, Clarke continued, "Why would anyone bother planting an heirloom? Mostly because they're hardy stock. They've passed the test of time." Clarke turned to face his helper. "Take a look at that seemingly decrepit hand pump over there, the rusty one. That was made no more than a couple hundred miles from here during the Great Depression. For three generations it's not once broken down on any of the Clarkes when they've needed to draw water. It's really a philosophical question you're asking, son. Why would you ever leave an heirloom if it never failed to yield for you?"

"Because people love progress," Jake said, working the handle on the old pump to find that the water did indeed come gushing out, just as Clarke had promised.

"Correction: people don't just love progress; they're *infatuated* with it. Infatuation and love are not the same thing. Take my love of politics as an example. I love the political process, but I'm not *infatuated* with it. Does that make sense?"

"Sort of," Jake allowed, wringing out his utterly soaked shirt-sleeve. Clarke's heirloom pump had worked too well.

"One of the things that appeals so deeply to me about politics, at least as we practice them here, is that they remain essentially an heirloom. Politicians still do stump speeches from soapboxes; they still decry the buffoon in the White House while standing atop a stack of hay bales; they still drink weak coffee out of Styrofoam cups with women's coffee klatches. And of course they still deceive, obfuscate, and misrepresent, and We the People do our level best to see through their web of lies to the real substance of the person. It's a tango, a pas de deux, and an heirloom at that."

"The thing is," continued the editor, "all that tradition is being washed away—literally eroded—right before our eyes. Do you know that during the last caucus season the candidates spent less than half of the amount of time they usually do on the ground here, meeting with voters face-to-face. And for all the talk about national elections giving a badly needed boost to local economies, each and every presidential primary the candidates spend less and less in states like this one, in terms of real dollars. Look it up. Just because you see their ads on TV doesn't mean they're catering town-hall meetings and pancake breakfasts in villages like Hereford, or treating their campaign staffs to a steak fry at a locally-owned café like our Cal Coolidge. Our business at the café should be up 100% with Cloward's campaign head-quartered here in town, but it's barely up 10%, and most of that is due to our locals' need to come into the café and vent about the foolishness they're seeing all around them. The same holds true at our grocery store. So where are the campaigns getting their food shipped in from? Des Moines, at the nearest, and more often from Omaha or Chicago."

"So if you can't beat 'em," Jake asked, "why not you join 'em? Put some California salads and avocado smoothies and arugula whatchamacallits on the menu at the Cal Coolidge and see if those fussy politicos don't start beating down your door."

"To what end?" Clarke asked, his face turning red with exertion. "So that we'd be left with a refrigerator full of spoiling food when they abscond after the election. And then there's the principle of it, Jacob. The simply fact is we don't drink avocado smoothies here. Mind you, perhaps we should, but we don't. Used to be politicians understood that to earn the vote of the people, they had to honor the character of the people, in deed as well as in word. These days the game is to get in and get out as quickly as possible, before the sophisticates on the Coasts begin to perceive the down-home candidate as pandering to parochialism. But if we're such noble, salt-of-the-earth people, why is it that candidates spend less time breaking bread with us, by and by?"

"Anyway," Clarke added, picking up a bushel basket filled to the brim with lime-green tomatoes. "I shouldn't get on my high horse out here in my weed patch. That's one of the great things about having this overgrown jungle of a victory garden to escape to. The plants don't talk back or write letters to the editor, and if they do, you know it's time to check yourself into the funny farm."

Jake picked up his own, significantly lighter basket. "That and growing your own saves you a trip to the store."

"More than that, it enfranchises you," Clarke added, heading back toward the house with his impressive haul. "If you can feed yourself, the politicians don't have you over a barrel. They can threaten and posture and preen all they want, but they can't take the food in your garden away from you. They can't even tax the produce from your homegrown garden, much as they would like. Some day the rest of America is going to remember the symbolism of the victory garden, and they're going to start applying the same logic to winning the war for freedom from our own government." Clarke stopped at the back porch, holding the door open for the not-so-willing volunteer trailing behind him.

"You sound like a libertarian," Jake said, knocking the dirt off his shoes.

"Not at all. Libertarians make it part of their creed that the government should do little or nothing for the people. They believe in the wisdom of the individual over that of the community. I, on the other hand, believe in an active, vibrant community made up of empowered individuals. There's an important difference there, Jacob, if you're patient enough to look for it."

"Just what we need," Katie commented when they walked into the kitchen with the day's catch. "More Zebras."

"Do I detect a note of irony?" her father asked.

The newspaperman's daughter stirred an oversized pot of soup simmering on a hot pad atop the table. "You most certainly do. Now can I turn this witches' brew back over to you? I got in a moment ago and found it bubbling over the sides of the cauldron while you were out in the garden looking for fresh sacrifices."

The old man took the spoon and good-naturedly thwacked his daughter on the wrist. "Leave the maestro to his symphony."

"You see," Katie said, turning Jake's way with a wry smile painted across her pretty face. "You see what I have to put up with? So long as you're staying here I have every intention of using you as a human shield."

"I don't blame you," Jake said, returning serve. "He's a dangerous man. A radical. You wouldn't believe all the incendiary notions he filled my head with out in the garden. Crazy stuff about people growing their own food, and caring for themselves and their communities."

"I know," she said. "He's simply intolerable."

"Downright criminal," Jake added. "The Thought Police will be breaking down the door of this farmhouse any minute."

"Good," said Herb Clarke from his station at the stove. "Maybe they can help make the soup."

Nine

Jake awoke to the sound of birdsong outside the otherwise silent farmhouse. The alarm read 8:30 AM. When he glanced outside the window at the gravel drive beneath his window, he could see that both Herb and Katie had long since flown the coop, leaving just him and the barn swallows who'd decided to stick around to see how the election turned out.

Downstairs he found a note from Katie. They'd left some steel cut oats on the stove for him, it said, and the newspapers would be arriving in the mailbox by 9 AM. He should relax for a day, she suggested, and get his bearings. Maybe the three of them could take a walk once they came home for dinner?

Jake had barely reached the bottom of his bowl when he heard the mailman drive up. Still in his slippers he walked out to retrieve the contents of the box, feeling spoiled at the leisure, like he'd checked into an all-expenses-paid bed and breakfast… or a funny farm.

In addition to heirloom tomatoes and sweetcorn, Herb Clarke's other weakness was newspapers, Jake surmised, glancing at the oversized bundle in his arms on the way back to the house. In today's catch alone he spied the *Times*, the *Post*, the *Journal* and the *Register*. The night before, the old editor had disappeared into his study after dinner with a bundle of newspapers tucked underneath his arms, and hadn't emerged again until bedtime.

Back at the table Jake eagerly sifted through the stack until he found the one he was looking for—the *Journal*. At the bottom of Page One his eyes landed on the headline. "A WOPPer in Iowa: Legal Sleeper Cells Threaten Outcome of Election."

By Mort McGreedy and Amethyst Gilchrest
A *Journal* and *Times* exclusive

As Milt Cloward, Mike Santoro, and Renard Kane do back flips to earn the votes of everyday Iowans, it may be the Wisconsiners to the north who end up stealing this year's primary season.

A group calling itself WOPP—Wisconsinites Opposed to Partisan Politics—announced yesterday in a *Times* and *Journal* exclusive that so-called voter sleeper cells made up mostly of Wisconsin voters numbering a thousand or more appeared set to sway the crucial first-in-the-nation vote across the border in the Hawkeye State.

Their ingenious if not inflammatory idea depends in part on the deep pockets of Milwaukeeians, Madisonians, and Chicagoans to keep the group fed, watered, and housed until election day, when this army of legally registered voters has pledged to vote for the least electable, most underfunded candidate on the primary ticket. "The political process asks us to pick our poison every four years, and gives us only those candidates who have been bought and approved by special interest groups and vetted by them, rather than by We the People. The only possible, legal recourse for non-partisan Middle Americans disheartened by our lack of real choice is to join us in registering a resounding protest vote that will be heard around the country and the world," a member of the organization's leadership told us on our recent visit to the WOPP compound, or, in their parlance, "national headquarters."

Unlike the "leaderless movements" of the recent past, WOPP isn't interested in disrupting the vote as much as it is in fully and legally participating in it to underscore the growing hypocrisies of electoral politics. "By election night, we'll be perfectly legal registered voters exercising our endowed constitutional rights. At most polling sites, you won't be able to differentiate us from your neighbors, because we are your neighbors," a credible source within WOPP told us.

WOPP leaders claim a thousand or more of their foot soldiers have been embedded inside the Hawkeye State for weeks if not months. Asked if their extreme geographic makeover has been a hardship, WOPPers, to a man and a woman, said no. "Iowans have made it almost too easy. While we haven't advertised our presence here, everyone we have encountered has been more than welcoming. Basically we've had to ask ourselves whether the 'sacrifice' of living in a friendly, affordable, accommodating state for sixty or ninety days was worth sending a message to the world about the way democracy ought to work. Put in those terms, it was an easy choice."

The group, consisting mostly of college-educated, highly mobile 20-somethings and adventuresome retirees with a long-latent radical streak, have dispersed their members across this sparsely populated, mostly rural state, taking full advantage of small-town demographics and economics in the Midwest, where Brain Drain has previously vacuumed up many of the homegrown, highly educated young professionals. "In many of our target communities residents have been visibly relieved to see us," commented one key informant. "Several of us have literally had people come up to us in the grocery and thank us for moving here. They tell us they pray at night that their grandkids would do the same."

But there's a rub in WOPP for native Iowans. The WOPPers for whom they've so graciously, and unwittingly, laid out the welcome mat are now threatening to run away with their sacred cow—the first-in-the-nation-vote that has been a fixture on the political calendar since 1972. WOPP has chosen now, the moment at which their reported numbers easily surpass the threshold needed to qualify as a swing vote, to declare its presence to the rest of the world in hopes of further growing its membership rolls. Once the word is out, WOPP recruiters suspect an additional 3000 to 4000 dedicated volunteers may yet join their ranks from all over the United States.

The political powers-that-be should expect an official statement from the group in coming days. That statement is likely to send state party officials here scrambling for ways to draw an even broader base of natives to the polls in an attempt to mitigate whatever influence these powerfully cynical, powerfully ideological out-of-state contrarians and iconoclasts may yet have.

In the meantime WOPP figures to rework the electoral math, as its frontliners move to Iowa in increasing numbers for an extended working vacation and geopolitical Kumbaya. Their reactionary social experiment is a literal manifestation of the old adage "you vote with your feet."

Either way, WOPP is coming soon to a corn poll near you. If you believe, as so many do, that politics is spectacle, get your popcorn, your extra-large Coke and settle in for what is likely to be an epic, a farce, a tragi-comedy, and a political thriller rolled into one admittedly foreign package.

Jake re-read the article in disbelief, his emotions stuck somewhere between betrayal and anger. The electoral scoop of the year had not put Jake Preston on the map; it had put Amethyst Gilchrest on the front page. McGreedy had told him a bald-faced lie, then sold him down the river.

He was livid, livid beyond the point of even knowing what to do. So he did the only thing he could think of that would offer some short-term solace: he drove the backroads into town at irresponsible speeds for some emergency pancake therapy.

When he opened the door of the Cal Coolidge he found Katie and Herb talking quietly at the counter wearing dour looks on their faces. "I'm so sorry, Jake," Katie said when he sat down heavily on the stool beside her father, who had the *Times* open on the counter. "One thing's for sure, Mort McGreedy and Amethyst Gilchrest won't be served another meal in this restaurant, I promise you that."

"It doesn't matter," Jake said, still in a daze. "They'll manage to subsist on the blood of their victims."

Herb Clarke chuckled ruefully. "Under ordinary circumstances I would say that was a bit harsh, but considering the depravity of what Katie has described to me, I'd say the shoe fits. Katie, any cloves of garlic in the kitchen?"

"Not enough for a bloodsucker the size of McGreedy I'm afraid," she said.

"I can't believe it," Jake lamented.

"And you won't, at least not for a while." The editor fidgeted absentmindedly with the salt and pepper shakers. "Happened to me once as a younger man, and I've never forgotten it. It's hard enough to get scooped on a story, let alone be lied to."

"If I'd been scooped, fair and square, I could live with that," Jake said. "But this was an exclusive. I offered it to McGreedy with the promise that he would share the billing with me. This is closer to a breach of contract, or an outright fraud, than a garden-variety lie."

"You may be right," Clarke replied, "but I'm afraid that kind of thinking won't get you very far. Politicians of the sort you and I cover get betrayed by their underlings and advisors all the time—defections, evasions, tell-alls, confessions, exposés. If every politician who suffered a leak or kiss-and-tell up and quit, we wouldn't have any left standing, or, more to the point, any worth electing. Remember Truman in 1948? General MacArthur betrayed him, and Truman was well behind in every poll you could name. Most men, especially those who had inherited a job they didn't necessarily relish, would have folded. Not Truman. He commissions himself a railcar, and gives 'em hell for 22,000 miles of cross-country campaigning. Next thing you know, Give 'Em Hell Harry is back in the White House."

The editor rapped his knuckles on the counter with conviction. "Jacob, you've got to go forth and do likewise. Figure out who and what you have on your side, and use your allies well and wisely. Truman figured on having the American people in his camp, if he could just hit the rails and meet them face-to-face where they lived."

"Daddy's right," Katie said. "You're still one of only three writers in the press corps who has access to the WOPP higher-ups. Give them a call."

"I don't have their number," Jake said, "and I have no idea how to get back to their headquarters. Our host in Holstein took so many turns on our little nocturnal goose-chase to their barn it practically made me dizzy."

"Then you drive to that meatlocker in town and camp outside until someone who looks like a WOPP shows up. You demand to speak to the Grand Poobah...the Big Cheese...whatever they call him... or her," Katie said.

"Whatever you do, Jacob, don't wait," the elder Clarke weighed in. "You've got to catch this tiger by the tail."

Jake looked up from the counter. "What do you say then, copilot? You up for a Holstein trip redux?"

Katie shook her head. "No can do. We're catering an event today, and I can't leave Bev alone again." She bit nervously at her lip. "Daddy, why don't you go?"

Herb Clarke looked taken aback. "I suppose I could," he said. "If Jake here would have me."

"Sure I'd have you. As long as you don't mind hearing me vent for forty miles."

"Not at all," Clarke said. "I'm a newspaper editor. I listen to people vent all the time."

"What if we drive all that way and can't find anybody?"

"We'll find someone, son. You don't live in a small community your whole life without learning a bit about how to dig up information when it's absolutely necessary. Now then, let's get while the gettin's good, shall we? Katie, will you lock up the newspaper offices for me, and leave a note on the door explaining that I'm away on a story."

"Will do."

"Well then, we're off like a dirty shirt," Herb Clarke said, hopping down from his stool and hitting the ground running.

They arrived just as the streets of downtown Holstein turned dusky, swinging by the meatlocker to find the back parking lot empty and the building shuttered. Herb Clarke pressed his head to the cinder block walls and listened hard.

"Not a peep," he said. "I didn't suppose there would be. Not yet anyway. If these WOPPs are determined to lay low so as to keep the rest of the political world in suspense for another day or two, they'll wait until everyone's in the barn for the night before any of them leave the compound and risk a trip into town. Why don't you let me buy you a coffee and we'll wait 'em out?"

"I appreciate it, Herb, but I don't want to have driven a hundred miles only to have them slip through our grasp while we're sipping our consolation Folgers."

"Trust me, they won't," the editor said. "Just park your car down the street, away from the meatlocker. We'll get us a nice warm cup of java, then we'll camp out at the meatlocker until, inevitably, the cows come home. Don't know about you, but I'd rather wait outside for a half hour stoked by coffee rather than wait outside for three hours with nothing but your conversation to warm me...no offense, Jacob."

"None taken. Alright, so we drop the car off and drink some joe. But if we miss them, you're paying for an overnight in Holstein's finest hotel."

"Deal," Clarke said. "And while you park the car, I'll grab us a booth over at the coffee shop."

A minute later Jake found his partner-in-crime camped out at a place called Freddy's Good Grind. Back in Denver, a name like that would likely have foretold a gay bar, but Iowans, to their credit, were mostly an un-ironic people.

"Can I ask you a question," Jake asked after they'd put in an order for a couple of tall coffees, blonde. "Why were you such a jerk to me when I first came to town?"

"I wasn't a jerk to you," Clarke replied. "That's part of the trouble with yours and Katie's generation. You use the word 'jerk' to basically mean 'someone who doesn't agree with me.' I wasn't being a jerk, I was merely asking you basic questions to ascertain your preparedness for the job."

"You still seemed like a jerk to me."

"I don't mean to be a grump. But when you edit a community newspaper your entire adult life, you come to learn that it's safer to have a chip on your shoulder, or at least pretend as if you do, than to be everyone's best friend."

"Is that so?"

"It most definitely is so. You write for a publication, Jacob…"

"Correction: I *wrote* for a publication."

"…yes, you wrote for a publication whose readers you were likely never to meet in person. By contrast, I know almost every single one of my readers. I recognize them on sight, in fact. The trouble is, when people start feeling as if they know you, it's natural for them to start asking things of you, almost as a way of cementing their relationship to you. Mostly, as I said, it's not a bad thing. Folks decide they like you, and they want to enter into some kind of mutually beneficial trade. Naturally they want to solidify that link with a quid-pro-quo that feels harmless enough to them. In a way it's not all that different from the preferential treatment constituents and lobbyists learn to expect from the influence-peddling politicians to whom they've contributed money."

"Except that you're no politician."

"And yet there was a time when I thought I might be," Clarke confessed. "In fact, I toyed around with the idea for years after I returned from the Service. Most newspaper editors who care deeply about their community, about shaping public opinion, about doing good for and by their readers, have a capable politician buried somewhere inside of them."

"So then why the gruff exterior if you have a politician in you at root?"

"Because like any good politician, I am aware of my tendencies—to want to be liked, to want to enter into quid-pro-quos with people as a substitute for real intimacy, to blunt the truth to make it more palatable to those you very much want not to disappoint. The difference is I'm resolved to fight against those inclinations. The kind of people who understand that, or can see past an otherwise prickly exterior, are exactly the kind of people you can trust to help keep you honest in the pulpit."

"You wouldn't last a day at the *Rocky Mountain Partisan*," Jake needled.

"Nor at the *Times*, nor the *Post*, nor the *Journal* nor a thousand and one other so-called major newspapers you could name. Nor would I want to. Those publications, while they're packed with celebrity writers like Mort McGreedy or rising stars like Amethyst Gilchrest, bear the same relationship to Main Street as Hollywood does to our little one-screen movie theater in Hereford. One is a projection of our need to create larger-than-life institutions of such scale and magnitude that we can't possibly comprehend them let alone belong to them; the other is a desire to create institutions that serve us directly, and whose size and shape and outlines we can appreciate at a glance, and up close."

"And that, Jacob, is what interests me so much about these... these WOPPers, as you call them. They're attempting to expose and even leverage the fraudulent nature of the system itself.

They're basically arguing that in a time when voter registration laws are so lax they're almost laughable, that anyone with a few weeks on their hands for an experiment in political tourism can now potentially alter the course of the world's most important presidential primary. That's not a quid-pro-quo stance, as much as it is a genuinely populist one."

"Speaking of WOPP," Jake said, checking his watch. "It's 7:30 and, judging from what I've seen looking out the window here, I'd say traffic on Main has pretty much slowed to a crawl."

"Right," Clarke said, scooting out of the booth with surprising agility for a man in his seventies. "I'll get the tab, and we'll commence our little nocturnal vigil."

Once out of the coffee shop they moved quickly in the chilly air, walking around to the back door of the locker where Ripon had met Jake and Katie just a couple of nights earlier. There they waited like two teenagers locked out of the house, their backs against the building's cinder block wall.

"I fear I underdressed just a little," Clarke said, shivering in his light jacket. "You see, back home I'm never more than a half a block from either the café or the newspaper, and I can duck in and warm up anytime I want. Here I'm a sailor away from port. Let's pray our stake-out doesn't last until election day."

Shortly thereafter Jake spied Ripon's pickup truck ease down the alley behind the store—checking to make sure the coast was clear, he assumed—before circling back. A couple of minutes after that she stood before them in her trademark hoodie, silhouetted by the streetlight.

"Well, if it isn't Jake Preston and…"—she stopped herself to squint at Herb in the darkness— "who's the old guy?"

"This is Kate Clarke's father, Herb," Jake explained, rising to his feet. "You got a minute?"

"I've got about fifteen of them," she said. "C'mon on into the ice chest." She unlocked the door and switched on the light to reveal a locker substantially cleaner, and more open, than the one Jake and Katie had visited just two nights prior.

"Let's just say we're having a moving sale. And everything must go," Ripon said, as her guests surveyed the room. "So what can I help you with," she asked, "that is, assuming you don't mind talking by flashlight. I don't want some Good Sam walking down Main Street to see the light on and call the sheriff. Not that I'm trespassing. I just don't want the PR."

"Have you read the article in today's *Journal*?" Jake asked.

"How could I miss it? Everyone in the organization has forwarded it to me."

"What did you think?"

"Way cool," she observed. "Though I was kinda surprised to see Mort McGreedy on the byline."

"You and me both," Jake admitted. "Weren't you equally surprised to see Amethyst Gilchrest's?"

Ripon furrowed her brow. "Should I have been? She was working with you, right?" Jake shook his head. "Well, that's what she told us."

"When did she tell you that?"

"A couple of nights ago…the same night we talked with you, actually, at the barn…. About a half hour after you and Kate left, Amethyst Gilchrest comes rolling up in a rental car, flashes me her creds, and tells us that she's working with you on the story…that you'd asked her to drive over for some additional fact-checking. Since Loretta had recommended her as one of the journalists we should consider giving the scoop to in the first place, we were like, 'C'mon in, girl.' She didn't stay long. Draper and I rehashed a lot of what I'd told you, and she was on her way, happy as a clam."

"She must have followed me here when I left the apartment that night…after our fight," Jake explained to Clarke.

Ripon watched them with interest. "I take it the two of you weren't actually working together on the story then?"

"Nope," Jake responded, adding, "I've been scooped by a careerist rat." He turned back to Clarke. "McGreedy always bets on the right horse, and he bet on the one that could get to the finish line quicker in this instance, not to mention the prettier one."

"Sorry about that, dude," Ripon said, giving Jake a consolation clap on the back. "If we'd known, I wouldn't have talked. I've been in your camp from the beginning. It's Draper that's all gaga over Gilchrest."

Jake glanced toward the walk-in coolers. "Do you still have the beef?"

"You betcha," Ripon replied. "He'll be the last thing we relocate."

"And there was nothing in this morning's article about the fact that WOPP had the Silver Steer in its possession?"

"Nope. Mainly because I kind-sorta-intentionally forgot to tell the Gilchrest chick when she came to the farm. Even if I'd told her we had the beef, I doubt she would have believed me without my bringing her back to Little Wisconsin here to prove it. 'Sides, in my book, the Silver Steer belongs to Jake Preston."

"Would you still trust me to take it?" Jake asked.

Ripon weighed her answer carefully. "I s'pose that'd depend on exactly what you'd want to do with it."

"I'd like to do with it exactly what we talked about at headquarters the other night…get it into the hands of a neutral party who can look after it."

"Who'd you have in mind?"

"The only logical choice is the state Republican party. They're the one whose nomination is being contested. They're the only one with jurisdiction, really. And they're the ones most likely to be able to keep it secure until election day. I hate it do it, but if the goal is to put the Silver Steer back in play before the voters forget about it, we've got to get it in the hands of the folks running the show and pulling the strings. Make sense?"

"Totally," Ripon conceded, "on one condition…that you promise not to tie its…"—she grinned mischievously—"its *borrowing* back to one of our members. If we publically declare we swiped it, it'll look like it's become the pet project of an opposition group, and people will turn against it. On the other hand, if you just sorta 'find it,' its legend only grows, you know."

"And this member who filched it…I take it this is someone who deserves your protection," Clarke asked.

Ripon chuckled. "Oh, most definitely. Trust me, this is the most innocent, well-intentioned criminal you've ever known."

Jake nodded toward the cold storage. "So, would you do us the honors?"

"Here she is…uh…here *he* is, the bull of the ball," Ripon said, returning from Little Wisconsin's deep-freeze carrying the prize.

"Go ahead, Herb," Jake offered, "why don't you stick him beneath that jacket that's two sizes too big for you, and we'll get the hell out of Dodge with our silver."

"Will do," the editor said, stuffing the steer into his windbreaker until only the tip of its horns poked through at the collar.

"Good luck tomorrow," Jake said, shaking hands with Ripon. "What time is the official WOPP coming out party?"

"Around 10 AM, on Facebook."

"Now you've got me even more intrigued," Jake said, holding the meatlocker door open for Herb Clarke as together they stepped into the darkened alleyway.

"And Jake," Ripon whispered after him, "as far as the Silver Steer goes, WOPP knows nothing, right?"

"Roger that," he said, smiling as he turned back to Clarke. "Stay here with the goods. I'll bring the getaway car."

"Never mind how I got it," Jake said into the receiver as the road rumbled beneath them. "But I have it…. Yes, I'm 100% sure it's not a fake…. I'll drive it down there tomorrow if you'll restore my full access as the winner of the Up Close contest. Deal? Good. I'll hand-deliver it to you then."

"He sounded relieved," Jake said after he'd disconnected with Pitchford. "Dubious but relieved."

"I don't blame him," Clarke replied. "The key to the state Republican party's stock has just fallen into his undeserving lap. I've known that boy since he was in diapers….he's no dummy."

"What if the Party tries to keep the steer under wraps?" Jake asked.

"Then you go public and demand that they go on record as to whether or not they have it."

"And if they won't?"

"Then you ask if they are willing to swear an oath that they neither have it nor know of its whereabouts. Trust me, if push comes to shove, they'll manage to produce it for public viewing."

Jake whistled appreciatively. "I didn't know you could play this kind of hard-ball, old-timer."

The editor looked pleased. "Remember, I'm an old Army man. We know how to play rough when needs be."

"So what did you make of WOPP?"

"You mean besides their atrocious acronym."

Jake grinned. "Besides that."

"They might actually be on to something," he said after a thoughtful pause. "You know about half of American voters claim not to identify with either party. In effect, they're non-partisan, so they find themselves round pegs in square holes in an era when most of the primaries require them to declare an affiliation. Look at this state. If you want to vote in the Republican primary, you have to declare your affiliation with the party, at least temporarily. That can't be in the best interests of the truly independent-minded voter. Actually, the open primary was the cause célèbre of our senator to the North, Fightin' Bob

La Follette…the closest thing we've had in a few generations to a populist, progressive Midwestern Republican."

"You sound like Mad."

The editor chuckled. "Everyone tells me I sound mad."

"No, I mean you sound like Mad…the bearded guy who tends bar at the Wagon Wheel."

"I know what you mean, Jacob. And as for Mad, I'm flattered by the comparison. Do you know he's the only entrepreneur under 35 who's bought a business in Hereford in the last decade? Not to mention the fact that he has good taste in politicians, and beer."

"But not carpet," Jake pointed out. "That crimson shag of his has got to go."

"We'll chalk his lack of aesthetics up to the follies of youth. In my generation, carpeting something in wall-to-wall red advertised yours as a den of ill-repute."

"So do you agree with Fightin' Bob that voters are more alike than different once they move beyond party politics?"

"Absolutely. As people we mostly want the same things. Fair taxation, manageable public debt, a safe and healthy place in which to raise and educate our children, roads that won't break the axles on our cars and trucks. What we disagree about mostly is how to get there, and that's where the differences between Republicans and Democrats become all too real."

Clarke continued, "You know, the really good marketing firms can predict party affiliation with something approaching certainty just by looking at what kind of alcoholic beverage someone drinks, what kind of radio they listen to, how much they watch television and which shows, or how often they attend church. Then they shamelessly but expertly go about targeting messages toward those niche groups that only serve to reinforce their ideologies. Every so often someone, or something, comes along that breaks those ideologies down and rearranges them completely. That's the sort of person, or the sort of phenomena, we wait generations to see."

"So why does it take so long for that transcendent figure to appear?""

Because the deck is stacked against visionaries in the primary process. Take the Republican candidates for instance. They're forced to run well right of where they really are to appease the conservative base that accounts for the bulk of caucus-goers. The primaries become a contest in who can say the most outlandishly conservative things, while finessing their position just enough that their inevitable move back to center for the general election won't look like outright hypocrisy."

"That's the beauty of our little trophy back there," Herb Clarke added, glancing over his shoulder at the Silver Steer nestled safely in the back seat of Jake's Accord as it sped through the night on its way back to Hereford. "If people would ever rally behind it, anything could happen. I may not always approve of that trophy, but even I have to admit it's worth its weight in gold."

"Or silver," Jake quipped, and together they agreed to let the bad pun die a graceful death.

Ten

Outside the offices of the *Gate*, the traffic on First Street had begun to heat up as Herefordians hurried home from their jobs at the distribution center and at the packing plant at the edge of town.

"Here it is," Herb Clarke said excitedly when Jake walked through the door to his office. "Straight from the newswire."

People Opposed to Partisan Politics, (POPP) formerly Wisconsinites Opposed to Partisan Politics (WOPP), are proud to proclaim our existence as a legitimate and legal voting bloc in the upcoming primary. What began as a movement of several hundred Wisconsiners willing to make the short drive across a shared border to express the strength of their populist convictions has now become a national movement. Individuals who learned of our existence a day ago in the *Times* and *Journal* have begun showing up by the dozens on flights from as far away from Seattle and San Francisco, New York City, and Washington DC in order to "vote with their feet." They recognize that grassroots politics is not a spectator sport, nor is it an exercise in meaningless and arbitrary protest. It is an outgrowth of civility and even domesticity…of informed, involved, and yes sometimes agitated voters taking a stance by growing roots, however temporary, while attempting to redirect an electoral process run amuck through positive, legal action.

POPP is a large and rapidly growing group of concerned citizens and legally registered voters who have relocated within the borders of the state of Iowa in hopes of affecting the outcome of the election in a peaceable manner that demonstrates pervasive voter dissatisfaction with the choices as they are, and the disappointment inherent in the pick-your-poison model of fielding candidates for public office.

POPP reminds our fellow voters that we are all in this together. We are a peace-loving group of friends and neighbors who want to see justice done at the polls. For those living outside the state's borders who would like to join our cause, there is still time to impact this historic election, if you act now. If you cannot join us in person, on the ground, we would gratefully accept your in-kind support. Effectively immediately, POPP will maintain a limited Facebook presence and website through which our progress to reclaim our rightful place within the electoral process will be documented. As of this time POPP has no plans to grant further interviews to the national media.

May the voter prevail.

"It's a good thing WOPP didn't print up fifteen thousand bumper stickers. What do you make of the name change and the statement, Mr. Editor?" Jake asked.

Herb Clarke stroked his chin before reaching a verdict. "It's concise, positive and nonthreatening…in short, I would bet my paycheck that our once quaintly grassroots WOPP has hired a public relations consultant who argued persuasively—and wisely I might add—for both a name change and a more carefully crafted public image."

"So the Big Cheese sold out, you think?"

"The Big Cheese has merely been better and more tastefully aged, you might say," the editor replied wryly. "This is the work of a more mature organization, though not necessarily a better one. WOPP, or POPP, or whatever it is they're calling themselves these days, has clearly gone out of their way to normalize themselves, though I very much doubt their statement will be read as such by the Republican party or the Secretary of State. And you can sure as hell bet POPP has set the FBI on edge."

"Seriously?"

"We underestimate the value of our little corn poll sometimes. But a disruption of any kind in the first-in-the-nation vote…it's not a stretch to call it a threat to national security. It's impossible to imagine what would happen if the caucuses didn't come off, or if there was some egregious error or systematic meltdown. Remember the whole sordid ballot business in Florida? That boiled down to hanging chads and invalidated ballots in a single county, and ended up in the most powerful nation on earth drifting for months without a presumptive leader. Before Bush v. Gore, such an unlikely outcome would have seemed to any sober political observer more the stuff of political fantasy than real-life headlines. And yet it happened all the same."

"Seems like Pitchford and the Secretary of State run a pretty tight ship, though."

"That's what they thought in Palm Beach County in 2000. That's what they assumed in Cuyahoga County in Ohio in

2004, when the Republicans turned up enough surplus votes to somehow defeat John Kerry. Something like that could happen here, Jake, it really could. And if it could happen in Florida, and Ohio, and Iowa, it could happen anywhere…. Anyway, it looks like we've got us a two-fer." Clarke pointed to the tiny television he kept in his office for, as he put it, "research purposes." The screen showed Matt Pitchford taking the podium backdropped by the first-in-the-nation banner which had lately been augmented by a likeness of the Silver Steer.

"The Republican Party of Iowa is pleased to announce that it has, acting on an anonymous tip, located and reacquired the Silver Steer statue that has become the symbol of this election season. From this point forward the trophy will be guarded by the party and secured until after the election on behalf of the voters."

"We would also like to take this opportunity to announce that the final debate of the season to be held next week in Cedar Rapids, Iowa, moderated by Donna Sawyers and George Agropolis, will be rebranded the Silver Steer Debate. More details on that live, interactive event will be forthcoming in coming days on our website and on social media."

Herb Clarke switched off the television set as Pitchford exited the stage without fielding any questions. "If they're feeling enough pressure from WOPP…."

"You mean POPP," Jake interrupted.

"Maybe we should call it WOPP+. In any case, to change the format of the debate on such short notice, you can bet there's some serious soul-searching going on at party headquarters right now. Chuck Sousage has already lost his job over this Silver Steer hot potato. I wouldn't be surprised if Pitchford gets pitched out on his rear end next if he botches things up between here and election day."

"He'll go down fighting, anyway," Jake said. "What's your take on the revamped debate?"

"I'll have to see it before I pass judgment. Besides I have a feeling POPP is just the tip of the iceberg."

"Why's that?"

"Because Dick Folsome, Rochelle Boxman's campaign manager, just sent out an email blast earlier this afternoon announcing that she's holding a primetime press conference of her own this evening."

"Do you think she's going to drop out?"

"Boxman? Heavens no! She'll duke it out until there's no blood left to spill."

"But she's at what, seven percent in the polls?"

"Depends on whom POPP-WOPP puts their votes behind now, doesn't it?" the editor said, a mischievous twinkle in his eye. "If they decide to throw their votes her way, as the candidate least favored by the establishment, she's right back in the game. In any event we should be getting ourselves back home. We've got company coming tonight. If we're going to be finished with dinner by the time Boxman takes the stage, we're going to have to mobilize."

"Company? I thought you were an anti-social bachelor farmer?"

"I am an anti-social widower-farmer-editor. Or is that nuanced difference too much for a black and white brain like yours to handle?"

"All I'm saying is you're slowly but surely ruining your reputation for curmudgeonliness," Jake shot back. "Before you know it, you'll be handing out fruit baskets and inviting the candidates over for a pig roast."

"Don't put it past me," Clarke said, putting on his jacket. "Rest assured, tonight is more about Katie than it is about me. By the way, we're supposed to stop by and pick her up at the café on the way home."

"Let me guess…. I'll end up either setting the table, washing the dishes, or both."

"That was our deal, was it not?" the editor replied. "Chores in exchange for lodging. Count yourself lucky I'm not having you clean the attic."

"How long has it been since we've had a proper dinner guest, Daddy. A year?"

Herb Clarke frowned, too focused on his meal preparations to be bothered with such calculations. "I think Grover Cleveland may have been president."

Jake handed Katie a bowl of freshly diced tomatoes to throw into the gargantuan tossed salad in front of her. "So tell me more about this favorite professor of yours."

"She was actually housed in the history department, but her specialty was elections. All of the political science students had her for at least one class. I had her for four."

"What's she like?"

"Quiet without being shy. Smart. Thoughtful. She's published dozens of books but you wouldn't know it. I guess what I mean to say is she's *real*. Some of the professors I had seemed larger than life, sort of like men and women behind the machine, or behind the podium. Anne seemed like, well…like someone you could have home to dinner!"

"As a rule college professors are full of themselves," grumbled Herb Clarke. "But Anne Templeton is different. I met her at Katie's freshman orientation and liked her from the start. She's always learning…always teaching herself new tricks."

Katie frowned as bits of salad achieved escape velocity, exiting the stainless steel bowl in favor of the pinewood floor of the old farmhouse kitchen. "Anne's been a widow for many years now. "

Jake couldn't resist a good-natured needle. "A further softening of the old gruff exterior, eh, Herb? Imagine…all our quality time in the car together on the way back from Holstein, and you didn't once mention this professorial flame of yours."

Herb frowned. "That's because there's nothing to tell, Jacob. Can't a man respect a woman's accomplishments and youthful, can-do spirit without necessarily implying romantic interest?"

"Daddy doesn't do warm and fuzzy, do you, Daddy?" pitched in Katie.

"I certainly do not…something I'd ask both of you to recall when she arrives, which she should any minute now."

"The thing I don't get," Jake said, putting out the placemats, "is who initiated this invitation? And why now, when things are getting so crazy with the campaigns?"

"It was pretty much synchronicity," Katie explained. "I've been telling Anne she should drive up to the farm for years, but between her busy teaching schedule at the college, and mine at the café, we just couldn't seem to make it happen. The last time she wrote me was right after your Silver Steer question at the debate…around the time Daddy published Marianne Meyers's first Silver Steer column in *The Gate*. In her letter she told me she was on sabbatical this semester and would love to come up. She wondered if she could meet you. And, of course, she asked about Daddy."

Herb Clarke grimaced. "You didn't tell me that."

Katie swatted her father playfully with a kitchen towel. "Because you're not at all interested in her, right? Besides, she said she wanted to tell me in person all about her latest research. I was her research assistant for a couple of terms in college, so we have a history together."

"Having a history with a history professor…now there's a novel concept," Clarke interjected.

"I think that's her now," Katie said. She swung around to face the window overlooking the gravel road, where a single pair of headlights slowed at the mailbox and turned tentatively into the drive. "Now I'm counting on you boys to behave yourselves."

The last piece of Herb Clarke's famous vegetable lasagna, Eva's Purple Ball tomatoes and all, lay uneaten in the oversized casserole dish alongside the night's first emptied bottle of red wine. At long last, Anne Templeton and Herb Clarke had begun to relax into the evening.

"What do you say we retreat into the soft seats?" the editor said, motioning his dinner guests into the living room before seating himself on the edge of the piano bench Katie had requisitioned for extra seating.

"Daddy, will you play for us tonight," she asked, pointing toward the piano. "Would you believe Daddy and I pulled that monstrosity of an antique from the back room of the Wagon Wheel before it was sold?"

"A member of our local history society discovered there was once a speakeasy in the back of our town tavern during Prohibition days," Herb Clarke explained. "And when Katie and I learned there was an old parlor piano there free for the taking, we got out the old truck and trailer and hauled this oversized piece of history back to the farm where, it seems, we have a sympathy for orphans."

"So will you play for us?" Katie repeated. Jake wasn't sure whether to chalk it up to the wine, or the stifling steam heat, but it appeared to him as if the editor blushed.

"Only if Professor Templeton will accompany me with that lovely soprano of hers."

"I'd be delighted to," the professor said, joining Clarke at the bench. "Shall we do a presidential theme song for Jacob...in honor of his first Iowa Caucus?"

The newspaperman struck a few opening notes, and signaled his accompanist with a nod of the head. A moment later the Clarke's parlor came alive with a vintage campaign song whose lyrics Jake was sure he would have remembered had he ever heard them before:

In a quaint New England farmhouse on an early summer's day,
A farmer's boy became our Chief in a homely simple way,
With neither pomp nor pageantry, he firmly met the task,
To keep him on that job of his, is all the people ask.

So "Keep Cool and Keep Coolidge" is the slogan of today,
"Keep Cool and Keep Coolidge for the good old USA.
A lot of politicians cannot do a thing but knock,
But Calvin Coolidge is a man of action and not talk.

So just "Keep Cool and Keep Coolidge" in the White House 4 years more,
We have a chance to do it in the year of '24.
He's been tried, he's never wanting,
He is giving of his best,
So "Keep Cool and Keep Coolidge" is our country's mighty test.

"Not bad for a couple of old geezers," Clarke said after a round of spirited applause from the evening's two audience members. "Always sort of liked Coolidge."

"I hope so," Jake said, "you named your restaurant after the guy…. I've been trying to solve that little mystery ever since I rolled into town."

"Most people do," allowed the editor. "Can't tell you how many passers-thru on First Street do a double take the first time they actually read our sign. I suppose that's part of why I picked the name in the first place…to get the attention of the drive-bys. That and Cal Coolidge was a sleeper, quite literally. The press called him 'Silent Cal.' He once told Ethel Barrymore, 'I think the people want a solemn ass as a president, and I think I will go along with them." Bottom line, Calvin Coolidge was so quiet people hardly noticed when he quietly went about passing civil rights legislation, granting Native Americans citizenship rights, and generally cleaning up the graft and greed of the Harding administration. He was tough on debt, frugal as the day is long, and unflagging in his support of the working class. He was another of our accidental presidents, Jacob—just like Truman—a man who never would have made it to the office of the presidency if Harding, that scandalous adulterer, hadn't died of weak ticker."

"Interesting," Jake said, turning to the professor. "But I have to admit to being even more interested in another sleeper of a candidate."

Anne Templeton looked please. "Which one?"

"I'm dying to know what Silent Katie Clarke was like when she was 21," Jake said, feeling his own face beginning to flush with merlot. "Did she get eleven hours of sleep at night and take two-hour long naps in the afternoon like Silent Cal?"

Dr. Templeton grinned approvingly. "Like Coolidge her reputation only improves with each passing year."

"Do tell, professor…. What was she like?"

"One of my brightest, and at the same time most modest students. Those two things seldom come in the same package. Perhaps she gets it from her father."

"She gets it from her mother," Herb said. "Modesty is not my forté."

"Was she popular?"

Katie mounted a feeble protest. "What is this...a Katie Clarke roast?"

Anne Templeton smiled. "I would lean towards *well-respected.* Katie was a natural leader...she wasn't always willing to make the concessions to win peer approval that would have made her popular in the literal sense, but she was, and is, principled, passionate, and purposeful. I tried to convince her that she should either pursue her considerable talents in writing and photography, or at the very least, consider a career in politics or public service."

"Along with the other frauds, and crooks, and glad-handers," Herb groused. "With all due respect, Professor, I did everything I could to undo your propaganda in that regard. I did my damndest to turn Katie into a journalism major, but the more I nudged her toward it the more she inched away from helping me at the paper and toward Anne's research. Probably was selfish of me, but I wanted her to apply those writing and photography skills at the *Hereford Gate*, so that one day I might hand over the reigns of the paper to her."

Katie looked intently at her father. "Maybe you should have asked me if I was interested. I might have surprised you."

Anne Templeton laughed. "Kate seemed resistant to a political path as well, and far too modest to effectively market herself and her work as a photographer, so eventually I gave up trying to persuade her of either of those two career options, and instead we focused on doing historiographies together, didn't we, Katie?"

"I always found it safer to be hidden away in books," Kate admitted, "rather than blathering on about my photography or standing at a bully pulpit for everyone to see. I guess I had seen the toll being a lightning rod in the community took on Daddy. History offered some anonymity to me."

"You know the perfect person to ask about career options," Jake said, topping off all of their glasses with the last of the red wine, "Dolph Heinrich. He went from being a history professor, to a state senator, to a college president, to a US congressman, to a popular author, to a candidate for president."

"Oh, Dolphus," Templeton said, looking off into a far-off corner of the ceiling as if she might find the candidate himself there spinning webs. "You know Dolph was a colleague of mine once."

Herb Clarke's ears perked up. "For God's sake where?"

"At Southwest Illinois State. It was my first professorship out of graduate school. He was a star. Even then you could tell he was much too big a fish for such a small academic pond. As faculty speaker he'd give these long, impassioned speeches that, looking back on them now, were nothing short of rhetorical genius."

"Tell us more," Clarke urged.

"Not surprisingly he made everyone around him uncomfortable. I dare say he was loathed by some inside the history department, though we universally acknowledged his gifts. Actually, though anyone with any intuition could see he was destined for better things, I, for one, thought public life would be out of the question for him, especially given the nature of his research."

"Which was what?" Jake inquired. "Attempts at political cloning?"

The professor laughed. "No, his specialty then was seditionist and secessionist movements in American history. He was fascinated with states that had pulled out of the federal system and decided to go it on their own."

"Like South Carolina in the Civil War?" Jake offered, hoping to impress.

"On an elementary level, yes. But perhaps Dolph's greatest contribution was pointing out how frequently these secessionist movements have cropped up in American history, and how, even when they failed, they shaped the nation's politics for many years to come."

"An example, if you please, dear professor," Herb Clarke prompted.

"My favorite is the Lost State of Franklin," the professor said in a tone that made it seem as if she might be confessing a long-held romantic crush.

"Never heard of it," Jake admitted.

"Very few have," she continued. "To make a long story short, not too long after the Revolutionary War, Franklin seceded from North Carolina and operated for a few years as a quasi fourteenth state, with its own constitution, governor, militia, you name it. In their way the Frankliners were radicals, but like most secessionists they were surprisingly learned, well-schooled men who were intensely proud of their home region, and didn't want to see it overruled, and unfairly taxed, by a remote government…in Franklin's case, the remote government across the Appalachians in North Carolina."

"Where was their capital?" Herb asked.

"For most of Franklin's history it was located in what is now Jonesbourgh, Tennessee. They actually had the audacity to set up their own houses of government a few doors down from their overlords from North Carolina. Anyway, the Frankliners saw things their own way. The first draft of their constitution barred doctors, lawyers, and preachers from running for public office, ostensibly due to the egalitarian impulse that ran so thoroughly through early Appalachia. Instead of having a central currency they insisted on the democratization of coinage. Bartering was actually the de facto unit of currency. You could use tobacco, furs, skins, liquor, farm animals, almost anything of truly local value as accepted legal tender. What Franklin really was, in so many ways, was an experiment in rule by the people rather than rule by the elites."

"Fascinating," Clarke commented as he leaned back in his chair. "Anne, will you come back for dinner next month, after the election is over, and regale us further?"

"I'd be delighted to," the professor said, adjusting the napkin in her lap. "And in the meantime I'll see if I can dig up Dolph's old paper and bring it along with me. It was never formally published, just circulated among a few of his colleagues for comment and critique. I think he was fishing for positive reaction, and when some of us responded with trepidation and even fear, he wisely decided to shelf it."

Herb Clarke rose to pour everyone a round of decaf. "We'd better have our next course in front of the boob tube if we're going to catch Rochelle Boxman's proclamation…. Homemade apple cobbler is on the counter. Help yourself."

In the living room Katie had already turned on the TV to the face of Bambi Bloomberg, who had dropped her daytime talk-show persona for the more sober visage of an evening news reporter. "Ms. Boxman's speech marks the first time a candidate in the Iowa Caucuses has bought a primetime slot to address potential voters. The purchase price for the time bloc is estimated to run in the millions, a substantial amount of the dwindling cash reserves of the Boxman campaign. As they say in the Midwest, she's putting her eggs in one basket."

"Utter foolishness if you ask me," Herb groused.

"But great fodder for political historians," the professor said, raising her cobbler-covered fork in tribute.

"Shhhh," Katie said, "she's beginning…"

> Ladies and gentlemen, fellow patriots, yesterday we learned of the existence of a group of what is being called "sleeper voters," within Iowa's borders, and I immediately booked time to address each of you on this importance issue. Since that time I, like you, have sought to understand the implications of this movement for our rapidly changing political landscape.
>
> Why would a group of concerned citizens uproot their families and their lives to live, work, and mobilize hundreds of miles away from where they keep their home fires burning? Over the last 24 hours I, like you, have tuned in as the pundits have ascribed to these fascinating citizens any number of motivations, many of them bordering on sinister. In fact, in vigorous discussions with my own campaign staff, our first instinct

was to dismiss this grassroots movement as a form of radicalism to be feared if not combated.

Fortunately, calmer minds prevailed within the Boxman camp, and I stand before you tonight urging you to consider the patriotism of this daring if not unorthodox group. In history books we read about the band of so-called radicals that became our founding fathers. We know that King George roundly condemned them as heretics, rebels, usurpers, even terrorists. And yet history reveals them to be our guiding lights, our patron saints in the political sense, not to mention the founders of our God-blessed Republic.

I was informed by my campaign manager that he had been contacted by a group from my home state of South Dakota calling itself SOD. Indeed, their acronym, Southers Organized for Democracy, or SOD for short, proclaims their proud embrace of a pioneering heritage in which their ancestors lived in sod homes and faced the most difficult conditions possible on an unforgiving prairie. For those of you who haven't traveled to my beautiful state, "Southers" is an affectionate nickname given us by the North Dakotans, and a term that also signifies a strong and forceful prairie wind. And that is what I believe this organization to be…a force for the winds of change.

Some five hundred strong of these SODS have already pledged to cross state lines in time to legally vote in the upcoming Iowa Caucuses, inspired by the powerful example of POPP before them. Immediately before I came on air tonight, my campaign manager,

Dick Folsome, was notified by a mutual contact that the first 'platoon' of three hundred strong had crossed the Missouri River at Council Bluffs. Again, while I do not align myself with this or any other movement, nor endorse the actions of my fellow Southers, I urge you not to vilify these proud patriots, who in many cases have left their families to live in our midst, becoming in effect strangers in a strange land.

Demographers tell us that many of you within reach of my voice this evening live within an hour's drive of a state border. You cross state boundaries regularly for work or for recreation, or to purchase groceries, or gasoline, or lottery tickets. Many of you have relatives living in neighboring states, relatives you love dearly and visit frequently despite what arbitrary boundaries may lie between you and them. As events unfold in the weeks remaining until Iowans cast their vote for the man or woman destined to become our next president, I urge you to sympathize with these new and visionary neighbors in our midst, knowing that they are driven not by greed, creed, or a desire for publicity, but to simply to share in the privileges Iowans are endowed with each and every four years—namely the right to cast a difference-making vote in a primary destined to impact the future course of our Republic, and therefore the world.

As your families begin washing the dishes after dinner this evening, doing homework, and packing lunches for tomorrow's long day at work or school, recall that we are all the children of God entitled to a vote in His kingdom.

Thank you again, good night, and God bless.

"Well," Katie said, reaching for the remote to mute the onslaught of post-press conference punditry, "what do our in-house experts think?"

Dr. Templeton scooted to the very edge of the couch cushions, her eyeglasses reflecting the image of the beatific Boxman on the screen. "What we may be seeing tonight is the further unraveling of the caucus system."

"What exactly do you mean, Anne?" Herb asked.

"What I mean is POPP and SOD are slowly, inexorably moving us toward a regional vote, which is the only logical outcome of the hyper-mobile, fiscally able activists and ideologues who are turning what used to be a single state's provincial election into a regional and national referendum."

The professor paused, searching for just the right words. "It's perhaps easier to understand by analogy. Suppose someone in Chicago is a huge fan of Iowa Hawkeye football."

"There are tens of thousands of them, unfortunately," Herb said. "And half of them have almost run me over on the Interstate with their lead foot."

"Imagine you're one of them, then. You live in Winnetka, or Lake Forest, or Joliet. You've got plenty of money, a top-of-the-line car, and no problem taking off from work early on a Friday afternoon. Indeed, chances are good that you probably got your degree from the University of Iowa, and supported it to the tune of tens of thousands of out-of-state tuition dollars. And you want to buy season tickets to cheer on your Hawkeyes, as would any other supporter. You're willing to make the drive to act on your allegiances, despite having plenty of choices for other teams to root for back in Chicago. Why should you be prevented from exercising your loyalties?"

"It's an interesting analogy," Herb conceded. "But I'm not convinced by it, not yet. The difference is that South Dakota and Wisconsin have their own elections, so there's no need to make a grab for ours."

"Just as Chicagoans have dozens of college and university football teams. But for reasons that are clear to all of us in this room, some folks are bound and determined to be Hawkeyes.... Herb, do you happen to know the date of the most recent South Dakota primary? I didn't think so, and yet as a newspaper editor surely you're twice, if not five times as politically literate as the average Midwesterner. In case you're wondering, South Dakotans don't get their say-so until early June—fully six months after our first-in-the-nation vote is held here. By then the nominee has already been anointed, if not by the number of pledged delegates, then by popular opinion. So the votes of these 'Southers' don't much count in the end."

"So Boxman is angling for the WOPP-SOD vote?"

"The POPP-SOD vote, and yes, it would appear so, Jacob," Herb said, sighing deeply. "It's a risky strategy, though... depending on and in some ways defending groups that might well steal the election, or tip it, while at the same time refusing to align herself with them. Even if POPP and SOD send all of their votes her way, she may not make up for the votes she's likely to lose from the natives who don't care to see their vote thrown to the Mongol hordes invading from the North and West."

"I think you may be underestimating her, Daddy," Katie ventured. "Let's assume the turnout this year is about what it's been in the past, 100,000 or so for easy figuring. Boxman is polling now at just under 10%, so that's about 10,000 votes. If POPP throws their protest vote to her as the most marginalized candidate, and SOD does the same, she could easily increase her share of the vote to close to 15,000 and that, given a large and diverse field like this year's, might well be enough to push her over the top."

In his head Jake worked on the math. "Here's the thing. Since when have you known South Dakotans and Cheeseheads to agree on anything? If POPP goes one way, SOD likely goes another. And if Boxman's stock in the polls looks like it might be rising, POPP might anoint someone else as its queen of unelectability."

"Like whom?" Katie said.

"Like Renard Kane, or, more likely, Professor Templeton's old colleague, Dolph Heinrich."

"One thing's for certain," Clarke said, rising from the couch for the first time since Boxman dropped her electoral bombshell. "We're not going to solve all the world's problems tonight. And as the oldest member of our little political coalition here, I'm afraid I'm going to have to retire and leave the further punditry to you young 'uns. And that includes you, Anne."

"What am I...a whole ten years younger than you, Herbert?"

"And infinitely more youthful," he said, kissing the back of her hand as she stood to see him go. "Thank you for coming. And good luck with that sabbatical of yours."

"Good luck to you with your election coverage," she said, holding the editor's hand warmly in her own.

"Alright, kids," Clarke said turning off the overhead light and ambling toward the stairs. "Leave the dishes until morning. Maybe the Silver Steer will do them for us."

"I suppose I should be going, too," sighed the professor after the editor had said his final good-byes from the top of the stairs and disappeared into the bedroom. "It's a long drive back to Des Moines and my eyes aren't what they used to be. Too much time spent in the archives…at least that's what my optometrist tells me."

"Can we get you something for the road?" Katie offered.

"Are you kidding? Any more calories tonight and the state patrol is likely to find me on the shoulder of Interstate 35 in a food coma No, I'm afraid it's time for this old political historian to hit the road. Please thank Herb again, from the bottom of my heart, for the homemade lasagna dinner. The tomatoes were divine."

"Green Zebras," Jake called after the professor as she found her way through the darkness of the barnyard to her car. "They're heirlooms!"

"Not unlike me," Anne Templeton called over her shoulder. "You two sleep tight, and may the steer be with you."

"And also with you," Kate called out, as the professor stuck her hand out the car window, and waved her last warm good-byes in the crimson glow of the brake lights.

Eleven

"Welcome back, everyone, to the final debate before the eagerly anticipated first-in-the-nation vote just two weeks from today," Donna Sawyers said, turning on the charm. "George, the third and final installment of tonight's debate is going to be something completely different."

"It certainly will be something," Agropolis said, raising his trademark furry eyebrows.

"So different, in fact, that we've decided to call it the Silver Steer Debate in honor of the trophy that has become the unlikely symbol of this spirited yet unorthodox campaign season. But that's just the beginning of what's different about tonight's debate."

"That's right, Donna," Agropolis said, taking the baton and running with it. "In this final installment Iowans from all walks of life stand ready to pose their questions to our candidates via live recording, identifying themselves by name and hometown only. And to make things still more little more interesting, we've asked the candidates to address their responses not to one of us, as tonight's moderators, but to the Silver Steer standing before us as a symbol of the shared concerns of the broader electorate…. So are you ready to play Silver Steer, Donna?"

"Ready as ever, George."

"Then let's get started. Everyone at home, now's the time to open up your email accounts, turn on your phones, key in your

Twitter hashtags, and submit to us the questions weighing most heavily on your minds. Tonight, we ask that you be as insistent and determined as our Silver Steer here in making certain that your particular questions get answered. This evening we're steering…"

"No pun intended, right George?"

"Right, Donna."

"…we're steering away from the questions these candidates have heard so often on the campaign trail…the hot-button issues if you will…in favor of questions that speak directly to who we are as voters, and who these candidates are as people. Donna, has our crack staff selected the first question posed by a viewer at home?"

"They have indeed, George. This first question comes from Kurt. Can we have the recording of Kurt posing his question?"

"Hello, candidates, here's my Silver Steer question: what would you do to make our small towns more lively and more interesting for people like me in their twenties and thirties. Most of our small towns shut down after dinner. It's no wonder young people move to places like California and Florida."

"Great lead-off question, Kurt," Sawyers enthused. "By virtue of our draw before the show, Renard Kane will have the first crack at answering the Silver Steer."

"Let me just say," Renard Kane began, "how happy I am to be here competin' for this hunk of silver sirloin. Down in Birmingham, Alabama, we'd slow cook 'im and serve 'im up with some homemade barbeque sauce. But seriously, Kurt…"

"Please address your responses to the Silver Steer," Agropolis reprimanded, patting the statue atop its horns as a visual reminder.

Kane repositioned his glasses. "Let me try that again, folks.... What would I do to liven up small-town life so people would stay, hmmm…I guess I'd begin by opening up the church in the evenings. The church is the lifeblood of the Black community."

"In all fairness, Mr. Kane," Sawyers interjected, "what if Kurt isn't Black, or especially religious, or doesn't feel comfortable socializing in church groups?"

"Then I'd tell him he'd have a helluva lot more fun with the Lord in his life." The businessman from Birmingham rocked back on the heels of his wingtips, wearing a self-satisfied look.

"And what about you Paul Paule?" Agropolis asked, turning to the gray-haired congressman who had once been a family physician. "What would you do to make small-town life more invigorating for young people?"

"I came of age in the Fifties," Paul Paule said, giving the Silver Steer a toothy grin. "We didn't believe in fun and excitement back then.... So, that's a tough problem, but I'd say you might have to reconsider what fun is. For us, fun was cruising the loop in a '57 Chevy. Or going to the river, fishing, maybe running the track at midnight. So I'd tell the young man not to have such high expectations… to be grateful for what he has."

"Thank you Mr. Paule. What about you Congressman Heinrich?"

Dolph Heinrich grinned impishly. "You know I've got to confess that at first I thought this Silver Steer stuff was a bunch of baloney, but now I'm beginning to enjoy it. What would a Heinrich administration do to make small-town and rural life more fun in places like Iowa and Wisconsin and South Dakota? First, I'd invest in our fiber optics, making it possible for cultural events in nearby communities to be viewed live right from the local small town café, community center, or convenience store. Second, I'd bring back interurban baseball."

"Baseball, Mr. Heinrich?" Sawyers asked.

"If it was good enough to help our Heartland towns forget their troubles in the Great Depression, it's good enough to help the Millennials forget the staggering loss of jobs they've suffered under a Democrat administration. Lastly—and focusing here on ideas now that would cost little or no additional money—I'd gather small-town mayors together at a regional conference, and I'd say, 'You know what…it's far more cost-effective to keep young parents and taxpayers in your town than to cede them to the nearest big city. So here's a limited pool of funds, and a streamlined application process…. Now you tell me what your homegrown ideas are for solving the outmigration problem. After all, you know your young people better than anyone."

"Time, Mr. Heinrich," Donna Sawyers interrupted. "Well, Round One went swimmingly, don't you think, George?"

"I do, Donna."

"Now, while a few candidates have been busying telling us how they'd enliven life in the underzied villages of the Middle Weest, our editors have been hard at work choosing the next voice recording of a live question from a viewer at home. Cue Question 2, folks." Sawyer pushed a button on the table in front of her, while, on the giant screen behind the candidates an animated version of the Silver Steer stomped and cavorted about. "Here's an interesting question from a gentlemen with an interesting name…Mad…from the now-famous town of Hereford, Iowa. And yet his question doesn't seem mad to me at all. Roll the tape please…"

"Candidates, in the last few days we've learned of two groups who have relocated to Iowa to lawfully participate in the first-in-the-nation-vote here. What is your position on such cross-border activism?"

"Senator Santoro, why don't you be the first one to take a shot at this thorny question," Agropolis offered.

"No problem, George. It's a fair question and one that I think all of us must grapple with. I'll be honest, these shadow groups are too new for me or my staff to comment on formally. But because I don't want to be caught giving the Silver Steer a load of bull crap on national television, let me share my gut feeling." Santoro paused long enough to let the drama of the moment become palpable. "As most of you know my wife Christine and I moved to the Hawkeye State more than six months ago to establish residency in a little town called Goodacre. In fact, we voted in our first local election as 'Iowans' last fall. As a citizen in a free country it's my right to move anywhere that's best for me, my family, or my career, and as long as I do so legally, within the laws set by the state, I feel called upon to vote my conscience. You know, we Republicans are traditionalists, and we're bull-dogs when it comes to law and order, but sometimes we need to realize that the law works two ways, providing all voters equal access even if they do and say things we traditionalists don't care for. So in case the Silver Steer is wondering, I say, so long as they're peaceable, bring on the political tourists and the electoral sleeper cells!"

"Rochelle Boxman, that brings us to you."

"Hello, Silver Steer, you handsome devil you! And hello to all of you watching at home. We send you warm Midwestern greetings. Now, as to the POPPS and SODS of this election, I agree with Senator Santoro…. I think it's fun. It makes the results more volatile, and while that's hard on us as candidates, it's more fun for you at home keeping score in your living room. Am I right? Let's hear it for the Silver Steer!"

"Thank you, Ms. Boxman. Your answer brings us nearly to the end of tonight's first segment. But before we go to our first extended commercial break, I'd like to squeeze in a third question. This once comes to the Silver Steer from Julie. Here is the recording."

"Candidates, some have said this is the largest and yet the weakest field assembled in many a caucus season. More and more people report wanting different choices. My question, then, is this: would you be open to something completely different this election cycle, for example a rule change in the way we choose our leaders?"

"Kudos to our producers," Agropolis said, "for selecting such a timely and provocative question. Candidates, we won't have time to hear from all of you on this one, so let's start with tonight's frontrunner, Milt Cloward. Mr. Cloward, how would you answer this Silver Steer of a question?"

"George," Cloward said, standing up straighter at his lectern, "around home, I'm a heck of a fun guy…. I can even be loose on occasion. But at some point we all have to play by the rules as written. You know, Blanche and I have been married forty-three years this July. Have there been times when one or both of us have wanted to change the rules of our union completely…for instance, just leave our five boys with their grandparents so we could jet off to Aruba. You bet! Was it within our power to do so? Absolutely. Should we have? Absolutely not. You see, sometimes we have to choose between two options we don't like very well, knowing that only we are to blame if we don't like the options as they are. So, no, I wouldn't support any changes to our current election procedures."

"Renard Kane," Sawyers said, inserting herself into the conversation, "you're running a close third to Mr. Cloward and Mr. Santoro in the polls right now and are known to be an unusually relaxed campaigner. What do you say on this issue?"

"Donna, you can break it to the bull there that I agree with Milt on this. You know, when we all agreed to compete for the Steer, I was willing to get on that cow and ride, so to speak. Now I've ridden it for a couple of weeks, and let me tell you it's been a wild, wild ride, and it's time to just settle down and live a little less dangerously. You know the wildest rides always look like they're gonna be the best, but you ride 'em and you end up losing your lunch, you know what I'm sayin'? No, I would not get behind any further changes to the current elections system."

"And you, Mr. Santoro? You're running a close second to Mr. Cloward. Are you up for a complete 180?"

"No, George, I am not. Despite what some folks think, politics isn't show biz. We're public servants, not movie stars. It's fair to ask a lot of us, and as we go from town to town, people do. But the difference between us and the stars people see when they go to the cineplex is that we're playing ourselves. So, no, if voters want to be disgruntled and have a chip on their shoulder about how we're not good enough candidates, let them go ahead and voice their dissatisfaction at the polls. It's like the last scene in the movie, you know, and if you haven't headed for the exit by now, you might as well stay and see it through, even if you don't like the outcome. I'm pretty sure nobody on this stage tonight is going to be handing out rain checks or refunds."

"Dolph Heinrich, I'm afraid yours will have to be the last word on this issue, as we've run out of time."

"You know, I'm standing here listening to my esteemed colleagues, and I've got to say I think they're dead wrong. The Silver Steer is all about change, and for us to stand up here, dig in our heels, and say we won't change; go ahead and pick the lesser of evils because the election is just over two weeks away is, in my mind, as heartless and hopeless as saying, 'Just throw in the towel, because you're sick and you don't have a prayer of getting better anytime soon.' Those kinds of take-it-or-leave-it ultimatums aren't going to bring anyone new to the polls or to our party. And, to use Senator Santoro's metaphor, I don't think we'd have gone to see that bummer of a movie if it had been fairly advertised in the first place. So, yes, if the party decides they want to make an eleventh-hour change in the way we run this race, and that change is affirmed by sound public opinion data, so long as we all play by the same rules, I'd be for it, whatever it is."

As the correspondents left their workstations to grab a few extra interviews in the makeshift spin room, Jake searched the crowd for Mort McGreedy. Normally, he could pick out the disheveled giant across a crowded convention hall, but tonight was pure journalistic Armageddon. The only way for Jake to catch journalism's Big Fish was to string his net across the pressroom's only door, the one beside the fake potted plant.

"Like pigs to slaughter," McGreedy grumped when finally Jake intercepted him. "It's getting worse every year. The bigger the politicians get the more sycophants they attract." He stopped, switching gears. "Upset about the WOPP story, I take it?"

Jake did his best to reign in his temper. "You know, I used to idolize you, McGreedy. Now I realize you're exactly like all the others you claim to hate, only worse. Most of these people," Jake said, spinning around to indicate the mostly empty newsroom, "would go to just about any length to get a scoop, but they wouldn't stab a colleague in the gut over it."

"Bullshit," McGreedy sputtered. "I could point you to a dozen guys in the room tonight who have joyfully scooped me over the years, and would gladly walk across my moldering, decomposing corpse to take my job. There's another half dozen who have impugned me, several more who I know for a fact have tried to get me fired, and one who gleefully slept with my now ex-wife."

"Let me make sure I understand your logic…. They're jerks and assholes, so that entitles you to be one as well?"

McGreedy shrugged. "You won't see things from my perspective, Mr. Sweepstakes Winner, until you've actually been on the payroll at a dog-eat-dog, shit-on-the-reporter daily newspaper."

Jake grabbed McGreedy by the sleeve of his jacket as the big man attempted to push past him in the hall. "Are you going to tell me why you swindled me out of my story or not?"

The oversized scribbler looked down menacingly at the hand on his sleeve. "I've got two minutes to indulge your asinine need for closure before I miss my filing deadline. In the meantime I suggest you *take your hand off me.*"

"So you sold me down the river in favor of Amethyst Gilchrest?"

"First off, she's got a better ass than you do," snorted McGreedy. "More importantly, though, she came to me first with the pitch."

"How is that even possible? I know for a fact she was at least a half hour behind me getting back to Hereford that night after tailing Katie and me to Holstein."

"What time did we meet at the bar?" McGreedy asked rhetorically.

"Shortly before midnight."

"And what time did you get back from your little nocturnal interview-rendezvous with WOPP?"

"About 10:30."

"So while you basked in the afterglow with your lady friend before deciding to meet me at the Wheel, congratulating yourself all the while on the manna that had been dropped in your lap, Amethyst got in at eleven, drove straight to my apartment, and showed up at my door saying she had a story that had the potential to blow the lid off this campaign. She had the notes, the interviews…she just wanted someone of my…shall we say experience…to make sure we handled the anonymous sources correctly and to share the blame if something went wrong . She sealed the deal while you were still putting on your make-up to meet me…. You snooze you lose in this business, Preston."

"Didn't you think it was a bit odd that I called you a half-hour after she arrived at your apartment with the same story?"

"Strange…maybe, exceptional…not at all. You know how many times I've had sources tell me all hush-hush and on the down-low that they were offering an exclusive, and the very next morning I see the same story splashed across the nation's front pages under a half dozen different bylines? I just assumed you and Amethyst had both been given the same tip, and she beat you to the punch."

"And yet you still agreed to meet me at the bar. You even allowed me to pay for your whiskey."

McGreedy smiled wryly. "I didn't ask you to pay for my booze. You volunteered. I did what any good reporter would do. I heard your story, and tried my damndest to see what part of it squared with Amethyst's. I even helped you write your damned awful copy, pro bono."

"So why did you agree to share a byline with me if you had every intention of following through with Amethyst?"

"Because I couldn't quite bring myself to break your yellow, sentimentalist's heart," McGreedy harrumphed. "Besides, I figured you'd figure it out for yourself when you saw the next day's papers. Look, if you've got a beef with anyone, it should be Gilchrest."

"Where is she?"

"How should I know? Probably scooping us both on a post-debate interview right now. Look, I'm sorry you had to get your lunch handed to you this way, Preston. My suggestion… pay close attention, so when it happens again, you'll be ready." He winked, disappearing down the hallway into the spin room.

"I take it that didn't go so well."

Jake spun around to see the familiar face of Herb Clarke, who stood before him holding a battered leather attaché case. "On the positive side, the Silver Steer just produced the most substantive debate yet, wouldn't you agree?"

"Yeah," Jake said, still stewing over McGreedy's unrepentant slings and arrows. He had expected—wrongly as it turned out—for the big grizzly to at least feign an apology once cornered. "What's your post-debate analysis?" Jake asked, trying to keep his mind off Amethyst's latest Judas act.

"I thought it was one small step for the *demos*."

"The what?"

"The *demos*, Jacob. It's Greek for the people of the state." Clarke patted him on the shoulder. "Trust me, something will come of tonight's little exercise in egalitarianism. I can feel it in my old reporter's bones…. Come on, let's go watch the campaign surrogates spin this thing. If you ask me, the only who didn't get dinged by that last question was Dolph Heinrich."

Dolph Heinrich, Jake thought to himself as he followed the editor into the fray, *the secessionist king.*

Twelve

"After last night's debate it is painfully clear to me that I can no longer remain a part of the Republican party."

Jake Preston looked on as a newly resolved Chuck Sousage, Mr. Breakfast Patty, endeavored to sever ties with the party for whom he had been a mouthpiece for as long as anyone could remember.

"What was it about last night's debate, specifically," a reporter asked, "that caused this decisive break?"

Sousage pondered the question. "I realized that, to a man and woman, they're all hopelessly enmeshed in the political machine. A viewer asked them whether they would favor changes in the election rules. And instead of asking what she might have in mind, or imagining what changes might be needed, they all piled on and said, no way…absolutely not. It's got to be the way it always was. Their posturing reminds me of the defensiveness of Donald Rumsfeld's quote during the Gulf War: 'You go to war with the army you have, not the one you might wish you had.' Here we have the same old company line. We can't change it now, they say, because that would be too much too soon. They then proceed to do nothing so they can pull the same trick at the eleventh hour of the next election cycle."

"A follow up if I may, sir. Could you blame the reporters in this room if they are a bit puzzled by what seems like your rather dramatic change of heart? Many of us have known you as a staunch supporter of the party line for more than two decades, and now all of a sudden you're asking us to believe you're disowning it."

Sousage flexed his empathetic muscles. "I don't blame you for your incredulity. But surely you understand that sometimes the veil gets lifted. As the Bible tells us, 'The people who walk in darkness will see a great light; Those who live in a dark land, the light will shine on them.' What can I say? I've lived in a dark political land for more than twenty years, but I'm not going to live in a dark land any more."

Another reporter raised his hand. "Will you be formally aligning yourself with the Democratic party?"

"Hell no," Sousage fired back, sounding briefly like his old, fiery self again. "The Democrats aren't one iota better. If I'm aligning myself with anyone, it's the voter at home who's sick and dog-tired of all the politician's evasions and obfuscations. I should know, because over the years I wrote more than my fair share of those duck-and-dodge statements."

Jake raised his hand, all the while fearing Sousage still held a grudge against him for the Silver Steer question that had lost the media relations guru his job in the first place.

"Does your change of heart have anything to do with rise of the Silver Steer?"

"Sure it does, Jake. I realized last night at the debate how much just having that piece of hardware, something the candidates actually had to face that wasn't a moderator they secretly hated or some carefully pre-selected studio audience member offering up a canned and carefully vetted question, has done to break things open. As the political cliché goes, the Silver Steer has leveled the playing field."

"What are your future plans?" asked a familiar voice Jake knew without even turning around…Amethyst Gilchrest.

"I plan to reengage the political process," Sousage said. "This time from outside of the existing party structure. Exactly what the nature of that involvement will be, I can't yet say. I'm hoping to continue to dialogue with folks who seek my input on how this broken political process can be bent to better serve."

"So you're saying individuals have already contacted you to serve in a consultative role?"

"Possibly," Sousage replied, slippery as ever. "What I can tell you is that I will not be working directly for any of the current candidates seeking the nomination for president."

The one-time PR guru turned anti-establishment champion looked around the room. "I'm afraid that's all the questions I've got time for, folks. But I hope to see all of you out there on the campaign trail. This election is too important for any of us to stand idly by and watch it go to the dogs again."

Jake heard the faux click of dozens of digital cameras snapping shots as Sousage waved, smiling broadly, before disappearing out the back door of the conference room.

As he watched him go, Jake felt a tap on his shoulder.

"Still pissed at me I suppose," Amethyst ventured.

She looked different. A new hairstyle maybe? Or had she just put a new pair of smart, sassy eyeglasses into the rotation?

"Do you actually want me to dignify that with a response?" Jake replied after a long pause. "Where in the hell have you been?"

"My mom passed away," she said, looking down at the floor. "I've been in New York the last few days helping my sisters tie up loose ends."

"Sorry to hear that."

"Me, too." A tear wandered down Amethyst Gilchrest's cheek. "She's the reason I got interested in political journalism in the first place. She practically raised me on CNN. Wolf Blitzer was like an uncle or something." She attempted a smile. "Anyway, here I am again…. Listen, I had a lot of time to think over the last few days, and I'm truly sorry for what I did to you. It was a low point in my career."

"You followed me, didn't you, after I got that letter at your place from WOPP?"

"Of course I did," she said. "When you said you were leaving to report on a story I knew something important was in that letter. You never leave on a story, especially not after dinner. And I knew there weren't any big media events scheduled for that night. So I did what any good reporter would do…. I gumshoed."

"But you didn't have a car."

"I borrowed McGreedy's…kind of without asking," she admitted.

"Are you going to reprint a retraction?"

She shook her head. "It was good reporting, Press. I did the follow-up and clean-up myself after you, per usual, left the scene early, and McGreedy and I wrote the copy on our own. Actually, I wrote 95% of it while McGreedy ate beer nuts and bitched about the state of the world. It isn't plagiarized…. It isn't falsified. To put it bluntly, you were scooped. There's nothing retraction-worthy in that." She paused, eyeing him carefully. "But you do have my personal apology. I was telling my sisters as we were sorting through Mom's things how awful I felt about it…about the way I treated you."

"Doesn't change the fact it was a low-down, dirty, sneaky, no-good thing to do," Jake said.

"Is there anything I can do to make it up to you?"

"Not that I can think of at the moment. The good news is, I was reinstated by the party, so I've got my credentials back."

"I figured," Amethyst said, "or you wouldn't be here. I'm guessing the 'emerging threat' of POPP and SOD to the status quo turned the Silver Steer, and therefore you, from a liability back into an asset, so the party brought you back into the fold."

"Pretty much. Only this time it's without strings attached."

"There are always strings attached, Press," Amethyst said, resting her arm on his shoulder. "Anyway, gotta go video-chat my sis. We've got a conference call set up with mom's estate attorney."

"Good luck with that," Jake said, meaning it sincerely, in spite of everything.

"Good to see you," she said over her shoulder. "By the way," she added as she reached the door. "The air mattress is still open if you need it."

"Press, how have you been?"

On the other end of the line Jake Preston's editor at the *Rocky Mountain Partisan*, Geoff Hickenlooper, sounded more energetic than usual. It was the first time in weeks Jake had heard his former boss's voice.

"What's up?" Jake asked, knowing Hick well enough to know he'd just as soon cut to the chase anyway.

"Got a letter here yesterday I thought you would want to know about."

"You open it, Hick?"

"Nope. It's addressed to you in care of the *Partisan*.

Good old Hickenlooper, Jake thought, *the last man on earth who played it by the book.*

"Go ahead and open it then."

On the other end of the line Jake heard the telltale sound of an envelope being ripped open, followed by the requisite rustling of paper and, finally, the long pause as his boss…ex-boss, unlikely friend…all the things Hick was to him…absorbed its contents.

"One of your fans apparently," Hick concluded. "Postmark's too smudged to make out. Somebody wanting you to view their Youtube page."

Jake rolled his eyes. "Uh-huh."

"Just a minute." More sounds of paper being shuffled coupled with the sounds of a couple dozen exploratory mouse clicks.

Then, in the background, a voice.

"This Is The Steer," a computer-generated voice began. "We are a citizens group determined that the voice of the everyday voter be heard. In the last debate the candidates spoke directly to voters via a statue known as the Silver Steer. Regrettably the steer did not have a chance to talk back. So we packed our cameras and went out to find out what the real Silver Steer had to say. And because he's camera-shy we shot him in partial darkness to protect his anonymity. Here is what he said to us, and by extension to you."

Hick paused the video as, hundreds of miles way, Jake listened close. "Do you want to hear what the cow has to say?" he asked.

"Let 'er rip, Hick."

Politics as usual belongs to a past where overlords and pedigreed elites make decisions for us. They told us how elections would work, and we blindly followed. They told us who the finalists would be, and we picked the least offensive. They told us if we didn't like the poison we picked we should stand by for four or eight years while *our* collective mistake, which was really their treachery, bankrupted a nation.

They all say the same thing. *I* say a different thing. I say down with the proxies and the middle men who are supposed to represent us, and don't. I say up with real democracy, where the people dictate the process rather than the process shackling and suffocating the people. Up with real choice not the lesser of two evils.... Over the next two weeks I will be recording several messages I hope you will take to heart. In the meantime let us take control of our own electoral fates.

"What do you see on your screen now, Hick?"

"Exactly what the video said…. It's a low-light shot of a bull…or a steer…in a stall. Shot straight on. You can barely make out the thing chewing its cud, then the computer-altered voice comes in."

"Anything in the comments field below?"

"Let me see…. Looks like the video was just uploaded 12 hours ago. There have only been a couple of views."

"Read me the rest of the letter."

Hick cleared his throat. "Jacob Preston, as it was you who helped give life to the Silver Steer, we want you be the first to share its first words directly with voters. Please let the voters of Iowa and America know where to find us, and to check here in coming days for future messages from the Silver Steer."

"What do you make of it, Hick?" Jake asked.

"Amateurish video…quite possibly a hoax. But there's a serious, well-crafted message behind it, and it's just resonant enough to catch on. What's your take?"

"I don't know what to think," Jake told him. "But considering I'm batting 0 for 1 on big-time scoops, I think we should run with this one…. Will you print it if I write it?"

Hick's reply reached him after a painfully long pause. "No can do, Press. When you got stripped of your credentials, the Big Boss nixed the idea of any more Jake Preston."

"So now that I've been reinstated as the Politics Up Close sweepstakes winner again, representing the *Partisan*, I'm not actually allowed to represent the *Partisan*."

"That's pretty much the extent of it. And, Press, I want you to know, I told the Big Boss that unless he changes his mind, and allows you to at least explain your position in the pages of the supposedly objective newspaper where your stories and columns have appeared for years, I would be submitting my resignation."

"You can't do that, Geoff. What about Samantha's college fund?"

"A daughter paying full tuition at the University of Colorado and a wife who's fallen in love with her $40,000 hybrid SUV, but, hey, I got into this profession to defend free speech, and to speak up for the little guy, and I'll leave it on the same grounds if that's what it takes to get the point across. Every man has to take a stand for something sometime in his life, Press."

"I can't believe you'd risk your job for me."

"It's not *for* you, Press, so much as it is *about* you. Legally, the Big Boss is just exercising his right to hire and fire as he sees fit, but underneath it, there's much, much more. And really, when you think about it, who are these corporate raiders anyway? Every few years they decide they want to add some mid-sized newspaper to their media conglomerate. Then a year or two later, when they realize what a messy, inefficient, downright maddening business journalism is, they want to 'downsize' and 'streamline' and 'maximize workflow,' and it falls to me to walk up to someone's desk late on a Friday afternoon—including most recently yours—and tell that poor person their livelihood has been sacrificed on the altar of corporate profits. Press, I just can't do it anymore…. It's rotting what soul I have left after thirty years in this merciless business."

"You've got plenty of soul left, Hick…probably more than is good for you."

"Like I said, maybe it's time for this grizzled old cowboy to get out of the saddle for a while, maybe become an intrepid explorer of the digital frontier, you know, start-up a Youtube channel like this revolutionary cow here, or a Facebook group like *Free Press*."

"So you've seen it?"

"Sure have."

"You know, a week ago if I'd asked you if there'd be a *Free Press* movement online with like 50,000 followers, would you have believed me?"

"Yes."

"Huh?

Hick chuckled. "I would have believed you because seven days ago pure unfocused, unfettered indignation caused me to ask my daughter to help me mount my first-ever Facebook page, which I proceeded to name *Free Press*."

"You didn't, Hick."

"I'm afraid I did, Jacob. And when the Big Boss finds out, as eventually he will, I'm as good as gone anyway. Officially I'm considering my potential resignation an act of preemption."

"So we might both find ourselves out of a job…?"

"And yet blessed with a cause," Hick said, adding, "and, Press, if you could see me now, you'd notice something very peculiar about me."

"Yeah, what's that?"

"For the first time in years I'm actually smiling."

Jake paused at the mouth of the lion's den again, wondering whether to knock.

"Yeah, yeah…keep your undies on," a familiar voice called out from the other side of the door. A moment later it opened to reveal Amethyst Gilchrest.

"Well, if it isn't the ghost of roommates past," she said. "Come on in."

She was mostly back to her jocular self, Jake noticed at a glance. "How are things back home in NYC…with your mom's estate?" he asked.

"Been better…. So what's up?" She took her traditional seat on the couch, Indian style, motioning him toward his old chair.

"At the debate you told me if there was anything you could ever do for me, just to let you know."

Am's eyebrows raised above her glasses. "And…?"

"Somehow," he continued, "another unbelievable scoop has dropped from the heavens into my hands. A big one, potentially…. And I think you're the only one who can help me get the word out."

"And you're willing to trust me because…?"

"Because I want to believe you're a good person." Jake paused. "Get your laptop?"

"What for?"

"Trust me, just do it."

"Cool your jets, Press," Am said. "It's right here."

Jake handed her a slip of paper with the This Is The Steer URL Geoff Hickenlooper had dictated over the phone to him a few hours earlier. Am's fingers flew across the keyboard and a second later the computer-altered voice of the Silver Steer echoed off the tin ceilings of Am's cavernous apartment.

"This can't be for real," she said, when the bull had finished its Youtube spiel. "It's way too corny."

"It may be corny, but it's potentially a game-changer."

"This is clearly the work of some nut job who lives with his parents trying to capitalize on the Silver Steer thing…. Still, it's so damn campy *Times* readers would probably go gaga over it. Maybe it'll go viral, like that dancing baby or the kid pretending to be a Jedi knight in his garage…. So you want me to forward this on to my editor?"

"I want you to write your editor and tell them you've got another exclusive. We break the story and we see what happens with the cow in the manger."

"Correction," Am said, getting up off the couch. "I'll write my editor and say that the late-great Jake Preston, reinstated winner of the Politics Up Close contest, has a stunningly good scoop that he's willing to offer to us and no one else. I'll volunteer to serve as consulting editor, but the byline, baby, is all yours."

"Not just mine, but also my editor's back at the *Rocky Mountain Partisan*, Hick."

"You're joking? Your editor's name at that backwater newspaper is really Hick?"

"Sure is."

Am rolled her eyes. "Okay, it'll be a Hick and Press byline, God help us all."

"And you're doing this for me because…?"

"Because I fooled you once, so shame on me" Am said, grinning. "And I'll even throw in a free dinner while we get it settled, that is, if I can persuade you to stay."

"I think I can," Jake said, looking out at the slow, cold rain falling outside—the first rain of the first week of November.

"So says the little political writer who could," Amethyst said, donning her 'I cook best alone' apron while she pre-heated the oven. "Hot-dish lunch special," she said, with a wink. "And that's in addition to the usual hot-dish…me."

For the second straight night Jake Preston and Herb Clarke found themselves dining alone at the farmhouse.

"Got a call from Katie this afternoon," Clarke told him. "She's having a great time with Anne."

"What exactly are they doing again?" Jake asked, draining the tall glass of milk on the table. He and Clarke had spent all afternoon removing the window air conditioners from the old farmhouse on what had been, ironically, one of the warmest days of the fall.

"Combination of scholarship and friendship," Herb explained. "Anne is moving into a new condo down in Des Moines, and Katie is helping her sort through the things in her old rambling Victorian. A lot of the stuff they're getting rid of belonged to Anne's husband."

"What happened to him?"

"The same thing that gets most of us sooner or later…. Heart troubles, or so I'm led to understand. She's been living in the house they shared ever since, accumulating stuff." The editor looked around the room and grinned. "Know anyone else like that?"

"Nope," Jake said. "So did you read my article yet in today's *Times*?"

"I did indeed, and it's an intriguing one. I haven't had a chance yet to look at the barnyard video though."

"No time like the present," Jake said, putting his and Herb's plates in the sink before booting up the editor's decrepit PC—the one sitting next to a pile of ancient *Life* magazines. Jake navigated to the Youtube page and pressed play, discovering a second video had been posted by—This Is The Steer, TITS for short.

"Another truly unfortunate acronym," the editor said, shaking his head mournfully.

"I don't think they're claiming it."

"I should hope not," he said. "Maybe that's a line of work an old fogey like me could get into—acronym consultant."

"And resident pun generator," Jake added, watching the image of the darkened manger come to life on the screen.

"That's it? That's the Silver Steer?" Clarke asked, reaching out to touch the screen. "You can hardly see anything more than a bed of hay and a stall. It looks like every state-fair stable I've ever seen."

Jake shushed him. "Hold on, let it speak."

> By now many of you all over the country have read about me. So what am I proposing? I am proposing anything, and I am proposing everything. I am proposing what-

ever it is that is the will of the people. Six candidates remain. One of these six stands a good chance of being the next leader of America, and the world. Is this what you want? Is this what you asked for? Is this what you are prepared to stand for? What message do you want to send the rest of the nation about voter responsibility, risk, and bravery? Which candidate, if any, are you prepared to recommend to New Hampshire and South Carolina, and the rest of the electorate waiting for you to make the first move? You have two weeks to decide whom you will be sending on with your endorsement. Rest assured, it could be anyone, anything, or nothing.

As the video clip reached its end, Jake gaped at the views tally since his story had hit the *Times* earlier in the morning—340,000—three times the number of likely caucus goers in the entire state he'd spent the last few weeks covering.

Herb Clarke couldn't resist a smirk. "I've worked with plenty of cattle on this farm and on others in my day, and I've yet to meet one who can talk as well as that one does. Hell, I can't even get our old milk cow to say 'Moo' anymore."

"She probably finds you intimidating," Jake quipped. "Besides, I don't see any fresh milk in the refrigerator."

"That's because the state government, in its infinite wisdom, forbids the buying and selling of unpasteurized milk. And then, too, Millie's past her prime...not unlike her owner, come to think of it."

"So what do you think of This Is The Steer?"

"I think it's a priceless piece of symbology," the editor said. "First off, the idea that some old steer somewhere is rallying Joe and Jane Q. Voter to do something other than submit to the will of the political machine is an idea whose time has come.... It turns the cows to slaughter analogy on its head, doesn't it?"

"More like on its tail."

"And the 'More Bull, Less B.S.' slogan is catchy, don't you think?"

"I do."

"What's not to like? It's a provocation, a goad. Bottom line, it's an appealing fantasy. Who hasn't felt, at one time or another, that an animal they were close to possessed an intelligence and perceptivity greater than their own. That's the beauty of the fable, isn't it, Jake? Strange as it sounds, animals can say things humans can't."

"It's the *Free Willy* thing, right?"

"I go back a generation earlier, to Shamu, the killer whale," chuckled the old editor. "Shamu was a star in the 1970s."

"I remember Shamu," Jake said. "My parents took me to see him in at SeaWorld when I was a kid back in Florida."

"I hate to be the one to break it to you, son," Clarke said, "but the real Shamu died in the early 1970s at the SeaWorld in San Diego. What your parents took you to see was a trademark...all the orcas were called Shamu for years after the real one's tragic death."

"Another childhood dream burst," Jake sniffed. "I suppose you're going to tell me next that there's no Santa Claus and no Silver Steer."

"I wouldn't dream of it," the editor said, patting him on the back. "Each of us is entitled to our necessary illusions. Besides, the Silver Steer is as real as Milt Cloward or Renard Kane. And in its way, probably realer, because by now it's an illusion collectively made and maintained by the people."

"Speaking of, we're still on for the Renard Kane press conference later tonight, right?" Jake asked, checking his watch. "It starts in less than an hour."

The editor nodded. "Wouldn't miss it for the world. Whatever it is, Renard Kane would rather have it soon forgotten. Why else would he call a news conference in the middle of the dinner hour?"

"Maybe to announce he's really Santa Claus."

"More likely," Clarke said, joining in, "that Shamu is a fake, that Santa Claus is fiction, and that the Emperor has no clothes."

Less than an hour later Herb Clarke and Jake Preston found themselves crammed into the basement of the old Calvary Lutheran Church the once-flush Renard campaign had not just rented as campaign headquarters but bought outright. Jake had been shocked to learn that in places like Hereford old steam-heated buildings like this could be bought for the price of a top-of-the-line pickup truck.

"Well, if it isn't the two most eligible bachelors in Hereford," Amethyst Gilchrest said, sliding into the folding metal chair beside them.

"A widower, not a bachelor, Ms. Gilchrest," Clarke retorted. "They're as different as an old maid and a virgin."

"I wouldn't know much about either, now would I?" Amethyst asked, needling him back. "So you came to watch the train wreck?"

"Should we be expecting political apocalypse?"

Am nodded. "Horsemen *and* the plague of locust. End times, I'd say, at least for Mr. Kane."

"What's your evidence?"

"The usual pre-mortem leaks. Supposedly it has something to do with Kane's wife, who's yet to be heard from, not even after the alleged affair."

"I don't get it," Jake admitted. "Why wouldn't she go public in defense of her husband?"

Am shook her head, equally bewildered. "Rumor has it she's a very private person….suspiciously private as a matter of fact."

Clarke shushed them. "Here comes the man himself."

The room quieted as Renard Kane strode to the podium, looking taller than usual against the low ceilings of the church basement. Kane found his sweet spot behind the podium, and proceeded to grab both sides of it, as if to steady himself. He adjusted his glasses, looked out at the crowd of journalists and well-wishers, then back down to the lectern again, as if the answers to whatever had brought him here might be printed on its thin veneer.

"Thank y'all for comin' tonight. I hope you got some of that good ol' popcorn when you came in. You know, when we bought this church, the popcorn-maker came with the deal. My campaign manager tells me they eat popcorn around here like it's going outa style." Kane's rich baritone laugh rumbled throughout the basement. "I called all y'all here tonight to address a few matters that you in the press seem to think are crucial to this campaign, and to discuss the status of my campaign moving forward."

"There have been numerous stories about alleged affairs that took place with coworkers at various positions I have held over the years. I admitted to these indiscretions at that time, asked for forgiveness from my God and from my supporters, and was gratified to find my honesty rewarded with the enduring love and support of my base. But I stand before you tonight to own up to another kind of wrongdoing that has weighed heavily on my heart since the race for the nomination begin. And I would like now to amend the record on that issue."

In the audience Amethyst nudged Jake and whispered "Cue fire and brimstone." On stage, Kane took a deep breath.

"I, Renard Kane, am not now, nor ever have been, married. Candy Kane, my wife, does not exist. She is a fiction that I alone perpetrated and for whose sinful invention I must now answer to my lord and savior Jesus Christ." The candidate bowed his head. "It would be unfair to the voters of this great state to continue to campaign on real issues, while having to repeatedly address my previous misrepresentations concerning my wife. Consequently, effective today I am suspending my campaign for the Republication nomination for the presidency of these United States."

Kane dabbed at the beads of sweat glistening on his forehead with a preternaturally white handkerchief. "We have a limited amount of time now to answer your questions, as I'll be flyin' back to Alabama this evening to be with my…well, to be with myself."

Amethyst's hand shot up.

"Does this mean that the extra-marital affair to which you earlier confessed didn't technically happen…" Am's voice trailed off, as if she herself couldn't quite wrap her brain around the paradox. "You can't have an extra-marital affair if you're not… *marital*, correct?"

Kane looked up from his script with hound-dog eyes. "I can see I'm gonna need to do a better job of explaining myself. As y'all know, I'm a former Baptist preacher. So to the extent that I was 'married' I was married like Christ was married…to the church. So when I say I committed the extra-marital affair, I mean that I cheated on my wife…the church."

Amethyst raised her hand for a follow-up. "Can you say more about how you cheated on the church?"

"I'm afraid I can't," Kane sighed. "That's between me and my Maker."

Mort McGreedy was next into the fray.

"So the bride you've mentioned throughout this campaign was merely a figure of speech?"

Kane nodded somberly. "She was a metaphor for my love of Christ."

"So Candy Kane is entirely a fiction, then?"

"Candy Kane is a symbol of my husbandly devotion," Kane said, returning to his talking points.

"But she is not your living, breathing betrothed?"

"That depends on how you define living and breathing and how you define betrothed. But no, she was not a flesh and blood woman."

"How did you create her?" a reporter in the second row asked as Amethyst muttered under her breath, *from Adam's rib*.

"As many of you are well aware, when my parents died, I lived for many years with my long-time friend, let's call her Candy, throughout my time at Morehouse and thereafter. By some definitions we were husband and wife under common law, but because Candy was rumored to be my cousin, we could not marry under the Alabama legal code, and yet at the same time we could not definitively determine her paternity as she was the product of a broken home and an absent father. When I went off to graduate school at Valparaiso, Candy decided not to accompany me nor to pursue what would have been her rightful status as my wife under common law—again had she not also potentially been my cousin—so I began to give her my last name in legal documents in honor of her years of devotion to me. She knew of my aspirations to one day take God and country as my bride, and realized that I stood a much better chance to win elections as a married man."

"So Candy Kane does exist?"

"If you mean exist in mind, she most certainly does. She also exists on paper in at least three states."

"For the record, there is no person who is your wife named Candy Kane," McGreedy pressed.

"That depends on how you define *wife*," Kane countered.

"So you're telling us there is a Candy Kane somewhere, and that Candy Kane may be your wife?"

"Candy is an alias," the candidate said, swallowing hard. "Candy is an alias used to protect her identity, while Kane is that alias's honorific surname."

"But Candy Kane is the name appearing on the legal documents you referenced earlier and in file photographs of you with the woman who you previously identified as Mrs. Candy Kane."

"Potentially," Kane said.

"Mr. Kane, will you be endorsing any of the remaining candidates?" Herb Clarke asked, trying a different tack. "Recent polls have you nearly tied with Mike Santoro for number of anticipated votes."

"I have weighed that decision carefully over the last week," Kane said, appearing as if the weight of the world were upon him. "As you know, Mike Santoro and I have had our differences, as have Milt Cloward and myself. Asking my voters to switch their allegiance to either man would, my staff and I have concluded, irrevocably tip the scales of this race in their favor. At the same time, arbitrarily splitting my votes among the existing candidates would be impossible on a practical level and politically presumptuous on my part." Behind the lectern Kane adjusted his tie and squared his shoulders, as if bracing himself for a stiff wind. "After considerable deliberation I've decided to throw my votes to…the Silver Steer."

Amidst the uproar that followed Amethyst Gilchrest turned to Jake and said, "Make that four horsemen, a plague of locusts, Santa Claus, a Candy Kane, and one hell of a strange race."

Thirteen

Beside them, the not-so-mighty Raccoon River flowed brown and muddy. After a drought that had lasted well into October, the cold November rains falling on Hereford had been almost Biblical.

Beside Jake on the path, bundled up tight in her yellow rain slicker, walked Katie Clarke, her hands shoved deep into her pockets. Jake had practically to shout at her to be heard above the wind. "So how was your time with the Dr. Templeton?"

Katie looked up at him, blinking into the droplets falling heavily from the sky. "Good," she said, "and then again not so good."

"Explain."

"Good because we got an incredible amount of sorting and cleaning done. I've never seen Anne happier and more contented."

"And bad because…?"

"Bad because helping her organize all the things she'd accumulated with her dead husband was emotionally exhausting, and more than a little sad."

"How so?"

"For starters, packing always makes me melancholic…. It's the this-is-what-my-life-boils-down-to moment. It's impossible to argue with the evidence of who you've been and what you care about staring you right in the face."

"That's not always true, is it?" Jake objected. "I mean I've moved a thousand times, and that disgusting old toilet plunger I've taken with me in each and every move doesn't reveal the essence of my life...at least I hope it doesn't."

"Still, it does say lots about you," Katie said, leaning against him now in an attempt to shelter herself from the wind.

"Like what, for example?"

"That you're frugal. Most people would simply throw it away and buy a new one, figuring that would be more hygienic anyway."

"You've got me there," he admitted.

"It also says you're a person who carries too much with him, and that what you carry increases, rather than decreases, with each move you make."

"Too true."

"It says that you're a person who prepares for the best but plans for the worst, and who prefers to fix things himself, especially when you might just as easily call the plumber."

"Thank you, Mr. Holmes," Jake said, bowing before her. "You've read me like a book."

"It's really true," she insisted. "The things you save speak volumes about you."

"So why does that fact bum you out?" asked Jake, following the path as it bent around an ancient oak tree.

"Because here I am with Anne, who's no more than a generation older than I am, and she's surrounded by memories of the past that she can't quite escape."

"Maybe she didn't want to escape."

"She was more than ready. But then to have to decide what to do with the keepsakes and mementos of the man you thought you would live with well into old age forces you to confront your own mortality, and the mortality of everyone around you."

"I guess it makes sense," Jake said. "Both you and Anne lost someone important in your life. You lost your mom. She lost her husband. Those losses can't help but shape a person."

"And someday I'm going to lose Daddy, too," Katie Clarke said, stopping in her tracks.

Jake laughed. "Are you serious? That man plans to live to be a hundred."

"When he's gone what will I have to show for it? Anne was telling me that when she was younger, before she got tenure, she wanted badly to run for public office."

"So what stopped her?"

"She had just married, and she was afraid her husband would think it was too selfish, or too ambitious or whatever. Then, too, that wasn't an era when a woman could just up and decide to run for office and expect to have the financial backing she needed. So she decided to stick to what she knew best, school, and went on to get her doctorate."

"At which she succeeded brilliantly."

"And yet she still has profound regrets," Katie pointed out. "You know, I was the same way when I was younger. I had big dreams. I either wanted to follow in Daddy's footsteps and write editorials for the newspaper, or do the thing Daddy could never quite get around to doing...running for public office."

"Maybe that's why she connects so well with you."

"Instead, what do I do? I live in the same farmhouse I grew up in, and I waitress for people who still believe 10% is a generous tip. If I died today, what would be left of me? A few boxes of my childhood toys up in the attic, mom's old keepsakes and theater props, some books, most of which I haven't read since I was in college, and an old beater truck that's a hand-me-down from my dad. No children, no husband. I haven't been on a date in years."

"Do you want to?"

"Want to what?"

"Go on a date?"

"Sure, I suppose."

"Than why don't we?"

"Why don't we what?"

"Go on a political date."

Katie's wind-whipped eyes stared directly into his. "Where would we go?"

"Where else," Jake offered, "but the Cal Coolidge Café? You still have another day of vacation before you go back to work, right? So we go in after closing, open back up, and have ourselves a proper political date…my treat."

"You don't have any money."

"But I have loads of time. You can tell me more about your time with Anne. What do you say?"

"I say it's a date," Katie replied, willing herself to smile.

"Jake Preston, Pitchford here."

"What's up?" Jake asked. The rain had stopped mid-afternoon, and the sun had shone briefly, so Jake had pulled his old Accord out of Herb Clarke's most decrepit hay barn, filled up a bucket with some dishwashing soap and water and strapped on the big furry car-washing glove that made him feel like he belonged on the *The Muppet Show*. He'd almost not been able to get the mitt off in time to answer the phone.

"Hey, is Herb Clarke around there?"

"He's inside," Jake answered. "Why?"

"Go get him and put him on speaker phone."

"What's this about?"

"Nothing to worry about, Jake. Just an idea I wanted to run by him, and by you, incidentally. Go ahead and call him."

Jake hollered into the house, feeling like Ralph Cramden in *Honeymooners*. A minute later Herb Clarke rounded the building looking more than usually agitated.

"What in the hell are you yelling for?" he asked, peeved. "I was all the way up cleaning the attic….sorting through Genevieve's old things. This cleaning and organizing binge Katie has been on down in Des Moines is downright contagious."

"Pitchford's on the line," Jake said, covering up the microphone with his hand.

"What the hell does that smug sonofabitch want?"

"I want to ask you what you think of an idea." Jake looked down as if his hand was talking, but it was Pitchford, of course, and he'd heard every word. He decided just to put it on speaker and save everyone the further awkwardness.

"So what's your idea, Mr. Chairman?" Clarke asked.

"We'd like to step up our Silver Steer promotions, while keeping the focus on the candidates…where it belongs."

"You're worried about losing control of your brand, is that it? You want to make sure folks remember that the Silver Steer is a trophy for the candidates, not the other way around."

"We wouldn't put it that way, but, yes, that's the general idea."

"So what's that got to do with me?" the editor asked.

"We were thinking it might be nice to reinstate the old candidate barbeque you used to throw. My father always told me about going."

Jake looked over at his host. *Barbeque?*

"That was ages ago," Clarke said, chuckling. "Back when dad was running the farm. He was the political animal of the family."

"Maybe," Pitchford replied, "but from what my father told me, the two of you, father and son, ran it together, and all the candidates and the candidates' men would attend."

"We did have some pretty amazing turn-outs," he conceded.

"Can I count on you to offer your farm up again, Herb? We feel like the symbolism of your farm, a Century Farm right there in rural Hereford, could help us reemphasize tradition…"

"…as a counterweight to supposedly radical upstarts like POPP and SOD. I get what you're driving at, Matthew. But if the party is in charge of the guest list, I'm not interested."

"The party has to be in charge of the guest list, Herb."

"Not if I don't take any party money."

"Trust me, you don't have the money to sponsor an event of this magnitude, nor does your newspaper."

"Issue tickets then," Jake interrupted. "Make them free to anyone from Hereford and surrounding communities, and charge a modest fee for anyone coming in from the outside… just enough to cover your expenses. That way you both win. The party gets their barbeque and a chance to rally the troops and turn out the vote, and Herb gets the autonomy to decide how he wants to throw his party and whom he wants to invite."

"And who, pray tell, is going to help me with the logistics?" Clarke asked.

"I'm sure the crack staff of the *Gate* and the Cal Coolidge would pitch in," Jake offered.

The editor shook his head. "Not nearly enough manpower."

"Then form a citizen's group. Open it up to anyone in the community with the desire and the time to help."

From the phone clutched in Jake's hand, Matt Pitchford was talking again. "So do we have a date then, gentlemen?"

"We do," Herb and Jake replied simultaneously. Jake checked his watch. "Which reminds me, I'm supposed to be in town for my own date in ninety minutes, and I haven't even showered."

"Before you hang up, I'm going to need to get this in writing from you, Herb. No backing out at the last minute, regardless of circumstances. I'm prepared to ask the same thing of the candidates."

"Fine by me, but I'm going to need a similar pledge from you. If we throw this clambake for you, we…meaning me and whatever committee…get to decide how exactly it's pitched."

For a moment all Jake and Herb could hear was the sound of Pitchford's heavy breathing. "So long as it's within the realm of what we discussed today," he said finally.

"So long as nothing," Clarke declared. "You're asking me to host a barbecue, and I'm not asking you for a cent to rent the farm. We decide what happens. Take it or leave it."

"Fine," Pitchford said flatly.

"We'll be in touch once we've formed our committee…. Now Jake, how in the hell do you turn this confounded thing off," the editor said, looking down at the phone as if it was a bomb needing defusing.

"Gotta run, gentlemen," Pitchford closed, conjuring up his own personal motto. "Drive safe, look out for bucks, and don't take any bull."

"There," Jake said, punching the 'end' button, "consider yourself disconnected."

"And not a bit too soon. Can't stand that boy or his slogans…never could. Didn't care much for his father, either." Clarke looked pointedly at Jake's phone. "Why don't you fire that gizmo up again and get Chuck Sousage on the line."

"What for?"

"Because I said so, that's what for. We're going to need Chuckles's help promoting this little weenie roast."

"Herb," Jake said, holding the phone at arm's length. "The Iowa Republican Party relieved Sousage of his job weeks ago. He's officially disgraced…put out to pasture."

"He's the best in the business, and has been for twenty years," the newspaper editor said. "That slick son-of-a-bitch could sell the fur right off a dog's back, and we need tickets sold fast to every voter and citizen and political observer who might want to drive to a farm in Iowa. That's the only way we make this hootenanny a people's picnic, not just a campaign event in disguise. Tell him we're going to do it like we did back in Dad's day… Pioneer games and all."

"Pioneer Games?"

Herb Clarke nodded decidedly. "The kind my ancestors, and probably yours, played to learn cooperation—to see what kind of stuff their neighbors and friends and rivals were really made of."

"Pitchford probably had in mind an afternoon of staged photos with obliging farm animals and plenty of flesh-pressings…. He's going to be plenty pissed."

"Let him be. I've known that boy since he was in diapers… Always was a cry baby."

Jake relented with a sigh. "Alright…. I'll call Sousage tonight on the way into town."

"Good. I'll get on the horn and form an executive planning committee with Katie as co-chair…Mrs. Meyers will want in of course, and Artie Shaw and his Cowtown Pickers would take care of the music, I imagine. We'll need someone to cater in the food and drink."

"Madison," Jake suggested before he'd quite got his head around the idea of the hirsute barman slinging beer and serving ribs at a big-time political event. "He's the only pub-and-grub option in town anymore."

The old newspaperman clapped Jack on the back. "We can get him working on the sound and video, too. He and Artie wired the sound and video system at the Wagon Wheel all by themselves, floor to ceiling. I've never seen so many wires crossed."

"I'll stop by the bar on the way into my date tonight and ask him myself. I'll put in a pitch to Amethyst, too. You'll want some media-types in the mix as minor celebs. Once Amethyst is in, she can convince her pals to help out, too—Loretta Draper, Alex… basically, the whole young-gun Wagon Wheel braintrust."

Clarke brushed a particularly clingy dust-bunny from his sleeve and looked at Jake quizzically. "Got yourself a date, eh? For God's sake, who's the victim?"

"Your daughter," Jake said, letting the screen door slam behind him as he hustled upstairs to the shower.

"Why didn't I hear about this?" Herb called after him.

"Because there are two timeless principles in life. One, politicians lie. Two, daughters never tell their fathers about their dates."

"I assume your interest is purely platonic…"

"It's worse than that," Jake called down from the stairs. "It's political."

A half-hour later Jake found himself in the Accord, hair still wet from the shower. He had, he congratulated himself, come to know the roads between the Clarke farm and town quite well in the couple of weeks he had lived out in the boonies with them. In any of the places he'd lived in before, knowing the route home by heart would have been a sure sign that it was time to move on, but this place was different. In Hereford, knowing your way was a point of pride.

As was paying your bills. And Jake resolved on his way that he wanted to pay Amethyst the remaining rent he owed her now, before his money ran out completely. When he knocked on the door of her apartment it was nearly 7:00 PM—well into the hours of her "cozy clothes" uniform: sweats and a sports bra with the radiator turned on full blast and the windows flung open.

"To what do I owe the honor of this visit?" she asked as she opened the door.

"Knock it off, Am. You know I enjoy coming here to see you."

"Which is why you never come anymore."

"I never come anymore," Jake corrected her, "because I live a dozen miles outside of town."

"I told you the air mattress is still available."

"And I appreciate it. But I couldn't pay you for it," he said, handing her his rent money. "Sorry this is overdue. I withdrew it…well, part of it anyway…on the night you told me to take a hike. Then I was mad at you for stealing my scoop, then you were back in New York, and…"

"Keep it," she interrupted.

"No can do. We made a deal and I'm bound by it. Take it."

Am closed her eyes and turned away, a kid refusing her spinach. "I'm not going to take your stupid rent money."

"Yes you are."

"Am not!"

"Fine," Jake said. "I'm leaving it the mailbox. You can either take it and put it to good use, or you can let the mailman have it."

"Then we'll let the mailman have it. I've noticed he's dressed a little shabbily lately."

"Am, that's his uniform."

She shrugged. "Then he definitely needs a makeover…all those boring blues and grays…yuck." She paused. "I know you well enough, Press, to know you didn't come all the way over here to argue with me. So…why are you here?"

"In part because I miss you. You're easily the most charismatic person in town."

"That's not saying much," Am said, pouring herself a glass of white wine. "But you're right of course…. And why else?"

"I was on my way into town…for a date."

Am raised her eyebrows. "Who's the lucky filly?"

"Kate Clarke."

Amethyst frowned. "The waitress who refuses to serve me at the café?"

"Don't take it personally. I think she's doing that in retaliation for your scooping me."

"Outwardly hostile but inwardly loyal," Am teased. "A winning personality if ever there was one."

"It's not a real date."

"No?"

"Just good company."

"Growing pretty desperate out there on the farm, are we?"

"Not desperate, just a little lonesome. Katie's been gone a lot and Herb's been burning the midnight oil at the newspaper."

"Gone where? I thought that chick was too provincial to travel."

"Down to Des Moines to help an old professor make a big life change.... Meanwhile, Herb's leaves for the paper at 6:00 AM, regular as clockwork. These Midwesterners are the most ritual-bound people I've ever seen."

"Tell me about it, partner." Amethyst moved to her walk-up apartment's most salable feature—the bay window overlooking First Street. Already its oversized panes had begun to fill with a dusky sort of twilight. "I've reached the frankly pathetic point where I can look out from my perch here at virtually any time of day and predict who's going to walk down the street next. I know, for example, when Hereford's favorite crusty newspaper editor walks the four doors down from his office to the café for his afternoon coffee. I know that he always leaves at 6 PM sharp, and that lately he's been working overtime, burning the candle at both ends on account of this wacky election. I know that waitress girlfriend of yours is going to drive up First Street in that God-awfully loud redneck truck of hers at exactly 5:55 AM for her 6 o'clock breakfast shift. And I can tell just by sniffing the gooey air wafting up through my floorboards what the crockpot soup du jour is below me in the Sweetheart Bakery—cheese potato, cheesy broccoli, chili cheese, French onion, or Wisconsin cheese. My God, I don't even miss Bravo and TLC anymore. Press, you've got to help me.... I'm one crocheting needle and ten cats short of becoming a spinster."

Jake felt a pang of something he had never quite felt before for Amethyst Gilchrest—pure, unadulterated sympathy. "I imagine you're chomping at the bit to get back to New York."

"See there," Amethyst exclaimed, whirling around to point an accusing finger at him, "you're even staring to talk like an Iowan!"

"No I'm not."

"Yes you are," she corrected him. "Since when do you say *chompin' at the bit*?"

"Since never."

"My point exactly," she said, folding her arms across her chest. "It's taken me months of fried-food and domestic beer therapy to be able to admit that I kinda-sorta-almost like it here, and Lord knows it's dirt-cheap living, but it's the sameness of it all, day after day, that drives me crazy. So, yeah, I'm ready to punch my ticket out of Cowtown on the first Conestoga."

"Could you leave early?"

"Why so eager to get rid of me, Jacob Preston? As a matter of fact, my editors at the *Times* have asked me to do a little investigative reporting while we wait for electoral D-day?"

"About Candy Kane?"

"No, as far as I'm concerned Renard Kane and his mythical wives and mistresses are done and over with. They want me to follow a warmer lead."

"Are you going to tell me?"

"Nope. I'm going to string you along until you beg for it," she said.

"Your usual M.O. then?"

"Exactly…. So do you want to know?"

"You know I do."

"I'm supposed to investigate who in the hell is behind the This Is The Steer videos."

"Sounds dangerous," Jake said. "Sometimes it's better not to depants Santa Claus."

"I think you mean unmask Santa Claus, to which I would say, true, as far as that goes. But shouldn't people have the right to know the man or woman behind the machine? Shouldn't TITS be subject to intense scrutiny? I mean, shouldn't a TITS video raise eyebrows." Am paused. "Um… let me rephrase that. Shouldn't we hold this shadowy This Is The Steer group up to the same rigorous inquiry we direct at all the candidates for prez?"

"Maybe," Jake conceded, "but the Silver Steer isn't running for political office."

"Could have fooled me," Am said, finishing off her first glass of wine and pouring another. "Isn't it our duty to arm the public, and disarm the folks who would try to manipulate their sympathies, and their vote?"

"It's more complicated than that, isn't it?"

"Not really." Amethyst paused. "And I haven't even told you the whole story yet."

"No?"

Am shook her head. "I left out one very important detail."

"Which is?"

"My editor asked you to help me. She liked the last piece you wrote with that Hick fellow, or whatever the hell his name is…she liked it a great deal in fact. She further pointed out that it would be fitting for the man who gave birth to the Silver Steer mystique to have a hand in demystifying it. I told her you probably wouldn't go for it."

"Why not?"

"Because, Dr. Frankenstein, I think you've fallen in love with the monster you created."

"Maybe," Jake allowed, as he moved toward the door and the stairwell beyond. "And hey, I forgot to tell you one very important detail."

"Really? Do tell."

"I officially volunteered you and Loretta Draper to help Herb plan a candidate barbeque Matt Pitchford has requested. You'll get to work with all your local favorites… Mrs. Meyers, Artie Shaw, Mad, and, of course, Katie Clarke…"

There was a long pause from the top of the stairs before Amethyst called after him, "I hate you, Jacob Preston!"

Across the table from him in the deserted restaurant sat the daughter of the grumpiest man in town.

"You look…you look beautiful," Jake said.

"You seemed surprised," Kate Clarke said, blushing a little.

"Not surprised. Just…impressed."

"Where I come from that's the same as surprised," she said, laughing. "Well, what do you think of the ambience?"

The Cal Coolidge Café had been transformed into a decently passable bistro, at least one booth of it anyway. Katie Clarke had hung a rustic lantern directly over the table, just above head high.

Beneath their elbows lay a thick linen tablecloth and on top of that a silver platter covering up the night's yet-to-be-revealed main course. In place of the Cal Coolidge's usually tinny sound system Katie had rigged up her own ad-hoc Ipod jukebox.

"What do you think of the new photos I hung for tonight's festivities?" she asked. Jake followed her eyes to the wall. "Out with the old and in with the new, right?"

He looked at the new telephoto shot of a luscious fruit with beads of fine dew clinging to its skin, and read the caption aloud to her. "Green Zebras on the Vine."

Katie nodded over her shoulder. "And there's another in the booth behind me."

Jake leaned over the table until his face nearly touched Katie's. "Silvered Steer," he read aloud as he took in the photo of what appeared to be a black and white shot of a milk cow gazing head-on into the lens. "How'd you achieve that nifty silver effect?"

Katie adjusted the napkin in her lap demurely. "I Photoshopped it."

"You mean the old-fashioned newspaper editor's daughter manipulated an image on a computer. Say it ain't so!"

"Guilty as charged. You know, hanging out with Anne the past week has really had an effect on me. She's, what, thirty-five years older than me, and yet she adores getting online and teaching herself new tricks. It's sort of amazing, actually."

Jake surveyed the semi-dark surroundings beyond the makeshift spotlight over their heads. "I take it she helped you come up with the Italian theme for tonight's political date."

"Maybe," his dinner date replied coyly. "And anyway, what makes you think we were going for Italian?"

"The Louis Prima playing on that Ipod of yours, and the not-so faint smell of scorched tomato sauce coming from the kitchen."

"Always think you have me figured out, don't you?" she needled. "Just this once, though, you got me. We're having that sumptuous Middle American repast known as the all-you-care-to-eat spaghetti supper."

"Perfect for a political date," he remarked. "And what does my fundraising ticket buy me."

"A night of sparkling political conversation, and a chance to woo a still skeptical constituency." She reached over and pulled the lid off the oversized platter on the tabletop between them. "Voila, spaghetti," she said in a faux Italian accent. "And for drinks…merlot."

"This stuff is like $40 a bottle," Jake said, taking note of the label. "Our executive publisher…the Big Boss we call him… used to splurge for this stuff at our annual meetings…. What's gotten into you, Katie Clarke?"

"I guess I finally want to enjoy myself a little. Is that such a bad thing?"

"Not at all."

"When Mom died she left me a little bit of money, and all it's been doing is sitting in a money market earning like ten dollars a year in interest. But what's the point of saving if you're never going to spend, right?"

"Right," Jake echoed, heaping her plate high with noodles before serving himself his own robust helping topped by some slightly scalded marinara. "Let me guess…. These are Eva's Purple Ball tomatoes from Herb's garden…. Only it looks as if Eva's been crushed by a meat grinder and put in the pot to simmer."

"Eva's ball didn't go so well apparently," Katie admitted. "Alas her fate was that of any unrequited lover…she spent too long under high heat and turned bitter." She adjusted the napkin in her lap, adding coyly, "You should know this isn't my first political date."

"Really? Who was your first?"

"Matt Pitchford."

Jake made a show of letting his fork drop noisily to the table. "Now you really are raining on my Eva's Purple Ball."

"I was 17…right at the peak of my rebellious stage."

"You, a rebel?"

She nodded her head. "I'm afraid so. The rebellion didn't last long, but it was intense. I remember one time I got so fed-up with Daddy I crumpled up the front page of the *Hereford Gate* and threw it in his face…. It hit him right in the glasses."

Jake whistled appreciatively. "I bet that didn't go over well."

"He said someday I'd realize that the thing I had just crumpled up was the very thing that had fed our family for two generations not to mention paid for my college tuition, and that next time I intended to throw something at him, he'd prefer if it was a hundred-dollar bill. Then he did the most infuriating thing I could have imagined at that point…. He walked away."

Katie adjusted the napkin nervously in her lap as she continued. "He was right, of course, about my ingratitude. Back then I never showed the interest in the newspaper that he wanted or deserved, and, now…all these years later, it feels as if the ship has sailed without me. It's sort of like forgetting someone's name. For a while it's awkward, then it's embarrassing, and finally it's downright shameful. Daddy stopped talking about wanting me to take over the newspaper years ago, and now I'm too ashamed to tell him I might be interested."

"Your old man might surprise you."

Katie chuckled wistfully. "Herb Clarke does not believe in surprising…he believes in consistency and predictability."

"So how did he feel when his high-school-aged daughter dated Matt Pitchford…. That must have rocked his world."

Katie smiled deliciously. "Oh, it did. It was two days before prom, and I had turned down both boys who had been brave enough to ask me. Then the phone rings, and it's Matt." She paused, twisting the noodles thoughtfully around the tines of her fork. "Daddy answered, and Daddy has always disliked Matt Pitchford…. He always said he was a people-pleaser and a sycophant, and that's the ultimate demerit in the book of Herb Clarke. Mom had been gone for many years by then, and so instead of rebelling against my mother, as most high school girls do, I had my dad to get belligerent with. So after poor Matthew got rejected by Goodacre's homecoming queen, he had the gall to call me up on the rebound. And I went…just to spite Daddy."

"Trip the light fantastic did you?"

His political date wrinkled her nose. "It was horrible. Matt dragged me around to meet the smart set from Goodacre like I was some kind of trophy, some status symbol he had acquired by his own cunning. I was so mad I wouldn't even let him kiss me when he dropped me off at the farm a half hour before my curfew."

"What did he say to that?"

"He took his hands off my shoulders, put them in his lap, and said in the most dejected tone possible, 'Drive safe, look out for bucks, and don't take any bull.' Then he started the car, and drove off into the darkness, kissless."

"You mean to tell me he was using that ridiculous mantra back then?"

Katie laughed. "I suppose his father, who was also a politician, probably told him at some point he need a slogan, so 18-year-old Matt Pitchford went out and found one even before he had found himself a date for prom. He still says it every time he drops by the café to flirt with me."

"He does?"

"I'm sure he'd love nothing better than to marry the gal he could claim was his 'high school sweetheart.' That'd give him the same pedigree as Milt Cloward, Rich Priestly, and Renard Kane...or at least the Renard Kane before the admission of the nonexistent political wife, right?" She paused to twirl her spaghetti smartly around her fork. "I mean, more power to them if they fell in love with their high-school sweetheart and never looked back, but I don't need my next president to have married the girl who wore his letter jacket. In fact, I don't need my president to be married at all."

"Now you're really getting radical. A single president in the Oval Office…. He or she would be hitting on hotties instead of dropping bombs on sleeper cells of alleged terrorists…. So now that you're divulging campaign secrets, tell me about your time with Professor Templeton."

"Remember when Anne said that she'd taught with Dolph Heinrich back at Southwest Illinois State?"

Jake dabbed at the blood-red tomato sauce at the corner of his mouth. He looked, he suspected, like an especially messy vampire. "How could I forget?"

"Well, as always, she followed through on her promise. She sorted through all her files until she found that old paper of his, the one he withheld from publication. She sent it home with me for us to look at together." She pulled a manila folder from a plastic shopping bag and put it on the table.

Jake read the title aloud, fork poised. "'Road to Sedition: Secession, Insurrection, and the Role of the Protest Vote.' Have you read it yet?"

She nodded. "It's pretty wild stuff. Anne said when she re-read the thing it seemed incendiary, but at the same time prophetic."

"Give me the *Reader's Digest* version then," Jake said. "I don't want to get tomato sauce all over a piece of history."

"He's basically offering a history of sedition in the United States, and projecting it forward forty years to today's political landscape."

Jake smiled ruefully. "My high school government teacher would kill me right now, but remind me again what sedition is."

"Basically it's any speech or organization that is deemed by the established authority to tend toward insurrection against the established order."

"That's a pretty broad definition."

"Broad enough to drive a truck through, at least according to Dolph Heinrich. And apparently that's where the danger lies."

Jake furrowed his brow. "Danger? How do you mean?"

"He points out that there have been something like four sedition acts passed in the United States, mostly during times of war, and mostly repealed."

"What's the big deal then?"

"The big deal is that there are at least two still on the books that have never been tested."

Jake raised an eyebrow. "Really?"

"In fact, my favorite president, Abe Lincoln, issued the first as an executive order back in like 1861. Heinrich quotes one of his orders…. Here, let me read you gist of what Honest Abe wrote to one of his chief Army generals."

> You are engaged in repressing an insurrection against the laws of the United States. If at any point on or in the vicinity of the military line… blah blah blah blah… you find resistance which renders it necessary to suspend the writ of habeas corpus for the public safety, you personally or through the officer in command at the point where resistance occurs, are authorized to suspend that writ.

"Sounds like mostly a wartime thing," Jake remarked.

"The problem," Katie said, her eyes still scanning the paper, "is that Lincoln's order was never really tested in the courts, and it contained no expiration date, meaning, technically, it's still on the books. And there's another piece of legislation, from 1940, that remains a federal statue. Basically it makes it a criminal offense if a citizen is perceived to be advocating the overthrow of an established legal authority… a government, or an arm of the government."

"Does the young Dolph Heinrich explain what constitutes advocating for the overthrow of a legal authority?"

"He does more than that. He explains how the act defines it. Here's his quote of the statute."

> Title I. Subversive activities. The Smith Act set federal criminal penalties that included fines or imprisonment for as long as twenty years and denied all employment by the federal government for five years following a conviction for anyone who:
>
> …with intent to cause the overthrow or destruction of any such government, prints, publishes, edits, issues, circulates, sells, distributes, or publicly displays any written or printed matter advocating, advising, or teaching the duty, necessity, desirability, or propriety of overthrowing or destroying any government in the United States by force or violence, or attempts to do so; or…organizes or helps or attempts to organize any society, group, or assembly of persons who teach, advocate, or encourage the overthrow or destruction of any such government by force or violence; or becomes or is

a member of, or affiliates with, any such society, group, or assembly of persons, knowing the purposes thereof.

"Interesting," Jake admitted, "but I don't get how Professor Templeton could call it visionary."

His dinnermate slurped up an unruly noodle that whipped her comically in the face. "The last section contains the bombshell…. According to Anne the major contribution Heinrich makes is that he anticipates the day when an organized protest vote could be prosecuted by the government, or an election commission, as an act of sedition."

"What does he mean by a protest vote exactly?"

"There's a section of history in Heinrich's paper about that, too. It's fascinating, Jake. He defines a protest vote as any vote cast in an election to demonstrate the caster's refusal or rejection of the current political system."

"I think I see where you're heading with this."

"He writes that a protest vote could take many forms. Abstention is probably the most common…people staying away from the polls because they're disappointed with their choices. Or there's a blank vote, where the disgruntled voter goes to the polls, takes the ballot, but leaves it blank or selects none of the above, if that's an option…. Then there's something called a Donkey Vote."

"You're kidding, right?"

Katie shook her head. "I wish I were. Technically a Donkey Vote is voting for the candidates in the order in which they're listed on the ballot, which is why candidates have always tried to get their name to appear first. But Heinrich points out that in

practice a Donkey Vote could mean any kind of protest vote…
and this is where it gets interesting…including voting for a
fictional character."

"You mean like…"

"Yep," Katie said, completing Jake's thought. "a fictional
character like Mickey Mouse, Donald Duck, or Bugs Bunny.
Heinrich delves into the whole fascinating history of votes that
went to completely fictional characters."

She paused a moment to let her words sink in. "He steps
right to the edge of calling for the first peacetime challenge to
the sedition acts. And he suggests the most likely test case would
be a future protest vote."

"A Mickey Mouse vote?"

"Or," Katie said, "a vote for the Silver Steer."

"You're not suggesting that a young Dolphus Heinrich was
actually advocating for an unlawful vote?"

"No, but Anne says he's an opportunist through and through,
with a real sense of the historical moment. If he senses the thing
he predicted in his unpublished paper back in 1972 coming to
pass, there's no telling what he might do."

"Tiramisu," she added, changing the subject as she whipped
off the lid to reveal two perfectly sliced pieces. "It's store-bought,
but it should do the trick."

"Don't mind if I do," Jake said, handing Katie her plate
before taking his. "So guess what went down while you were
working wonders on this amazing spaghetti feast."

"Bambi Bloomberg announced her retirement from *The
Scoop* to devote more time to her plastic surgery?"

"I love it when you're nasty," Jake said. "No, try Matt Pitchford calling out to the farm to ask your dad to host a candidate barbeque."

"You're kidding…. Daddy refused, right?"

"He tried to, but Pitchford, with a little assist from yours truly, convinced him otherwise."

"But Daddy hates crowds."

"So he claims. Apparently back in the day your grandfather and your father hosted a candidate pig roast to beat the band. Pitchford said he remembered anyone who was anyone being there."

"I remember seeing pictures of it when I was girl," Katie recalled. "But Daddy's never said much about it."

"Probably because it reminds him of his dad, which in turn reminds him how much he misses him. Anyhow, we're on, and—spoiler alert—he intends to ask you to co-chair the planning committee."

"How soon?"

"Nine days…. Crazy, isn't it?" Jake admitted. "Which reminds me, your dad wanted me to have you home early tonight. He wants our help sorting out some of the details of this last-minute shindig."

The newspaper editor's daughter looked up at the glowing hands of the clock over the short-order counter. "It's almost 10:00…. I suppose we should be getting back. Let's just leave the plates here. I can take care of it in the morning before we open."

"So should we put this place to bed," Jake said, waiting for her as she gathered up her coat and Dolph Heinrich's long-lost political manifesto.

"Definitely," she said, fishing in her pocket for her keys.

"May I escort you home?" he asked, bowing slightly.

She pushed him aside playfully. "It'd be a pretty weak political date if you didn't."

"My chariot awaits." He pointed to the Accord parked under the flickering lights of First Street. "So are you going to let me come in when we get back to your place?"

"I might," she said, winking, "but only if you promise to keep your hands off my heirloom tomatoes."

Fourteen

"So Anne Templeton sends her regards," Dolphus Heinrich mused, walking to the plate-glass windows of his temporary quarters for the election season. Unlike Cloward and Santoro, the cosmopolitan Heinrich had kept his campaign headquartered in the city. Thirty floors below him now lay Iowa's capital, Des Moines, basking in the early November sunlight. "How is my old colleague, Mr. Preston?"

"She fine," Jake told him. "Just moved to a condo downtown. We're probably no more than a mile from her house actually."

Heinrich returned from his eagles-nest view, sitting down heavily in an overstuffed leather recliner. "She was the star of the history department at Southwest Illinois State, and don't let anyone tell you otherwise."

"She says you were the real political genius…that you were at least a generation ahead of your time. Anyway, when she learned I was coming to visit you she asked me to give you this." Jake reached in his pocket for the jewelry box he had been dispatched to deliver. "Apparently she bought it a few years ago at a curio shop in DC when she was there doing research at the National Archives."

Heinrich eyed the box quizzically "Why didn't she just stop by my legislative offices and give it to me herself? I would have been delighted to see her."

"She tried," Jake explained, "even despite her aversion to K. Street. Apparently your secretary said you weren't in, and sent her away." Jake passed the miniature box to the politician with a shrug. "Anne wouldn't tell me what was inside."

He watched as Anne Templeton's former colleague withdrew a silver coin from the box and held it up to the light.

"Is that a cow on the tails side of the coin?" Jake asked. "And a donkey on the heads?"

"Correct on both counts," commented the former professor. "Except that it's no ordinary cow…. It's a steer." Heinrich brought the coin down to eye-level again. "The casting is very old…probably from the 1876 celebration of the centennial of George Washington's inaugural year in office." He paused to let the import of the gift sink in. "Mark Twain was right. History doesn't exactly repeat itself but, at least where presidents and steers are concerned, history does indeed rhyme."

"I imagine there's a story behind it," Jake remarked, and Heinrich motioned him toward a leather couch.

The one-time college president cleared his throat. "After retiring from the presidency to his farm at Mount Vernon, George Washington made it a personal quest to locate the finest jackasses in the world…"

"I see the election parable already," Jake interjected.

"So he finds himself searching the world over for mates for his mares in order to create a line of super mules. King Charles III of Spain catches wind of Washington's quest, and sends him two Andalusian donkeys."

"With a stubborn streak and a weakness for sangria, right?"

Heinrich smiled wanly. "Only one of the stud Spanish donkeys makes it across the Atlantic alive, so Washington dubs him Royal Gift. That's Royal Gift on the tails side of the coin."

"The ass end," Jake quipped. "So who's the handsome hunk of steer on the heads side?"

"That was Charles the III's attempt to make amends for the other royal jackass…the one who couldn't last the rough ride across the Atlantic. He next sent Washington a royal steer, a showpiece really, to reign over the pastures at Mount Vernon as a symbol of American freedom and independence."

"So what happened to them…Royal Gift and the steer who shall remain nameless?"

"The steer outlived Washington by a dozen years and ended up spending a leisurely retirement at the farm of Washington's grandson-in-law George Washington Parke Custis. As irony would have it George Washington, like the steer he inherited, was infertile, so he and Martha eventually adopted his step-grandson John, as a boy, after John's father died. You'll be amused to learn the unnamed steer was stolen from Custis's farm after Washington's death in 1799, and an attempt was made to ransom the bull, but to no avail, and the star-crossed steer was ultimately returned."

"Royal Gift, however, is another story altogether," continued Heinrich. "He was too shy, or too proud, to mate with the mares. So Washington, gentleman farmer that he was, figured out that if we waited until Royal Gift was, shall we say, *excited*, he could swap out an infertile donkey for a fertile mare. By

1799, Royal Gift had sired more than fifty of the best mules in the country by Washington's ingenious method."

"It's a great story," Jake commented. "And an even better gift. It's your very own silver steer."

"Politically fitting, isn't it?" remarked the professor. A hint of a smile played at the corner of his lips. "Please convey to Anne my deepest thanks."

Jake nodded his assent. "You made a big impression on her all those years ago. She still remembers some of the ground-breaking stuff on electoral politics you wrote, some of which you opted not to publish, as I understand it."

"Yes indeed," the candidate said, casting his eyes up at the ceiling. "The ideas flowed out of me back then. That doesn't mean, however, that my research was of the most orthodox kind."

"Anne shared this one with me," Jake said, digging into his messenger bag to hand Heinrich the ghost of academic papers past: "'The Road to Sedition.' Do you remember writing this?"

"My goodness," Heinrich said, as if Jake had handed him a picture of his teenage self all dressed up for the homecoming dance. "This takes me back a few years."

"You remember it then?"

The candidate flipped through the pages of his long-ago opus. "I do now," he said. "This is one I would have been proud to publish."

"But you didn't…. Why?"

"Because my senior colleagues at the time thought it was far too much of an ideological hot potato," said the congressman, a touch of bitterness entering his voice. "You learn that sometimes discretion is the better part of valor, at least where one's superiors are concerned."

"There's some fascinating stuff in there," Jake prompted him.

"You know you're probably one of only a dozen people on the planet who's read that work." He paused. "The tone is a bit on the prickly side, wouldn't you say?"

"I'd say *edgy* is a better word for it," Jake commented. "Personally, I had no idea there were sedition acts still on the books."

"You're not alone. Back when I was a college president, the faculty would invite me to deliver one class per year to our undergraduates. Naturally, I'd teach a course on American politics. And each time I'd take a couple of class sessions to talk about sedition and secession. Most of the students were juniors and seniors, meaning they'd been through fifteen years of schooling without once being taught how our government treats would-be dissenters and civil disobedients. In their minds abstention meant not having sex, rather than refraining from the vote out of protest." Heinrich chuckled. "We do a poor job of educating even our brightest young people about what to do when they feel the political process is irrevocably broken."

"Did you feel that way then...that it was broken beyond repair?"

"We're off the record, right?" Heinrich asked, crossing his legs to reveal a freshly polished wingtip. "You're correct that I did detect a certain brokenness back then, but unlike many of my students, I saw a potential future in public service, so I was more about channeling that dissatisfaction into reforming the process itself."

"Instead of resisting an established political authority, you'd change it from within, was that it?"

"That's the general idea, yes."

"Which brings us back to the Silver Steer. You've been one of the few candidates to truly get behind it. Santoro seemed like he was gung-ho, but at the last debate he distanced himself from it if it meant changing the way we elect our candidates."

"Mike Santoro is a friend of mine," Heinrich said. "In fact, some would claim he's a disciple. But I'm afraid he's much like any other politician who got his lunch handed to him in his last senatorial election. He's finding it more fruitful now to position himself as an outsider, mostly because he's suffered a loss in the very system that once promoted him. He's a progressive Republican, but only inasmuch as he fits within the established fold of the party."

"And where does that leave you?"

Heinrich laughed. "I've been asking myself that same question now that I'm hovering at what…ten percent in the polls."

"About eight percent as of this morning."

"Suffice it to say, not where I want to be." The candidate leaned forward, put his elbows on his knees, and sighed heavily. "I suppose you'll want to publish excerpts of that long-ago paper I wrote. Is that why you've sought me out…to float a trial balloon at me? You don't need my permission, you know, and I'm sure you'll find plenty of takers. The question is, what will publishing that mothballed paper do to my campaign?"

"I won't run it if you insist I don't."

"You'd be a fool not to. I would have at your age," Heinrich conceded. "There's no telling what breaking a story like this one could mean to your career."

"It could give your campaign the shot in the arm it's needed," Jake pointed out. "There's a lot of voter dissatisfaction out there…. They might actually rally around you."

"I hardly think so," Heinrich said, getting up to pace his well-outfitted penthouse. "They're angry enough to reject anyone who smells like K Street or Washington DC, especially when there's a protest vote in the works."

"You mean the Silver Steer?"

"That's exactly who…or rather what…I mean. No, I'm afraid publication of that paper would pretty much sound the death knell for my campaign, especially among the rank and file, who would regard it as plainly unpatriotic if not frankly subversive. You can see why I tried for many years to bury that little opus."

"The offer still stands," Jake reiterated. "I'm willing not to run it…especially for a friend of Anne's."

"Don't be so diplomatic, Mr. Preston. It's a good paper, and one that could get some real traction at a political moment like this." Heinrich turned his back on Jake to look out the window. "It looks like after all these years I've come full circle back to being a provocateur. I suppose I could get used to that role again." Heinrich returned to the coffee table to pick up the treatise. "You know if I suspended my campaign, and threw my votes to the Silver Steer, this thing…this race could get very, very interesting."

"What would happen if…if the Silver Steer actually won?" Jake asked, feeling like he was back in college again in his American government class.

"That's just exactly it, Mr. Preston.… I don't know the answer to your question. No one does. And that," he said with a hint of a smile, "is what makes the idea so incredibly appealing to a veteran campaigner like me. If I stay in the race, the outcome is virtually assured. Milt Cloward will win, and Mike Santoro and Paul Paule will duke it out for second. Of course, neither of them have the politics or the policies to run a truly national campaign, so whatever momentum they may achieve here is likely to be reversed by the outcomes in New Hampshire and further down the road in South Carolina. But if the Silver Steer wins…well, it's almost too radical a notion to even consider."

Heinrich wandered over to an elegant china cabinet and reached up to remove a wooden box from its top shelf. "I've been collecting these since I was a teenager, never dreaming that someday I'd have my own pin.… Ah yes, here it is." He pulled a button out of the box and handed it to Jake. "You'll enjoy this."

The button showed a picture of a large-nosed cartoon dog, wearing an Uncle Sam cap and a bowtie, raising his doggie arms aloft in triumph. The caption read, "Huckleberry Hound for Vice President."

"Probably Huckleberry would have made a better president than LBJ," Heinrich observed. "Anyway, it's a good example of a donkey vote, at least colloquially speaking."

"It's an incredible piece of memorabilia," Jake observed, putting the button carefully back in the cigar box from whence it came. "I guess someone needs to start printing up campaign buttons for the Silver Steer."

"Someone indeed," Heinrich repeated, adding, "if you came here, Mr. Preston, to ask my permission to print portions of my paper…go ahead. I'll wait and see what happens. In the unlikely event there's a swell of voter approval, I'll ride it. In the likelier scenario that I'm pilloried and vilified by my own hypocritically righteous party, I'll suspend my campaign in a blaze of equally righteous glory." He extended his hand. "I couldn't have predicted what our meeting would bring, but in the end I'm glad you knocked on my door. One reaches a certain stage of one's life, and he begins to reflect on the person he was before he began making concessions for what he assumed would be a greater good. Do you know what I mean?"

"I believe I do," Jake said.

"You'll understand even better when you're on the other side of 60," Heinrich said, walking his guest to the door. "Remember, Huckleberry Hound for President," he said, offering Jake a wane smile as he closed the door.

"And then there were five," Amethyst said darkly into her beer. "Sianara, Dolph Heinrich."

Less than forty-eight hours had passed since the *Times* had run the damning excerpts of Dolph Heinrich's long-mothballed academic paper, and the reaction from the hard-liners in Heinrich's party had been swift and merciless. He had been labeled a "traitor," a "closet radical," and a "fox in a henhouse."

Over beers at the Wagon Wheel, Jake and Amethyst listened as, for the umpteenth time, the wonks and pundits rehearsed and rehashed the contents of the allegedly seditious position paper. "Here he writes, 'And in the tradition of the Boston Tea Party, National Hale, and even John Brown, the time will soon come for a truly American people, somewhere in one of America's most forgotten and neglected places, to reclaim the sovereignty their founding fathers intended for them, and engage in the greatest protest vote this land has ever known, at a political and social consequence they themselves can barely fathom.' Well, I've got news for Mr. Heinrich, John Brown was a *traitor,* and so, sir, are you!"

Across from Jake in the booth, Amethyst flipped the channel to a somber network interview with RNC Chair Prince Reebus. "Bottom line is that Mr. Heinrich has always been something of a firebrand, and while there's room in our party for free-thinkers, there's no place in our party for the sort of unpatriotic and frankly dangerous sentiments he expresses in his paper. I suspect Mr. Heinrich himself would be in danger of being prosecuted under the very sedition acts his so-called scholarship brings to light."

Amethyst pointed the remote at the television. "Heinrich's press conference should be coming on any minute." She glanced at her watch. "The email blast said 8:00 PM Mississippi-time.... Okay, here we go."

"Give 'em hell, Dolph!" Mad enthused, bringing Jake and Amethyst a refill on their popcorn and a couple of Dolphus Heinrich Stouts as a bon-voyage tribute. "You know I hate to see that dirty old bastard hang 'em up," the barman lamented. "Minus all the affairs and the scandals and shit, he's about the only one of 'em that has any real policy initiatives."

"Who says he's going to put himself out to political pasture?" Jake cautioned. "Maybe he'll become the opposition candidate he always was, and just swim upstream for what's left of the race."

"Everyone who's ever worked with him says he's obstinate, idealistic, and prone to wandering off whenever a piece of legislation ceases to command his interest, or when a blonde begins to attract it," Amethyst observed. "But they also say he has one of the most brilliant intellects...for a politician, anyway...of his generation."

"It's the obstinate part that makes me dig 'im," Mad said. "He's just different enough to throw a wrench in the business-as-usual crowd in Washington."

On screen Heinrich rested his hands on the podium like it was an old friend he didn't plan on seeing in a while. "Thank you all for coming. Thank you. Tonight I intend to speak briefly and directly to the American voters about their options as I see them, and about from whence these venomous and mean-spirited attacks against me originate."

Heinrich looked directly into the camera—seemingly right into the Wagon Wheel itself, where Jake, Amethyst, and Mad looked on, rapt at the historical moment they were witnessing.

> In a state that's often overlooked by the rest of the nation but for the six months leading up to the presidential primary season, something very interesting, indeed

historic, is underway. As a former history professor and college president, I could offer you a historical lecture on why the country should pay close attention to the momentous events unfolding in the Midwest, but you would find much of the same content in the paper whose more radical excerpts have been cherry-picked and quoted ad nauseam in the yellow press these last few days.

Fortunately for the American voter, history is happening now, right before their eyes, in Iowa, where polls increasingly indicate an electorate that may, if they indeed possess the liberties to do so, close up ranks around a symbol of the very independence and autonomy they themselves once practiced. That symbol is, of course the Silver Steer, and, as the Steer itself has made clear in its recent videos, it is very real.

American voters are a courageous people, brave enough to elect a man like Lincoln. Of course, many of our best presidents have been 'accidental' presidents initially considered unfit to be at the top of the ticket and thereby relegated to vice-presidential status. These include many of the presidents best loved by the American people and rated most highly by my fellow presidential historians—Teddy Roosevelt, Harry Truman, and some would even say Cal Coolidge. My question to you, my fellow Americans, is what bravery you might exercise when the choices themselves are not worthy of your vote, when to choose between Candidate A and Candidate B is to sell yourself short in either instance.

There will be plenty of pundits who will tell you a protest vote is a good vote spoiled, but they would be wrong when the protest itself becomes the only just action among thoughtful and well-intentioned people. The party faithful may call you traitor, but that is merely their way of acknowledging the independence in another that they find wonting in themselves. Their vitriol is only the rhetoric expected to be directed at one who would dare to leave a club based on enforced loyalties, conspiratorial handshakes, and the smugly congratulatory back-slaps traded among those who assume the party machine is more powerful than the divine will of the people.

I, on the other hand, stand here tonight to remind you that history forever supports the American voter when he or she acts their conscience. And so, with all due seriousness and with an abiding belief that the people indeed know best, I urge my supporters in Iowa who are dissatisfied with the options as they are to consider casting their vote for the Silver Steer, with the confidence that history will judge them well for their audacious courage.

As of tonight I am officially suspending my campaign for President of the United States, as the recent attacks against me and my character cannot help but distract from the race as it moves into its final, crucial days. I thank the good people of Iowa, and of all the states where we have campaigned, for their patience, their open-mindedness, and their forbearance, and I urge them now as ever to vote their conscience. This election season, teach your children, and your children's children, what it means to be a citizen of vision. And while you are at it, write a chapter in the history books your great-grandchildren will someday read about in open-eyed wonder.

Good night, be brave, and may God be with you, and these United States.

Amethyst Gilchrest switched off the television, duly impressed. "That man can give a speech, can't he?" She took a long pull on her beer. "He's got me fired up to go vote, and I'm not even a Hawkeye."

"So what happens now?" Jake asked. "We're just a little over a week from election night."

"Don't know, partner. But I do know if I'm going to unmask the person behind the Silver Steer videos before our little corn poll happens, I'll need a breakthrough, and I'll need it soon."

"Did your editor at the *Times* phone Youtube about the This Is The Steer video?"

"Yeah, but they're not required to release the name of an individual posting a video unless there's unlawful or offensive activity, or unless those records have been subpoenaed in court. If TITS could be tried for sedition, I might be in business. As it is, though, it appears I'm going to have to wait for an admission from This Is The Steer…a clue, a bread crumb trail, or a vicious lawsuit."

"Any suspects?" Jake asked.

"None as yet," Am said, floating her icy mug back and forth across the table. "It's a needle in a haystack."

"Speaking of haystacks, how are things going on the barbeque planning committee?"

"Just ducky," Am said. "Between me and Mad, Herb Clarke's pig roast is turning into a silo—no pun intended—for anything and everything we've ever dreamed of wanting a candidate to do or say but were afraid to ask."

"Like what."

"Like milk a cow."

"You're kidding."

"In this case, yes. Herb Clarke claims his last remaining cow is dry, whatever the hell that means. I can tell you between castrated bulls and dry cows, the Midwestern farm seems a pretty macabre affair to me, just sayin.'"

"But you feel like it's going to come off without a hitch?"

"Oh, I wouldn't say that…. No, I wouldn't say that at all. They'll be more hitches in our little barbeque than in a two-mile-long coal train, but it'll happen all the same. We stuffed half the ticket envelopes last night, which is exactly why I'm here, drowning my sorrows with you, under the pretext that I have an urgent story to write about Heinrich's calling it quits, so that I don't have to experience Envelope-Stuffing, the Sequel."

"So the rest of the committee, minus you and Mad, is stuffing envelopes and you're here revealing top-secret information about what's happening behind the scenes in the biggest little campaign event of this election cycle?"

"I figured you'd get all of the information from that chick, Katie, anyway," Amethyst said, "who I've got to say I'm sort of warming up to. She's so thoughtful it just about makes me sick."

"I've hardly seen her these last few days," Jake confessed. "She's either at the restaurant, planning for the barbeque, or down in Des Moines helping her old prof fix up her rambling old Victorian so she can put it on the market."

"And on the subject of old profs, a toast," Am said, raising her glass of stout high into the Wagon Wheel's stale stratosphere.

"To what?" Jake asked.

"A toast to your breaking the Heinrich story with an archival assist from your girlfriend and your girlfriend's crusty professor."

Jake clinked Am's glass. "I'll drink to that, but, just so you know, she's not my girlfriend."

"Really," Am said, raising an eyebrow, "could've fooled me."

"Speaking of friendships, how's Mad?"

"Oh, Mad Mad Mad Mad Mad Mad Mad," Am said, glancing at the bearded barman busily serving up a group of equally hirsute friends who, he'd told them, had driven down to see him for election week. "He's so full of that Up-With-the-People progressive bullshit it's coming out the holes of that ratty-ass Army jacket he wears around everywhere. But he's a force to be reckoned with, I'll give him that. He's like a really good Limburger…good in small doses, but with an unpleasant capacity to linger and turn to funk."

"As a cheesehead, you mean he's young and sharp," Jake offered.

Am nodded appreciatively at the metaphor. "He's definitely not mild." She paused. "You see, that's what I miss so much about you, Preston. You're like my very own Silver Steer."

"Cold and metallic?"

"No, right here in front of me…but just out of reach."

Fifteen

"So will you be my political date for the afternoon?" Katie Clarke asked.

They were sitting in the living room at the farmhouse, a steady stream of VIPs too proud to use the porta-a-johns walking past them to avail themselves of Herb Clarke's first-floor toilet. At the moment, none other than Chuck Sousage stood waiting his turn in the water closet.

"Looks like you worked your magic, Chuck," Jake said, looking out the window at a crowd that easily numbered in the thousands. "Nine days isn't a lot of time to shake the trees, but you did it."

"Daddy knows how to pick his PR men," Katie said.

Sousage had grown in a beard in the weeks since he had been relieved of his duties, and, Jake couldn't help but notice, his entire demeanor seemed to have changed. In his hiatus from ceaselessly promoting party politics, he had almost, but not quite, become a sympathetic character.

Behind Sousage, the door to Herb Clarke's bathroom clicked open, and one of the hundreds of anonymous, well-dressed young staffers that had descended on the farm exited without making eye-contact.

"Kinda relieved to discover I've still got the ol' promotional mojo," the PR guru said. "Man, when I got your call last week,

Jake, I thought you might be pulling my leg, or rubbing salt into the wound." Sousage beamed—the confident, professional smile Jake remembered from his abbreviated breakfast with Rhymes-with-Corsage weeks earlier. "Nine days later I'm out of the shitcan and about to go into Herb Clarke's exclusive shitter as a credentialed PR man again. That's life, son...one moment someone or something takes a mighty dump on you; the next you're taking a prodigious dump on them. Now, if you'll excuse me I've got some business to attend to that's almost, but not quite, as messy as politics."

As soon as Mr. Breakfast Patty had closed the bathroom door behind him, Jake turned gratefully back to his political date. "Be forewarned, friend, I may try to get to political second base today."

"Which is what exactly?"

"A flesh-pressing with the candidates."

"I'd hate to know what a home run is then."

"Yes you would," Jake replied conspiratorially. "There are some things an Innocent like you should not know."

"So now I'm the political naïf?"

"Let's just say co-chairing the planning committee for the Herb Clarke Candidate Barbeque doesn't exactly qualify you as a Washington insider."

"Fair point," Katie allowed. "But neither does squatting in the farmhouse of the young woman who headed up the executive planning committee of the Herb Clarke Candidate Barbeque.... C'mon mister sweepstakes winner," she said, grabbing him by the wrist, "let's go out and wallow in it."

"I don't know why the committee chose that title in the first place," Jake said, grabbing a program from the end table on their way out. "It sounds like we're actually barbequing the candidates."

Katie grinned wickedly. "Who says we're not?" She snatched the program from Jake's hand. "Far be it for the girl who planned the lay-out of this whole she-bang to offer up an itinerary, but I suggest we begin on the east side of the property with Brad Charger's Tolerance Tent."

"Charger dropped out of the race weeks ago, right?"

"He's still living over in Sweet Loam, doing some consulting on diversity for the local school district.... He contacted us first and Pitchford said it would be a publicity headache not to invite him." She pointed back to the hand-drawn map on the day's schedule of events. "Then we head over to Santoro's Born in America tent."

"Barn in America is more like it, don't you think," Jake quipped.

"Then we make a bee-line from there to Cloward's and Box-man's big-tops."

"In between can we stop by Renard Kane's Church of the Immaculately Hypothetical Wife and Mistress?"

"Would you believe we actually issued him a courtesy invite, but he's hidden himself away from the pitchfork-wielding mobs back in Birmingham."

"I can imagine," Jake said. "There's nothing really to feel good about forgiving him for, since his sins were mostly of the imaginary nature."

"So we end up here," Katie said, tracing their proposed route with her index finger, "on the west side of the farm at the Rich Priestly Fifties Drive-Thru."

Jake scratched his head. "I'm not sure I get that one. Everybody but the VIPs had to ride the shuttle in. How do the Priestly people expect anyone to drive up and order a malted milk?"

Kate shook her head ruefully. "Awfully literal today, aren't we, Mr. Preston? The Priestlys wanted to highlight the fact they're high-school sweethearts. So they ordered a vinyl tent to look like a 1950s drive-in malt shop, chrome and all. Who knows, if you behave yourself, I might just treat you to a True Blue Cheeseburger and a side of Freedom Fries."

"Delivered by a wholesome maid roller skating on pasture grass…?"

Katie winked. "Or delivered by the wholesome maid who lives on this farm. We'll see. Let's go…. Forward toward Charger!"

It took them less than five minutes to locate the Brad Charger Tolerance Tent beneath the shade of Herb Clarke's 150-year-old oak grove. As they entered Charger was holding court with a group of school kids who had been bussed in from Sweet Loam for a celebrity civics lesson.

"Hey, everyone, look who's here. It's celebrity journalist Jake Preston and the young lady who lives on this beautiful farm, Kate Clarke."

"Hey, I've seen you on TV," one of the kids said, standing up to point at Jake. "You're the Silver Steer guy."

Jake bowed. "At your service."

Brad Charger looked intently at them. "Jake and Katie are perfect examples of tolerance."

"How?" asked one of the little girls, clearly puzzled.

"Jake came to us all the way from Rocky Mountains, and Katie is a farm girl born right here in Iowa. They're different people from very different places, but see how well they like one another?" Katie cocked her head and smiled goofily at Jake for Charger's benefit. "Kids, that's how tolerance works. The fact that someone is different than you are, or comes from a different environment, adds spice to life." Charger raised his hand in acknowledgment. "Thanks Jake and Katie, for reminding us what tolerance is."

"I've got to get out of here," Jake whispered urgently into Katie's ear. "It's so over-the-top sweet I feel like I'm about to gag on cotton candy." She nodded, and together they slipped out of the tent past a couple of heavily pierced college interns manning Charger's Rainbow of Diversity table.

"When the candidates learned that we expected all of them to give something back to the barbeque attendees, the Santoro camp requested a tent for his Born in America stuff," Katie explained on their way to the next destination. "Then Milt Cloward had to have one, too. And pretty soon tents were the gold standard. They kept one-upping one another until Rich Priestly used his oil money to build that vinyl temple of a malt shop over there." She pointed west to where the early November sun glinted off Priestly's chrome-trimmed monstrosity.

"Where to next?" Jake asked.

"I think we'll skip Santoro for the time being." Katie stopped to size up the eager crowd waiting to have their picture taken with a costumed Uncle Sam, to get their free copy of the Constitution, and to test their knowledge of American history at the Know Your Country booth.

"Shall we visit Paul Paule's libertarian wonderland then?"

"Gee, can we?" Jake teased, following his political date through the maze to a byzantine series of what looked like carnival games. "What…no tent?"

"They tried," Katie explained. "But they discovered their Slipping Dollar slide was too tall to fit underneath even the bigtops they could get trucked in from Des Moines. It was either cut a hole in the top of a very pricey rental or go tentless. Paule ultimately decided it would be wasteful to rip up a perfectly good big-top."

"He would, wouldn't he," Jake observed, taking in the magnitude of the outsized metaphor that was the two-story inflatable dollar slide, whose top denoted what a dollar was worth in gold one hundred years ago compared to the slide in value of that same dollar represented today. As he watched, blissfully unaware kids zipped down the slippery slope while their parents looked on, anxious about the prospect of a sudden deflation of a more literal kind.

Kate pointed across the Paule carnival grounds to the other end of the makeshift midway, where it appeared as if a mini Woodstock might be underway. There several shirtless high school boys, pale as the day God made them, stood shivering as they awaited their turn in the dunk tank.

"Press, pretty please, won't you please win one for me?" Jake's political date asked, all mock-schoolgirl.

Meanwhile the kid impersonating the Fed Chairman hurled abuse at him and the other contestants loitering on the slippery grass, awaiting their shot.

"I want to deflate your dollar," the kid whined, sounding like a high-pitched, pre-pubescent version of Mr. Potter from *It's a Wonderful Life*. "I want your money so I can make it worthless. Give me your cash, you no-good gold bugs." Beside, him another kid, this one clearly picked for the power of his pipes, shouted in Jake's ear as he handed out softballs to the willing participants. "Step rrrright up. Dunk the Fed Chairman. Get the Fed Chair All Wet. One-time. Ooone-time. Taaaake your chances here. Give it a whirl, big guy."

Jake took aim at the bulls-eye as the kid hurled insults at him. "You can't hit me," the kid on the hotseat taunted, sticking his thumbs in his ears and wiggling his fingers. "You can't even make your deadlines."

Jake smiled gamely. The kid was going down. Behind him, Katie Clarke egged him. "Nail him, Press," she whispered.

"I'm gonna rock your money-changer's world," Jake said, grunting as he let loose the first fastball he'd thrown since suiting up for Babe Ruth baseball as a kid back in Florida.

"Better luck next time, chump," the punk catcalled as Jake's high heat missed the target by a good six inches. "You can't take me down!"

"I'm worthless," Jake said, handing his second ball to Katie, who proceeded to underhand the Fed Chair to a watery grave on her first attempt.

"Piece of cake," she said, dusting off her hands.

"Where'd you learn to pitch like that?"

"Hereford High state softball champs, 1990-something."

"And how come you never bothered to tell me about this hidden talent of yours?"

"Because you never bothered to ask. You never ask about a lot of things, Jacob Preston…. C'mon, I want to take you out back to the barn."

"Behold," she declared when they reached their destination a moment later, "the Silver Cow!" Katie pointed to a sorry-looking Guernsey staring mournfully off into the shadows of the old dairy barn. "Jake this is Mildred, Mildred, Jake. It's okay, Millie, Jake is domesticated."

Jake scratched the beast between the ears as kid after kid stepped up on a plastic footstool so that Marianne Meyers, third grade teacher and occasional newspaper columnist extraordinaire, could snap their souvenir pic.

"Saint that she is, Mrs. Meyers agreed to fill in for me as photographer until I had at least toured you around the grounds," Katie explained.

"Why didn't you tell me you had this beautiful specimen of an over-the-hill bovine?" Jake asked.

"I hope you're not referring to Mrs. Meyers," Katie whispered.

Jake frowned. "I mean why didn't you tell me about Mildred?"

"Daddy and I both did. And, as usual, your mind was else-where."

Jake stepped back so a kid could get his picture without a journalist spoiling the mug shot.... Or maybe cud shot was more like it. "This was your idea?"

"Start to finish," she said, putting her hands on her hips. "Actually, this was a compromise. Pitchford explicitly forbade any use of the Silver Steer's likeness at the barbecue."

"How in the hell did Herb let that fly?" Jake asked, incredu-lous. "I thought the old man and the planning committee were completely calling the shots."

"We were," Katie said, "until we heard from the attorney, or more accurately the attorneys, the state Republican party keeps on retainer. Pitchford pulled out the big guns, and the big bucks, apparently, to make sure the likeness of the Silver Steer didn't undermine the last big political event on the calendar, especially with all these television cameras rolling."

"So you subverted the paradigm."

"As they say in Wisconsin, 'you betcha,'" Katie said, motion-ing toward Mildred. "Have cow, will politic. We knew the kids would be disappointed if the Silver Steer wasn't here in some fashion, so we settled on the Silver Cow. It's Millie's shining moment. Anyway, I carried some of my photographer's lighting out here to brighten things up, and we're off and running, and speaking of running.... The Pioneer Games begin in ten min-utes."

"Are you going to reveal to me what these mysterious trials entail?"

Katie laughed. "Patience, Jacob Preston. All mysteries shall be revealed in time."

Jake had never seen Herb Clarke so animated.

"Welcome, welcome, welcome," the editor barked from atop the makeshift pitcher's mound his volunteers had built for the candidate barbeque. "Come on over for the afternoon's main attraction, the Pioneer Games."

"Each of the candidates and their staffs have graciously agreed to set aside partisan bickering for a few hours this afternoon in the spirit of good old-fashioned play, and to cast themselves back in time, along with the rest of us. By agreement of the candidates all cameras and recording devices, including those from the major media outlets, must be put away at this time."

Jake looked at Kate, puzzled. *No recording devices?* She shrugged. "Pitchford again," she whispered.

On the pitcher's mound Clarke was ready to get things started. "Several high-profile national journalists based in Hereford this fall have generously agreed to emcee each of our competitions. Here to explain the first of our pioneer games to you is Amethyst Gilchrest of the *Times*.

"Thank you, Mr. Clarke, and heellllloooo, Hereford!" Amethyst shouted, hamming it up. "It's great to be here on this sunny day in November. Many of you know me as that sassy yet sophisticated…okay, somewhat snarky political columnist for the *Times,* but today I'll be leading the candidates in a pioneer game known as the Railroad Spelling Bee. Basically it works like this…all the participants line up next to the wall. The person in the front of the line can spell any word they want and the contestant following them must spell a word beginning with the letter on which the previous contestant's word ended. So suppose I decide to spell the word "silver," ending in "r." The person coming up behind me would then have to spell a word beginning with "r," as in "Republican." The next person in line would have to correctly spell a word that begin with the last letter in the word *Republican*, in this case the letter 'n.'" Whoever misspells their word must sit down, and the game continues with the correct spelling."

"Now because we're all adults here, or most of us are anyway, we've added a couple of additional rules to make our pioneer game more apropos to the occasion. First, every word the candidates spell must be at least three syllables long, and, second, the word must have something to do with elections or campaigns. Candidates, are you ready? Congresswoman Boxman, ladies first."

Rochelle Boxman stepped atop the square hay bales that had been set up as a makeshift stage. "Ms. Boxman, what three-syllable, campaign-related word will you spell for us today?"

"B-a-l-l-o-t."

"Uh-oh, that's two syllables. Judges, your ruling please." Amethyst looked to the sidelines where Herb Clarke gave her a reluctant thumbs-up sign. "Good enough!" Amethyst enthused and the crowd clapped dutifully.

"Next up, former governor of Connecticut, Milt Cloward!"

"Gee, I haven't been this nervous since the first time I asked Blanche out on a date," gushed the frontrunner. "Let me see. How about this?"

"P-r-e-s-i-d-e-n-t-i-a-l…. Did I get that right?"

"You sure did," Amethyst said, ringing a cowbell to signify the correct answer. "Mr. Paule, remember now your word must begin with the last letter of Mr. Cloward's word."

"Which was what?" Paul Paule asked.

"An 'l'."

"L-i-b-e-r-t-y."

"And explain to us what your word has to do with elections," Amethyst prompted.

"It has to do directly with my election," Paule replied grumpily.

"Alrighty then," Am said as the next candidate mounted the bales. "Senator Santoro, tough one here…. How about a three-syllable election or campaign word that begins with a Y."

"Y me?" Santoro joked. "No seriously, how about Y-s-a-b-e-l-l-e. That's the Italian spelling of my great-grandmother's name. It means 'consecrated by god.'" Santoro beamed.

"Can you tell us what Ysabelle has to do with our elections?"

"Because I wouldn't be here, in America, running for President if it hadn't been for my nonna."

"That's good enough for me," Amethyst said, ringing her cowbell. "And now, last but not least is Rich Priestly. Mr. Priestly, why don't you join me up here for a go in the hay."

"Don't mind if I do," said Priestly, grinning ear to ear. He looked to Jake like he'd just been chosen for the lead in the school play. "Just tell me what you need me to do."

"You need to spell a three-syllable word relating to elections that begins with the letter 'e'."

Priestly thought hard. "I can't think of anything," he said finally. "My mind's just a big fat blank."

Jake caught Amethyst's eye. She was finding it hard to resist the needle. "What about 'empathetic' as in an empathetic electorate?"

"P-a-t-h-e-" Priestly stopped, clearly stumped, and Am mercifully waved him off. "You can stop there, Mr. Priestly. 'Empathetic' begins with an 'e.' 'Pathetic', by contrast, begins with Congress."

"Oops," Rich Priestly said, shrugging his shoulders endearingly.

"Again, the prompt is a three-syllable word having something…anything to do with elections."

"E-x-c-e-l-l-e-n-t, which is what I'm striving for in my campaign. Pure excellent."

Amethyst gave a dispirited wave of her cowbell. "That concludes our first round of pioneer games. With a little creativity, all five of our candidates have kept their railcars on the track in our Railroad Spelling Bee. Next I'll turn it over to Kate Clarke to tell the candidates about the next agrarian game to be played in our little backyard, barnyard Olympiad. Katie, why don't you come up here and tell these Railroad Spelling Bee pros how to play Shadow Tag, and then, as our final pioneer game of the afternoon, Herb Clarke will host an inning of flatboard and twine baseball with the candidates divided up into two separate teams with consummate waffler Jake Preston on the mound. You won't want to swing and miss it."

"That's one run for the Republicans," Herb Clarke announced from his perch atop the bleachers that had been brought in for the final pioneer game of the day—flatboard and twine baseball where the flatboard was a three-foot-long barnboard the editor had wiggled loose from one of his many semi-descrepit barns. "And we also have one run for the True Conservatives." Clarke held up an index finger on each hand to indicate a dead heat, though it looked to Jake as if he might have been making the universal sign for the Silver Steer. "We'll have to end it in a tie, I'm afraid, to stay on time with our program. Later tonight we've got a bluegrass band for your enjoyment, Hereford's own Artie Shaw and his Cowtown Pickers, but please turn your attention now to the Jumbotron in leftfield. Each of the candidates has put together a five-minute video especially for barbecue attendees in order to introduce themselves to you and your families. And to those of you in the media, this is the point in the proceedings when you may begin filming again. Madison, cue up our candidate videos, if you will."

In the distance the army jacket-clad Mad raised his hand, punched a button, and the Jumbotron displayed the words "Welcome to the Candidate Barbecue" with the insignia of the state Republican party embossed just below.

"First on our list alphabetical list is Rochelle Boxman, the Congresswoman and environmental lawyer from South Dakota."

As the crowd looked on, the big screen flickered on, then off, until a random smattering of illuminated pixels decorated the board like fireworks.

This was definitely not Rochelle Boxman.

Instead, projected in front of the crowd was the enormous image of a person wearing a mask that made them look like a minotaur. On closer inspection, Jake noticed, it wasn't a minotaur, but a cow's head, and the man—or was it a woman—behind the mask in the video was beginning to speak.

"I am the Silver Steer," the cow's head said in an otherworldly, digitized voice. In the crowd children screamed—some out of fear, and some out of pure, starstruck delight. Even Jake had to admit the Silver Steer in its semi-human personae was a little bit spooky.

"My agenda is your agenda. My cause is your cause. The planks in my platform are your platform. My victory, or my defeat, will be yours. What do I want? Only a fair, open, and transparent election. A chance to do right by the voters of this and other states. A chance to represent a true alternative to the establishment candidates for the first time in modern American history…. Friends, Countrymen, Citizens, the Silver Steer heartily accepts the people's nomination for the Presidency of the United States."

Sixteen

"Welcome back to *The Scoop*, I'm Bambi Bloomberg and this, as always, is my cohost Venus Jones."

"Yo, yo, yo," Venus Jones called out.

"Venus and I are delighted to bring back Jake Preston, the upstart reporter whose innocent question in one of the first presidential debates gave rise to the phenomenon we now know as the Silver Steer. We're going to bring out our second guest, political history professor Anne Templeton, in just a moment, but for now we'd like to get Jake's reaction to the latest video produced by the ballot-inspired bovine…. Jacob, how have you been the last couple weeks? Managing to stay on top of this upside-down campaign?"

"Getting a little dizzy, Bambi."

"Time to get off the ride then, boy," Venus quipped.

"Jake, why don't you catch our viewers up on what's been happening with the Silver Steer over a weekend that included a barbeque on the farm of the editor of the *Hereford Gate* newspaper. Hidden-camera footage shot at that event has been making its way around the Internet ever since, and not all of it is flattering to the candidates. Is that fair to say?"

"I'm afraid so."

"Why don't we start there before moving on to talk about the man or woman behind the mask in the latest, and most life-like, incarnation of the Silver Steer yet. So let me start by saying I've seen the videos shot at the barbeque, and I'm not quite sure what the fuss is all about."

"The fuss, girlfriend, is that these Republican candidates are nothin' but a chain of fools," Venus piped up. "They're petty, back biting, and worse at spelling than I am, and let me tell you that's saying something. This girl can't even spell FYI."

Bambi smiled patiently at her charismatic cohost. "Jake the general impression from the videos leaked to the press is that the candidates seemed rather inept at things many voters do on a regular basis…like playing baseball."

"Or spelling *potato*," Venus added.

"As you know, Jacob, I was there, too. And I must say even I found the candidates a bit off-putting once they were forced outside their tents."

"Some see it that way," Jake said, doing his best to be diplomatic.

"But the big surprise of the barbecue was undoubtedly a new Silver Steer video, this one somehow spliced or smuggled into the campaign bios the candidates had produced especially for this climactic event. Are there any indications yet as to how that slight of hand may have been accomplished?"

"It could have been anyone. The tape was apparently produced off-site, and no laws were broken so far as we know. Each of the candidates did sign a document supplied by the Republican party in which they were promised, for example, that their videos would play, but they were not contracts, just memos of understanding. And their videos did play, though, as you know, Bambi, the crowd was in such an uproar over the Silver Steer video announcement of its candidacy that by that point the other candidate bios hardly seemed to matter."

"The big question appears to be the degree to which this video has changed the dynamics of the race with the iconic Iowa Caucuses less than a week away now. Has it, in fact, changed the electoral math?"

"There's no question but that it has," Jake surmised. "Until this latest video most of the pundits believed the Silver Steer was a flash in the pan, a corny media fad that went viral among a Midwest electorate and would play itself out when voters realized, or were made to realize, the stakes."

"No pun intended, right?" Venus interjected, wagging her finger at the camera.

"What do you think has changed?" Bambi asked, rolling her eyes at her cohost.

"Now it's not just some homemade video of a cow in a stall somewhere. Now someone is actually assuming the role of the Silver Steer, which means the Silver Steer has a human face it lacked before. Bottom line: this Silver Steer seems much more real to voters, myself included."

"And what do Republican party officials have to say about this?"

"We'll see," Jake said. "They're due to release a statement later this evening. I can imagine they're not at all happy."

"As unhappy as when you first mentioned the Silver Steer?"

"Likely even more," Jake conceded.

"And do you suppose we will be seeing any more videos from the Silver Steer prior to election night?"

Jake shook his head. "I doubt it. It's simply too risky for… for whoever is assuming this personae. There's a rumor going around the press corps that the state Republican party and the Iowa Secretary of State have asked the FBI to investigate whether this Silver Steer poses any immediate threat to the election."

"Do you think there's any merit to that charge?"

"It depends on how you define threat. Do I think the voters are tired of being scared and bullied away from voting their hearts? Absolutely. But do I think the party's inevitable scare tactics will work on a certain subset of the voters, yes, I do. What happens on caucus night now is anyone's guess."

Bambi Bloomberg turned to face the camera. "Fortunately, we don't need to guess. We've got an expert in election history right here in our studio, Dr. Anne Templeton, professor emerita from Central Iowa University."

Anne Templeton sat down on the couch beside Jake. "Emerita?" Jake asked, turning to greet her.

"Retired effective the end of this semester," the professor said, "which, since I'm on sabbatical, effectively means now."

"'Bout time you came down out of that ivory tower, girl," Venus interjected. "That place will rot your brains."

"Too true," Templeton said. "Though I must say I've had some wonderful students and colleagues over the years."

"So what's your take on the viral barbeque videos making the media rounds, and the emergence of the first Silver Steer video in over ten days?" asked Bambi.

"I'd defer to Jake on the effect of the hidden-camera footage of the barbeque," Templeton said. "But speaking personally, I found myself turned off by the candidate's extreme competitiveness."

"Yes, but wasn't competition the whole idea behind the Silver Steer trophy in the first place?"

"Not exactly," Jake said. "It's safe to presume politicians that have succeeded at this level are ultra ambitious. The Silver Steer was really about their not pretending that their competitiveness didn't exist."

"What'd he just say?" Venus asked. "Boy, it's a good thing you didn't follow the professor here into teaching."

Professor Templeton continued, "I'm just one voter, but I found myself reminded how normal these candidates are, and that produced an interesting internal debate. On the one hand, the fact that Milt Cloward can't hit a twine ball makes him more relatable and real to me, because I can't hit a ball either…of any kind. On the other hand, seeing a man who stands a good chance of the being the next President of the United States whiff in his first at bat makes him seem less the superhuman talent we need him to be to restore the reputation of the United States in a new world order. Does that make sense?"

With a sympathetic nod from Bambi, Anne Templeton pressed ahead. "I think that's the process a lot of voters are going through right now. And now comes this new video from someone now not only adopting the personae of the Silver Steer, but actually embodying it. By contrast, this new representation feels like a superhero or a myth. It has no voting record to live down, no rebellious kids who have been in and out of jail, no checkered past as a corporate raider, a failed senator, or a philanderer real or imagined."

"The thing I don't get," Venus said, "is how some dude or chick wearing some cowhead mask can enter themselves into an election. I can't put on my tiara and be Miss Universe, know what I'm sayin'?"

"Barring a last-minute election change on the part of the Secretary of State, the law is clear on this matter. The only realistic way the Silver Steer could win next Tuesday's caucuses would be by write-in vote."

"And isn't such a write-in campaign looking increasingly likely?" Bambi asked.

"Yes, but the problems with the write-in are well understood by political scientists. First, it relies on spelling."

"Game over then," Venus said.

"For some, it might be," the professor said, smiling wryly. "While 'Silver Steer' is not difficult to spell, in an era of printed ballots, handwritten responses make the chances of potentially ambiguous or invalid ballots exponentially larger. If the person helping with a hand-count of the votes can't read the handwriting on the ballot, it would likely be considered spoiled."

"Are there any examples in American history of successful write-in candidates?" Bambi asked.

"Oh my, yes! Name me virtually any past president between Hoover and Kennedy and I can point to at least one state primary they won on a write-in. Most of these fascinating instances are known only to presidential historians. Why? Because in most cases the candidate in question was unable, for procedural reasons, to get on the ballot in only one or two states out of fifty. You'll remember we saw this in Virginia in the 2012 campaign for the Republican nomination. At least two of the major candidates failed to certify the required number of signatures, so they were left with no choice but to mount a write-in campaign in that particular state."

"Go ahead, professor," Venus coaxed, "name names."

"Okay," Templeton said. "Iowa's own Hebert Hoover won the Massachusetts Republican primary as a write-in 1928."

"Somebody besides a dead white dude who caused the Depression," Venus insisted.

"I suppose FDR winning the Democratic New Jersey primary as a write-in in 1940 would count as a dead white guy, too."

"You got it, girl."

"Nixon, Kennedy, and Johnson…all dead but getting warmer; all won state primaries as a write-in. Then there's Ralph Nader."

Venus widened her eyes. "You mean he ain't dead yet?"

"Not yet, hard as that may be for some to accept." The professor laughed. "In fact, Mr. Nader may be the best contemporary example we have. In 1992 he ran in the New Hampshire primary as a write-in on both the Democratic and Republican tickets simultaneously. Actually, his name never appeared on the ballot to my knowledge. He ran as 'None of the Above.'"

"So if 'None of the Above' won, Nader would have claimed victory?" Bambi said.

The professor nodded. "Precisely. And therein lies the volatility of the write-in candidate, especially if it's a donkey vote."

"A donkey what?" Venus asked.

"A donkey vote, Venus. Colloquially it's come to mean a protest vote. So while the write-in may be the only truly democratic option American voters have left at their disposal, our history is so driven by the two-party system that voting for a candidate who's not either a Republican or a Democrat is considered whimsical at best and wasteful at worse. Protest votes in the past have attempted to own and in some ways celebrate their perceived eccentricity."

"Explain," Bambi urged, leaning back in her couch.

"Remember *Mad* magazine?"

"Are you kidding," Bambi said. "My little brothers practically grew up with it."

"Mine, too," Templeton agreed. "You'll remember that *Mad* ran Alfred E. Neumann as a write-in candidate for almost two decades. Neumann never got so much as single delegate, so far as I know, though he helped sell a lot of magazines. And then there's the obvious fact that, while he's the personae for the magazine, he's completely a fiction. And of course Huckleberry Hound, George Jetson, and Captain America have all at one time or another thrown their fictive hats into the ring.... But the Silver Steer is different than all those examples I've named. Here we have a fictional character who has at least a distant shot of pulling this off if the voters resonating to its message don't get cold feet on election night. And at the same time there are echoes of Ralph Nader here."

"Not him again," Venus sighed

"I'm afraid so. In the almost unthinkable event that the Silver Steer would win the caucuses as a write-in, the natural legal question would be: who is the Silver Steer?"

"My goodness," Bambi said. "Kids, don't ever let anyone tell you history isn't interesting. I'm so pleased you agreed to be our guest, Dr. Templeton, to share with us the fascinating history of our most fundamental civic right: voting. And there you have it folks, if you're thinking of casting your vote for the Silver Steer, there *is* a historical precedent. One way or another, make sure you get yourself out to the polls next Tuesday night and tune in here the following morning for all of your post-election analysis. Special thanks tonight to our amazing guests, journalist Jake Preston and history professor emerita Anne Templeton."

Jake turned to his seatmate on Bambi Bloomberg's couch as soon as the cameraman signaled the commercial break. "Congratulations on your retirement, Anne. I'm so happy for you!"

"Things have moved pretty quickly these last few weeks," she said. "But I'm confident it's the right time."

"What caused you to pull the trigger?"

"Lots of things, really—the move to the condo, all the sorting of the keepsakes and souvenirs making me remember all the things I wanted to do in my youth. Things I wanted to accomplish, or witness, rather than just study…. That and spending so much time with Katie. You know, I see so much of myself in her, Jake, that at times it's a bit scary."

"How do you mean?"

"For starters, she reminds me how old I really am. We figured I was about 45 years old when I had her in class as a senior in my elections history course…a mid-career academic. Now, almost twenty years later, my life is really nothing like I expected it to be. I thought I'd be married forever, then Michael passed away. I thought I'd be in the classroom forever, then I became a part-time administrator. If I've been wrong that many times in my life, I realized maybe my plan of waiting until I was 70 to retire was equally off the mark. That proved to be the kick in the pants I needed."

The professor continued, "Then there was something else, too. Katie has so many dreams, and I see her putting a lot of those off, or at least seeming to. Maybe I'm just projecting myself onto her, but I think back on the girl who wanted to run for political office some day, the daughter of a man who once also had political aspirations, and I wonder sometimes where some of our early impulses go."

"Maybe they just get channeled into other things," Jake offered. "Take Herb as an example. He's a newspaper editor. In terms of community involvement, that's pretty close to a politician."

"True, but Katie is a waitress. Now I suppose you could make the case that she minored in journalism and majored in political science and that both fields have a lot to do with the study of humans, but I fear that may be stretching it…. And what about me, or any of us? On the one hand, I'm a successful professor and a productive scholar. On the other hand, I'm a widow who's lived in the same house for the last twenty-five years. Of course some of my life possibilities changed when I lost Michael, but I've never had any children. I've never known any career other than teaching or research. In short, you could say I haven't truly lived."

"That's some serious soul searching for sure," Jake conceded.

"And long overdue," the professor observed. "But now look, I've gone on about me, and Katie, and Herb, without asking about you. How are you, Jacob?"

"Confused," Jake admitted, and the professor emerita laughed heartily.

"I'm so glad to hear you say that, because I am, too. You know, my time in academe has taught me one thing above all else."

"What's that?"

"You've got to fight confusion with more confusion. You've got to invite more productive chaos into your life until the chaos mixes with the confusion and the confusion mixes with newfound certainties and all of a sudden you have a pretty flavorful stew."

"Or a big fat mess," Jake said.

"Can you believe it was me giving a press conference up there just a few weeks ago?" Jake pointed toward the stage of the Hereford High auditorium where, in a few minutes, Matt Pitchford and Prince Reebus were due to issue a joint statement.

Herb Clarke smiled. "Seems like longer ago than that."

"So you've covered almost a half century of campaigns…"

"Quit saying that, will you?" the editor groused. "It makes me sound ancient."

"When I first met you, those battle scars were a point of pride," Jake pointed out. "I remember the old curmudgeon who, in this very auditorium, on just my second day in Hereford, took me to task for being a whippersnapper who didn't know his head from a hole in the ground where politics were concerned."

"Yes, but the last few weeks have done wonders for me, Jacob."

"Must be your heirloom tomatoes."

"It's many things, I suspect, but perhaps the principle driver has been this election. As a young man I dreamed of this kind of race."

"How do you mean?"

"Unpredictable. Utterly free-wheeling. Filled with a cast of characters and one true underdog."

"You mean the Silver Steer."

"Precisely."

"Someone's had a change of heart. I remember the Herb Clarke who said the Steer was nothing but a gimmick…a passing fancy. I also recall a Herb Clarke who had to hold his nose just to help Marianne Meyers write her pro-Steer column."

"I've evolved, Jacob, however belatedly. While I don't always approve of the Steer's methods, I've come to see them for what they are—a good-natured thumb in the eye of the presumptive nominees and the presumptuousness of the candidate-selection process itself, which is largely over before it even begins."

Jake felt the row of fold-out chairs shift beneath him, and looked over to see the girth of Mort McGreedy land in the chair beside him.

"Hello, Morton. Long time no see, " Herb said, acknowledging his weighty colleague. "I invited you to my barbeque but I never got your RSVP."

"Had to fly back home to recharge the batteries," McGreedy replied enigmatically.

"You're getting old, Mort," Herb said, mischief playing in his eyes. "You know I've been at this game almost twenty years longer than you, and I'm loving every minute of it."

"And I can't wait till it's over, so I can get back home and walk the dog," McGreedy said. "What's your point?"

"My point is if you can't enjoy this election, you can't enjoy any election."

"That so?" McGreedy grumbled. "You want me to get all juiced up because a bunch of back-benchers have survived the guillotine to be the last five candidates standing. Meanwhile, some nut job has made himself a cowhead mask out of paper mache and craft paint and horsehair and whatever else he's got in his garage and is threatening to turn the whole shebang upside down. I fail to see what's so great about that."

"It's great because you're alive to take part in it. But more than that it's great because it's different, and half again as exciting as any campaign you and I have ever covered."

"You're seeing things through rose-colored glasses, Herbie," McGreedy chided. "You sit in your office there on First Street, with your Norman-Rockwell view and your cactus sitting in the windowsill and Darlene out front at your beck and call, and it's easy because once every four years the political world comes to you. The rest of us have to follow these artful liars around the country and suffer all their peccadilloes and fibs. Let me tell you, it gets more than a little wearying."

"I suppose you're right in some respects," the editor conceded. "I do have certain advantages, though for every advantage there is an equal and opposite disadvantage. For example, virtually every college journalism student in the United States knows who Morton McGreedy is. Mort McGreedy already merits a couple of lines in their Introduction to Journalism textbooks, while the work of Herb Clarke is known largely within a twenty-mile radius of the farm where he grew up. Still, I'm not sure I'd trade places with you."

"And vice versa," McGreedy grumbled. "Now, if you don't mind, I'd like to return to my cynicism."

"Don't let us stop you," Jake interjected. "Half the time I'm right there with you. Same is true of this guy, by the way," he said indicating Clarke with his elbow, "until he found the journalistic fountain of youth somewhere a few weeks back."

"Gentlemen," Chuck Sousage called out. "If it isn't the big three of caucus journalism," he said, reaching out to shake each of their hands in turn.

"Chuckles," McGreedy said. "Hardly recognized you in that beard you're wearing these days. How in the hell are you?"

"Squeezed a decent little severance package out of the tight asses at the state G.O.P., so all and all things are looking up.

And Herb's candidate barbecue lit a fire back under me, I can tell you that."

"A man grows a beard, Chuck, and it's a sure sign an inward change has come over him," Herb Clarke observed.

"Damn straight. A man drags a goddamned piece of sharpened steel across his razor-burned face for thirty years to keep up appearances, and just like that he doesn't have to report to the office anymore…doesn't have to answer to anybody."

"Sounds like old Herbie's life over there," McGreedy said, nudging Herb Clarke beside him. "Or, better yet, Jake's. Preston, that dog, doesn't even have to show up at an office."

"Quiet, you three," Herb Clarke whispered, "here come the kingmakers."

Jake followed the editor's gaze to the stage where Matt Pitchford and Prince Reebus, both wearing red ties and blue blazers pinned with miniature American flags, strode to the podium. "Ladies and gentlemen of the press," Pitchford began, "thank you for your time and attention this morning. It is our intention to read a prepared statement and, as time allows, to answer a few of your questions. Prince Reebus, chair of the Republican National Committee, is here with me to field any inquiries you may have requiring a national perspective."

At the podium Pitchford cleared his throat and donned a pair of reading glasses. Gone was the Pitchford of humble agricultural anecdotes and back-slappy aphorisms. In his place was a serious, sober professional. "Our joint statement," continued Pitchford, "reads as follows:"

The Republican National Committee and the Iowa Republican Party wish to inform voters of the rapidly changing dynamics of the precinct caucus scheduled to commence this coming Tuesday evening. While it is not our intention to influence the outcome of the upcoming election, we hope and trust our perspective in this matter will be heeded.

This past weekend an individual adopting the personae of the Silver Steer hijacked an official video jointly produced and paid for by the Boxman, Cloward, Paule, Priestly, and Santoro campaigns. That individual used the video as a means by which to launch what he or she declared was a campaign for the Republican nomination. The RNC, in concert with the state Republican party, wishes to remind voters that the deadline for filing election papers passed many months ago.

We also wish to announce that we are launching a full-scale investigation into whether any criminal wrongdoing may have been involved in the creation and distribution of this most recent tape, and whether, and if, such a tape might have voiced a credible threat to the security of the upcoming election. We have requested the FBI's help in this matter. Again, we wish to remind citizens that this investigation, while serious, does not at present allege any specific criminal wrongdoing, though we reserve the right to allege so in the future.

We wish to remind voters that we do not, at this time, believe the video in question to be the work of terrorists, domestic or international, though that possibility exists. There is a chance, however remote, that the masked individual or individuals may be acting as agents for a foreign government or its proxy. While state and federal law enforcement are working hard to determine whether this may be the case, it is unlikely that the identity of the masked individual will be learned prior to voters going to the polls on Tuesday night. As such, we advise extreme caution and vigilance on your way to and from your polling place. To that end we are establishing a hotline where you may report any suspicious or unlawful activity. Again, we rely on vigilant voters to protect and uphold the democratic processes we hold dear.

Further joint statements from our offices may be forthcoming as events warrant between now and the first-in-the-nation vote. In the meantime, individuals wishing for up-to-the-minute news concerning the Silver Steer are urged to sign up for our text alert system.

A weary Matt Pitchford looked up from his prepared copy. "Mr. Reebus and I will be leaving shortly for further meetings with the Secretary of State. But we do have time to field a couple of your questions. Yes, Mr. McGreedy."

"Are you aware of any direct threats made against the caucuses?"

"We are not," Pitchford answered somberly. "Yes, Mr. Clarke."

"Have either you or Mr. Reebus given any thought to the deleterious effects your statement today may have on voter turnout on Tuesday."

"Our statement seeks merely to inform voters, not to persuade or dissuade them from participating."

"But don't you understand that language like that…gobbledygook you just read…is likely to scare or intimidate voters, and have the de facto effect of suppressing the vote."

"We do not share that assessment," Pitchford said flatly.

"We have time for one last question. Yes, Ms. Gilchrest?"

"What kinds of state and federal resources have been directed toward this investigation that might in any way effect the experience voters are likely to have at the polls on Tuesday night?"

"In terms of resources, we are giving this matter our highest possible priority. Voters are likely to notice increased security around many polling sites, especially in urban areas."

"It sounds like a police state," Herb Clarke muttered under his breath.

"So much for your ideal election," McGreedy deadpanned.

At the end of the front row Sousage stood, raising his voice before the state party chair could even think about recognizing him. "Matt Pitchford and Prince Reebus are frauds!" he shouted, his complexion gone from pale to ashen. "This is McCarthyism. It's a witch hunt, and all over what…someone making videos wearing a cow's head."

Out of the corner of his eye Jake noticed a sudden buzz of activity among the well-muscled security guards and polo-shirted party officials that had previously been standing unobtrusively in the wings.

In front of them, Chuck Sousage, Mr. Breakfast Patty, was in the process of flipping his lid. "The people of Iowa demand the resignation of the traitors Matthew Pitchford and Prince Reebus. The only way to a free and fair election is the immediate removal of these unaccountable election-fixers."

No sooner had Chuckles finished his diatribe than two burly rent-a-cops walked briskly down the front row past where Jake and Herb where seated, tripping over McGreedy's tree-trunk limbs along the way.

"Jesus, watch where you're walking, you apes," McGreedy said, standing up to glare at the security guys. "This is a press conference not a Nazi rally."

The officers grabbed Sousage by the forearms, one on either side, and held him tight. "I'm not going willingly," Sousage declared, as he attempted to root himself to the gymnasium floor. "You're going to have to drag me out of this auditorium…. Down with the fixers," Sousage called out again as the glorified bouncers escorted him away. "Up with free will and the Silver Steer!"

Another hubbub, this one from the back of the room, reached Jake's ears as yet another familiar voice echoed in the rafters of the undersized high school auditorium. "The people reject Milt Cloward. The people reject Mike Santoro and all the back-door deals by which they have been elevated to the status of frontrunners without the people's endorsement, without the people's blessing. We demand our country back. We demand to choose without undue influence."

Jake wheeled around to confirm his suspicions. The voice belonged to none other than Loretta Draper.

At the lectern Pitchford smirked as another group of security officials led the intransigent editor of the quasi-mythical *Weekly*

Badger out of the gym. "Let me apologize on behalf of Mr. Sousage for that unprofessional outburst. As most of you know, Mr. Sousage was dismissed from his post several weeks ago for conduct unbecoming a party official. We had all hoped he would come to see the folly of his ways, but apparently not.... As for the young lady there, I think perhaps she had better quit living with her parents and find something more productive to do with her energies. In any case, I'm afraid that is all the time we have for questions. Please direct any further inquires you may have to either my office or to the RNC. We ask for your full cooperation in our investigations as they proceed."

"This whole tawdry affair is going to the dogs," McGreedy grumbled, breathing heavily as the red drained from his cheeks. "I had half a mind to clock those goddamned storm troopers."

Herb Clarke nodded solemnly. "It's an abomination. Chuck Sousage may be a little unsettled at the moment, I'll grant you, but Hereford High is public property paid for by the taxpayers of this county.... Pitchford and Preebus should have been prepared for some blowback, and if they weren't, they should have held their little presser behind closed doors, on private property." The editor stood from his chair with surprising vigor. "C'mon Jacob, let's see if I can bend Mr. Big Shot's ear for a tic," he said, marching toward the stage with Jake in tow.

A moment later the old editor had the state party chair in his crosshairs. "Matthew," he began, "you and I both know the statement you delivered here today will be damaging, to say nothing of your heavy-handed and uncharitable handling of your former colleague."

"That's your opinion, Herb, not the opinion of our lawyers," Pitchford said, shaking hands with well-wishers and boosters as they left.

"So even though you grew up ten miles from here, and have been helping with elections in this state since you were barely old enough to reach the ballot box, you're going to take the counsel of some attorney in New York City or Washington D.C. over the welfare of your own people?"

Pitchford fixed the editor in a cold stare. "It is the welfare of our people I am worried about,"

"Bullshit it is," the old newspaperman shot back. "It's your career you're worried about. If this election goes to the Silver Steer on your watch, we both know your future in the Republican party is over. That's what this is about."

"I'm not going to dignify that with a response, Mr. Clarke. You've made your point, now kindly get out of my way." Pitchford pushed past the editor, glowering at Jake for good measure as he went.

"This is what it all comes to, is it?" Clarke said, in a tone Jake had never heard from him before. "All the freedoms and the enthusiasms and eccentricities of the last twelve weeks end in accusations of illegality, investigations, broken friendships, professional self-preservation, and policemen with guns guarding the polls. This is not at all what I imagined."

"Me neither," Jake said, adding, "I'm sorry, Herb. I'm sorry I ever mentioned the Silver Steer."

"Don't be, son. Come what may, people have finally woken up from their collective political nightmare. And while there will surely be a hangover effect, eventually they'll come to realize that the nightmare they emerged from is far, far worse than a brave new world of Silver Steers could ever be."

"I hope you're right."

"I know I'm right. And Jacob," the editor, said, leading him toward the door of the auditorium and the bright sunshine beyond it. "No matter what the next few days bring, let's remember to keep a sense of humor amid all this nonsensical fear-mongering."

"We'll try," Jake said, relieved to be in the fresh air again. "Now what do you say you join me in my post-press conference stress-reduction program."

"And what, pray tell, does that entail?"

"What say you and I eat us some pancakes?"

"Go ahead and knock already, you kook!" came Amethyst's voice, muffled by the solid wood door of her apartment. "I'm watching you through the peephole, you political perv."

"How'd you even know I was here?"

"You tell me," Amethyst said. "Between the telltale squeak of your Walmart shoes in the hallway and your heavy breathing as you hemmed and hawed about whether to let the deal go down, you announced your presence quite clearly.... So, are you going to stand there, or are you going to come in?"

"Thanks," Jake said, taking off his stocking cap and holding it at his waist as if he were about to sing the national anthem.

"You are aware it is 6:30 AM on a Saturday morning, right?"

"Sorry about that.... I couldn't sleep."

"So what's up," Am asked, cinching up her robe as she nestled into her favorite comfy spot on the couch with a steaming cup of what smelled like chai tea.

"I need another favor."

"Go on…. I'm listening."

"I got a call last night…from Pitchford. He wants me to come down to Des Moines to meet with him and whoever else…about the Silver Steer video."

"On a Saturday?"

"Yeah, I'm supposed to be there…" Jake checked his watch "about three hours from now."

"Did he say exactly what he wanted?"

"Nothing more than what I just told you."

Amethyst furrowed her brow. "Something is definitely rotten in Denmark, or Des Moines, as the case may be."

"I know," Jake said. "I was hoping you might be willing to go along with…you know, for moral support."

Amethyst smiled. "I'm flattered by the offer, Press, really, but I'm afraid it's a no-can-do. My editor is riding me hard—not literally, mind you—to discover the identity of the Silver Steer before the caucuses on Tuesday night. I've got all of thirty-six hours now to shake the trees on this God-forsaken treeless prairie."

"Are you getting any warmer?"

"Maybe," she said. "The video could be a big lead."

"How so?"

"If Youtube would play ball—and they likely won't unless they're subpoenaed or otherwise dragged into court—we could get a location for the he, she, or it who posted the original video, maybe even an I.P. address for the computer used. But even if we could finger the culprit behind the Youtube caper, it doesn't mean that same individual donned the mask to produce the hacked video from the barbecue." Amethyst took a slow sip from her tea. "Now, the barbecue video may yet turn out to be our smoking gun. A good criminal physiologist and psycholinguist, I'm told, can glean quite a bit of evidential material once a human being appears in the picture. The government has whole departments who specialize in this sort of thing. In fact, my phone interview with a counter-terrorism expert in DC later this morning happens to overlap with your little inquisition in Des Moines, otherwise I might just be dupable enough to help you out."

"What could a counter-terrorism expert possibly tell you?"

"Well, the gender of the person portraying the Silver Steer might be gettable—something to do with masculine versus feminine musculature and kinetics, I guess. I don't claim to understand it all myself." She pointed with the remote toward the muted TV on the coffee table. "Apparently men and women hold themselves differently. The voice is a more difficult problem, but I guess there are ways to work backwards from a digitally altered recording and try to reconstitute something of the original."

"You make it sound like a crime scene," Jake said.

"Personally, I don't think it's even in that ballpark. But then again I'm not running for high office. I can bet you each and every one of the campaigns are treating this as a Code Red, if for no other reason than to keep the money flowing from donors all too willing to drown the Silver Steer threat with a boatload of cash. Here's an example," she said, turning up the volume on the television in time for a campaign ad. "This started running yesterday afternoon. Listen."

At certain times even competitors must pull together in the face of common foes. That's why Rochelle Boxman, Milt Cloward, Rich Priestly, and Mike Santoro have joined forces for a cause greater than themselves. Tell the person behind the Silver Steer to stop playing childish games. On Tuesday, Vote No for the Silver Steer and Yes for the candidates who played by the rules. Paid for by AASS, Alliance Against the Silver Steer.

Am re-muted the television. "AASS here is a good example... and, again, no comment on the acronym. For the average Joe or Jane sitting at home, that kind of targeted insinuation is a powerful weapon. Meanwhile, our Silver Steer has a budget of exactly $0, and he, she, or it is going to be outspent like a million to one in the next two days."

Am switched off the TV for good this time, turning toward him. "Sorry, Press, I'd like to help you out, but investigative journalism first, friendships later....you know the drill. And anyway, you keep showing up at my apartment like this, unannounced, just as I'm on the verge of cracking another part of this mystery, and I might begin to suspect that you're the Silver Steer...or at least running interference for him/her/it."

"What about Artie Shaw as a prime suspect?" Jake suggested, only half kidding. "He volunteered for Herb's candidate barbeque committee; he used to be the mayor of Hereford, he's got the audio-video skills to mount a multi-media campaign, and he's got a handlebar mustache."

"You see!" Amethyst exclaimed, springing up from the couch to point a melodramatic finger at him. "There you go again... shifting the scrutiny onto someone else."

"Or it could be Mrs. Meyers," Jake added, playing along, "a radical-in-sheep's clothing if ever I met one."

"The nerve of you!" Amethyst exclaimed with mock indignation, "throwing a grade-school teacher under the bus no less."

"Or how about one of the campaign managers back in the pack hoping to undermine one of his or her rivals...someone like Dick Folsome from the Boxman camp. Boxman has nothing to gain and everything to lose from a resurgent Silver Steer."

Amethyst snapped her fingers. "I've got it! The Silver Steer is Brad Charger, which means the Silver Steer is actually gay. No wonder it's taken the poor impotent thing so long to come out of the closet."

"Be serious."

"I am," Am said, still pacing as she gumshoed. "Someone inside one of the campaigns would have too much to lose in the subterfuge...they'd risk taking their candidate down with them. No, I think the Black Hat behind the Silver Steer is someone outside the fence, but still on the ranch. Someone like you, actually."

"Or Loretta Draper," Jake suggested, ignoring the finger Am had dramatically poked in his face again. "By the way, where is she?" he asked, glancing over his shoulder at Am's spare room, the one that had lately been hosting The Sexy Badger, as Amethyst called her friend, in the days since the two diva reporters had joined forces to work on Herb Clarke's candidate barbeque. "The last time I saw her she was being politely escorted out of the press conference at the school auditorium by a couple of meathead security guards."

Amethyst waved her hand dismissively. "Oh, that. That was strictly a-catch-and-release operation… Matt Pitchford putting on a show of force for Prince Reebus's benefit. They had no real cause to hold her. She was back here by yesterday afternoon begging me to go out and drink some beers with her." Amethyst sighed. "We went for a girl's night on the town last night… you know, just two red-blooded American news-babes a few days from shipping out, drinking Old Milwaukee, cow-tipping, doing donuts in the cornfields and howling at the Man in the Moon. Then this morning she up and pulled a Preston on me."

"Which means what?"

"She left."

"Why?"

Am rolled her eyes. "All the truly sexy ones turn up missing in the morning…. Seriously, though, I get the impression there's a power struggle at the top of POPP."

"The POPP-top?"

"The very tip of the dill spear, if that's even kosher for me to say. She needed to go back to Holstein, I gather, to be among her Cheesehead brethren and thwart some sort of eminent coup d'état…you know, shore up the esprit de corps."

"The brie de corps?"

"Anywho," Am continued, ignoring the pun, "I'd love to loll about all morning long and chat with you about this, that, and the other cheese, but this extra sharp young cheddar has got a serious story fermenting here. Don't just sit there like Little Miss Muffet, Press. You're welcome to keep me company here if you'd rather not return to wherever tuffet you call home these days."

Amethyst walked to the window, opened the blinds, and stretched like a cat. "Which begs the question. Why darken my door at the butt-crack of dawn when you could just ask your little girlfriend to go with you to the inquisition and stand by her man?"

"You mean Katie?"

"Who else would I mean?"

"I keep telling you, she's not my girlfriend. She's my political date."

"Then here's a perfectly romantic Saturday outing for the two of you Sad Sacs... a grilling at the hands of the state Republican chair ought to be, pardon the pun, a regular party."

"I can't ask her to go," Jake said. "She's been emotional lately."

"If she's a true politico, the two weeks before the election should be her Valhalla and Nirvana and Grateful Dead Reunion Tour rolled into one."

"She's not like you, Am."

"You mean tough, sexy, and charismatic to the max?"

"I was thinking more like unflappable, emotionally detached, and professionally prickly."

"I'll take that as a compliment," Amethyst said, breezing past him into the kitchen. "You're afraid your little Iowa wildflower will wilt under the political heat from Pitchford and company, is that it?"

"Maybe," Jake said, moving towards the door. "Anyway, I'll figure it out. Good luck with your interview."

"Won't need it," she called back.

"And, hey…"

"Hay is fodder for horses," Am said, poking her head through the door as Jake paused in the stairwell with an afterthought.

"What if Renard Kane is the Silver Steer? We know he has a tendency toward willful fabrication and delusional behavior."

"Deflect and distract all you want, Bub. We all know you're the Silver Steer."

"I don't understand what this is all about," Katie Clarke said from the passenger's seat. "Jake, I'm a little bit scared."

"There's nothing to be scared of," he insisted, not entirely sure he believed himself. "Pitchford probably just wants to read me the ground rules for the next two days. Besides, if he tries to play rough, you could always melt his heart by reminiscing about your long-ago prom date together."

Jake pulled into the relatively deserted parking lot of Pitchford's office for the second time in as many weeks. The first time he'd come he had merely been delivering the Silver Steer for safekeeping, but this—this hastily called meeting on a Saturday morning—felt palpably different and strangely threatening. He put the car in park and turned to look at Kate. "It means a lot to me that you would come. But if this is intimidating to you, or frightening, or whatever, you can just stay here in the car, or take the car and go get a coffee, and I'll give you the blow by blow when the witch trial is over."

"I want to come inside with you. I just…I don't know. I feel like everything is beginning to spin out of control." She stopped to look out the window. "And then…"

"And then what?" Jake prompted.

"And then it's beginning to dawn on me that once the election is over, everyone is going to leave."

"Katie, it's going to be all right. How many Caucuses have come and gone without the world breaking into complete anarchy or political meltdown? If your grandparents could get through all those primaries, not to mention grasshopper plagues and horse thieves on the prairie, I'm sure we'll survive."

"But that's what's going to happen, isn't it?" she persisted. "Everyone is going to leave town, including you."

Jake gazed out the windshield, searching for the right words to reassure her. "Yes, most everyone is going to leave. Amethyst will be gone. And McGreedy. Apparently Loretta Draper already left town."

"She did?"

"And the streets are going to be a whole lot emptier and the café is going to slow down. But all the regulars, the people who really make a difference in your life, are going to be there. Artie's still going to be spinning cringe-worthy tunes at the Wagon Wheel on karaoke night. Mrs. Meyers is still going to be teaching Hereford's third graders to be little critical thinkers. Your second cousin, Cynda, is still going to be the odds on favorite for prom queen this spring. And nothing is going to stop Herb

Clarke, firebrand extraordinaire, from holding the politicians' feet to the flames at the *Hereford Gate*."

"And what about you?"

"What about me? I haven't spoken with my mom and dad since I lost my job in Denver. I have no gig, officially, and the sublettors I found for my apartment back in Golden aren't graduating until May…. What I'm saying is, I don't know what my immediate future holds. It's possible I could stay. But right now all I know is that my stomach is tied in knots, and I need to get in there and face this firing squad before I throw up."

She nodded. "You're right. First thing's first. Let's get you through this meeting."

Jake reached for Katie's hand, and together, they walked toward the door, where Matt Pitchford stood waiting to receive them.

"Katie…this is a surprise," he said, looking intently at Jake, leaving the "why on earth is she here" unspoken on his lips.

For reasons he couldn't quite fathom Jake felt compelled to offer Pitchford an explanation for her presence. "We're going out to do some shopping afterwards," he said.

"Shopping?"

"Christmas shopping."

"My God, I haven't even thought about Christmas!" Pitchford exclaimed, his face breaking into a tight little grin. "I suppose they'll still be a few weeks for bargain-hunting after the election…. Come into the conference room and make yourself comfortable. Help yourself to some coffee if you'd like."

"Don't mind if I do," Jake said, and when he reached for the Styrofoam cup he noticed his hands were shaking.

"I think both of you know Dolph Heinrich." Jake and Katie looked up from their coffees to see the former congressman and college president enter the room dressed in a sport coat and tie, as always.

"Good to see you both," he said, extending an enthusiastic hand.

"And this," Pitchford said, "is the Iowa Secretary of State, Mark Schulte. He's here mostly in a support capacity."

Support for whom, Jake wondered, as Pitchford continued with the preliminaries. "For now it's just the four...er...the five of us." Pitchford swiveled around in his chair to push the door shut. "We just want to have a little conversation."

"What kind of a conversation?" Dolph Heinrich asked, his eyes narrowing.

"About what you may, or may not, know about the latest developments with the Silver Steer."

"Now hold on, Matt," Heinrich said. "My staff told me you wanted to consult on a matter of importance to the election. If my role here is anything more than consultative, I'm afraid I must be leaving."

"Relax, Dolph," Pitchford said, his palms pointed downward like a conductor trying to quell an unexpected swell. "My questions are mostly of a consultative nature."

Heinrich arched an eyebrow. "Mostly?"

"I want to ask both of you, directly, whether you have any information as to the identity or whereabouts or plans of the man—or woman—behind the Silver Steer video shown at the barbecue."

"Absolutely none," Heinrich said.

"Ditto," Jake volunteered.

"Mr. Heinrich," Pitchford began, "we've read your paper on sedition very carefully since Jake here published it in the *Times*. It strikes us that the Silver Steer, whoever he is, is following your words like a blueprint."

"What are you suggesting, Pitchford?"

"That it seems something more than coincidence that this paper would come to light at exactly the time when a widespread protest vote stands the first chance in American history of actually succeeding."

"Look," Heinrich said, his face growing flush. "I wrote that paper when I was a junior professor. I had forgotten it almost completely, in fact, until Mr. Preston here brought it to my attention. Is there some original scholarship in it… some visionary thinking? I like to think so. But is there any conclusion in that paper that a seditionist, or a libertine, or an egalitarian, or a populist wouldn't arrive at by their own common sense? Certainly not. The truth is, there were probably only a handful of people in the world that had read it prior to its recent publication in the *Times*. The chances that the man or woman behind Silver Steer could have digested it, and used it as a manual of some sort, are infinitesimal."

"Mr. Preston," Pitchford asked, turning to face him. "You first broke this story, but beyond the short paragraph that accompanied the text of Mr. Heinrich's paper in the *Times*, you've said nothing about how you came into possession of it."

Jake considered the question. "The editors at the *Times* were strictly interested in the document and Congressman Heinrich, not me."

"But I'm interested in you…specifically, how *you* came upon a document that Dolph here says less than a dozen people had ever read prior to its publication."

"I told Mr. Heinrich exactly what I'll tell you," Jake replied, feeling his pulse quicken. "I learned of his paper from a friend of a friend, a professor…at least she was, or will be, a professor, for another day or so."

"*Was* she a professor or *is* she a professor, Jacob?"

"Both…sort of. I don't know exactly. The last time I saw her she said she was retiring."

"And does a sudden retirement strike you as at all odd?"

"Not really…I mean, sure, a little, but then again I don't know her that well."

"But you mentioned that she's a friend of a friend, so you must know her somehow."

"Right," Jake said. "The professor is a friend of Katie's." He turned to look at his companion though Pitchford's eyes never left his.

"Does this professor have a name?" Jake looked again at Katie for a cue, but her eyes were in her lap.

"It's Anne Templeton. She teaches…or taught…at Central Iowa."

"Now we're getting somewhere."

"Dolph," Pitchford asked, "have you kept in touch with Professor Templeton over the years?"

"I would run into her every few years at a conference or a colloquium. She's one of the foremost presidential historians in the Midwest, if not the country."

"I take it she, too, studies acts of sedition."

"Not really. Her work was never as specialized as mine, which was probably a good thing for her academic career." Heinrich's self-effacing rumble of laughter temporarily lifted the tension. "No, Anne is more of a generalist—presidential biographies, quirks, election history, that sort of thing."

"Election history?"

"Sure, but that's not the least bit unusual for a political historian."

Pitchford's attempt at a smile turned into a smirk. "Dolph, I don't want to take up too much more of your time, but before you go I wanted to ask your opinion on a historical question."

"Go on."

"Based on your research, what does a seditionist want?"

"That's not an easy question to answer," Heinrich replied, folding his arms atop the table. "Certainly, there's no boilerplate seditionist. In general, though, theirs is a corrective impulse. Seditionist waves usually strike at times when government is perceived to be too overarching, too intrusive, or too ineffective, especially when such excesses are amplified by a foreign or domestic war and its accompanying domestic upheaval. At certain points in history those two criteria for sedition—war and a keen distrust of government—are satisfied at once, and you have a perfect storm of sorts for the insurrectionist's message to take hold."

"Are we in such a storm now, do you think?"

Heinrich's eyes drifted to a far-off corner of the room. "We're in a foreign war, we're just beginning what figures to be a historically contentious election, and there's a healthy libertine movement underway. Yes, technically speaking, I'd say the moment is ripe."

"Is it possible, Dr. Heinrich, that a seditionist could seek to disrupt our little corn poll on Tuesday night?"

"It's possible."

"But you're not worried that may be the case here?"

Heinrich took a deep breath. "I am not. So far as we know there have been no specific or credible threats against the Caucuses or any other primary. We have a donkey candidate…a steer candidate, I should say…but even that is not all that unusual. In this country we've had rock stars encode their intentions to be a write-in candidate in their song lyrics and superheroes announce their desire to run for the presidency in the pages of comic books. If you're asking for my professional opinion, Pitchford, I'd advise letting this situation play itself out. If you crack down too hard, history says the seditionist only gains more power as the authorities are seen as militant enforcers of an increasingly intolerable and authoritarian status quo."

"I'm afraid we can't let things play out, Dolph," Pitchford said, leaning back. "If it were solely up to me, I'd be tempted to take your advice. But the Secretary of State and I are both under some serious pressure from the RNC to make sure this election comes off without a hitch. And the Federal Election Commission is watching closely. I'm determined not to be the guy on whose watch the first-in-the-nation vote is brought to a screeching halt.... Mr. Preston, you are the only one we are aware of who has had contact with every person who has been mentioned thus far in connection with the Silver Steer: Dolph, Professor Templeton, Barton Trinka…"

"I don't know a Barton Trinka…"

"You might know him better by his middle name…Madison or Mad. He's the local bartender whose job it was to coordinate the candidate videos at the barbeque."

Jake drew in a sharp breath while Pitchford pressed on. "You can understand how you might be seen as a person of interest."

Underneath the table, Jake felt Katie squeeze his hand.

"We also made a phone call to your editor at the *Rocky Mountain Partisan*, Geoffrey Hickenlooper. He wouldn't agree to speak with us, but his boss, the executive publisher, tells us you've not been on the payroll there for six weeks, nor have you filed a single story for the *Partisan* during that time."

"We want to make it clear," Pitchford continued, "that we do not, at this point, consider you a suspect, just someone with whom we would like to speak further. Of course, you're entitled to obtain the services of an attorney, but we would prefer that you accept our assurances and cooperate as fully as possible with federal law enforcement agents. Again, all this is all strictly off-the-record. Are you willing to tell us what you know?"

Jake swallowed hard. "I already told you…I don't know anything."

Pitchford grinned. "Chances are good that you know more than you think."

"He can't help you," Katie said beside him, squeezing Jake's hand so tight it hurt.

"What makes you say that, Katie?"

"Because it was me. I was the Silver Steer.... I made those videos."

Jake spun around in his chair to face her, but Katie Clarke's gaze remained on Matt Pitchford. "I made the first three videos, the ones with the cow in the stable."

"Why?" Jake asked, incredulous.

"I guess the idea of the Silver Steer ran away with me. I thought it would be fun," she said, "and make a positive difference...in terms of keeping people involved in the race."

"And the steer in the Youtube video?"

"It's our dairy cow," Katie explained. "I set our video camera up on her and let her do her thing."

Pitchford leaned forward, his voice lowering. "Did you have any help you would like to tell us about?"

Katie Clarke cast her eyes down to her lap. "No. I did the videography, uploaded the video, and wrote the text."

"And the computer-altered voice?"

"It took me about an hour one night after work using some free software I found on the Internet." Her eyes met Pitchford's again. "But I had nothing to with the video at the barbeque. And I don't know anything about who did."

Across the table the state party chair looked relieved. "One Silver Steer confession should be more than enough for our purposes. What we're going to do then, Katie, is keep this little bit of truth-telling between us, okay?"

"I would appreciate that, Matt, truly," she said.

"Don't get me wrong…we're going to need to announce your confession as widely as possible in the next two days. But as you have not been charged with any crimes, and as it is not a crime to post a Youtube video, it won't be necessary to release your name. Gentlemen, do you agree?" Pitchford turned to the Secretary of State, who had been quietly absorbing the questioning. Schulte tented his fingers and nodded his agreement. "Dolph?"

Dolph Heinrich considered the situation. "I think the lower key you can keep things the more likely you are to have a successful vote come Tuesday night, if that remains your ultimate objective. "

"We're agreed then," Pitchford said. "We'll call a press conference for early this evening, in time for the Monday morning news cycle. We'll announce that a young woman has come forward to party officials with an admission of posting Silver Steer videos, that she deeply regrets her actions and retracts all her previous statements. And, as no laws have been broken nor formal charges filed, the party has agreed to respect her wishes for anonymity and looks forward to a free and fair election come Tuesday night."

"You know people like Amethyst Gilchrest and Mort McGreedy will be all over you to release the details, right?" Jake pointed out. "You'll have the full weight of the editorial departments at both the *Times* and the *Journal* on you to disclose names."

"They'll do their job; I'll do mine," Pitchford said. "Besides, if we disclose Katie's name, she could turn around and sue us for defamation. So our hands our tied." Pitchford smirked at a job well-handled. "All of you are free to go. I think after tonight we'll be able to announce the death of the Silver Steer." He shook hands around the table. "Let the post-mortem begin."

Seventeen

The text messages from Amethyst Gilchrest began rolling in around 6:30 PM on Saturday night, and continued for the next two hours unabated—in something dangerously close, Jake noted with a chuckle, to what Am called a text avalanche—a *textvalanche.*

> Press, don't see u. R u here at the p conference?
>
> Big news breaking. Get in yr Honda and ride.
>
> Steer turns out to be a prank sayeth P'ford.
>
> Get yr ass over here. Herb Clarke just asked P'ford if he's 100% sure. U should see the look he gave him.

Jake switched off his phone and walked slowly down the hall to stand in front of the door to Katie's room.

"You okay?"

"I guess," she said, attempting a smile. "I feel pretty stupid."

"You shouldn't," Jake said. "You didn't really do anything wrong. It's Pitchford's duty to paint the picture as darkly as possible. After all, his job is on the line."

He sat down beside where Kate had perched herself at the window overlooking the side yard and the two old walnut trees that had weeks ago dropped their leaves. "Look, there are thousands of videos uploaded to Youtube every day where people pretend to be someone else." Katie looked up hopefully; Jake could tell she badly wanted to believe him. "The only difference," he continued, "is that your video helped sustain a movement. It actually helped make something happen. You should be proud of that."

"Looking back, it all feels pretty juvenile."

"As are the acts of most revolutionaries. What could be stupider, or goofier, when you think about it, than the Boston Tea Party? A bunch of white colonists dressed up as Indians to dance around a little bit before dumping British tea into the harbor. Sure, it was juvenile, not to mention novel, which is probably why so many school kids are fascinated by it hundreds of years later. It was incredibly brave, in addition to being a little hokey."

"I guess you're right," she admitted.

"Even in the unlikely event your name is released long after these primaries are a distant memory, you're more likely to become a folk hero than a goat. Think about it: you might actually end up in some Masters thesis some day…with your own footnote and everything. Your granddaughter will be researching her dissertation, and she'll come upon the name of her Gran right there on the front page of the *Register*. And she's not going to think, *how juvenile*. She's going to think, *My grandma rocked!*"

"I don't think a granddaughter is in the cards for me."

"My point is, if you're discovered once, someday someone is bound to rediscover you. That's the nature of notoriety."

"Infamy, you mean." She reached for his hand. "What do you say we go downstairs and make some dinner? Daddy said not to wait on him. He didn't expect to be back from the press conference until late."

"He shouldn't be that late. It's only down in Des Moines.

"Either way, let's eat. I'm starved."

Jake checked his watch. "You mind if I flip on the tube? I didn't watch the press conference out of solidarity with you, and the Steer, and because I knew it would only piss me off. But I really should tune into the punditry, at least to see what the talking heads are saying…. It's kinda part of my job, or what's left of it anyway."

"I understand," Katie said. "I'll close the door to the kitchen and do my best to plug my ears."

Downstairs Jake turned on the TV just in time to hear Donna Saywers and George Agropolis anchoring the post-press conference coverage, suggestively titled "Steer's Clear?"

"It's been another absolutely fascinating news day, hasn't it, George?"

"Fascinating is an understatement," Agropolis said, glancing down at his notes.

"Go ahead and catch our viewers up on what's happened thus far in this remarkable news cycle."

Agropolis gazed unblinkingly into the teleprompter. "Well, the news day really picked up this afternoon when news was leaked by the Iowa Republican Party that they had received a full confession from an anonymous individual who had allegedly played the role of the Silver Steer in those cow-in-the-barn videos we all remember from a few weeks ago. The individual, who will apparently not be charged, has allegedly retracted all her previous statements and rescinded any and all ties to the Silver Steer. Observers are saying this confession and another received hours after the story broke is likely to close the barn door, as it were, on what had been the growing momentum of the Silver Steer protest vote."

"Tell our viewers what we've learned about that second confession," Sawyers prompted her cohost.

Second confession? Jake turned up the volume.

"This one is equally interesting in many ways. A professor specializing in election history has come forward to say she exercised undue influence in convincing the unnamed Silver Steer impersonator to go through with the videos. She says she, acting as an employee of the Central Iowa University, provided logistical and technical support. She insists her actions and the actions of the unnamed masquerader are consistent with the actions of historical protests votes, her research specialty, and has freely given her name to the press. She is Anne Templeton, a recently retired professor emerita. A statement posted on her professional website this afternoon says she is proud to stand in solidarity with the region's voters, and to act in the interests of a free and fair election."

As Agropolis finished the jaw-dropping updates, Katie poked her head through the kitchen doorway. "Did I just hear what I think I heard?" she asked. She walked over and sat quietly beside Jake, reaching for his hand as the name of her most beloved professor ran across the news roll at the bottom of the screen.

Jake turned to her and said, "You should have told Pitchford. He's going to feel betrayed, and angry."

"And rat out Anne…never. Anyhow, it doesn't matter much, does it? I'm proud of my professor. I'm proud of both of us. We did something we thought needed to be done. We stood up. What can be wrong with that?"

"Nothing," Jake said, cheering up. "That's exactly what I've been trying to tell you."

Monday, the day before the caucuses, dawned with the eerie stillness of a calm before the storm. Per usual, the mailman drove in as Jake ate the leftover oats the Clarkes had left on the stove before heading off to work. He had learned to love these few morning hours to himself in the old farmhouse, the light streaming in, the sparrows and red-winged blackbirds noisy in their punditry outside his window.

As a kid, this is how he had dared imagine his future. Not in some tony, soulless Florida town, but in something more like his grandparents' farmhouse, where the day didn't begin with a breakneck commute to Tampa at dawn, but with oatmeal and good mornings before walking across the barnyard to report to work. It had been a beguiling image then, and it was an equally beguiling one now.

Still, it was all well and good to be your own boss and report at 6 AM to your job in the barnyard, quite another to wake up at 8:30, eat breakfast in your boxers, and report to no job at all. The trip to the mailbox, then, had become a daily highlight for him, bringing with it Herb Clarke's bevy of national newspapers with which Jake could easily while away the morning with the built-in pretext of keeping current in his would-be profession.

Election eve day had brought the expected surfeit of newsprint in the mail, Jake discovered as he bent over to peer inside the box—the *Times,* the *Post*, the *Journal,* the *Tribune*, all addressed to Mr. Herbert Clarke, and all bearing head-turner headlines in cant-miss bold print: *Tall-Corn Throwdown; History to Be Made in Hawkeye State; Shocker in Iowa!* It was a sort of guilty pleasure to sift through someone else's mail, Jake decided. It allowed you to step into their world for an instant, imagining what it would be like to wear their clothes and smoke their pipe and read their *National Geographic* in the bathtub while eating their chocolate chip ice cream.

Today, though, a letter arrived addressed to Jacob Preston. When Herb and Katie had first invited him to stay, he had dropped into the Hereford post office to fill out a mail delivery form. Exactly why he had done so wasn't clear to him, only that it seemed natural for a man to set down some roots who had previously spent two weeks sleeping on an air mattress. He intended it, he supposed, as an act of citizenship, akin to saying "I'm a real person with a real address. Here's where you can reach me." He hadn't needed a forwarding address from his apartment in Denver. It would just be bills anyway, and he still had his graduate student sublettors there to filter through which of the envelopes were on fire, and which could wait until after the election when not only his own bills, but the nation's, would surely come due. Thus far the imperfect filtration system he had put in place had worked perfectly, as nary an invoice or statement had arrived.

Eagerly, he opened the padded package with his name on it to discover several DVDs. The first one out of the envelope carried a typed label that read *For Immediate Distribution* and the other two, marked "Victory" and "Defeat" warned in bold type *Not To Be Viewed Until Election Results Are In.* No name. No handwriting. No legible postmark on the envelope even. Hustling back inside, Jake stuck the immediate-distribution DVD into Herb Clarke's computer and waited for its seemingly ancient processor to digest the data. And when it did, the image on the screen took his breath away.

The video showed the same man, or woman, with the cowhead on, its movements and sound broken by the old computer's anemic memory. "Rumors of my death have been exaggerated," the Silver Steer on the screen began. "As predicted, the establishment's campaign of fear and false accusations and innuendos has begun in earnest." The computer froze and Jake instinctively pushed the eject button, praying that the DVD would come out. It did.

He looked at the kitchen clock—it was nearly 10 AM. He needed to get this to someone who could broadcast it, or at least evaluate its suitability for broadcast. Wherever he took it, he needed to get there by early afternoon if the producers were to have time to insert it into that evening's news. If it missed the Monday evening news cycle, it might be too late for the video to get any real traction. The Caucuses opened around 5 PM on Tuesday, and most voters would be stopping by to cast their lot on their way home from work—too late to have seen the footage for themselves if the video waited until election morning to air.

Jake threw on some jeans and a wrinkled collared shirt, pulled a comb through his hair and headed out the door, still buttoning.

He waited in the station lobby for what seemed like a full half an hour, his leg pumping like a nervous jackrabbit, until at last Bambi Bloomberg emerged from the newsroom, looking perfectly put together as ever. "I imagine this is important," she said. "My assistant pulled me out of an editorial board meeting to talk with you."

"Trust me it is," Jake said. He held the battered package of DVDs aloft. "This came in the mail this morning addressed to me. It's another video from the man or the woman…the person…wearing the cowhead mask…the Silver Steer."

Bloomberg smiled patiently at him. "You must have been away from your TV last night, Jake. That was all cleared up. A person…two people actually…have already come forward claiming to be the Silver Steer. One of them is Anne Templeton."

"Those two posted the first few voice-over videos…the ones with the steer in the darkened barn stable. But they're not the same as the person behind these recordings. I know it for a fact."

Bloomberg raised an eyebrow. "Listen, we've loved having you on the show, Jacob. But as far as my producers are concerned, the Silver Steer train left the station twenty-four hours ago, killed by the RNC and the state Republican party. We've got around-the-clock election coverage planned for tomorrow, and reporters spread out in each of the campaign headquarters. What I'm saying is we're maxed out." Bambi smiled ruefully. "Any other time, I'd do what I could for you, but I'm afraid it's a non-starter or us."

"I don't get it," he said, rising from his seat. "A week ago the Silver Steer was all you wanted to talk about. Now it's toxic? Did all the producers receive a memo from the RNC or the FBI or something?"

Bambi put her hand gently on his elbow. "A week ago this was just an idea, a trophy the candidates were competing for. It was all in good fun… a human-interest story embedded in an otherwise humorless campaign. But now there are real people involved. How are we supposed to verify identities, cross check facts, report both sides, and triangulate the story if we don't know who or what we're triangulating? All of a sudden we're reporting news that's not news, but fiction. If I walk in there right now and tell my producers I've got a guy in the lobby who says he has another Silver Steer video…this one from the real McCoy…they wouldn't touch it."

"It's coming from me, though," Jake reiterated, pointing at himself. "I'm not exactly an unreliable narrator."

The veteran talk-show host smiled a matronly smile at him—the one that made him feel as if he was just some no-account kid begging for a special favor. "You are, and then again you are not. Remember, you're the one who gave birth to the Silver Steer movement, and you were the one most closely identified with it for its first couple of weeks in the news cycle. In a sense that makes you its creator. A responsible news outlet isn't going to turn to Dr. Frankenstein as an objective source about the latest alleged actions of his monster."

Bambi paused, summing up her case. "Look, Jake, I believe you're a journalist with a lot of potential, a true up and comer, but I can tell you how the people inside that conference room would view your eleventh-hour bombshell—they would see a young man who's working...or not working...for a newspaper they've never heard of, a weekly no less. It's not the *Times*. It's not the *Journal*. It's not even the *Tribune* or the *Star* or the *Register*. I'm sorry, Jacob. The best I can do is call WBCC across town and tell them to give your pitch a listen. But I can't promise anything, okay?"

"Don't bother" Jake said, tucking the package of DVDs beneath his arm and making a beeline the door.

He glanced at his watch. 1 PM. He had one more shot. The ace up his sleeve. The devil in his deep blue sea.

He had Mort McGreedy.

"Rumors of my death have been greatly exaggerated..."

"Jesus Christ, Press," McGreedy said as he watched the image of the Silver Steer flicker to life on his laptop.

They were at McGreedy's crash pad, his flophouse as he called it, in Hereford, and it was an unholy mess. Dirty clothes hung from every possible surface. Dishes lay undone, moldering in the sink. Newspaper after newspaper covered the dirty shag carpet, with a depth and breadth that reminded Jake of the littered floor of a hamster cage housing an exceedingly large varmint. "Not much to look at, is it?" McGreedy conceded, considering the tsunami of scattered broadsheets and half-eaten food around him. "I've spent more time at the Wagon Wheel the last few months than in this dump."

On screen the Silver Steer was speaking:

> What is my message to the voters? To remind you of the power you possess, a power great enough to bring the party, the secretary of state, law enforcement officials, and even the FBI out on high alert. A power so great that armed patrols have now been ordered to the polls. The powers-that-be suggest a terrorist plot. They threaten that your status as the first-in-the-nation vote might be compromised if you act your conscience and lodge the protest that is in many of your hearts. In short, they treat you as unruly children who cannot decide for themselves, who require their paternalistic protection and overwatch, children who cannot be trusted to see the difference between truth and lies.
>
> Who am I? I am you. Who am I not? I am not an emeritus history professor with an expertise in election history. I am not an anonymous individual who recorded a harmless milk cow in a darkened barn. I exist because you willed me into existence, and I will stop existing the minute you stop believing. I am an article of faith…your faith.
>
> Twenty-four hours from now you will go to the polls with two choices—one practical choice, a vote for the status quo, a vote for the political machine your mothers and fathers and grandmothers and grandfathers yearned to end. The other is a choice for you, for

your potential, for the possibilities of a democratic government by the people, for the people—the promise of our founding fathers and mothers. A vote for the Silver Steer is a vote for you, and your neighbors, and your neighbors' neighbors. It is a not a vote for fortunate sons, for lawyers, or legislators.

Me, I'm just a person wearing a mask—neither more real, nor less, than the candidates who have appeared in our high school auditoriums and public libraries and cafés asking for your vote. Consider me, in the final analysis, your cheerleader. Fancy me a coach. All I ask of you is that you get out there and throw the Hail Mary pass you've long dreamed of, the one all the naysayers have claimed would be nothing short of a miracle.

Mort McGreedy was first to break the silence. "You said you've shown this to no one."

"Not a soul. I tried to play it for Bambi Bloomberg but she shot me down."

McGreedy snorted derisively. "The TV talking heads wouldn't know what to do with something like this. They'd cut it down to a 15-second sound bite and finish it off with a 'gee ain't that something' and a smile. They're media whores of media whores."

McGreedy took a swipe at the clutter on his coffee table, sending a dozen beer cans sprawling. "We've got to get this to my editor at the *Journal*, pronto. Is this the only copy you've got?

Jake nodded, and McGreedy checked the time on his phone. "The pages get uploaded in about 45 minutes. I'm going to try to copy this thing, and send it to them as a video file. What I'll need from you is context. A couple of paragraphs, tops."

"What do I say?"

"Tell the readers what you told me…how the package arrived, how the first network you talked to turned you down. Tell them the RNC has it wrong. Basically tell them the Silver Steer is alive, kicking, and poised for election night." McGreedy ran his fingers through his hair. "Jesus, I'm a word-guy not a video tech, Press. Give me a copy deadline and I can meet it with my eyes closed, but give me video feed to upload, and I'm as hopeless as a college intern…. C'mon, C'mon, C'mon, upload already, you son of a bitch."

"Alright," McGreedy continued, cracking his knuckles. "Upload successful. The Silver Steer should be winging its way to DC as we speak in the form of millions of 1 and Os. Romantic, isn't it?" McGreedy turned to Jake. "How's that context paragraph coming?"

"Done," Jake said, inserting the final period. "You want to retype it?"

"Retype it? You mean you hand-wrote the son of a bitch…. Forget it, just give to me." Jake passed the spiral-bound and watched as McGreedy, a man in his element, pounded on the keys. "Done and…done!" he declared, hitting the return key with a flourish a few minutes later. "I marked it extremely urgent. If that doesn't get my editor's attention, I don't know what will."

"What do we do now?" Jake asked.

"We do what all great reporters do while they're waiting for their editor to call them at the eleventh hour…. We drink," McGreedy said, pulling a bottle of Scotch down from the top of the refrigerator. "Grab a tumbler. And if you can't find a tumbler, grab a Dixie Cup."

"There's our call," McGreedy added, pounding his first draught of whiskey in order to answer the phone buzzing in his pocket. "Jim, yeah, you got it? Yep, it's legit…matches the previous videos to a 'T.' Run the story on page one. Jacob Preston. Yep, he's the reporter out of…" McGreedy put his hand over the receiver and whispered, "Where in the hell are you based again?"

Jake mouthed the words *Denver*.

"Sorry about that. Uh-huh, Denver. The *Rocky Mountain Partisan*. Check your inbox…you should have his blurb. Can we get the video up on the web pronto? Forward it on to PBS and all the TV partners. Good. Yep, just ducky. Regular twelfth day of Christmas. And a Cloward and a Santoro in a pear tree. Don't worry, I'm not going anywhere unless it's to the bar. Okay. And, Jim…thanks for this."

McGreedy punched "end" and pitched the phone over his shoulder onto the couch. "It'll make tomorrow morning's papers, front page. The video will be launched simultaneously on the *Journal's* website…drive more traffic to it that way. All our partner TV stations will get a heads-up about the footage coming down the pike."

"So that's how it's done? Twenty minutes and the big head-line that this morning I couldn't get aired for love or money will be read by 2 million people over breakfast."

"Closer to three," McGreedy said, swirling his whiskey, "but who's counting."

"And millions more TV viewers."

"Pretty much," the veteran reporter said, slamming his empty glass down atop the thrift-store furniture. "Intoxicating, ain't it?"

"Where have you been?" Katie shouted through the window, meeting the Accord in the Clarke's graveled driveway before the car had even come to a stop. "I was getting worried about you."

"You wouldn't believe me if I told you," Jake said, slamming the car door behind him. "C'mon, let's go inside. It's freezing out here!"

She had been waiting for him on the porch swing, in her winter coat and boots. Caucus eve, the newscaster's called it, even giving it its own forecast. The forecast for tonight was chilling—rain changing to snow.

"I was going to make some hot cocoa to warm up," she told him. "Want some?"

"Anything to chase the whiskey."

"Whiskey?"

"I ran into Mort McGreedy. And when you run into Mort McGreedy, you run into whiskey. Or rather whiskey runs into, and over you." Jake hung his jacket up on the hook. "Herb home yet?"

Katie frowned. "He's not home either. I've got two, too-hard-working journalists."

"One hard-working journalist," he corrected her. "And one pretender who's realizing just how much is involved in being the real thing." He put his arm around her shoulder. "I had an amazing day."

Katie brightened. "You're joking?"

"Nope, I really did have an amazing day. And weirdly enough, so did you."

"You're going to tell me about it, right?"

"That depends on whether I can leverage my story for some of your leftovers."

"And that depends on whether your story is worth a hill of lima beans"

"Add some pancakes to those limas and you have yourself a deal." Jake bent down and kissed his dinnermate on the cheek.

"What was that for?"

"That," he said, "was a kiss for Caucus eve."

Eighteen

"There's a big breaking story out of the Hawkeye State this morning," Donna Sawyers announced when Jake switched on the TV on Tuesday morning, the morning of the election. "Hello, everyone. This morning and throughout the day we'll be reporting live from political ground zero, Des Moines, Iowa, where this morning the pundits and politicos are abuzz with news from the late edition of the *Journal*. It seems yet another Silver Steer video has surfaced, mailed to the rural route address of the reporter, Jacob Preston, who began the movement with his debate question one month ago on this very network. We begin our coverage with a clip from the video itself."

"Isn't this the kind of news day you'd give your right arm to be in television?" a voice said from behind him, causing Jake to jump.

"Herb! You scared the bejesus out of me!" Jake put his hand to his pounding heart. "I thought you'd be at the paper by now."

"Another late night last night," he said, "and another one to come this evening. I figured I'd catch some winks while the catchin' was good. Besides, I wanted to see the video all the talking heads are prattling on about."

"Well, what do you think?"

"It's brazen. Whoever is behind it has a lot of chutzpah, I'll give him or her that. I might not always approve of their methods, but I can't question their patriotism."

The editor raised a glass of orange juice to his lips. "Still, I suspect the Steer may be a day late and a horn short. Caucus day is a slow news day by design. No new arguments, no new facts coming to light…just folks going to the polls to vote their preference. I'm afraid the Silver Steer there"—he pointed to the image of the masked person on the muted television—"may be lost in the get-out-the-vote shuffle. But for one glorious moment it was one for the record books, wasn't it…one you and Katie may be telling your grandchildren about someday."

"I'm afraid we're both a little behind in the grandchild-generating department." Jake spooned up the last of his steel-cut oats, making a half-hearted attempt to conjure a smile.

"Not every race is to the swift," the editor said, giving him a consolation pat on the back. "Every campaign has its dark horse."

"Where parenting is concerned I'm worse than a dark horse, Herb. I'm the horse that never left the stables."

Clarke smiled. "A regular bum steer."

"Someone's in a good mood this morning."

"What can I say? I love Caucus day. Always have. Reminds me of my dad."

"Yeah?"

"I remember him coming in from the barnyard smelling like diesel fuel and fermenting corn, getting cleaned up and into a fresh pair of overalls, then driving me and mom down to the old schoolhouse to greet our neighbors, and cast our lot. Dad was a staunch Democrat, and on the Dem's side, after each of the campaign's representatives had said their peace on behalf of their candidates, all of your neighbors sectioned off in the room according to the candidate they were backing. For a kid it was pretty heady stuff to witness. On one blessed night all the questions your child's mind had puzzled over for years regarding the secret lives of your neighbors—what they believed in, what they worried about losing, what hopes they had for the future—got answered. It's one of the only nights in the Corn Belt where everyone has a voice."

"Now the Republicans," he continued, "don't section themselves off in the corner of the room. You fence a Midwestern Republican off at your own peril. And I should add that Caucus night is not always pretty. Midwesterners are about the most civil people you can find anywhere south of the Canadian border, but I've seen a lot of bottled up tensions and ugliness vented over the years, too."

"So will you and Katie be voting tonight?"

"You betcha," the editor said. "Wouldn't miss it for the all the silver in the Silver Steer."

"I thought you two agrarian radicals were independents."

"We are, though like most folks who live on farms we lean conservative. Doesn't really matter on Caucus night, though. If you're willing to register Republican you can have your say-so this year, and that's a beautiful thing." He paused. "Even you could vote if you wanted to, Jacob."

"I don't know, Herb."

"What's not to know? You've got a physical address and an intention to stay at least a while longer. There you have it. The State of Iowa makes it almost too easy for would-be voters."

Jake looked down at his lap. "The trouble is, I'm not sure I want to stay."

The editor raised an eyebrow. "That so?"

"Being here the past month has caused me to remember what I enjoyed so much about visiting my grandfolks on the farm," Jake began. "But the truth is, as much as we moved around when I was a kid, I'm not sure I belong in any one place. When it comes down to it, I'm probably more like the Milt Clowards and Mort McGreedys and Amethyst Gilchrests of the world than I care to admit—always restless, always on the move, always curious about what might lay around the next bend." He paused. "In other words, I'm not enough like you and Katie."

"Katie and I are probably much more like you than you realize," the editor confided, sitting down beside him on the couch. "That's a common mistake folks make with us, by which I mean all of us hobbits who live in places like this one.... That we're perfectly content with our lot. That we've never traveled beyond our home state's borders. That the only book on our shelf is the Bible. It's a myth, Jacob. I can't entirely speak for Katie, but I think, homebody though she may be, she would love to travel, if the right opportunity presented itself."

Jack turned to look the editor in the eye. "So why doesn't she?"

"Probably because she feels she needs to stay here and look after her decrepit old father and the café. It's a lot to feel tied down to." He paused. "On the other hand it's a helluva lot to live for. You know, Katie and I are actually incredibly free. We don't have a spouse. We don't have a mortgage. The extent of my farming these days is my heirloom tomatoes and my sweetcorn. And as far as the newspaper goes, I like to think I'm indispensable, but for a few weeks Darlene could probably run the old dog-and-pony show if she had to." Herb Clarke chuckled. "Truth be told, I'm more of a figurehead than anything...the token old guy with gray hair and glasses and a chip on his shoulder. Sometimes it seems like a newspaper can't be legitimate without at least one of those dinosaurs roaming the office."

"I know exactly what you mean," Jake said, thinking of his own editor, or ex-editor, or erstwhile editor, and co-columnist, legal defender, cheerleader and friend...all the things Geoff Hickenlooper was to him.

"Well," Herb said, patting Jake on the back. "Better get back to work at the old building and loan. Gonna be a long day, but a hell of an exciting one." He paused. "I admire your refusal to vote in our little corn poll, Jacob, I really do, but if you want to caucus with us God-fearing, gun-toting Middle American Republicans as an observer, you'll find us at the old township schoolhouse. Hereford has its own separate caucus site for the folks who live in town, so ours will be a pretty intimate affair. Probably a couple dozen of us old farmers and their wives and a few of their adult children. No media allowed inside. Besides, we're far enough out in the boondocks they wouldn't know how to reach us if they tried."

"Observing I can do," Jake promised, turning back to the television, where Sawyers and Agropolis continued to decon-struct the latest Silver Steer video.

When he heard the back door click shut, and the sound of the editor's jalopy turn down the gravel road that would take him to town, Jake got up, put his bowl of oatmeal in the sink, filled it with enough water so it wouldn't shellac, and turned up the television loud enough that he could hear it while he shaved. Whatever election night held for him, he had an inexplicable urge to look his best for it.

He was in the middle of attacking an especially tough whisker when he heard an excited exchange of voices coming from the TV set. Shaving cream still clinging to his cheek, he raced to the end of the couch to see what the commotion was all about.

"George, each time it seems that tonight's Caucuses can't get any stranger, we receive word to the contrary. Unconfirmed sources are now telling us that earlier today a claim of responsibility was made for the latest Silver Steer videos by the group of activists known as POPP, People Opposed to Partisan Politics. The group's new leader, Chuck Sousage..."

"I think that's pronounced to rhyme with *corsage*," Agropolis interrupted.

Sawyers smiled disarmingly into the camera. "Mea culpa, George. I'll bet the folks gathered on the street outside our Des Moines studio—she turned to acknowledge the crowd of camera hounds behind her—"could educate me on the difference between a sausage and a Sousage."

"I think one's been involved in generating political pork and the other is just plain pork," said Agropolis, grinning. "Apologies to Chuck for the awful pun, but up until assuming the leadership of POPP, Sousage was considered an entrenched establishment figure in the Republican party."

"No longer, it seems," Sawyers said. "This morning the organization he now leads, POPP, released a statement claiming responsibility for the latest videos." She paused. "Let me read some brief quotes from lengthy release. 'The Silver Steer's latest video, which debuted at the Hereford Candidate Barbeque, was produced and filmed by POPP's Barton Madison Trinka.' It was a 'creative statement of voter discontent and a protest against the options as they are.' Sousage goes on to claim that the current slate of candidates for the Republican nomination 'does not present the voters with a real choice,' merely a list of 'unacceptable non-choices.' The group is urging voters to join them in backing 'the one candidate that is by the people, and for the people...the Silver Steer.' Sawyers looked up from her notes.

"George, a major, major development out of Iowa this morning just a handful of hours before the polls open from a group previously expected to throw their votes to Rochelle Boxman. How will this play among the electorate?"

"Too soon to tell, Donna. But it may backfire."

Sawyers raised an eyebrow. "How so?"

"If voters feel as if the Silver Steer belongs not to them but to what is arguably a fringe organization, they could be less likely to get behind the movement as they cast their lot."

"You mean the moo-vement, don't you, George?"

"That's right," Agropolis said, looking like he might be sick. "We still don't have a definitive ID on the person in the video. And we do not have an independent verification of POPP's claims. What sense voters will make of these eleventh-hour declarations is still anyone's guess."

Madison, Jake said as he pointed his chin upward to shave his neck. *It had been POPP, and Mad, all along.*

But then again, Jake thought, turning his other cheek to the mirror, it wasn't Mad that had given the Silver Steer life. The Silver Steer had been his question at the debate, just as it had been Dolph Heinrich's white paper from 1972. It had been Professor Templeton's bully pulpit and Katie's cow in the barn and, finally, Mad's chutzpah and video savvy at the candidate barbeque coupled with the opportunistic Chuck Sousage's—Mr. Breakfast Patty's—expertise at taking credit for things he hadn't done himself that had, in sum, breathed life into the Silver Steer.

"So you're coming to the Caucuses after all!" Katie enthused. She walked into the farmhouse kitchen and sat down wearily. "The café has been jammed all day with the national media. My regulars couldn't even get in the door." Halfway through pulling off her tennis shoes, she stopped, looked up, grinned. "Daddy must have persuaded you."

"A little bit," Jake confessed. "It took some of your dad's proding, but I agreed to go as Herb's guest, and as an observer only. I'll admit I'm curious to see how this whole thing works, if it works at all."

"That's the spirit," Katie called from the bathroom. "Just changing into my jeans. Be right out."

"Did you hear the news about Sousage?"

"How could I miss it? That's all anyone wanted to talk about today. Daddy came in for a coffee around 3:00 expressly to tell me it was a bunch of bunk."

"What was?"

"POPP's claim of responsibility."

"Why does he think that?"

"He said he's known Sousage for twenty-five years, and that, while he's a bang-up PR man, he's not enough of an outside-the-box thinker to concoct a scheme as intricate as the Silver Steer."

"Is that what he called it…a 'scheme'? He still won't give himself completely over to Steer, will he?"

Katie shook her head as she buttoned her jeans. "Daddy seldom gives himself over to anything, at least not completely. When I was a teenager dating for the first time, do you know what his most frequently given piece of fatherly advice was?"

Jake grinned amiably. "I shudder to guess."

"He'd quote the Irish poet W.B. Yeats and say solemnly, 'Never give all the heart.' And yet he has one of the biggest hearts I know."

"Anyway," Jake said, "I don't agree with him. Maybe the pre-firing Sousage wasn't whimsical enough to dream up such things," he conceded, "but the post-firing, rogue Breakfast Patty might be. Prolonged unemployment does funny things to a man. He might just be loopy enough to don the mask."

Katie emerged from the bathroom again, balming her lips and puckering for good measure. "Do you really think it's loopy?"

"You tell me. Didn't you feel a little bit crazy when you were shooting a video of your old milk cow and posting it on Youtube for the world to see."

Katie leaned against the door jamb, thinking. "I felt exhilarated mostly, and a little bit anxious. Mostly I felt alive, though. More alive than I've felt in years." She walked to the stove and started the tea kettle. "Looking back on it, sure, I felt a little bit silly, but at the time it seemed perfectly rational, even sensible. Anne and I had talked about the Steer phenomenon so much while we were packing and unpacking all her boxes that by the time we actually went through with it, it seemed almost like an inevitability. Like why wouldn't we shoot a Silver Steer video and post it on the web, you know?"

Jake shook his head. "Honestly, I don't. Maybe I'm not made out of whatever the rest of you—you, Anne, Heinrich, Mad, Sousage—are made of."

"That's ridiculous. You were the one who dreamed this whole thing up in the first place."

"Hardly. All I did was ask a question."

"And that, Mr. Preston, is how revolutions begin." Slowly she poured the boiling water into her cup, bobbing the tea bag up and down thoughtfully. "Want some?"

"Sure," Jake said. "If this vote is as close as they say it's going to be, I'm going to need a caffeine IV to stay up for the results."

"Grab a mug and take it with you," she said, turning off the lights. "Time for the rural Hereford Tea Party."

Herb Clarke hadn't been kidding.

The caucus site was like nothing Jake had ever seen before. In every election he could recall he had voted in some cavernous suburban school auditorium, or some gleaming, taxpayer-funded public library, and even once at shopping mall next to a Gap outlet store. The building in front of him now, by contrast, looked barely habitable.

Katie pulled her truck up not so much to it, but off the road in front of it, where a few dozen other vehicles, mostly Chevy and Ford pickups, lined the road's muddy shoulder.

"It's an old schoolhouse," she explained, grabbing her fleece from the back of her truck. "Bring your coat. No use firing up the boiler for one night in early November, right? There's an oven in the kitchen, though, and someone usually turns that on to take the edge off the cold."

Jake shivered in the November air. "Where are we?" he asked, turning around in the starry night to see nothing but an abandoned railroad, two derelict buildings with gaping holes in the roof, and back behind the schoolhouse, what looked to be the silvery, moonlit zigzag of the Raccoon River knifing through good Iowa loam.

"There was a little town here once called New Liberty," Katie explained. "Depot, feed store, pharmacy, general store, school… just about everything you could need."

"What happened to it?" Jake asked, feeling as if he'd accidentally stumbled onto the set of a slasher flick.

"Passenger train quit coming, Depression hit, school closed, kids left, basically New Liberty dissolved…then died."

"But it's not a ghost town?"

"Not yet," Katie said. "Midwesterners won't usually let a schoolhouse or a church go to seed….bad karma. The farmers in our township volunteer the maintenance on the building every year, and the historical society chips in a little, too." Katie pointed to a steel roof that looked more like it belonged atop a machine shed than a turn-of-the-century red-brick schoolhouse. "That's what happens when you allow farmers to take over the upkeep. They stop every leak and fix every hole, but they'll use whatever they have leftover around the barnyard to do it. I keep suspecting one day I'm going to drive by and all the red brick will be painted John Deere green. Anyway, it's not as bad as it looks on the outside. Come on in."

They had arrived in time to get the last of the popcorn that had been popped up in a saucepan on the old school stove. They checked in at the makeshift desk, and took their seat amid a room full of men in Carharts and hoodies chatting amiably, a smattering of mostly older women, and a few kids who looked to Jake like they couldn't be more than a few years out of college. Cloward, Santoro, and Paule had each pledged they would have a representative from their campaign at each and every one of the hundreds of polling sites across the state, and by the looks of it, one or two had somehow managed to reach even this far-off outpost.

At one minute till seven, the front door opened and a hooded man burst in, rain sheeting off his slicker. "Ghastly night out there," he said. "Never understood why we hold elections in November." The man turned to face them as he took off his coat.

"Thanks for waiting, folks, and sorry to cut things so close. Came straight from the newspaper. Got here as quick as I could," Herb Clarke said.

"You say that every four years, Mr. Precinct Captain," replied a beefy farmer sitting at the table behind Jake's and Katie's.

"That's because it's always true, George." He smiled. "You all don't need me to tell you how the process works."

"Works the same as it does every four years, right Herbie?" another of the farmers asked.

"We'll give folks a chance to say a few words on behalf of their candidate, then we'll vote."

"Anyone here want to speak for Mr. Cloward?" Clarke asked, rubbing his upper arms briskly to warm himself.

"We need a businessman," a voice from the side of the room said. "Someone with executive experience. I don't much care for Milt Cloward, but I'm not voting on personality. I'm voting know-how."

"Thank you, Dean. A man of few, but choice, words…. Yes, Helen, you have the floor."

"I'm here to speak for Mike Santoro," she said. "He's the only one of the candidates who comes from a working-class background. He understands that agriculture can't employ everyone around here. We need some manufacturing close enough to home that we don't have to drive to an hour to work at a plant, and he'll help us get it."

"All good points," Herb said. "Anyone here for Paul Paule?

The young volunteer in the back of the room stood up. "He's the only candidate who would end the Federal Reserve and get us back on the gold standard. And he's the only candidate who understands what truly limited government means."

449

"Thank you, young man," the editor said. "Anyone for Rich Priestly? No one for the big man from Oklahoma? Then what about Rochelle Boxman?"

"She's a farmer's daughter, from a neighboring state. She comes from our culture. She's one of us."

"All true things," Herb said. "Thank you, Len." The editor stopped to clear his throat. "This year, as you all know, there's an elephant in the room…or more accurately a steer. Is there anyone else here who would like to say something on behalf of the write-in candidate?" Herb looked directly at Jake and Katie. "Anyone?"

"I'll do it," a guy in the back of the room said just as Jake readied himself to testify.

"And who are you?"

"Name's Drew," the kid said. "I'm here representing POPP."

"Why don't you tell these good folks what POPP is," the editor coaxed, "in the event they've been living under a rock these last few weeks."

"People Opposed to Partisan Politics," the kid said proudly.

"That's that sleeper group who moved here to sway our election," an older woman grumbled.

An angry voice called from the back of the room, "We can make up our own minds."

"Now, Grace," Clarke cautioned, "you may be right that we don't need POPP's help, but let's hear this young man out. He's come a long ways to speak his mind, so let me him speak it. Any of you here going to deny him that right?"

"I am," a big man said, standing from a tiny school desk upfront to loom over the proceedings. The man turned menacingly toward the kid in back. "We've lived here our whole lives to earn this vote. I don't care if you are here legally, what you're doing isn't right."

Herb Clarke held up his hands. "What do you propose I do about this, Murray. The young man there—Drew—is an eligible voter. I can't very well deny him his right, or I myself would land in a heap of trouble, and so would our proud little caucus here." Herb eyed the big man closely.

"Don't know about any of that," Murray said. "But I know I don't like what I'm seein'. We've been doin' this for how many years now without any newcomers sticking their noses where they don't belong. We ought to be able to keep doin' it like we have been."

"I may agree with you," the editor allowed, "but it's worth considering that maybe we haven't been doing as well as we thought, at least as far as the rest of the nation is concerned. POPP is here because they believe, rightly or wrongly, that we've failed in our jobs as citizens to demand the very best candidates and to raise an unholy fuss when we don't get them. Would you agree that we don't always vote for who's in our heart, Murray?"

"S'pose so," the big farmer grumbled. "But I don't like givin' up our rights to out-of-staters."

"Me neither!" a woman shouted from the far wall. "Tell the kid to go home!"

"Folks," Herb said, holding his hands up for calm again. "No one likes a hostile takeover less than I do. And if we do our job, next time maybe—hopefully—the POPPS and the SODS of the world will stay home. But for now, as your precinct captain, I'm obliged to follow the election rules as they're written. If anyone would have me do otherwise, I'll need to step down from my post, which means one of you will need to step up to replace me."

The newspaperman looked sternly around the old schoolhouse. "Would anyone care to replace me as precinct captain so as to deny this young man his Constitutionally guaranteed right? Anyone? Alright then, proceed young man, but let me advise you to walk lightly, and speak respectfully."

The kid looked twice as spooked as he had a moment earlier, Jake noticed. Still, he had to give him credit—he was determined.

"Most of you are older," the kid managed to begin. "You remember a time when politics didn't seem so broken, and scary, a time when you actually admired the candidates personally, and felt like you knew them. A lot of voters are scared to go the polls these days. Scared of protests, scared of seeing neighbors they've either never seen before or don't want to see, scared of being judged for publicly standing up for who and what they believe in." The kid paused. "I'm young enough not to care about any of that…about what others may think. I want my country back. And I'm voting for the Silver Steer."

"But you don't even live here," a woman said, eyeing him critically.

"I've been living here for twelve weeks," the kid said.

"How come we've never seen you then?"

The kid shrugged. "Probably 'cause you weren't looking."

"Let him finish, Barb," Herb said. "Unless there's some reason you've got to get home in the next two minutes."

"Nope. Young man can waste everyone's time if he wants to." Barb leaned back in her chair, arms folded across her chest in the classic prove-it-to-me pose.

The kid continued. "I'm voting for the Silver Steer because sometimes you've got to send a message that the system is broken beyond repair, that it's not working for us anymore, that the choices we're getting aren't the ones we've earned." He paused. "I'll bet there are a handful of you here tonight who are gonna have to hold your nose when you vote. You don't really like your candidate, but he or she is the best there is. Imagine if you didn't have to make that choice. Please consider voting your heart tonight by writing-in your vote for the Silver Steer."

Herb Clarke patted the young man squarely on the back. "Well said, young man. Now there," he said, addressing his neighbors, "is some courage. How many of you would be willing to travel across a state border and steel yourself to speak in front of a crowd of frowning locals you've never laid eyes on in your life. I for one wouldn't have had the guts to do it at this young man's age."

"Yes, you woulda, Herbie," said an ancient man sitting at a table near the back of the room.

"Maybe so," the editor admitted. "But we should thank this young man. As we should thank Jake Preston here, who's also lived among us for a while now. He's the reporter who had the guts to ask the Silver Steer question in the first place…. Well, if there are no other words on behalf of the candidates, I suppose there's not much left to do but pass out the ballots, eh Katie?" Kate Clarke stood with a handful of what looked to be scrap pieces of typing paper. "Just write the name of the candidate you fancy, and Katie and I will collect 'em, same as always."

Katie quickly scribbled something on her ballot, smiled, and stood up. "No copying, Press," she teased, and she began picking up her neighbors' slips with one hand, and popcorn bowls full of old maids with the other. A moment later she was at Jake's side again while Herb went into the kitchen to tally the votes.

"That's it?" Jake asked. "This is the legendary, iconic vote envied all across America?"

"Glorious, isn't it?" Katie commented, checking her watch. "Like most things, I guess it's sexier to people who aren't afforded the luxury." She turned in her chair to face him. "So how do you feel after witnessing your first-ever Caucus?"

"Anxious," Jake said, nodding toward the room where Herb Clarke counted the votes under the watchful eye of the men and women who'd spoken on behalf of their candidate moments ago.

A minute later the editor poked his head through the kitchen window. "Looks like we've got ourselves a tie between Milt Cloward and the Silver Steer, with six votes apiece. Mike Santoro comes in second with 4 votes, Paul Paule with 3, Rochelle Boxman 2, and Rich Priestly 1. That's all she wrote, folks," Herb said. "Hope to see you at the same time and place four years from now."

"Thank you, Herb," a woman said, standing to put on her coat.

"Yeah, thanks," another man chorused. "One of these years we've gotta draft someone to give you a break." He patted Herb on the back on his way out.

"Glad to do it, Bob, so long as I'm here."

"You planning on going somewhere?"

The editor cracked a wry grin. "Been here the last 70-odd years, haven't I? Probably couldn't tear myself away even if I wanted to."

Jake and Kate grabbed their coats and added themselves to the line of folks processing past Herb Clarke into the cold, drizzly night.

"What'd you think of our caucus, son?" Herb asked when finally Jake stood before him, the last in line.

"Not what I expected," he replied. "On the one hand, it was quicker than I ever imagined."

"Folks don't dilly-dally much around here. For better or worse, they know their mind."

"And at the same time it was more contentious," he added. "I thought the kinds of people who would respectfully tell their neighbors to sit down, or tell them they think they're full of it, were dead and gone, but I guess they live on in places like Hereford."

"And maybe only in places like this Hereford," Herb said. "In most of the rest of country you vote behind a curtain without ever talking to your fellow voters at the polls. Not here."

"So the Silver Steer held its own in the end," Kate said, her face breaking into a grin.

"It did indeed," Herb said. "Frankly, I'm surprised. I thought folks would jump ship with all the competing Silver Steer headlines of the past couple of days muddying the waters."

"It's a little bit like Christmas for adults this year, isn't it?" commented Katie. "Everyone will have a reason to stay up late… to watch, and to listen."

"And that, my dear daughter, is exactly my concern. Tomorrow, when we all wake up, there's going to be a terrific amount of disappointment, assuming, of course, that the Steer fails to deliver."

"Shame on you, Daddy," Katie said, wagging her finger him. "If you believe in it, it exists. That's what the old man with the white hair and the reindeer teaches us every year."

"You two youngsters had better be on your way back to the farm. Weather Service says the rain's supposed to change over to snow."

Katie looked closely at her father. "Would you like some help tonight, Daddy…at the paper, I mean."

The old man shook his head. "As my father always said, no rest for the wicked and the good don't need it…. I'm afraid I wouldn't know what to do with an extra pair of hands."

"See there…. All these years you've been trying to con me into helping you with the paper, and when I offer, you come up with some lame excuse."

"Your offer is music to an old newspaperman's ears, Katie, believe me. But tonight you two should go enjoy yourselves. Besides, I'm accustomed to being a one-man show on Caucus night." The old editor leaned over to kiss his daughter on the forehead. "Don't you worry, I'll be home sometime before the rooster crows, and sooner if Santa and his reindeer somehow manage to deliver."

"Be careful out there," he said, calling after them from the doorway as they emerged into the clear night air outside the schoolhouse. "Look out for voters intoxicated by their own power."

Back at the truck, Jake asked his political date the question that had been on his mind since the newspaper editor's daughter had first distributed the ballots. "I'm dying to know who you voted for."

"On just our third political date you want to know my voter preference? That's rushing things a little, Press, don't you think?"

He put his hands on his hips. "You're going to tell me, aren't you?"

"I wrote-in who I always write-in." She grinned mischievously. "I voted for Daddy."

"But he didn't read out your vote in the results."

"He never does," Katie said, clambering into the pickup truck and turning the heat on full-blast. "Herbert Jefferson Clarke can be counted on to discount himself."

McGreedy, me, and Special Guest u know and won't want 2 miss @ the Wheel watching polls. Git yr bunz over here quick. —Am.

Jake read the text message twice, debating whether he wanted to leave the farmhouse they had only just returned to in order to venture back out into the black night to a bar of darkly humored journalists.

"An invitation from my fellow journalistic brethren," he explained, answering the unspoken question hanging on Katie's lips. "They want me to meet them at the Wheel.... Want to go with?"

"No, but you should go. I'll be fine here, and besides, Daddy should be home before too long. He and I always make a home-made pizza and stay up late to watch the results roll in together. It's a father-daughter tradition."

"I don't know if I can stand three hours of unadulterated reporterly cynicism."

"Who says you wouldn't get that here?" She smiled. "Go, Jacob. In a way it's part of your job."

Another Amethyst Gilchrest text lit up his phone.

Just 2 titillate u...I know who the Silver Steer is. Consider yrself baited. —Am

He had been snared by yet another Amethyst Gilchrest trap. Who could the special guest possibly be? Knowing Amethyst Gilchrest, it could be anyone...his parents, an ex-girlfriend, a former grade school teacher, someone her perverted and twisted sense of humor would delight in dredging up from the past.

Now there was no choice. He would have to join the hyenas dining on the carcass of this supposedly maggot-infested, rotting Republic.

Nineteen

First Street was surprisingly deserted as Jake cruised its length, as if the good citizens of Hereford had been expecting an air bombardment rather than a free and fair election.

He managed to park right out front of the Wagon Wheel, stepping almost directly from his Accord into the belly of the Wheel itself, whereupon a blast of humid air laced with the smell of warm domestic beer washed over him. Before him lay a scene uncannily like the one Am had dragged him into upon his arrival a month earlier—the big table upfront dominated by the larger than life figure of Mort McGreedy and his hangers-on, and Amethyst Gilchrest surrounded by a few of her handsome and quirky journalist friends who would fly out tomorrow morning and remember their time in Middle America, if at all, with the pleasant fondness of a brief weekend in the country.

As soon as Amethyst spotted Jake loitering just inside the door, she put her thumb to her lips, tipped back her head, and wordlessly pointed him to the bar…the universal symbol for 'beer me.' And just as he had the very first night he'd come to the Wheel to hear Herb Clarke's unexpected recitation of "Get on a Raft with Taft" and McGreedy's sarcastic serenade sung to the tune of "Desperado," he simply nodded and did Amethyst's biding. And just like that first night, Hereford's favorite ex-mayor, Artie Shaw, stood on stage in his cowboy boots, spinning tunes.

"Well look what the cat dragged in," Mad said, meeting Jake at the bar with a series of hand-grabs and fist-bumps and salutary squeezes that together constituted his inimitable hand-shake. "Where ya been, stranger?"

"Been out on the range, partner," Jake said, flipping a little of the cowboy stuff back at him. "I figured by now you'd have an FBI agent attached at your hip, or one of those ankle bracelets that tracks hardened criminals and wild animals."

Mad grinned. "When they put you under surveillance, that just means you're finally worth them worrying about." He paused. "C'mon back to the back, I wanna show you something."

"Who's gonna tend bar?"

"Got Ripon helping me pull pints for tonight," he said, gesturing down the bar to the dishwater blonde with the nose ring that had first introduced he and Katie to Little Wisconsin a little more than two weeks earlier. "C'mon, follow me."

The tavern-keeper led Jake down the hall toward the bathroom Jake had traveled to dozens of times in his stints at the Wheel, past the room where Mad kept his mad laboratory of brewing equipment to where the hallway dead-ended at a wood-paneled wall. There, Mad knocked four times and the panel slid out of the way on a track to reveal the one and only Sexy Badger, Loretta Draper, and behind her, a couple dozen young people noisily watching a big-screen.

"Never told you about my speakeasy, did I?"

"No you didn't," Jake said, whistling appreciatively. "So the night I was here with McGreedy, and knocked on wood about my big secret…. I really did here someone knock back, didn't I?"

"You knocked three times if I remember right," Mad said. "Our secret knock is four…one for each year of a presidential term, or one for each of Dolph Heinrich's ex-wives. Whoever was back here sleepin' on the job and snarfing down cheeseballs that night you met up with McGreedy was just makin' sure you weren't one of us who had somehow missed a knock, which of course you hadn't. Anyway, this is the thing that really sold me on the place. First time the realtor showed it to me, I was like, 'I gotta have it.' C'mon, let me show you inside," Mad said, ushering Jake into the hideaway as he called out, "Hey, Loretta, what's shaking in the stronghold? See any G-men coming to bust up our little election party?"

"That's a negative," she said, reaching up to give the burly brewer a hug. "Congratulations, Madison. You're back in as our first-in-command."

"Well, I'll be flogged and feathered," Mad said. "How many ballots did it take to get my hairy ass reinstated?"

"One, but first we had to splinter off from POPP. It was either that or the original, founding Cheeseheads had to accept the slicker political sausage made by the new Chuck Sousage regime, and they weren't about to do it." She stepped back to look around the room. "So here's what's left of the loyal followers of the once mighty WOPP."

Jake looked around at the old speakeasy, which, minus the big-screen TV, looked like it had been mothballed since the days of Calvin Coolidge and his famously long naps.

"Welcome to our Hereford headquarters, man," Mad said, clapping Jake on the back. "I guess you've already met my bodyguard, handler, roadie, attack dog and advocate-journalist, Susan Koehler, a.k.a. Loretta Draper."

"So this is where the magic happened," Jake remarked. On the screen in front of him Donna Sawyers and George Agropolis announced 75 percent of the precincts were now reporting.

Mad rested his booted foot on a folding chair and looked around the room proudly. "Yep, this is ground zero for the WOPP movement. See what I mean about bartenders and their secrets? We've been here all along, pretty much right under your nose."

"So why'd you send me and Katie on a wild goose chase to Holstein?"

Mad grinned. "'Cause I wanted you to meet Ripon and Loretta Draper of course, and to see the barn at our Holstein headquarters. Don't you think you would have begun to suspect something if the note had said to come to the Wagon Wheel to pick up the beef?"

"So it was you in the Nixon mask that day outside Bambi Bloomberg's studio…the one who pressed the note into my hand about WOPP having the Steer?"

Wordlessly, the barman pointed to a Nixon mask hung on a peg beside the secret door to the speakeasy. "Had that mask since I was a teenager. Used to dress up as Tricky Dick every year for Halloween."

"Speaking of disguises…you're not really the Steer, are you?"

"As I confessed to the G-men when they got around to asking, I spliced that barbecue vid, sure," confessed the barman, "but I didn't wear the mask. I had my hands full here trying to run a populist movement while tendin' bar. Let me tell you, it ain't easy."

Jake gestured toward the oversized TV, still clutching the pitcher of beer Mad had pulled for him, and which he was now long overdue to deliver to the table of thirsty journalists. "So what are you going to do once the fat lady sings and we have a winner?"

"Gonna keep on truckin,'" Mad declared. "Little Wisconsin is a state of mind, man. Look, you go anywhere in the U.S. and you'll find people drinking 'Sconsin …New Glarus, Leinenkugels, Miller. Same thing's gonna be true of WOPP. What I'm trying to say is… the WOPP doesn't stop here."

Madison put his big bear paw on Jake's shoulder. "Hate to cut the tour short, Press, but I'm expected to watch the results roll in with my loyal foot soldiers here," he said, nodding toward the WOPP faithful. "Everybody's caucused by now, so all that's left is to stand by and see if the Silver Steer wins by a hoof."

"I should probably be getting back out front, too," Jake admitted. "I'm sure the table of jaded scribblers is getting anxious."

"Then you gotta beer 'em, man, and beer 'em good," Mad said, as Loretta Draper walked Jake back to the door that wasn't a door.

"There goes Mort McGreedy now," she said, peering through the peephole, "on his way to the bar. He looks kind of pissed."

"That's because his blood-alcohol had dropped below .2," Jake joked, as Loretta opened the door in time for Jake to exit and intercept the big bear of a reporter en route back to the scribbler table.

"Jesus Christ, Press," McGreedy said, "I could've written a Pulitzer Prize-winning, three-part feature story in the time it took you to fail to get us a pitcher."

"I got distracted in back."

McGreedy grinned lasciviously. "Whoever she was, I hope she was gorgeous. Now grab a seat," he said, "right here between me and the treacherous Amethyst Gilchrest."

"Why, so you can both have a shot at me?"

"Exactly," Amethyst said. "Slide your skinny ass down here and regale us with tales of how you spent the evening telling war stories with the Silver Steer himself, just the two of you buckaroos rustlin' up them doggies known as votes."

"I'm beginning to think the Silver Steer may be my only friend."

"And an imaginary one at that," quipped Amethyst. "Speaking of which, the Special Guest I promised you is due to arrive shortly. I sent Alex over to fetch them from my apartment."

"You're not going to tell me who it is?"

"Of course not. That would completely ruin the drama, and, Press, I'm all about the drama. All I'm going to tell you is the *Times* agreed to fly this person in so I could interview them as part of my little ongoing investigative reporting, and to do a little business with them as well."

Jake ran his fingers through his hair. "What kind of business?"

"Cat got my tongue, I guess," Amethyst said.

McGreedy poured a round of beers. "A pint of Silver Steerage Porter for each of you to help settle your election night nerves… Mad's latest and last limited edition campaign swill, brewed just in the nick of time, too. If the Steer wins, this stuff is gonna be drained by the keg."

"And if he loses?"

"Then we all head to New Hampshire with a collector's item case in our trunk to warm us on all the cold New England nights to come."

"So what'd you think of Mr. Breakfast Patty's bombshell this afternoon?" Amethyst asked, a mischievous twinkle in her eye.

"You mean this morning?"

"No, I mean this afternoon." She stared at Jake, incredulous. "Don't tell me you haven't heard the latest."

Jake shook his head. "I had dinner with the Clarkes, then I went straight to their caucus."

"Turns out Sousage's claim of responsibility has more holes in it than Swiss cheese." Am leaned in on her elbows. "Reader's Digest version…the Silver Steer is AWOL, still at-large and in-charge."

Jake eyed her carefully, badly wanting to say, *but you said in your text you knew who the Steer was,* but he couldn't, not with McGreedy and the other journalistic vultures circling so close.

"Imagine what it must feel like to be Milt Cloward right now," she added. "You're sitting at your campaign headquarters surrounded by your million-dollar advisors, and strategists, and wonks, and you're trying your damndest to be light-hearted and optimistic, but deep in your heart of hearts you're absolutely terrified…"

"Terrified that you're going to be get beat by a freakin' fictional cow," McGreedy added, plainly delighted by the irony. "This is beautiful stuff, and we have you to thank for it, Preston…. And so a toast…." McGreedy raised his glass of Silver Steerage high over his head as he locked eyes around the table. "To our very own Desperado…the greatest accidental journalist of all-time."

"And a legend in his own mind," Amethyst added. "To Jake, the best roommate who never was!"

"So where do things stand?" Jake asked after he too had found the bottom of his pint. "The polls closed, what, a half-hour ago?"

"Let's see," Am said, squinting at the big-screen. "With 77 percent of the precincts reporting, it's Milt Cloward at 25 per-cent, Silver Steer 23 percent…That's hilarious," she said, pointing at the TV graphic. "There's Milt Cloward's Ken Doll mug shot, and Santoro's, but they didn't know what picture to use for the Steer, so they just left it as a question mark. It's like the Steer has become The Riddler or something."

"More like The Enigma," Jake added.

"And yet no more an enigma than you, Press," she fired back, keeping her eyes glued on the numbers updating on the big-screen.

"How's that?"

"Where do you want me to begin? You're from Bradenton, Florida, but you're really from all over. No one's quite sure where you live. Your best friend in a town temporarily full of journalistic hotties looking to hook up far from port is a grumpy old man. You're a reporter who in the last three weeks has published in both the *Times* and the *The Journal*, but you don't have a job, at least not really, and no one's quite heard of this sketchy Rocky Mountain rag you supposedly write for." Am winked. "Admit it, you are the Silver Steer."

"If you are, you played me like a fiddle," McGreedy declared, clearing out a throat full of phlegm, "convincing me to help you get your video played on every television station from here to Hell and back."

"You don't seriously think it's me, do you?" Jake asked, incredulous.

"I'd be lying if I said the thought hadn't at least crossed my mind," Am replied. "But then again, I've also wondered if McGreedy here wasn't our corn-fed Clark Kent of the Caucuses, driven by the desire to make this, his so-called Alimony Tour and his last campaign as a journalist, one for the record books. Why else would a man who has risen to the pinnacle of his profession agree to report on yet another Iowa Caucus unless, beneath that snide, cynical, nihilistic exterior, he wanted to play a new role to ensure his legacy...the good guy." She pointed her mug at the screen.

On stage Artie Shaw turned down the tunes to call out, "Here we go, cowboys and cowgirls, with 87 percent of the precincts reporting it's...drum roll, please...Cloward at 27 percent, Silver Steer at 26 percent, Mike Santoro 21, Paul Paule 18, Rochelle Boxman 5, and Rich Priestly a whoppin' 2."

"And some sad son of a bitch in the remaining one percent is probably voting for Ralph Nader," McGreedy lamented. "Never understood the mentality of people who would throw away their vote on the same guy for twenty years running."

"Then again you've never seen the logic behind keeping the same wife for more than ten years either, have you, Mort?"

"Painful," McGreedy said, raising his glass in acknowledgment of Amethyst's professional barb, "but true.... So Gilchrest, what if I told you I've harbored a suspicion that the Silver Steer might in fact be you."

Am did a spit-take. "You mean you'd throw the book at little ol' me before you'd consider, say, our very own WOPPer and Sexy Badger, Loretta Draper... accomplice of one Barton Madison Trinka, and herself a known rabble-rouser, couch-surfer, rogue journalist, hopeless ideologue, and shameless purveyor of that shabby-chic style all us other fashionistas in the press corps admire but are powerless to achieve."

McGreedy shook his head. "Loretta Draper isn't the mastermind type. No, I'm sticking with you as my number one suspect...close associate of one Jacob Preston, to whom the suspect originally gave the idea of the Silver Steer...the one assigned to discover the identity of our masked avenger, but who herself has existed above suspicion while quietly building a relationship with nearly all of the major players in this twisted political mystery."

"Yeah, and like any super-chick I've got the ass to pull off the black tights…. By the way, did Artie Shaw just wink at me, or am I imagining things? And should I be concerned about said wink, or simply totally creeped out by it?" She paused, thoroughly vexed. "So what do you say, Press? Who's your number one suspect?" Am asked, turning on him again. "Maybe that girlfriend of yours, who, I would be remiss not to point to, confessed to being only a part of the Silver Steer…like a tenderloin is only part of the whole Iowa hog…while she cleverly throws the government hounds off her trail by sort-of-partially, and preemptively, falling on her dagger. Well, what say you?"

"Or it could be Colonel Mustard in the conservatory with the lead pipe," McGreedy grumbled. "What I want to know, Gilchrest, is what's the first thing you're going to do when this dog and pony show is over and you get back to your bachelorette pad in NYC?"

"Who says I'm going back? I may just stay in Iowa forever, like Dorothy."

"That was Kansas," McGreedy corrected, "but then how would you know. You were born in what, like 1983?"

"Right and you were born somewhere around 1893," Amethyst fired back. "Seriously, the first thing I'll do when I get back, after checking to see if Jake's relationship status has turned from 'Single' to 'It's Complicated…In love with the Silver Steer,' is

469

probably take a week off work and live at Zucker Bakery. I can't tell you how much I've had a jones for their Chocolate Roses. I'll hang out there, consume twice my weight in middle-eastern pastries, go get my pooch from the doggie day care, let him dog-hump me for days, shamelessly sleep with him, then take him back to the kennel so I can fly out for the New Hampshire primaries."

"In other words, exactly how you treat the men in your life," McGreedy deadpanned.

Amethyst's face lit up with the usual mischief. "Precisely. What about you, McGreedy?"

The veteran reported snorted. "Sleep, drink, eat, and try to be merry, though not necessarily in that order."

Just as McGreedy finished answering his own question, a draft blew in from the front door behind the reporters, and Jake turned to see Amethyst's reporter friend Alex hanging his coat up on a peg on the wall and, behind him, a figure that qualified as sight for sore eyes.

"Hick!" Jake shouted. "What in the heck…?"

Amethyst Gilchrest rose to help her special guest off with his coat.

"Hello, Press," Geoff Hickenlooper said sheepishly, his cheeks still red from the cold outside. "Fancy meeting you here."

After giving Hick the kind of hug he'd always assumed he'd reserve for a long-lost relative if and when they showed up, Jake sat down to stare, disbelievingly, at Amethyst Gilchrest, who seemed more than usually pleased with herself. "So, are you going to continue to keep me in suspense?" he asked.

"What's there to be suspenseful about?" She kicked off her boots and put her stockinged feet up in Jake's lap. "In case you forgot to remember that you had one, this is your boss...well, ex-boss, technically."

"Sooo, as you know," she continued, "the world's most trusted news source, who just happens to pay me in a relationship that may be foreign to you, Jacob Preston, but which is conventionally called employer-employee, has retained my services over the last ten days to find the man, woman, or skunk-ape behind the Silver Steer."

Jake stared, wide-eyed, at his former boss, who merely raised an ironic eyebrow. "Well, due diligence dictates that I would contact your former employer—standard reporting techniques, as I'm sure a seasoned news pro like you would know. But come to find out there was no man manning the ship at that venerable little rag known as the *Rocky Mountain Partisan*, only an empty captain's chair where the news editor should have been. It wasn't hard to find out from a staff still indignant over the loss of its beloved head man that someone very important to them all had recently been let go for unspecified reasons, and that juicy tidbit led me, in turn, to the executive publisher, the Big Boss, a man who just happens to be a major Milt Cloward donor, who curtly informed me that both Jake Preston and his unnamed editor had both recently been...how did he put it...*terminated*. Of course, the aforementioned Executive Publisher refused, citing confidentiality, to disclose name of his former editor, or the reason for his unceremonious sacking."

"Naturally, an investigative reporter always has more than one iron in the fire, and another of my red hot pokers, you might say, was at that very moment turning molten—Facebook responded to our journalistic probe, disclosing that the creator and site manager of the page cleverly titled *Free Press* was one Geoff Hickenlooper, who a quick online cross-check revealed to be the very same editor who had recently been relieved of his duties at the *Rocky Mountain High*.

"*Rocky Mountain Partisan*," Hick interrupted.

"Whatever," Amethyst said. "Of course Hick, as you call him, had recently coauthored an important article in the *Times* with one Jacob Preston, so it was as simple as getting in touch with our payroll department to determine his mailing address." She paused to take another self-satisfied swig of her Silver Steerage Porter. "My queries at that point were merely informational until another fact came to light. Our fellow news organization, the *Journal*, known, among other dubious distinctions, as the employer of one Morton J. McGreedy, had in its possession, and was willing to share, the original envelope that the Silver Steer DVDs had been sent them in, an envelope that, while it did not contain a return address, was fairly easily traced to the postal facility outside Denver. All things seemed to put a bulls-eye, no pun intended, around the otherwise remarkable cowtown of Golden, Colorado, home to one Geoff B. Hickenlooper, and one Jacob Truman Preston."

"A regular goddamned Nancy Drew," McGreedy scoffed, kicking back in his chair as he watched the polling numbers update on the screen. "Press, just so you don't think I sold you down the river twice, I'll have you know I had nothing to do with handing over that padded envelope. Zilch."

Jake regarded his nondescript boss with utter incredulity.

"*You* mailed those DVDs to me, Hick?" Jake asked, and across the table his mild-mannered mustachioed editor nodded his head slowly.

"Here we go, boys," Amethyst interrupted, holding up her hand. "Everyone…a moment please," she said, turning around in her seat to quiet the bar. "They're going to call it!"

On the screen Donna Sawyers and George Agropolis exhibited that strange combination of giddiness and exhaustion common to good politics and good sex. "At 11:57 PM Central Standard Time, it looks like we can call it. With 27 percent of the vote, Milt Cloward has bested the Silver Steer by just over 1,000 votes, a mere 1 percent margin. To all of you Silver Steer supporters out there, George and I want to be the first to congratulate you on a historic run, and for you Milt Cloward boosters watching tonight, let the party begin!"

From somewhere in the far-off reaches of the Wagon Wheel a loud and sustained groan—the groan of the collectively disappointed—traveled through the walls to every nook and cranny of the tavern that had been offering consolation to the people of Hereford since the days Silent Cal Coolidge had napped in high office.

"Hell of a race," McGreedy said, slamming his glass down to the table. "I'd say a few words to raise the spirits, but then again I know this group of hard-hearted sons of bitches won't be down in the mouth for long…. Just think of the headlines we'll soon be asked to generate, "Cloward Wins…No Bull!"

"Cloward to Cowherd, 'No Use Crying over Spilt Milk,'" Amethyst added, giving Jake a playful punch in the arm.

"'Cloward Closes Deal; Steer Buys Farm,'" Hick pitched in.

"Don't know about the rest of you, but this dark horse has got to piss like a racehorse," McGreedy said, rising noisily from his seat to head for the toilet. "Be right back. Don't do any more political crack without me."

Jake excused himself, too, on the pretense of ordering another beer, but instead circled back to intercept McGreedy on his way back from the can.

"Jesus, Preston, you sacred the shit out of me," the giant exclaimed as Jake practically leapt at him along the shadowy back hallway of the Wheel. "If you wanted to see me with my pants down that badly, all you had to do was ask."

"Listen to me, McGreedy," Jake said, withdrawing a slim case from his jacket pocket. "You remember when we forwarded the Silver Steer DVD to your editor in its original envelope?" Jake paused to gather himself. "Well...I lied to you."

"You what?!"

"I told you a white lie," Jake repeated. "There were actually three DVDs in the original package Hick apparently mailed to me."

"You're shitting me."

"The other two were labeled 'Victory Speech' and 'Concession Speech.'"

McGreedy arched an eyebrow, his mind working fast. "I'm assuming you're willing to give me another exclusive on the concession."

"Of course," Jake told him. "It's not my story anyway. It's Hick's. But if Amethyst gets wind of this, she'll either try to run with it, or hold it back as part of her grand, and I'm sure soon-to-be-forthcoming, exposé of Geoff B. Hickenlooper."

"Exposé, hell, she'll make a book out of it," McGreedy scoffed, seeming suddenly to sober up. "My editor at the *Journal* will be happy to run all or part of the text of the concession speech and upload the video itself for the website and for our TV partners. It'll be all over the country by tomorrow morning."

"I appreciate it, McGreedy, I really do."

"No skin off my nose," he said. "I'm the one who comes out smelling like a rose instead of a feedlot. Another killer story falls into my undeserving lap and the seemingly invincible Amethyst Gilchrest gets scooped at long last."

"Not quite undeserving," Jake said, resting his arm on the big man's massive shoulder. "You were the only reporter with the balls to run the Steer's election-eve video. That took some guts."

"You want a shared byline on this one?"

"No," Jake said. "It's all yours...and Hick's...if he wants it."

"Did you watch it, Preston...the concession speech?"

Jake shook his head. "I was tempted to, believe me, but it says right on the DVD 'Not to be viewed until election results are in.' Besides, part of me didn't want to...you know...acknowledge that the legendary steer might meet an inglorious end."

"Ever the sentimentalist..." McGreedy shook his head. "You know I don't think I've ever met a reporter I like so much that's so completely goddamned different from me. Anyhow, thanks for the lead. I'll make sure the vid lands in the right hands and that we do right by Hickenlooper with it."

"Thanks," Jake said, pushing past him down the darkened hall.

"Hey, where are you going, Press?" McGreedy called after him. "The bar is that way."

"Need some air," Jake told him, with no intention of stopping once he hit the alley. "Let Hick know I'm looking forward to having breakfast with him tomorrow morning at the Cal Coolidge…all-you-can-eat pancakes on me. And do me a favor…don't let Amethyst parade him around town like a war prisoner while she's pumping him for more information."

McGreedy laughed darkly. "She's hell on her male captives, isn't she?"

Jake opened the back door of the Wheel to a bracing rush of November air, and a globe of stars sizzling above him. Part of him couldn't quite believe that the Silver Steer was over, that it hadn't somehow managed to win over a disbelieving electorate, as if politics itself were an especially convincing fairy tale.

On the other hand he doubted whether he would have believed the result if the Silver Steer had won. Even as it was, the poll totals were incredible, more than a quarter of caucus-goers in an unusually sober Midwestern state had voted for a hope, a dream, a vision, a symbol with no real life other than the life the citizens had given it.

Jake ambled down First Street in a post-electoral daze, past the Sweetheart Bakery, under the window of the walk-up apartment that not so long ago he'd shared with the indomitable

Amethyst Gilchrest, past the offices of the *Hereford Gate*, before circling back to the Calvin Coolidge Café.

He reached in his pocket for the key Katie had mercifully loaned him the night he'd been locked out of his apartment, and the door unlocked without a hitch. He turned on just enough light to find his way back to the grease-stained office PC Katie used to do the restaurant's accounting and inventory, and sat down wearily in the office chair, pulling one of her long strands of ginger hair from its fabric. From his coat pocket he withdrew the last Silver Steer DVD, the one marked "Victory speech," and put it into the drive.

Before him, like a djinni teased from a long-corked bottled, materialized the familiar figure of the man—Hick, he knew now, and yet part of him still couldn't believe it—wearing the cow's head mask, his computer-altered voice so familiar that it seemed to Jake purely human. Leaning forward in the chair he pushed play and turned up the volume.

> Voters, Citizens, Neighbors, mine is no ordinary victory speech. There are no balloons, no screaming campaign boosters, no trophy spouses and adoring children looking up admiringly as we stand at the podium. There could be no venue large enough to house a victory rally the magnitude of what we have accomplished tonight.
>
> Had we had a rally to celebrate this, your victory over the tyranny of mundanity and mediocrity, the journalists would no doubt have peppered us with questions. *What are your plans from here? Will your campaign be moving on? How will this victory help your*

position with potential financial backers? For us these questions happily do not apply.

I address you this evening in the only way I know how, directly and with deep and abiding respect for your will, your intelligence, and your moral courage. In voting for us, when all the voices of so-called reason were telling you to disbelieve and do otherwise, to persist in your faith despite all evidence to the contrary, means you have summoned the spirit of the original voter, the one that drafted General George Washington, reluctant hero, to run for highest political office, the same spirit that demanded the best, most honest candidates from the birth of this blessed Republic, and refused to hand over their sacred and God-given right to proxies and pundits.

I am deeply humbled by your vote of confidence and honored to continue to be what you would have me be. Since its inception, our campaign, such as it is, has been about putting into practice a revolutionary idea—the idea that our candidates don't need vetting and spinning as much as they need unrestricted access to the very people from whom they presume to solicit a vote. Our enduring fight has been to empower voters to band together and say, 'This is not what we asked for. Take it back and bring us something better. And if you don't we'll exercise our right to a protest vote.' The Silver Steer merely dared to give a name to that mobilized voter when he or she at last chose to exercise their first right of refusal.

And now, in this glorious moment after our improbable victory, I want you to have the satisfaction you've earned of putting a face to that which has merely embodied your wishes in a campaign that otherwise threatened not just to ignore your independence of mind but to punish you for it. I want to unmask myself so that you, yourselves, can begin the good and glorious work of undoing decades worth of rigged primaries and pre-ordained frontrunners. Only in this way will the powers-that-be come to reckon not just with one man dressed like a minotaur, but millions of men and women too strong to have their liberties trifled with.

"I'm not sure I'm ready for the unmasking, are you?"

Jake spun around to see the familiar figure of Herb Clarke leaning against the office door. "I'm afraid I already know who Santa Claus is," Jake said. "A know-it-all girl in my class told me."

The editor grinned. "Is that so?"

"How long have you been standing there anyway?" Jake asked. He paused the video to turn fully around in his chair.

"Long enough," the editor said. "I was walking back to the car after setting the last line of type in our election edition, and saw the light on at the café. I fancied I'd find Katie here, not you." He paused. "So your candidate lost tonight, eh, Jacob?"

"Afraid so."

"But what you're watching there doesn't sound like a concession speech."

"That's because it isn't," Jake said. "It's the tape that would have been played had the Silver Steer won."

"I presume that more hopeful tape was delivered in the same batch as the DVD McGreedy's rag and its TV affiliates ran yesterday." Jake nodded. "Well then, shall we finish the viewing together?"

"Sure," Jake said, suddenly feeling very sheepish. "Curiosity got the better of me, I guess."

"No need to explain on my account," the editor replied, settling into the chair beside him. "It's the romance of alternate histories, of what would have happened had the stars been aligned differently, or the people drunk a little bit more deeply from whatever intoxicant caused them to believe in the Silver Steer in the first place. Remember that night Professor Templeton told us about the still-born State of Franklin? I suppose, in a way, this video is our own Lost State."

"Perhaps," Jake said, taking a deep breath before pressing 'play' on the unmasking.

Twenty

"Why'd you do it?"

"For a thousand reasons, Jacob, that are so complicated and yet so simple that I'd surely be at a loss to recite them to you now."

Herb Clarke patted him gently on the back as he continued. "That's one of the problems with this culture…. We assume that the old have lost all romantic impulse, that they don't wish and hope and dream just as actively as they did when they were younger. In my own case it's quite the opposite, actually. The older I've grown the more I've urgently longed for many things…true freedom, justice, fairness…that seem more and more emblems of the past. If one began as an idealist, as I did, they eventually become something of a wizened old ideologue, a priest without a pulpit. I'm afraid donning that mask," he said, pointing to the image frozen on the computer screen, "was the best way to get people to listen."

"But how did you…"

"How did I manage to video the thing? Katie didn't help me, if that's what you're asking. I couldn't break it to her, especially when things looked as grim as they did for her after her own authorship of the cow-in-the-barn videos came to light. In a way, I was just doing what any loving father would do who enjoys a close ideological kinship with his daughter. She couldn't go on any longer without endangering herself and her professor, so, unbeknownst to her, I picked up her mantle."

"And the DVD?"

"You're correct to assume that the technical challenges of producing this kind of video are well beyond an old fossil like me. That's where Madison came in. When Mad volunteered to be on the executive committee for the candidate barbeque, I pulled him aside and told him what I had in mind. He was more than willing to assist."

Jake smiled. "I bet he was. Two rabble-rousers separated by two generations and one state line. So what about the cow's head mask?"

"One of my wife's old theater props I pulled down from the attic. Made out of paper mache and fragments of a real steer's skull she discovered many years ago on our farm. The mask is what gave me the idea in the first place. When I put it on, I immediately sensed that she was there with me, and fully behind my revolutionary theatrics."

"And you weren't worried that you'd wake up some morning to flashing lights in the barnyard and handcuffs around your wrists?"

Clarke chuckled darkly. "The thought did cross my mind. But some things that would terrify you at 30 or 35, with a young spouse and a child dependent on you, seem perfectly insignificant when you're staring down the barrel of 72. I knew I wasn't breaking any laws, and I was prepared to go to court against Matthew Pitchford, the RNC, the State of Iowa, or whoever else would have tried to deny me the rights due me as a citizen.

Part of me is sorry the authorities didn't try to drag me kicking and screaming from my family's one-hundred-and-fifty-year-old farm. It would have made for one hell of a news story."

"Editor Refuses to Be Cowed by Federal Agents," Jake said, unable to resist.

The old editor cocked his head thoughtfully. "No, my biggest scare came just two nights ago. I had stashed my mask in the storage closet at my office, back where not even Darlene dares venture. I was leaving the *Gate* at such an ungodly hour that it didn't occur to me that anyone would ever see me with my superhero gear in tow."

He stood to pace the room. "It must have been almost midnight, and without thinking I left the mask on the hood of the car for no more than a minute while I loaded up the newspaper bundles to be delivered the next morning. Out of the corner of my eye I saw one of the lights go on in the apartments across the street. I looked up, and there stood Amethyst Gilchrest looking directly down at me from her bay window. I could tell from the look on her face that she recognized the mask on sight, and quickly put two and two together. After about thirty seconds of staring intently at me, she drew the blinds. Naturally I assumed I was going to end up in the *Times* the next day, the subject of one of her famously hard-hitting, tell-all exposés. You cannot imagine with what trepidation I opened the following day's issue only to search in vain for the shocking revelation of the demented old man behind the mask."

"So Amethyst has known for days?"

"I assumed she would probably tell you first. But, just watching and listening to you the last couple of days, it dawned on me that she hadn't."

"Nothing but a teaser in a text she sent a few hours ago. Why on earth would she fly Hickenlooper in, then, if she already had the answer to her question?"

"Some part of her, it's clear, wants the Silver Steer to live on, and prosper. Still I'm sure she, like anyone, feels obliged to go through the motions, keep up appearances. The logistics people at the *Times* probably booked his flight days ago, long before she caught me with my mask down, as it were." The editor grinned. "So she either cancels Hick's flight at the last minute, draws unwanted attention to herself, and fritters away the *Times's* money, or she does nothing, and flies him out here for a Caucus night reunion with you, and the thrill of a newsman's lifetime."

Clarke paused to look intently at him. "It would have made a great story, Jacob. I'm guessing she held it back because she thought it would hurt you too much, or hurt this community. She's a good girl at heart, Amethyst is. Don't let exteriors fool you."

He hated to admit it, but the old editor was right. "Weren't you tempted to expose yourself?"

Clarke frowned. "A rather unfortunate turn of phrase, don't you think? But yes, I wanted you to know, I wanted Katie to know, and the longer it remained my little secret, the harder it was to bear." He paused. "Now it's my turn to turn the tables and ask you a question, Mr. Preston."

"Me?"

"Yes, you. I want to know whether you viewed the concession speech I arranged to have mailed you at the farm, with an assist from Hick, your loyal editor back in Colorado, who graciously acted as the go-between to keep you and Hereford's long-time and unfailingly nosy postmaster off my trail and thus the anonymity of the Silver Steer intact."

"Couldn't bear to watch the tear-jerker, Herb. My heart belongs to the Silver Steer, you know that."

"A pity you didn't view the concession," the editor said. "I've discovered I'm a much better writer when I'm writing the part of the failed underdog."

"I passed it off to McGreedy before I came here. I…I thought for sure the gig was up, that it was Hick who had donned the cow's mask…that Amethyst flying him to Hereford pretty much meant she had him by the balls, or by the horns." Jake paused to shake his head in wonderment. "I'm sure I'll see it tomorrow, but since you and I are two of only three people on the planet right now who know of the tape's existence, how about a preview?"

"Lots of pulpit-beating and spirited vows to carry on," Clarke summarized, adding, "but no unmasking. After all, a thwarted Zoro would be a fool to abandon his mask when there are villains left to fight. Basically, I make the point that the Silver Steer lives on even in defeat."

"Will it?" Jake asked.

"See that car out there?" the editor said, pointing to the old Buick sedan parked on the street. "It's packed to the gills and ready for the New Hampshire primaries. If you look closely,

Jacob, you'll see the Silver Steer Express has already picked up one of its two scheduled passengers."

Jake squinted hard into the midnight gloaming outside the café. "Is that Hick?"

Clarke nodded. "Two grizzled old editors with a powerful dream for their country, and nothing to lose…what could be more revoluntarily than that?"

"I take it Katie will be your third…"

"Heaven's no. I dare say my daughter is not the type to relish last-minute trips. No, in a week or so we'll offer to fly her out to Manchester if she's ready. And of course the same offer applies to you."

Jake eyed the editor curiously. "Who's the 'we' in that statement?"

The newspaperman looked from Jake out to the car. "The first mate's chair is reserved for the Silver Steer's original historical consultant, Dr. Anne Templeton."

Jake stood from the office chair to shake Clarke's hand. "You couldn't have chosen better coconspirators. Between the three of you, the political powers-that-be in the Granite State will be rendered defenseless."

"Which leads me to a rather more serious favor I must ask you."

"Name it, Herb."

"Will you serve as an editor of the *Gate* in my absence?"

"I'll do my best," Jake said, bowing slightly. "Though keep in mind my journalistic trajectory is something less than stable. I've gone from the back pages of the *Rocky Mountain Partisan* to the front page of the *Times* without much of anything in between. I'm not sure I'm prepared to be editor."

The old man grinned. "I said *an* editor, Jacob, not *the* editor. *The editor* is someone I've had my eye on for almost thirty-five years."

"Marianne Meyers?"

Clarke rested his palms on Jake's shoulders. "Katie Genevieve Clarke. She doesn't know it yet, of course…. I'm hoping you'll break the news to her once we're safely down the road." He paused to look at the dark, empty street running south out of town toward the highway. "Hick and I are supposed to pick up Anne in Des Moines tonight…or, more accurately, this morning. We plan to leave for New Hampshire by first light. As for you, buckeroo, you might want to head on back to the ranch. I'm sure Katie is beginning to stew about you."

"I'll text her and let her know I'm on my way," Jake offered, as he walked the editor to the door, and turned off the lights of the café as he'd seen Katie do a hundred times. Just beyond the door, the getaway car gleamed in the moonlight.

"You need a pair of longhorns to put on the hood of that jalopy, and a bumper-to-bumper silver spray-paint job," Jake commented, looking at the "experienced" car that proposed to take the rabble-rousers twelve hundred miles across a half dozen states.

"Don't give an old man any more whimsical notions," Clarke warned, wrapping Jake in a warm embrace beside the car. "Thank you, Jacob. If it weren't for you, none of these rusty old wheels would have ever started turning again."

Jake clapped the editor squarely on the back. "Get in that Silver Steer and ride, old man," he said, kicking the tires for good measure. Then, pointing into the Buick's interior he said, "And that means you too, Hick, you closet radical, you!"

The car door half-opened and Jake reached in to shake his old boss's hand. "I told you the Caucuses would change your life, Press…. I just didn't expect when I called you into the office that night that they were going to change mine." Hick turned to Herb. "You ready to hit the campaign trail, geezer?"

"Hi-ho, Silver, and away!" Clark whispered from behind the wheel, and eased the Buick down the very street by which Jake had cruised into town scarcely more than five weeks earlier.

As soon as the taillights had disappeared down First Street, Jake glanced down at his phone to discover it was well past midnight, and when he looked up again he found himself blinkered by two high-beams pointed directly at him. He watched as a silhouette stepped out of a truck and walked slowly towards him.

"He didn't want me to know, did he?" Katie Clarke sighed, stepping out of the darkness and into the light.

"He didn't want you to worry."

"Did he realize I'd begun to suspect him?"

"Had you?"

Katie nodded. "There's something about a father a daughter always knows. When you live with someone for thirty-five years and share his DNA, you can't help but develop a kind of sixth sense."

"When did you begin to think it might be him?"

"The video that came out yesterday morning. The ideas were so much Daddy's."

"What tipped you off that he might be leaving?"

"For that I have to thank an email from my old professor," she explained, adding, "women are the worst secret-keepers. Anne emailed me about an hour ago, thinking, I'm sure, that I wouldn't read the message until tomorrow morning. She knows my early-to-bed habits all too well, or thinks she does anyway. I suppose I would have waited to check it then, but when neither you nor Daddy were home by midnight, I thought maybe you'd written me a message. So I checked my inbox."

"What did she write?"

"'Off to New Hampshire with a Hick and your stubborn, silver-haired steer.'"

Jake whistled appreciatively. "Pretty clever, that one."

"The thing I haven't figured out is why my grammatically correct professor would capitalize the word *Hick*. Daddy can be a bit of a redneck, but still…"

"Probably because it's a proper noun, as in Hickenlooper."

"Your old boss at the *Partisan*?"

"One and the same. Amethyst flew him in for a Gotham-styled grilling then let him loose. Now he's up and joined forces with your old man."

"And the Silver Steer leaves for its next campaign in the wee hours of a Wednesday morning." Katie paused. "Oh my God…. It's Wednesday! Who's going to put out the newspaper?"

Jake smiled. "The newspaper editor's daughter has become the newspaper editor, or so it would seem. I got the news straight from the horse's mouth just now before the horse left the stables."

Katie Clarke wiped at a tear that had begun to form at the corner of her eye. "Will you stay and help me, Jacob?"

"Not that you need it, but sure…. I mean, I am the newspaper editor's assistant…. You okay with that?"

"I'm more than okay with that." She rested her head briefly on his chest and said, "Shall we then?"

She held her hand out for him in the middle of the street opposite the Sweetheart Bakery, a street so still and silent they might have run its length like two modern-day Paul Reveres sounding the alarm against the latest political tyranny.

Jake heard a soft tap above him, and when he looked up he saw Amethyst Gilchrest and Mort McGreedy peering down at him curiously from the bay window of her apartment. Then, arm in arm with the newspaper editor's daughter, he watched as Amethyst performed a charade whose meaning could only be understood by the four of them. She held up a silver spoon, made two horns of her index fingers, and put them above each of her ears, like a bull ready to charge.

Then, slowly, she raised a triumphant fist into the air.

A Citizens' Discussion Guide to
Corn Poll: A Novel of the Iowa Caucuses

The food-for-thought questions that follow have been created as an alternative to partisan bickering for free-thinking, independent-minded citizens who prefer substantive dialogue and discussion during election season. Public libraries, schools, book clubs, coffee klatches, and other citizens' groups and not-for-profits that would like to host a discussion about the issues raised in *Corn Poll: A Novel of the Iowa Caucuses* should feel free to select from the prompts that follow those most relevant to you, your patrons, or your organization; feel free to photocopy and distribute them. If you would like to invite the author to participate in your discussion, book club, or forum, or for help making copies available for your event, please feel free to contact the publisher at steve@icecubepress.com

Q: In *Corn Poll: A Novel of the Iowa Caucuses*, the candidates agree, however reluctantly, to compete for a "people's trophy," in this case the Silver Steer, to lend a greater sense of drama, transparency, and engagement to the campaign. What other creative ways might there be to increase voter turn-out and political participation? What changes in the current electoral system would cause you to vote with greater enthusiasm and/or frequency?

Q: Fightin' Bob La Follette from Wisconsin championed the cause of primaries in which voters are not compelled to choose a party affiliation in order to participate. Would such an open primary system be an improvement? Why or why not?

Q: In the book McGreedy tells Jake Preston, "Ambition is an easy target, Press, because the people who don't have it, or never have it, or have given up on ever having it, resent it when they find it in others." Is McGreedy's assessment of ambitious people mostly true or untrue? In what particular ways would you want (and not want) your Presidential candidate to be ambitious?

Q: When Jake jokingly labels him a "libertarian," Herb Clarke counters, "Libertarians make it part of their creed that the government should do little or nothing for the people. They believe in the wisdom of the individual over that of the community. I, on the other hand, believe in an active, vibrant community made up of empowered individuals. There's an important difference there, Jacob, if you're patient enough to look for it." Do you agree with Clarke's definition? How would you characterize a libertarian?

Q: Katie Clark, the newspaper editor's daughter, tells Jacob, "I don't identify with either party, at least not exclusively. I identify with people, and places, and principles." Does Katie's point resonate? What are the advantage and disadvantages of voting for the person over the party, and what role does place play in our taste for presidential candidates?

Q: On their ride home after meeting with WOPP, Herb Clarke tells Jake that people mostly want the same things from their government—"fair taxation, manageable public debt, a safe and healthy place in which to raise and educate our children, roads that won't break the axles on our cars and trucks. What we disagree about mostly is how to get there, and that's where the differences between Republicans and Democrats become all too real." In what ways could it be claimed that Republicans and Democrats are actually more similar than different, making them, in effect, two sides of the same coin? What would a truly alternative candidate look like?

Q: In a nationally televised TV debate Herb Clarke tells the viewing audience watching on the Coasts, "We're not yokels, hicks, rednecks, isolationists, provincials, or any of the other unfair stereotypes directed our way." To what extent does the nation continue to harbor these stereotypes about Midwesterners? To what degree do the stereotypes ring true, if at all?

Q: In his controversial paper, history professor-turned-presidential-candidate Dolph Heinrich argues that conditions in America make a widespread protest vote possible for the first time in American history. Do you agree with him? If so, what conditions are responsible for creating a growing sense of voter dissatisfaction in the Midwest and around the country?

Q: During her appearance on "The Scoop," Professor Anne Templeton cites a number of presidents who won at least one state primary or caucus as a write-in candidate. Why do more voters not avail themselves of the write-in option, and how might the American political landscape change if a greater diversity of grassroots candidates mounted successful write-in campaigns?

Q: If you were to write-in a true darkhorse candidate on your ballot in an upcoming election, who would it be and why? Is there anyone among your circle of friends and family members that you think would make a great candidate for office? Who? And why?

Q: Herb Clarke claims that candidates make their positions more extreme to "brighten the contrast" between themselves and the rest of the field in the primaries, then move back to center in the general election when it suits them. Is this true? If so, does this fact alone account for why our Republican presidential candidates, for example, so often appear to us as caricatures—i.e. the rich business mogul, the working-class firebrand, the Hawkish neoconservative, the brilliant yet impractical intellectual, the strict, often overliteral constitutionalist, etc.?

Q: In his press conference party chair Matt Pitchford justifies the involvement of the FBI at such time as a protest vote can be construed to represent a "credible threat" to the security of the Caucuses. Where is the line between a widespread protest or protest vote and the supposed treason of sedition, defined as "conduct or speech inciting people to rebel against the authority of a state"?

Q: *Corn Poll* anticipates a major shake-up in the way we elect our presidential candidates in the not-so-distant future, and whom we elect. In the next ten years, what are the prospects for a woman being elected president? A celebrity? A sports star? A business tycoon? A citizen without a prior political record? Would you be willing to elect a president under 45 years old? A president without children or spouse? Which of these or other eventualities do you consider desirable, if any?

Q: Herb Clarke tells Jacob that he's much better at writing the part of the "failed underdog," and, further, that many of our accidental presidents, such as Truman, Roosevelt, and even Coolidge, have been among our best despite leaders, despite being widely considered "unelectable" on their own. Does the candidate branded with the label "underdog," "accidental" or "loser" compel you in ways more orthodox, conventionally "successful" candidates do not?

Q: In *Corn Poll* a number of impassioned, politically active citizens travel across state borders in an attempt to sway state primaries by legal means. Would you be willing to move to a neighboring state for sixty or ninety days to positively influence an election or work for a candidate or cause you believed in, assuming you could afford to do so? For what political or ideological cause, if any, would you be willing to travel out-of-state to campaign for (or against)?

Q: Both McGreedy and Clarke lament the fact that presidential candidates spend significantly less time on the ground in states like Iowa than in the past, and yet Midwestern voters still have an exceptional opportunity to meet candidates in person. What candidates, past or present, have you met face-to-face, and what impression did you come away with? Did that in-person meeting, good or bad, make a difference in your ultimate vote?

Q: At one time in their lives, both Herb Clarke and his daughter Katie harbored political aspirations. Have you ever considered running for political office? If not, why not? If so, what kind of candidate would you be?

Zachary Michael Jack's analysis and commentary on Midwestern politics and culture have appeared in many periodicals nationwide, including the *Cedar Rapids Gazette*, the *Des Moines Register*, the *Daily Yonder*, *Front Porch Republic*, the *Iowan* magazine, and the *Middle West Review*, among many others. Zachary has been a featured speaker or presenter at the Hauenstein Center for Presidential Studies, the Herbert Hoover Presidential Library, and the Iowa Conference on Presidential Politics. The author of over twenty award-winning books and many works of fiction, including the 2010 *Foreword Reviews* runner-up novel-of-the-year in its class, Zachary is a seventh-generation resident of Iowa and a recipient of a Hoover Medal from the Herbert Hoover Presidential Library. He teaches in the graduate and undergraduate Leadership Studies programs at North Central College and in the graduate and undergraduate writing programs.

The Ice Cube Press began publishing in 1993 to focus on how to live with the natural world and to better understand how people can best live together in the communities they share and inhabit. Using the literary arts to explore life and experiences in the heartland of the United States we have been recognized by a number of well-known writers including: Gary Snyder, Gene Logsdon, Wes Jackson, Patricia Hampl, Greg Brown, Jim Harrison, Annie Dillard, Ken Burns, Roz Chast, Jane Hamilton, Daniel Menaker, Kathleen Norris, Janisse Ray, Craig Lesley, Alison Deming, Harriet Lerner, Richard Rhodes, Michael Pollan, David Abram, David Orr, Frank Deford and Barry Lopez. We've published a number of well-known authors including: Mary Swander, Jim Heynen, Mary Pipher, Bill Holm, Connie Mutel, John T. Price, Carol Bly, Marvin Bell, Debra Marquart, Ted Kooser, Stephanie Mills, Bill McKibben, Craig Lesley, Elizabeth McCracken, Dean Bakopoulos, and Paul Gruchow. Check out Ice Cube Press books on our web site, join our facebook group, follow us on twitter, visit booksellers, museum shops, or any place you can find good books and discover why we continue striving to, "hear the other side."

Ice Cube Press, LLC (est. 1993)
205 N. Front Street
North Liberty, Iowa 52317-9302
steve@icecubepress.com
twitter @icecubepress
www.icecubepress.com

to Laura Lee & Fenna Marie
my two best votes for
all that's good